With love from Sophia Worden xxx

Collodian Star

By

Sophia Worden

Part III of The Valerian Trilogy

Little Red Hen Books, Cornwall, UK

Copyright © Sophia Worden, 2024.

Copyright notice © 2024 by Sophia Worden. The right of Sophia Worden to be identified as the Author of the Work has been asserted by her in accordance with the Copyright, Designs and Patents Act, 1988.

All rights reserved. No part of this book may be reproduced, stored in or introduced into a retrieval system, or transmitted, in any form, by any means (electronic, mechanical, photocopying, recording or otherwise) without the prior written permission of the publisher, except in the case of brief quotations embodied in critical articles or reviews.
A catalogue record for this book is available on request from the British Library.
Published by Sophia Worden, Little Red Hen Books, Cornwall. LittleRedHenBooks75@hotmail.com

Cover lettering and design, back cover image by Alexander Hiett
Front cover image and interior design by Sophia Worden
French Proof Reading by David Madell

ISBN: 978-1-4457-73635-8

Thank you to everyone who has taken an interest in the *Valerian Trilogy*. Your kindness and support are the lifeblood of these books.

Collodian Star

1. Codename: Rose Thorn
2. The Purple Book
3. Honolulu Nights
4. Sophia, Robot Girl
5. Lady Elridge's Last Administrator
6. Operation: Golden Claw
7. Cylinders of Memory
8. In Guelder

Additional story: Nettled

Codename: Rose Thorn

If Rose Thorn had met Tallulah Mae Jackson before, in their other life, her blue eyes now didn't give away a flicker of recognition. She had spent years with the Sisters of Valerian, after all, schooling her responses for situations just like this.

'Soooo....' drawled Tallulah to her prisoner, glancing down idly at her perfectly manicured, silver nails, 'anything you want to tell me?'

From the floor, crouched and bound, Rose Thorn looked round the musty, disused rail carriage where Tallulah had decided to hold her interrogation. Craning her neck upwards, towards the window, she glimpsed disused rail tracks, overgrown with long sweeps of grass and tangled weeds. In fact, this sweet-smelling grass, mingling with the clear, sharp scent of nettles, and the overripe mulch of rotting fronds made her eyes water. Beyond that, there was an old railway track, half off its rails, though two of its four wheels were still spinning.

Just for a moment, Rose Thorn thought she could hear the turn of wheels along the track, a passenger, stretching and yawning, another, whistling defiantly at whatever this place could devise.

'This is stupid,' Rose Thorn said, as waves of anger rose within her. Then she reminded herself: controlled anger is a weapon, anything else, a waste of energy. 'You know you can find everything out with celestine memory clips.'

Tallulah ran her fingers through her golden helmet of hair, that formed a striking contrast to her dark skin. It felt springy, vital, alive. 'Let me put it another way,' she said, after a moment. 'Everything you tell me voluntarily is another memory we don't have to take from you.'

'You need to remind yourself of the Political Prisoners Act of 2323,' said Rose Thorn. 'Confession via coercion is illegal. Celestine memory clips are deemed coercion.'

Outside their window, a crow screeched. Rose Thorn followed its erratic progress past pieces of decaying machinery and old sheets of corrugated iron, to a row of electricity cables, with poles jerked asunder by what fierce giant, striding his way through this forbidden zone.

The Collodian.

'That legislation don't count for diddlysquat in the Collodian,' said Tallulhah. 'Only in Valerian.'

'There are a number of potentially illegal practises taking place in the Collodian that the Sisters of Valerian are concerned about,' said Rose Thorn.

'Now we're getting somewhere,' said Tallulah, her eyes gleaming. 'More of this and I can go home early. And you get to sleep in a nice, comfy cell for the night. So, you admit to your involvement with the Sisters of Valerian?'

Rose Thorn tried to stretch, then started to laugh. It wasn't a happy sound. 'Anyone still alive has to have had some kind of involvement with the Sisters of Valerian,' she said.

'Queen Morgana also offers generous protection to her supporters,' said Tallulah, frowning. She really did want to go home early. The latest episode of *Collodian Star* was on tonight: there was pepperoni pizza and soda waiting for her in the fridge.

'Is that before or after she's wiped their memories as fodder for her television show?' asked Rose Thorn.

'Enough of this,' said Tallulah. 'You're here to answer questions, not ask them. You were picked up by our search party trying to break into the Winter Palace. You've been given ample opportunity to tell us what you were up to, but you're not playing *Jabberwocky*. So get up now and come with me.'

Rose Thorn arched her eyebrows at the reference to a game she hadn't played since she was a teenager.

Tallulah had to haul Rose Thorn to her feet, then prodded the small of her prisoner's back with the butt of her bayonet, right where the flesh was tender and likely to bruise. In this way, she pushed her down the steps from the train carriage.

'So,' grumbled Rose Thorn. 'It seems we have a problem. You want to kill me, but I'm not prepared to die.'

'Of course I don't want to kill you,' said Tallulah. 'Even I can't interrogate a corpse.'

'Then less of the bayonet action, please,' said Rose Thorn as she stumbled down the last step, shivering as the cool wind whistled, bringing up goose flesh. On the breeze, came the tang and taste of smoke, from old, exploded fireballs, perhaps.

'I will conduct matters as I see fit,' said Tallulah. She pushed and prodded her prisoner alongside the disused rail-track, past the intertwined, skeletal branches of a grove of trees that smelt of oak, pine and sweet, rotting leaves. Hung from one of the branches, Rose Thorn could see a pink neon sign which read 'LOVE.' She paused to look at the L, which wouldn't light up, and the E, which kept flickering, on-and-off, on-and-off.

'What you looking at, Dorothy?' asked Tallulah. 'This ain't no Oz.' Then she relented for a moment. 'That used to be the sacred grove of Avalon.'

'Yeah,' said the spiky-haired brunette. She had been here before, but there was a pang in her heart to see what the place looked like now. Then she added, 'They call me Rose Thorn, and that's all you're getting from me.'

'When we get back to the Mothercrystal,' said Tallulah, 'I have a pair of celestine clips that says something different.'

Rose Thorn shrugged but kept on walking. She hoped that the defence shields she had spent the last few years perfecting would be strong enough to survive the upcoming memory interrogation.

The Winter Palace's courtyard was immense and paved with coloured stones. In a far corner, Rose Thorn recognised the Arch of Regeneration, all painted over and beaded with symbols, signs of the zodiac, and hieroglyphics of prayers. However, it was the Mothercrystal, at the centre of the courtyard, which was truly impressive. It was lit up by pillars of quartz crystal, selenite and white limestone, immense and glittering.

At the heart of the Mothercrystal sat a familiar blonde woman in a red samite gown lined in ermine, with a necklace of rubies round her white neck. There were a thousand glass eyes shining down upon her and she was known and loved by millions. But, for the moment, she was only a hologram, a stand-in for a later broadcast.

Rose Thorn steeled her heart, rubbed her eyes, and concentrated on her mental defence shields.

Tallulah switched off the hologram, then sat down in the chair.

'You, there, Dorothy,' she said, jerking her head at the chair opposite. Then she reached into a shelf cut into the wall of crystal and took out a pair of celestine clips. She clipped them onto each of Rose Thorn's index fingers.

'All these years spent refining them, and they still pinch,' Rose Thorn, said. The steel wires attached to the celestines smelt like the metal of blood.

'Yeah, said Tallulah. 'I've tried them. They pinch, but they don't hurt.' Then she plugged their wires into a socket beneath a huge vastscreen.

Rose Thorn steadied her mind against the onslaught of pulsating energy. Yet, despite her best efforts, a moment later, blurred, colourful images began to appear onscreen.

'What the fuck is that?' asked Tallulah, frowning at the kaleidoscope of colour.

'I'm hardly likely to tell you,' said Rose Thorn.

'So - we play guessing games?'

'You guess,' said Rose Thorn. 'I already know.'

'But it's not anything,' said Tallulah, rubbing the joint that was slightly out of alignment in her neck.

'Not my problem,' said Rose Thorn.

Tallulah twisted her hand in front of the screen. The image resolution grew sharper.

'It's a stained glass window,' she said, at last. She squinted at the screen a bit more. 'Hey, I know that window,' she said. 'It's from that fancy co-ed school they have here. You one of those Brunwych girls? You gonna do magick, voodoo, on me?'

The rose bloom of the onscreen window fell upon them both, all splendid dyes and vivid hues. It was from Queen Guinevere's Hall at the school, high, triple arched, and garlanded with flowers.

'If I could do that,' said Rose Thorn, quietly, 'do you think I would still be here?'

'A queen, a princess, a window,' said Tallulah. 'A yawn, yawn, yawn. Show me something worth seeing.' She adjusted the celestine clips with a precision born of many years practise and waited for the next image to appear onscreen.

It came, soon enough. It was evening and a hand was lighting a silver taper.

'That's it?' said Tallulah. 'That's it? Other people have their most precious memories, their most heartfelt secrets ripped right out of them - and with you, I get this?' Her dark eyes narrowed. 'You're doing something, aren't you? You're blocking it, somehow.'

'Think of it as being for your own protection,' said Rose Thorn. 'I don't think you'd like what you saw.'

'You don't get to decide that,' said Tallulah, 'I do.' She stretched out her thumb and index finger in front of the screen, and a moment later, a room in a castle appeared. The uneven flagstones on the floor were strewn with grass and flowers, and the posts of the bed were ivory. The bed itself dominated most of the room. The mattress looked to be of brocaded silk, deep, plush, burgundy, and the coverlet was sable.

'Better,' said Tallulah. 'Much better.'

Onscreen, the sudden flame of a lantern flared up, and in the castle chamber, a dark-eyed man with dark, tousled hair began to pull off his shirt. Then the lantern blew out.

'Who he?' asked Tallulah, genuinely interested.

'The wrong man,' said Rose Thorn. 'A long time ago.'

'Before or after you joined the Sisters of Valerian?' asked Tallulah.

'Oh, after,' said Rose Thorn, then stopped, realising her mistake. Now the celestine dug down deeper into the neural pathway that her mistake had opened up, so that onscreen there appeared a singer, in a gallery, a girl with hair like flame, and sad, expressive eyes. She began to sing:

'The guide who cannot find her way,
The spirits who come out to play,
Ghouls who relinquish their sweet flesh,
The horse he drags who is himself.

Where's the castle down the dark road?
Damned if you do, damned if you don't.
There's no heaven, try not to mind -
In heaven, it's the devil you find.

What if the devil is the knight?
Who is the angel in the night?
Did she put your dreams on a rack?
Cast her off and the sky turns black.'

When Tallulah spoke again, she sounded oddly moved. 'There's a lot here, isn't there?' she said. 'Too much for one evening's interrogation. At any rate, you've earned your cell for the night.'

She called to the guard stationed at the entrance to the Mothercrystal.

'Admiral Tevlev,' she said, 'take Rose Thorn to the Inner Reception and ask them to find her a bed.'

Tevlev nodded and came towards them. Just before he pushed her ahead of him, Rose Thorn gave him a curious glance. His hair was dark, his forehead, gaunt, and his black eyes, mournful, and rimmed with kohl. But his cheeks were round and painted with black and white diamonds, very precisely, to emphasise the contours of his face.

Admiral Tevlev handed Rose Thorn over to a female prison guard; her fingerprints were taken, and there followed a few minutes in the BOSS chair (Body Orifice Security Scanner), a kind of metal detector. Then she was led into her cell, dingy but clean, and lay down on its narrow bed.

Her pillow smelt faintly of lavender, and she wondered if the scent was to calm nervous prisoners. In fact, the place reminded her of her Little Hut in Valerian - except that there, the doors and pillars were to be blessed, ritualistic rites were to be performed, and there were chants to be sung, nightly. The routine had been comforting and interspersed with those rare moments when she had truly felt herself to be in communion with the Goddess.

Perhaps it was the celestine clips' disturbance to her neural pathways, but that night, for the first time in ages, she dreamt. A lot.

Queen Morgana had largely forbidden mirrors in Avalon, since they were doorways into other realms, and yet Rose Thorn dreamed she was staring at herself in a slither of glass. There she was, pale face, dyed black hair, outraged blue eyes. Then she dreamt she had to carry a chalice of water or wine, entirely full, through the dark to someone who was thirsty, but she could never reach that person. And yet she pushed through the darkness, until she beheld a glimpse of sky, and in that glimpse, there were stars.

In the morning, Rose Thorn woke up, thirsty, and poured some water from the pitcher into a glass. It was clear and sweet, flavoured with elderflower, and she comforted herself with the thought that some sacred springs still flowed in Avalon. Then the female guard she had seen the night before brought her a better breakfast than she would have hoped for, on a tray.

So she sat on her bed, eating eggs with dark yellow yolks that spurted down the side of their eggcups when she dug in her spoon, as well as toasted rye bread with salted butter. Next came porridge, and she shut her eyes and savoured the wholesome oats and surprising cream and honey, all the while basking in the pale flood of light through the rectangular window.

She had just begun her second cup of tea when Admiral Tevlev came to escort her back to the Mothercrystal.

'Sit,' Tallulah said a few moments later, scowling and nodding at the opposite chair from the heart of the crystal sphere.

Rose Thorn sat, whilst Tallulah adjusted something on the control screen. 'Last night's *Collodian Star* was a big disappointment,' Tallulah complained. 'Just some knight who went into the wrong room and lay down next to a girl. You couldn't even see much, the screen was so dark. Anyway, the next day, he thought he had to marry her, and so, eventually, he did, and so yawn, yawn, yawn... As far as opium for the masses goes, it was hardly crack cocaine.'

'Sir Sagramore,' Rose Thorn said, but so quietly that Tallulah didn't hear.

As Tallulah continued to complain, she pinched the celestine clips open almost viciously, and placed them on Rose Thorn's fingertips.

'Loving the ergonomic design,' winced Rose Thorn.

'Wriggle your fingers a bit - once the circulation comes back, they won't pinch so much. Anyway, I hope you've got something good lined up for me today.'

But, as on the previous day, a blur of bright colours appeared on the screen. Red, blue, purple, green, yellow, fuchsia, all shimmering. 'Fuck that,' said Tallulah, but as she swore, the image became sharper and the colours were revealed as pieces of silk, with heraldic devices and fantastical borders of branches, buds, flowers, and yellow-throated birds. A silken case.

'That must have taken hours to make,' said Tallulah, impressed, despite herself, as she tried to imagine the cool touch of silk, like breath, on her aching neck.

'Hours and hours,' said Rose Thorn. Tallulah's moment of interest seemed to break down her defences, because then, onscreen, a hand, her hand, was removing a shield from that silken case. A magnificent shield, with three azure lions on it, crowned with gold, rampant in the field.

'No fucking way,' said Tallulah. 'That's the Prince Consort's coat-of-arms.'

'The Prince Consort?' asked Rose Thorn.

'Yes' said Tallulah, 'how can you not know? Queen Morgana just got married to Lancelot Dulac. The wedding was broadcast on all the major channels last month.'

Rose Thorn paused. 'I was... on a retreat,' she said, at last. 'Major spiritual training programme. No television.'

'Well,' said Tallulah, 'from what I see here, it looks like the Prince Consort would be able to identify you.'

'I doubt it,' lied Rose Thorn. 'That's a wooden copy of Sir Lancelot's shield, that my brothers painted.'

'But the embroidery...' said Tallulah, savouring the fancy Valerian word, because it evoked for her the tilt of towers and turrets, old castles, old picture-books, old fairy-tales.

'He never saw it,' said Rose Thorn. 'C'mon, I can't have been the only teenage girl in Valerian with a crush on Sir Lancelot.'

'That must have been some almighty crush,' said Tallulah. 'Anyway, you had brothers, thanks for that piece of information.' She typed something onto the screen, and a moment later, a cypress tree set amongst the cobblestones of a courtyard appeared. Tallulah adjusted the focus angle, and then it was as if they were standing at the base of that tree, the ridged bark at their fingertips, the leaves shifting and turning above their heads. A pair of dark grey eyes peered out from among the leaves above them, accompanied by gales of laughter.

'One of my brothers liked to climb trees,' said Rose Thorn, off-handedly.

'Yeah, but that tree, those cobbles,' said Tallulah, 'they're like the embroidery, something fancy, something old. You're one of them Precursor Valerians, aren't you?'

14

Suddenly, without warning, the screen in front of them turned blood-red. Then Tallulah realised that the red mist was in fact a veil of samite, which was removed to reveal a chalice. It shone with a light so bright that the candles around it seemed less radiant. And the chalice itself was of pure gold, and inlaid with many jewels, stones so rare and precious, from such far-flung corners of the earth and sea, that no-one even know what they were.

Rose Thorn glanced across at Tallulah now. She was lit up by the light of the onscreen Grail, so that, for a moment, her face looked softer, kinder.

Then Tallulah swallowed hard. 'I ain't no religious nutjob,' she said. 'Show me some cup and I grovel at your feet, ain't gonna happen to me. I've worked too long and too hard for that.'

'Not a cup, but a sacred chalice,' Rose Thorn quoted.

'Not a sacred chalice, but the Holy Grail,' said Tallulah, repeating the next line of the prayer before she could stop herself.

'So,' said Rose Thorn, 'you know the Creed of the Sisters of Valerian?'

Whilst Tallulah sat there, shaking her head, Rose Thorn quickly removed one of her own celestine clips and attached it to Tallulah's index finger. A moment later, a nun's dark robe appeared onscreen, and someone was lighting incense in a burner in front of an altar. The nun was Tallulah herself, breathing in those sacred herbs burning there, dancing in their smoke, all alone. She was dancing for spirits she could not see, though Rose Thorn saw them, now onscreen, crowding in the air all around her, following the turn and spin of her feet and the circling gestures of her arms.

'I knew I recognised you!' said Rose Thorn. 'You're Sister Golden Claw. But we thought you were dead.'

'Guess again,' said Tallulah, snatching the celestine clip from her finger. 'You ain't trickin me with all that mumbo-jumbo. Sleeping in a hut, worshipping a chalice, hoping for a glimpse of some goddess that no-one except the Leader ever sees. And all out in the sticks, in the marshes of Valerian. But here - here in Avalon, I got a nice, big house see, a proper job, friends, and television.'

'A proper job, torturing people?'

'Harvesting memories ain't exactly torturing people. It's creating mass entertainment until Queen Morgana finds us a new planet.'

'You seem to have swallowed the party line pretty well,' said Rose Thorn. 'What happens to all those who are left brain-damaged by the harvesting process?'

'Collateral damage,' said Tallulah, swallowing hard. 'Besides, brain damage is overstating it.'

'You take away people's best memories,' said Rose Thorn, 'those that make them feel happiest - and proudest of themselves, the things that make them who they are. And then you expect them to cope in the grey drabness you leave behind.'

'But they get to watch everything on *Collodian Star*,' said Tallulah, 'they get to see everyone's best days.'

'It doesn't mean the same, like that, though,' said Rose Thorn. 'You see a random boy; I see my brother.' Before Tallulah could reply, Rose Thorn said then, quietly, but with steely determination, '*Tirra lirra*.'

At the sound of those words, all the harshness and meanness in Tallulah's face, the calculating expression, fell away. She looked again at Rose Thorn, as if with new eyes. 'You're her, aren't you?' she said.

'Who?'

'The Leader. The Priestess. Elaine of Astalot.'

Rose Thorn nodded, and grabbing hold of the celestine clip, she concentrated hard. Now onscreen, new images rose up. They saw in front of them, unsteady sunlight, shining aslant in the chill and brittle air. Bindweed, which had forced its way between mosaic tiles, their blue engravings outlined with frost and snow. It caught on the passing robes, long and black, of the Sisters of Valerian.

The sisterhood made its way, two-by-two, down the vast hall between double rows of columns. Rose Thorn and Tallulah could hear the drums, beating rhythmically. Dark-robed girls carried torches that burned reddish in the shafts of sunlight pouring through the narrow, arched windows. Only women were allowed through the great doors, robed, hooded, proceeding towards the altar.

Two tall women, one, thin and precise, the other, swaying as she walked, accompanied a young woman with fair hair who wore a straight, dark robe. At the foot of the steps leading up to the altar, the two taller women halted and pushed the girl forwards.

The altar itself was comprised of another seven steps, austere and gleaming. Alone, the girl climbed the first four of those steps. They were so broad and high that she had to get both feet onto one step before clambering onto the next. On the middle step, she paused. The three highest steps above her had never been climbed by mortal feet.

They were the steps by which Valeria, the Goddess of Light, might one day descend and walk among her followers, in answer to their prayers. But for now, these steps were thick with dust, the grooves of their white and blue marble tiles hidden.

The drums began to sound again, beating to a quicker pace. Whilst the girl was gazing up to the empty alcove, that lacked offerings of frankincense, myrrh, or even jars of wildflowers, the two priestesses that had accompanied her threw a red cowl over her shoulders.

'Behold the Girl given unto the Goddess,' they chanted. 'Let her always be acceptable in the eyes of the Goddess.'

The girl turned and descended the four steps laboriously to face the assembled maidens. The two priestesses took hold of her hands and raised her arms in the air. 'Let her find the stolen memories. Let her restore them to those who are lost - and in doing so, let her make Valerian whole again.'

'As the Goddess wills it,' said the new priestess.

Silently, the procession formed and moved away from the altar, eastwards, towards the bright, distant rectangle of the doorway. Among the sisterhood, their Leader now walked, her bare feet treading solemnly over the frozen weeds and icy stones. When the sunlight flashed through the domed glass roof and down onto the new priestess, she did not look up.

Female guards held the great doors wide open. The procession came out into the light of the morning. The line of priestesses, two-by-two, wound down the hill, softly chanting.

Now Tallulah and Rose Thorn watched, as, onscreen, the new leader was taken from room to room in the Compound of the Sisters of Valerian. Finally, as the evening star began to set, she was brought to the Little Hut, and there, she rested.

The screen faded to grey, and then turned black. 'So,' said Tallulah softly, 'you were trying to find the harvested memories in the Winter Palace when we caught you?'

Rose Thorn nodded. 'We knew the celestine clips were mined and manufactured close to the Mothercrystal. We were working on a hunch that the harvested memories were stored there, too.'

'*We?*' said Tallulah.

'You don't expect me to tell you their names, do you?' asked Rose Thorn. 'Besides, a few of them you would know anyway, from the early days of the Sisterhood.'

Tallulah shook her head. 'The cylinders of memory aren't here,' she said, a worried note to her voice. 'And you shouldn't be, either. Queen Morgana's fucking renegade granddaughter. What the hell am I supposed to do with you, now?'

'Help me escape?' asked Rose Thorn, hopefully.

'I know you said the Prayer of Undoing,' said Tallulah, 'thanks and all, but why should I help you escape?'

'Because since I said that prayer, already you feel better,' said Rose Thorn. 'Already, you have some hope that there's a better way.'

'Goddesses, priestesses, chalices... my better way is *me*,' said Tallulah.

'Come with me, then,' said Rose Thorn. 'You know a lot. I could do with your help.'

'I ain't coming with you,' said Tallulah. 'There's a really good episode of *Collodian Star* on TV tonight. And besides, you're assuming I'm going to set you free.'

'Point One: You don't want to give me up to Queen Morgana,' said Rose Thorn. 'Point Two,' she continued, counting them off on her fingers, 'You know I don't know where the cylinders of memory are so I'm no real threat.'

'At the moment, you don't know,' said Tallulah. 'I'm pretty sure that might change in the future.'

'And Point Three,' said Rose Thorn, starting to smile, 'You're hoping, beyond hope, that the Sisters of Valerian can make Valerian like it used to be.'

'Say it like that,' said Tallulah, 'and you make me sound like a double-agent.'

'Sister Golden Claw, that's a role for you, if you want it.'

'Not now,' said Tallulah, shaking her head again. 'Maybe not ever. But I'll let you go. I personally think the queen should treat her kinsfolk a little better. Just don't ever tell her I said that.'

'As a knight once said to me,' said Rose Thorn, 'where Morgana is, it's best that I am not.'

'Dark Eyes onscreen?' asked Tallulah.

'No,' said Rose Thorn. 'The other one.'

'Yeah, I didn't buy that *my brothers' painted shield* bull,' said Tallulah. 'Probably Morgana would like you more if the Prince Consort liked you less.'

'That's unlikely to happen, though,' said Rose Thorn. 'He and I go way back.'

Tallulah helped Rose Thorn to remove the celestine clips. Then she tapped something onto the screen in front of her.

Rose Thorn looked across at what her friend was doing. Onscreen, there was something which resembled a map of Avalon. She glimpsed triangles representing forestland, as well as an oval for the great glass building that was the Mothercrystal Broadcasting Studio, at the Winter Palace in Beaurepaire, deep in the heart of the valleys that made up the Collodian. Then too, there was the village of Beaumain on its outskirts, once a fine duchy, and finally, the rivers and seas that flowed out to Valerian, Ravenglass, the Westward Isles, and then on to the wider world.

'I'm arranging a pickup for you, somewhere where there's enough landing space,' Tallulah said. 'It's on the outskirts of Beaurepaire - you got your walking shoes? I can't risk my car being seen and reported.'

'I can walk,' said Rose Thorn, 'but landing space?'

'For the starship. I'm getting you as far away from Queen Morgana as I possibly can.'

'Good plan,' said Rose Thorn. 'But I'm not a stowaway. Tell them onboard the starship that I'm a constellation class flight navigation officer.'

'Tell them yourself. This is just standard Mayday protocol - I can't give out too much information on this frequency channel.'

'Of course not,' said Rose Thorn. 'Sorry, I didn't mean to sound ungrateful.'

'Fucking Precursor Valerians,' said Tallulah. 'You think the entire fucking planet revolves around you.' But she was grinning, and a moment later, as the screen shuddered and beeped, she cheered. 'Yes. They're going to take you on board. We *rendez-vous* at 7pm.'

'Thank you,' said Rose Thorn. 'You've done a lot.'

'Yes, I saved your sorry ass,' said Tallulah. 'Just don't come to the Winter Palace again till it's safer.'

'Which is when?' asked Rose Thorn.

'I'm not getting into any treason,' said Tallulah, firmly. 'Anyway, I'll go and sort us some packed lunches, then we better get going.'

They spent all day crossing the valley, following the path the rail-tracks had laid out before them. At one point, there appeared a crowd of spirits, silent and devout. The eyes of each were dark and hollow. Their visages were pale, and so lean, that their bones showed through their skin.

And then at last, one, a knight, broke free of the rest, and on his skeletal horse, galloped forwards, with lengthening strides, as if eager to display his chivalry. But as he neared them, his armour began to fall off, piece by piece, and where it fell, it vanished, to be followed by his arms, his hands, and all his remaining limbs, until there was only that sorry horse fleeing out in front of them.

'I hate this place,' said Rose Thorn.

'It is fucking awful here,' agreed Tallulah. 'It's for the spirits who didn't make it into Hell. Imagine not even being good enough to get into Hell!'

'When I was a little girl, I wasn't considered good enough to be a sixer in the Brownies,' said Rose Thorn, 'only a seconder.'

'That's kind of a lame anecdote,' said Tallulah, swiftly, turning to face her. 'How much did you want to be a sixer?'

'Not very much at all after the age of ten,' confessed Rose Thorn, frankly. 'I knew I was destined for better things.'

'You knew this at the age of ten?'

'I was quite precocious. And holy,' she added, lest there be any mistaking her meaning. 'You know, quite spiritual, and, sort of, well, *special*, with that indefinable radiance and grace, that, you know, is granted to very few young girls at that age and...'

'After you found the Grail, you had a vision of the Goddess and you grew angel wings... blah, blah, blah, I read the brochure when I joined the Sisterhood. Where are your wings, anyway? I'd have known who you were sooner, if I'd seen them. And if you hadn't dyed your hair.'

'After Queen Morgana closed the borders to Avalon, and things got really, really bad in Valerian, I started to feel quite down, and my wings sort of disappeared. I mean, I think they're still there, somehow, because I can feel them itching along my shoulder blades and down my spine, but, then, they're not there, too.'

'Phantom wings?' asked Tallulah.

'Exactly,' said Rose Thorn.

Later, as they walked out into the evening sky, Rose Thorn thought first of her mother, and then, as the rosy hues turned to flame, her grandmother. And then, as the sun began to set, she recalled her last visit to the Collodian, when she, Lanval and Lancelot had emerged from the underworld into its valleys. Then her grandmother had summoned her and Lancelot to the castle, leaving poor Lanval behind. She remembered how her grandmother had kept calling for wine, and then, ever deeper in her cups, she would tell ever wilder tales, seeming to enjoy the look of confusion on her granddaughter's pretty, pious face.

Just as the rays of the setting sun began to fall gently on their foreheads, and Tallulah was starting to tell Rose Thorn that it was nicer out where she lived, that she should really come visit sometime, they heard a rapid noise, like a bell beating. For a moment, Rose Thorn wondered if it were a hawk, a peregrine, or even a merlin. Then she remembered what the sound was, an approaching starship, and her heartbeat quickened with excitement.

Slowly, like two tiny spiders on a great wall, the two women toiled across the valley, until, at its top, they stood on dry ground, streaked with long shadows across its gorse and sage. Wordlessly, Tallulah pointed to the east, where the sun was sinking lower and lower, behind rolls of cloud. Though the sun grew ever more hidden, still, there was a glitter on the horizon, something like the dazzle of the crystal sphere they had left that morning, and yet, vaster, more immense, a glorious shimmering on the edge of the world.

'The starship,' said Rose Thorn.

'Yes,' said Tallulah. 'It's here for you. Three starships were orbiting in the vicinity. I sent your coordinates to your old ship, the *Joyous Gard*.'

'How can I thank you for everything you've done?' asked Rose Thorn.

'Stay alive,' said Tallulah, 'and keep in touch.' Rose Thorn stepped towards her, as if to hug her, but Tallulah shook her head. 'Goodbyes make me crazy,' she said.

'Then it's not goodbye,' said Rose Thorn, smiling. Now she looked ahead, to where the starship stood.

It was massive, and unfathomable as a mountain, dark as camouflage, except for that welcoming shimmer of light. The two women halted for a moment, then one set off, back over the rugged tufts of sage and gorse, only turning once to pause and wave. Meanwhile, the other moved forwards, over the crest of the valley, finally out of sight of the Winter Palace and the Mothercrystal, and on towards the starship's opening square of golden light.

The Purple Book

Rose Thorn ran forwards, through the starship's hatch and into its beam of light. As she crossed over the threshold of the *Joyous Gard*, a sudden thought gave her pause. If Captain Dulac was now the Prince Consort of Avalon, who was in charge of the ship?

A moment later, she had her answer. In the reception bay, the new Captain, new to Rose Thorn, anyway, stepped forwards to greet her. A woman, not too tall, with a few more lines around her eyes, and slimmer than she used to be, though with that same soft blonde hair, now worn in a bob. Her uniform was different too: navy trousers, a black polo neck top, a navy tunic with the Conglomerate triangle insignia. There was an A inside it, surrounded by the customary laurel wreath for officers. Rose Thorn would have known her anywhere: Aurélie De Lys.

Excellent. Her friend's heroic exploits at the sanatorium in Shoreditch a few years ago, back when she was still the ship's History Officer, must really have opened the Conglomerate's eyes to what she could do. And it was about time there was a female captain.

'It *is* you,' Aurélie said, beaming, and catching her hand. 'I thought it was.'

'What do you mean?' asked Rose Thorn.

'Ms Jackson sent us a picture. You can cut and dye your hair all you want, you're still you.'

'Do you like it?' asked Rose Thorn, twisting her head from side to side.

'I'm not sure,' said Aurélie. 'It makes you look tougher. I suppose that's the idea.'

'Yeah, well, getting older suits you too,' said Rose Thorn.

'There's nothing about arthritis that suits me,' said Aurélie. She smiled. 'Being Captain does, though.'

They walked along a corridor to the main turbo lift bay.

'Tomorrow,' said Aurélie, 'you can look over the details for a planet in the Delta quadrant - see if it's worth the time and fuel for us to have a look. Not every planet that's capable of sustaining human life is worth it. But for tonight - we put you in your old quarters.'

'I'd be really glad of a shower,' said Rose Thorn, 'but I'm not ready to sleep.'

'Maybe you could catch a movie, then?' said Aurélie. 'Or no - I think they're showing some programmes from Avalon tonight - we're trying to give the crew insight into Queen Morgana's mindset.'

Rose Thorn rolled her eyes. 'Good luck with that one.'

'You knew she has her own TV show now?'

'Yes, but... the Sisters of Valerian don't watch TV. We have spent years perfecting our neural pathways against that kind of savage onslaught.'

'All the same,' said Aurélie, 'Officer Pluto is showing a triple bill of episodes tonight in the Viewing Theatre. Might be worth a look?'

'Oh, Valeria, is he still here?'

Aurélie nodded and sighed. 'Yeah. I know he can be a bit... off... but he's too clever to get rid of.'

'I suppose,' said Rose Thorn, sighing. 'Just he gives me the creeps. Anyway,' she said, brightening, 'do you care to join me? There's safety in numbers!'

'Oh, I'm not off duty for a few hours. I'll catch you later, though. Meet you in the officers' canteen?'

'Sure. Do they still have those dark slabs of chocolate cake?'

'It'll be too late for them to serve that, this evening, but I'll ask someone to bring a slice over to your quarters, now.'

'Captain Dulac would never have done that,' said Rose Thorn.

'Oh, I think he might have,' said Aurélie, and then she added, so softly that Rose Thorn didn't hear her, 'for you.'

After her shower and her slice of chocolate cake, Rose Thorn walked back along the corridor to the turbo lift, then down a floor, to the Viewing Theatre in the recreation suite. Her memories of the place were flooding back, and it was pretty easy for her to find her way around - but then, her sense of direction had always been good.

She sat in one of the plush velour tip-up seats in the viewing theatre whilst the lights went down. Up came the vastscreen, then flashes, zigzags, flickers, then the opening credits which revealed the name of the programme, *Collodian Star*. The programme that Tallulah obsessed about. And tonight - oh fuck. The specially harvested memories of... fuck. Lieutenant Lanval. Really? Then again, he had lived for centuries. Easily enough material for a triple bill. And when Rose Thorn had met him again, five years ago, he'd been well and truly in the clutches of Queen Morgana. So... Rose Thorn sighed, then sat back, anticipating yet more propaganda promoting, sigh, Granny's family values.

There Lieutenant Lanval was, up there onscreen, huge and mournful, tying tomato plants to canes in his greenhouse, then pruning roses that were half-strangling the garden gates of his semi-detached villa in, where was it? Rose Thorn struggled to remember. Oh, that's right, Battersea, in Valerian.

Offscreen, a telephone rang, setting a dog barking. Lieutenant Lanval put down his pruning shears, and the camera tracked him back into his house's shadowy interior. He picked up the receiver, grinning broadly.

Rose Thorn remembered then that Lieutenant Lanval had always prided himself on his gadgets, and on possessing *sufficient wherewithal* for their purchase. But then - closeup: the cradled receiver, his fallen face, his dismayed expression as the strident tones of Queen Morgana blasted his ear.

Without much preamble, the queen announced that she was in the process of devising a reality TV show called *Collodian Star.* Then, of course, she had to explain the concept of television to the Victorian Lanval, which took a few minutes.

Very knowing, very intertextual, thought Rose Thorn, from the plush comfort of her seat. Her attention wandered for a moment, but returned just as Lanval was nodding, 'Yes, television then is a sort of miniature music hall of wondrous variety in our own front parlour! But what's that, Queen Morgana?' he continued, 'you want Blancheflor to be a television show hostess? Because of her frankness, her charm, her candour, etcetera? Well yes, I know all about that. I am married to her.'

The camera hovered on his uncertain smile, as he began to ask about salary and living arrangements, then cut to a shot of Uxbridge, the golden retriever at his feet, who, with downcast head and sorrowful eyes, was whining slightly. 'Oh yes, and about the hound,' said Lanval, bending down to scratch Uxbridge's ears, 'how long will he need to be quarantined in kennels before he can join us in Avalon?'

'*Us*? There is no *us*, Lanval,' said Queen Morgana. 'I'm only inviting Blancheflor and Uxbridge.' She began to explain about the immigration problems in Avalon in the twenty-fourth century. Rose Thorn groaned. Granny didn't even begin to address the real reasons why Avalon was closing its borders to Valerians and Precursor Valerians alike. 'If I let you in,' Queen Morgana concluded at the end of a long speech extolling the *Avalon Way of Life*, 'I could be judged as showing favouritism to in-laws, and that could create such a political stink, I might never recover.'

'But Uxbridge is from Valerian too,' Lanval said earnestly, and then, when she didn't reply, he asked, 'what do you suggest *I* do?'

'I don't know, Lanval,' snapped Queen Morgana. 'Do I have to think of everything?' All the same, she paused for a moment, whilst onscreen there appeared some old stock footage of her adjusting her rubies. Then she continued, 'You could make yourself useful to the realm. Use the Travelling Candle to go forwards into the future and join one of the starship recruiting programmes. I'm commissioning a fleet of starships to seek out a new planet which might be inhabitable for people from our world.'

Next came a sorrowful montage sequence shot in sepia, splicing Blancheflor and Uxbridge packing their portmanteaux with shots of Lanval clumsily searched for the Travelling Candle in dainty baskets of pot pourri scattered about the two-up, two-down semi. Once his wife and dog had departed and the candle was fairly in his grasp, he began to mouth some words, which appeared onscreen as:

'North, South, East, West,
A starship space program is my request.'

There came a flash of lightning, then, fade to black.

Now the camera craned upwards to show storey upon storey of a magnificent skyscraper, that shone with windows of raven-glass.

Rose Thorn knew the building at once, since she had been there herself for the starship recruitment: Willis Towers, in Ipswich. Onscreen, its entrance doors slid open, Lieutenant Lanval gasped, and stepped inside.

He was greeted coolly by a woman with yellow hair, seated behind a desk in the building's lobby. When he gave his name, she tapped a few things onto her computer keyboard, then directed him to *Office Suite E*. She pointed in the direction of a lift down the corridor. 'It's on the eleventh floor,' she said. 'You really can't miss it.'

Lieutenant Lanval glanced at her name-badge, pinned neatly to the front of her turquoise blouse.

'Thank you, Miss Cordelia,' he said.

'It's Dr Maladroit to you,' she snapped.

The camera panned after Lieutenant Lanval as he paced across the lobby, then stood beside the lift doors. They opened and a tall golden monkey emerged. Lanval stepped inside, and the doors shut on his bewildered expression. But a moment later, the lift was soaring upwards, and a caption appeared onscreen:

'Today the lift: Tomorrow the stars!'

Another montage sequence followed in which Lieutenant Lanval was shown seated in a booth, filling out an application form for the role of Captain of the Starship *Joyous Gard*. In the section entitled Previous Experience, he wrote, 'I've read the collected works of Messrs Verne and Wells. My great, great, great uncle was a rear admiral. And last Sunday afternoon, I successfully paddled a canoe all round Hyde Park's boating lake.'

Spotlight then on his crestfallen face when the Recruiting Officer, Pluto, informed him that he had only been successful in securing the position of second-in-command. For Captain, they wanted Lancelot Dulac.

'Where *is* Captain Dulac?' Lanval asked. 'Didn't he become a monk and die?'

'An excellent question, Lieutenant Lanval,' said Lieutenant Pluto, who, onscreen, was even more unprepossessing than Rose Thorn remembered. 'Your first mission for the Conglomerate can be to search him out in the afterlife.'

'But, how, exactly, am I supposed to do that?' Lanval asked.

At that, Lieutenant Pluto pressed his fingertips to the temples of his bulbous forehead and opened his pale blue eyes very wide. 'Why, I should have thought the answer was obvious, Lieutenant Lanval,' he said, 'you still have one of Queen Morgana's Travelling Candles, don't you?'

Cut to a shot of the lobby. Now the lift doors slid open once more; Lanval gave Cordelia a little wave, then stepped out and lit the remaining stub of the Travelling Candle. Onscreen, the words appeared:

'North, South, East, West,
Take me to where Lancelot is,
That would be best.'

The screen turned black, but a moment later there was an exterior shot of an overcrowded platform, and a train, hissing into it. The crowd surged forwards and Lieutenant Lanval found himself propelled onto the train. But now he was grinning, and Rose Thorn remembered something he had once said, that even if the destination was unknown, still, the journey itself was a capital thing.

Onscreen, the train wrapped its sinuous way through cities and into coastal towns. The white sun shone down on white houses by the sea. Overhead, gulls circled in the endless blue of the sky, their ravenous caw-caw mingling with the chime of a faraway clock, or the tolling of a bell from a distant tower. Or else again, came the hum and rattle of a train approaching on the other line, or the chug of a motor-boat, ripping through the bays, and always the surge, wash and song of the sea.

Suddenly, the camera panned from a shot of Lieutenant Lanval, half asleep in the sunshine, to the seat behind him. Here, a man with dark grey hair and aquiline features, who Rose Thorn recognised, placed an order in a dry, refined voice.

'A cup of English breakfast tea, if you have it, please,' said Sir Sagramore as the tea trolley ceased trundling and clanking down the carriage aisle and stopped at his side.

'Tea, capital idea,' Lanval said, waking up, and when it was his turn, he ordered a cup of Earl Grey and some shortbread biscuits. As he took a sip, inhaling the scent of charred bergamot, Sir Sagramore spoke to him through the gap in the seats.

'Excuse me,' he said, 'my memory's not what it used to be, but aren't you one of the Camelot fellows?'

Lanval swivelled his head round to speak to him. 'Yes, I'm Lanval, remember? And you're Saggy!'

'Oh yes,' Sir Sagramore replied, 'that's right. You married one of Queen Morgana's granddaughters. Well, good luck with that, old fellow.' He cleared his throat, then glanced quickly round the carriage to make sure no-one else was listening. 'Of course, I'm to be married myself,' he said. 'In fact, I'm travelling to the town where the wedding will be.'

'Really?' Lanval said, 'who's the lucky bride? The Kumquat Damsel?'

Sir Sagramore had the grace to blush to the tips of his ears. 'Ah - you remember that?' he said. When Lanval nodded, Saggy added, 'Well, yes, actually, it is. I was selling some horses to her father, and there was a bit of a mix-up about the old sleeping arrangements, eh what, and well, the long and short of it is, honour must be satisfied, and the chapel is all booked for this Tuesday. I say, old chap, you wouldn't like to come to the wedding, would you?'

'That would be splendid,' replied Lanval, 'but, you see, I'm on a bit of a quest of my own. I'm looking for Sir Lancelot.'

'Oh him,' said Saggy, yawning slightly. 'Well, that was a bad business, make no mistake. I was glad to be out of it all and catapulted into the nineteenth century. Some of us more promising chaps were sent on to prepare for the King's Second Coming.'

'Yes, I know all about that,' said Lanval, 'and I wish I'd been one of them. I've been stuck serving Mordred for centuries, with no hope of promotion.'

'That's what happens when you get mixed up with Queen Morgana,' said Sir Sagramore. 'I did try to warn you. Still, I daresay you and the Lady Blancheflor, was it? are happy enough.'

'We would be,' Lanval retorted, 'except that she's had to go and be a reality television show hostess in the twenty-fourth century.'

'Really?' said Sir Sagramore. 'Rum sort of a thing, if you ask me.'

Lanval tried to smile but the effort hurt his mouth.

Sir Sagramore stood up, reached over the seat and clapped him on the shoulder. 'I suppose you know your own business best, old chap,' he said.

'I'm in training to become a starship officer,' Lanval replied, somewhat stiffly, but he saw Saggy was no longer listening. He had sat back down and returned his attention to the *Valerian Literary Supplement.*

Outside the train window, the sun still shone, the gulls still wheeled and circled, and children still buried themselves in sand or busied themselves with buckets and spades. As the train rounded into the station, which bore the sign, *Plain Ease*, everything glittered like champagne. The light glinted off the rocks, washed porpoise-slick by the turquoise shudder of the waves.

Far ahead lay the great towers and rugged walls of an unknown castle, crowning a sheer, rocky crag, overlooking the dunes below. It stood there majestically, as if waiting for the tide to turn and the distant sea to come and lap at its feet once more. Behind it, the peaks of mountains towered into the sky, a ladder for giants to climb.

'Please, what is that place?' Lanval asked, turning to speak to Sir Sagramore through the gap in the seats once more.

'You don't want to go there, dear boy,' said Sir Sagramore, lowering his newspaper, the corners of his mouth trembling. 'That's the gateway to the City of Dis. Eternal fire burns within that tower. It's in that place, you know...' His voice became a confidential whisper, 'Hell.'

'Hell?' Lanval gasped.

'Ah, but *Plain Ease*, this is my stop,' said Sir Sagramore, gathering up his newspaper, his sandwich wrappers and his valise. 'Peggy, that is to say, the Lady Margaret, and her family are all waiting for me at a nice B&B just down the road. And if you're sure you won't join us, old boy...'

Sir Lanval gazed longingly at the beach outside the window. It was postcard pretty: there was a dog padding at the water's edge and children running up and down, their feet shivering and slapping the springy sand. There they were with their fleeting castles, boys and girls, kingfishers and moving jewels.

Always came the surge and retreat of the deep blue, dark blue sea.

'Quickly, quickly, make up your mind,' said Saggy, but now his voice was less the fluting vowels of the aristocratic knight, and rather more irritable, testy even. In fact, he sounded more like, like...

'I'll stay on the train,' Lanval sighed.

'Excellent, excellent,' said the man, who suddenly wasn't Sir Sagramore at all, but rather - the magician, Merlin. There he was onscreen, just as Rose Thorn remembered him, with his beard of winter, and his eyes like petals drowned in rain. But now came a swirling fog, like something out of an early Hitchcock classic, and when it had dispersed, the two men were no longer on the train, but standing at the foot of a hill.

In front of them on the path was a leopard. Rose Thorn was forced to admire the cinematography that depicted the creature's amber fur, sprinkled with black dots, gleaming against the gorse and bracken. Everywhere that Merlin and Lanval tried to go, there she was, blocking their path.

'Morgana!' cried Merlin. He turned to his companion. 'But she is here for me, not you, Lanval.'

'If you say so,' Lanval replied. 'But I am here at her bidding.'

'Are you?' said Merlin. 'I thought you were here to find Sir Lancelot. That is why Elaine of Astalot, the Leader of the Sisters of Valerian, sent me to you.'

The mention of her own name onscreen gave Rose Thorn a sudden jolt, and then a hollow, uncanny feeling in the pit of her stomach. It also made the leopard bare her fangs and snarl, then turn tail and pad away.

'I should be grateful for your help,' said Lanval, 'but why is Sir Lancelot, a virtuous knight and true, here among the tormented souls and burning shades?'

'Alas,' said Merlin. 'Know ye not that our greatest knight was our most flawed? Know ye not the sin of which he is guilty?'

'No,' Lanval replied to the sudden, rousing accompaniment of a full string orchestra, 'and I will not hear it. For I must believe in him if I am to lead him from this place.'

'Lanval,' said Merlin gently, 'we are all of us flawed, to a greater or lesser extent. Even I. Which is why I can only lead you so far, and no further. The Lady Elaine will be your next guide upon this sorrowful path.'

'O bright star, Elaine,' Lanval murmured.

Thus the two men continued along that deep and rugged road. Presently they passed through a great, leaden gate. On the gate, there was a sign with words inscribed upon it in Avalon: *'L'Endroit de l'Espoir Perdu.'*

Lanval cried out then, 'Merlin, those words are cruel!'

But Merlin, inexorable as Death, touched the peridot head of his staff to that gate, and it opened without resistance from within onto a courtyard of utter pain and ugly anguish. It was not Ipswich. It was not Brighton. It was not Reigate. It was not any of the places where Lanval had ever been, no, not even Ravenglass.

'This, dear Lanval,' cried Merlin, 'is Hell.'

Through that courtyard, the wizard began to pace, with the moon and stars of his robe throwing out glimmers of light onto suffering souls.

Now the screen turned black, and the closing credits began to roll upwards.

Next came some intermission music, which was a mash-up of the *Collodian Star* theme tune with the lyrics from *Star Trek: Enterprise*: 'Cause I've got faith of the heart/I'm going where my heart will take me...'

'Why did they pick an Eighties power ballad?' Rose Thorn wondered.

Then came a new set of opening credits, in which all the characters were shown in various poses: Merlin, holding aloft his staff, Lanval, his pruning shears, then a glimpse of a brunette lady in a red swimsuit, reclining by a sunlit pool whilst a dark-haired man poured her a cocktail. Elsewhere, a fair lady cuddled a kitten, and then finally, golden words swirled onto a purple background: Special Guest Appearance: *Sir Lancelot Dulac, played by himself.*

'The big reveal,' thought Rose Thorn. 'The Great Knight of Misbegotten Means.' And then, 'Did I really used to wear my hair like that? And where did the kitten come from? The props department? Although - this is *Lanval's* harvested memories of me. Perhaps I once told him about a kitten. I had to say *something*, anything, to distract him from his woes, to get him through the Inferno and later, the Collodian. Unless, of course, that was Blancheflor? We did used to look exactly alike. Did she ever have a kitten?'

Then the programme proper began with a wide angle shot of - an abyss. Merlin and Lanval were circling round it, whilst the diegetic sound was howls and cries.

Merlin paused a moment and said, 'Those poor souls that came before the birth of Christ. They are cut off from hope, and yet they live on in desire.' He sighed heavily. 'This might be where I end up, too.'

'Oh, but why?' asked Lanval.

'Well, it's the living backwards that's the problem,' said Merlin. 'At the rate I'm going, I'll be a tiny child before Christ is born.'

'You could convert to Christianity?'

'But I will still be born before Christ, and it is hard to believe in someone who won't yet exist.'

'But that is the nature of faith,' cried Lanval, 'I think you should try.'

They passed then into the second round, where a mighty storm raged, sweeping and driving its spirits, whirling and lashing them. Lanval stopped and asked Merlin, 'What souls are these, who are punished in this way?'

Merlin began to call out a list of names, quite as if he was a schoolmaster with a register: *Sir Ironside, Sir Patrise, Sir Persant, Lady Lavender, Dame Nikura, Princess Petunia.* Then Rose Thorn realised that many of these names were the knights and damsels of Camelot, her former companions. Her heart sank, and Lanval's face onscreen grew more melancholy: the light went out of his eyes, and he clutched at Merlin's sleeve.

A pair of shades whirled onscreen. They were both dark, striking, beautiful, but unknown to Rose Thorn - and Lanval, who asked his guide who they were. At the sound of his voice, the female shade lifted her head, and the camera moved in for a close-up of her dark, mournful eyes. She had been weeping.

The shades left their flock of tormented souls and flew over to the watchers from the world of men. Their wings were raised high and poised, like those of ravens returning to their nest.

'Why are you here, dear souls?' Lanval asked them.

The tumultuous wind grew silent to allow their voices to be heard.

The lady began her story in a murmur, like the wind stirring autumn leaves. 'Know you this, gentle strangers, that I am Francesca Da Rimini, and this is my kinsman, Paolo.' She paused for a moment, but the names meant nothing to Lanval. 'Love made this Paolo enamoured of my great beauty,' she continued, unselfconsciously, 'and Love made me delight in him. We were inseparable. And thus we went straight to sudden death together, murdered by one who envied us our delight.'

She bowed her head again, the epitome of the sorrowing, gracious lady, except that Rose Thorn caught a glimpse of malice in her tearful eyes.

'There is more to this than she tells you,' the wizard said to Lanval. 'Do not fall for her wiles.'

Lanval turned back to the lady and said, 'Tell me then, how did you know it was Love that you felt?'

Francesca sighed. 'You ask me in my present grief to recall my past happiness? That is cruel indeed, and yet I will tell you the root of our great love.'

As she spoke, further images appeared onscreen. There was a younger Paolo and Francesca, cloistered in a nook in some great hall. On Francesca's lap lay a great book with purple binding. She was reading aloud the story of - oh - Lancelot and Guinevere. Her face flushed then paled as she began to read of longed-for lips being kissed by such a famous lover. Then the book fell from her hands, the screen turned black, and Francesca concluded, 'That day we read no more.'

Cut back to the sorrowful shades circling the knight and the wizard. Now Francesca took the book from a fold in her robe, this book, that by her own account, was the cause of her downfall. She showed it to them: it had a dark purple cover, and inscribed upon it in golden, curling letters was the title, *Lancelot Dulac*.

'When I read from this book, this man,' said Francesca, nodding to the silent Paolo, 'kissed my mouth, trembling all the while.'

Lanval turned to Merlin, the lines of his face softened with compassion and woe.

'Tell me,' he said, 'what must we do?'

'You have heard the name of Lancelot,' said Merlin, 'and yet you do not ask for the book?'

Lanval hung his head in sorrowful confusion.

Merlin took the book from Francesca and handed it to the knight.

As Lanval began to read, a vision rose up from the book's very pages. There was the lady again, with hair as black as shadows, that writhed about her head in serpentine coils. She seemed to want to take the book back from Lanval, but when she touched its pages, she dropped her hand, as if it had burned her. As she twisted her tormented head this way and that, sometimes she had the look of Francesca Da Rimini, but at other times indeed, she resembled Queen Guinevere.

And in those other times, this vison revealed that it was not Sir Lancelot who had first kissed the longed-for mouth of Guinevere, oh no, it was the queen herself who had placed her hand on Lancelot's chin and kissed him.

Different expressions flitted across Lanval's face as he read this, but Rose Thorn knew her friend and judged he was shocked to his heart's core. From her seat in the Viewing Theatre, she tried to recall if he had ever divulged any of the contents of this scandalous book, then shook her head, filled with strange misgivings. She knew her own time onscreen was coming soon.

'But Lancelot?' Lanval said at last, when his eyes could read no more. 'Where is Lancelot?'

Merlin opened his eyes very wide. 'Surely you know,' he said. 'Surely you realise that our Lancelot is imprisoned here in Hell. Here, inside this very book.'

'What must I do to release him?' asked the knight.

'Burn the book,' called Francesca, with such sudden spite, it enkindled her face to life.

The Dark Lady of Lanval's vision seemed then to toss the book upon the flames in front of her, there to watch it burn and blaze. Her very eyes were lambent flame as they gazed into those red, yellow, orange and black depths.

Now the burning pages rose up in sparkling whites and swarms of fireflies. Now the Dark Lady, this Francesca, this Guinevere, this shade who represented all men's fears of the witchery of womenfolk, exulted in what she had done, smiled at the charred book, smiled at its ashes, that carried yet the memory of those glorious flames.

Finally, the cinders blew away in a wind turned black with burning.

'Fled is that vision,' murmured Lanval, faintly. 'Do I wake or sleep?' But no, the book was still grasped in his hands and Francesca, the shade of the real Francesca, still stood before him, though now her head was once more bowed.

Merlin clasped his staff to himself. 'Burning is indeed a form of purification,' he said, 'but only for the souls in purgatory. For the damned, it is their punishment.' He paused. 'We will take the book from these sorrowful souls, and we will ask the Lady Elaine what should be done.'

Merlin and Lanval thus departed, with the purple book now tucked into a fold in the magician's cloak.

Then came another montage sequence of hail and snow, tumbling in torrents, and then the screen split into three to depict the three heads of Cerberus, guardian dog of the place. He howled from his three throats and tore at wayward spirits. But the mage stayed his jaws with fistfuls of mud, flung down the dogs' greedy gullets.

Afterwards, the weary shades danced around these mortals, whilst the extra diegetic music was that of a fateful roundelay. It reminded Rose Thorn briefly of Queen Morgana's account of a Tarantella that she had once danced in Valerian, just before she'd burst into flames - and perhaps, indeed, that was the point. For then Merlin began to speak of Queen Morgana, and since his words did not flatter her, Rose Thorn decided their inclusion was to strike fear into the viewers: 'There may come a time when the people of Avalon no longer remember the fairy-tales told to them in their horse-chestnut cribs. They may see them depicted on screens, but they will not understand them. And then all the magick of Old Valerian will shrink to the size of a thimble, and Queen Morgana will wear that thimble round her neck, and thus will her dominion be complete.'

At these words, Lanval's expression grew yet more hangdog, and when Merlin noticed his companion's sorrow, he cast his cloak around the knight's shoulders. Then he said, 'When at last angel wings unfurl on new soil, you will understand all of this, dear Lanval, and indeed, your own life's purpose.'

'I thought my purpose was to rescue Sir Lancelot,' Lanval replied, reaching inside the cloak, and running his fingertips over the swirling letters emblazoned on the book's purple cover.

'With the Lady Elaine's assistance, that will not be such an arduous task,' said the Magician, kindly. 'And when it is accomplished, there will be all of your life left to live.'

'And yet a story cannot have two heroes,' Lanval replied.

'I do not think you are at the point where you can call yourself a hero,' said Merlin, still kindly, whilst Lanval shivered in the folds of his cloak.

'Now, onwards,' the magician cried. 'The fish are shimmering over the horizon.'

'They are?' said Lanval, with a look of bewilderment which Rose Thorn had once found endearing.

So Merlin explained that some stars of the zodiac, Pisces, lay in front of them. Moreover, the sun would presently rise in Aries. For each sign of the zodiac covered about two hours of the journey, and so, he surmised, they were nearly two hours before sunrise.

'We are?' said Lanval.

Now, onscreen, Merlin and Lanval continued on their path, along the banks of a crimson river, wherein shrieks arose from boiling souls, up to their throats in blood. The camera panned across their anguished faces: a bloodshot eye here, a tangled fringe there, a gaping mouth, dripping crimson. Once again, Rose Thorn thought she recognised one or two faces from the court of Camelot.

Presently, the tide lowered, and the two men found the ford by which they might cross.

They passed over into a great forest which grew all around them. The leaves of its trees were blackened and charred, and its branches were entangled, bearing no fruit, but only twisted thorns. Cries of grief echoed, but who was there to make the sound? Only the shades, hidden in the trees.

Then Merlin said, 'Lanval, break off a little branch.'

Lanval reached out and snapped off a twig from a great thorn bush.

Now its trunk cried out, 'Why are you tearing at me, yon hapless knight?'

'That's torn it,' Lanval said, as the blood began to grow dark around the wound. 'Who are you?' he asked, but the voice in the tree did not answer.

Merlin shook his head and now his eyes were grim. 'The shades imprisoned here were once caught coupling in the sacred groves of Avalon.'

Lanval gasped, but his hand stole once more to the purple book, and as he ran his fingertips over its cover, there was a knowing look in his once innocent eyes. But now Lanval turned and looked askance at the magician.

'Were you not once imprisoned in a mirror, yourself?' he muttered. 'Should those in glass houses throw stones?' When Merlin did not answer, Lanval inquired, more tactfully perhaps, 'Do you know of any way by which a soul may leave these thorny branches?'

'My former student, Rose Red, would know,' said Merlin with a sigh. 'She was gifted in forest lore. Yet whether it be right to free such souls such as these, I cannot tell.'

Whilst they stood there, contemplating the tree's leafy ire, there came a sound like smashing branches and the crash of a boar, followed by the blast of a hunting horn. Then two shades appeared in front of them.

The shade in front cried out, 'Quickly, quickly.'

Rose Thorn knew him at once: this was tall Sir Tristram, with his forest brown hair and forest green eyes. Lanval had once beaten him in the Tournament of the Blood Rubies. His shield still bore the design of a spear, a harp and a bugle, but on his head, he wore a holly spray, which scattered berries.

'You were not so swift when last we jousted,' shouted his companion, Sir Pinel Le Savage himself, with his froth of dark hair, his pale eyes, and the points of his fangs, gleaming beneath the stars of Aries.

The next moment, Sir Pinel had fallen in the mud.

Now onscreen appeared a whirlwind of black dogs. They pounced upon Sir Pinel, and so, once again, in death as in life, he was torn to pieces.

The hounds ran off with his limbs protruding from their jaws.

Sir Tristram rubbed his unbelieving eyes, as if he were trapped in a nightmare from which he could not wake. A moment later, a noose appeared on the branch of the talking tree. Meek as a lamb, Sir Tristram climbed on an upturned bole and placed his neck inside that noose. The branch creaked upwards; his feet swung away from the bole; and thus was Sir Tristram hung.

He swayed there, slowly, backwards and forwards, resplendent still in his livery of forest green whereon tripped a thousand, tiny, silver deer.

Onscreen, Sir Lanval began to gather up the leaves scattered by the swinging corpse. As he placed them at the foot of the bleeding trunk, Merlin gave a bark of laughter.

'Lanval,' he said, 'tell this tale of the end of Sir Tristram to your sons. One day, your boy William will travel back in time to this knight's native Cornwall. There he will paint a sign for his public house, which he will name after this Hanging Man.'

'I'm to have sons?' Lanval asked. 'Not just Uxbridge? And why will my son become a pub landlord?'

'Why not?' cried Merlin. 'Making men and women happy through drink and song is a noble aspiration, and Lostwithiel would be bleak enough without a pub.'

'If you say so,' Lanval replied. He might have said more, but there came again the sound of snarls and snaps, the sudden whirl of midnight hounds. 'Merlin!' shouted the knight, 'you need to turn us invisible!'

'Not today,' said Merlin, 'it's a lot of effort. And in my haste to obey the Lady Elaine, I didn't bring the right spell - or my reading glasses.' Still, he grabbed Lanval's arm and forced him over the stony bank, then on, through the forest that was engirdled by the river of blood.

Presently they reached a line of stepping stones and crossed over to the other side of the river.

On the other side, there was a dry expanse of sand, and over all that sand land, fire flakes fell. They kindled the sand like tinder under flint sparks so that fires sprang up. All around them now there were flames, floating, falling.

But the hands of wretched souls were forced to brush away those flames.

Now they began to scale another bank, and then, all of a sudden, a vast pit opened up before them. The camera cranked down inside to reveal a terrible confusion of serpents and sinners, all coiled about in knots.

Suddenly, two six foot serpents shot up out of the pit, one with the face and aspect of Sir Pinel, and the other with the likeness of Sir Tristram. Their limbs were so entwined they began to melt and fuse. The two heads of the serpents became one, and the features from each blended into one loathsome face.

In their desire to escape the pit, the men crossed over a bridge, and then continued on, a full bow shot's length. Eventually they came out upon a lake of ice, more like a sheet of glass than frozen water. Here, there were shades stuck in the ice, up as far as their waists, with their heads bowed, their eyes, downcast. Yet there was a figure with dark hair flowing down to the ice who Rose Thorn thought she recognised. Her wicked uncle. *Mordred*.

Mordred inclined his neck and raised his face towards the two men. His eyes were dropping tears that turned to ice and his breath was too frozen for the utterance of his words.

The shade pointed to the dagger through his heart, but all the blood that should have poured forth from this wound was congealed and frozen.

'Mordred!' cried Merlin. 'Staked - and that put an end to your vampirism!'

Now Mordred wept again, and his tears filled the hollow part around his eyes, like a visor made for them in crystal. Lanval stooped, and, as a last service to his old master, scraped away the clusters of glass tears. Maybe it was the action itself that made him inquire, 'Whatever happened to Mordred's son, Morleon?'

Perhaps the warmth and kindness of Lanval's action melted the words frozen in the shade's throat. 'The boy's not here,' sighed the shade of Mordred. His voice sounded like drips of water, falling onto ice, in a cavern, far distant.

'He escaped into that other timeline where Queen Victoria was assassinated,' replied the wizard with a dismissive shrug. 'But I expect he'll end up here, sooner or later.'

'Morleon is the purest incarnation of evil that ever was,' Lanval said, nodding.

'No-one could accuse you of too fine a subtlety, Lanval,' sighed the wizard.

'Meaning?' said Lanval.

The magician shook his head, then gestured that he and Lanval should walk out across the souls, trapped in ice. And by dint of pacing, trudging, stumbling, they at last arrived at the City of Dis, known as, the words across the screen informed the viewers, the *City of Flame*.

Merlin seized hold of Lanval's arm and half hauled him up a flight of steps to the top of the tower that the knight had glimpsed from the train. Thus they came out, not onto a palace promenade, but rather the rocky ledge of castle battlements, which was, the magician intoned, the central point where the Man whose birth and death were free of sin was sacrificed.

'Then our great journey through the Kingdom of Grief has taught you at last to believe in Christ?' asked Lanval.

'Yay,' replied Merlin, 'but also nay, since there are other things to believe in, more beautiful and more impossible than you could ever imagine. Look yonder, Lanval!'

Next came a shot of Lanval frowning out across a ruined city. So Merlin seized hold of the knight's forehead, and pressed the central point between his eyes, then rubbed his fingers across his eyelids. 'Now,' he said. 'Now do you see?'

Now the camera tracked Lanval's line of vision. There had been no budget skimping on this episode, for, in full, glorious technicolour, a lady of silver and white began to approach them across the water, sometimes with the aspect of a nightingale, sometimes like a star, and sometimes like an angel.

As Rose Thorn realised that there, onscreen, was herself, she gripped the armrests of her seat so hard, her knuckles became knife blades.

The lady grew in size and brightness as she approached, and then it became possible to discern, unfolding and opening out, the form of her wings. So bright was she, that Rose Thorn was forced to drop her eyes, yet when she raised them again, there onscreen was a small boat, swift and light. The winged lady stood at its helm, and steered herself towards the two men, whilst spirits darted all about her, pale with wonder. As they too neared the shore, the lady waved her hands, and then all the spirits were sent flying off, like a flock of wild pigeons.

'When she joins us, I must leave you,' Merlin said to Lanval. Close-up then of the face of the wise old man, the sorrowful glint in his watery eyes, his long beard, mixed with hoary white, falling in double-folds upon his robe.

'But, but, but,' said Lanval with a beseeching note to his voice, so that the wizard smiled kindly.

Merlin continued, 'Yet I have one more thing that I must tell you, Lanval, before we say goodbye.'

'Which is?' asked Lanval, making a manly effort to steady himself.

'The sin you will commit, it is forgiven.'

'Which sin?' cried out Lanval, 'and what forgiveness?'

The lady moored her boat, then picked her way across the shingle until she stood beneath the cliff. She unfurled her wings once again, and with light, graceful movements, she soared up to the rock where they rested.

As the winged lady landed beside them, Lanval held out his hands to her, and she grasped them, warmly.

'Elaine!' he said.

'Dear Lanval,' she replied. 'You must bid farewell to Merlin now, for I am here to guide you on your path.'

'I think I will be getting back down the mirror corridor to my eerie,' Merlin agreed. 'My slippers will be nicely toasted by the fire, and there are roast chestnuts waiting for me.'

'But King Arthur always said, sitting softly cushioned was no way to win glory,' said Lanval.

'Wise words indeed, from the Fisher King, tucked up in his bed,' said Merlin. 'Anyway, he was referring to knights,' he added, nodding at the purple book of sin in the cloak he had given Lanval, 'not Kings - or elderly wizards.'

'Well, if you're sure,' Lanval said. 'It's been good to see you again, Merlin. Let's not leave it so long, next time.'

'Maybe things will be easier now they've built the new A11 timeline,' said Merlin, clapping him on the back.

Then Lanval reached out to grasp his hand and give him a bear hug in that *hail fellow, well met* way that Rose Thorn remembered from her time at court in Camelot. Somehow, however, Merlin slipped right through his fingers. Lanval was left clutching empty air. Apart from his cloak, there was no trace of the wizard left, not even smoke upon wind, or bubbles upon water.

'He's gone,' Lanval said, sorrowfully to the Lady Elaine.

'That's right,' she replied, brightly. 'And I believe Sir Lancelot is imprisoned in that purple book? If you could just hand it over. Thank you.'

She sat down, cross-legged, on the rocky ledge and placed the book upon her lap. Then, with a puckered frown, she began to leaf through the book's pages. When she found the section she was searching for, she began to intone the Charm of Undoing from memory.

'*Tirra lirra*,' she concluded, quietly.

After she had spoken the sacred charm, all the words rose up from the books' pages, swarming into the shape of a Knight - and this Knight was the very image and likeness of Sir Lancelot. Up to the surface of the book he swam, a thing to startle even the most stalwart of hearts, as he spread out his arms and doubled up his legs.

He emerged from the purple binding of the book, gasping for breath, his flesh now the only source of light on that rocky ledge.

As Rose Thorn watched the events unfolding onscreen, she felt the most curious sensation in her arms. It was hard to comprehend, but it was as if her arms were burning, set aflame, full of love. The feeling radiated into her chest, as if a door were opening up inside her heart. And, behind the door, was the most perfect, pure, exquisite distillation of love: there was no need, no want, not even desire, just a sudden rush of feeling in her heart for everyone and everything. She stretched out her legs beneath the seat in front of her, at ease for once in her delicate frame, and strummed her fingers on her knee.

Sir Lancelot glanced round at the steep, towering cliffs in bewilderment but then his gaze alighted upon Elaine, and his expression cleared. 'You!' he cried. 'Where is my shield, that I asked you to keep safe for me?'

Before Elaine could answer, Lanval interrupted.

'Excuse me?' he said. 'The Conglomerate wanted me to ask you, Sir Lancelot, to captain our Starship, *Joyous Gard*, and help us to discover a new planet where we can all be happy.'

After a moment or two of gazing at Elaine, Sir Lancelot replied, 'I'm already happy.' Then he frowned. 'But what is this thing called starship?'

'Ooh, I know, I know,' said Elaine at once.

Back in the Viewing Theatre, Rose Thorn groaned. Is that really what she used to sound like?

'I glimpsed one in a vision,' said her onscreen incarnation. 'It is a Great Bird of the Goddess, and we must fly in it to do the Goddess's work.' Her wings beat back and forth in measured time with her words, creating a gentle flurry of breeze across Lancelot's face.

'You have wings now?' he asked, pausing to look up from the contemplation of her perfect face.

'The Goddess Valeria granted them to me after I found the Holy Grail,' replied Elaine.

'So you have some flight navigation experience, then?' Lanval said, eagerly. 'One of us needs to have - I've only just learned how to work a lift in the twenty-first century.'

'Yes,' replied Elaine.

'When I was young,' interrupted Sir Lancelot, 'I squired in many jousts before I became a knight. Perhaps further training for the captaincy of this starship will be provided?'

'That's an excellent idea,' said Sir Lanval. 'And it sounds as though you're agreeing to join me?'

'Where you go, dear Lanval,' said Sir Lancelot, 'I shall surely follow.'

Elaine sighed. '*I'm* the next guide on the path.'

And so the party of three entered that hidden road to make their way back up to the bright world. Weary though they were, as they climbed, they never once thought of resting. Finally, through a small portal ahead, they glimpsed again the lovely things that the heavens hold, until at last, they clambered through it, to emerge with the stars.

Closing credits rolled up the screen, followed by some more stirring interval music. Rose Thorn sighed and stretched in her seat. There had been a moment there when Sir Lancelot had swum out of the pages of the book, and she had hoped, oh, how she had hoped, that he might step right down from the silver screen. But no. Things like that only happened in books - or the movies.

She stood up to find the Ladies - and a vending machine. Then she came back with a can of Sprite and a strawberry cornetto. A gulp of lemon and lime, a crunch of frozen strawberry, then she settled back into her velour seat, just in time for the next episode.

The next episode began with an exterior shot of rusted rails in a valley, the accursed place that was Queen Morgana's realm of enchantment, her playground. The Collodian. Then the camera moved in for a close up of Lanval's sorrowful face.

From her seat, Rose Thorn surmised he was missing his departed companions, Lancelot and Elaine, as well as his wife, Blancheflor, grievously. Queen Morgana had spirited them all away. Rose Thorn remembered, Lanval had hoped he might see Blancheflor, but as one of the new hostesses of Queen Morgana's entertainments, and as an example of the new laws the queen was trying to impose about intermarriage, the princess was now closely guarded.

And yet, Rose Thorn recalled what Merlin had told Lanval in the previous episode. That one day, Lanval and Blancheflor would have a son, William, and the boy would grow up to be the landlord of a tavern, *The Hanging Man*. It would have been better if, holed up in a flimsy tent in one of Collodian's numerous valleys, Lanval had been able to derive some comfort from the old man's words. Instead, close-up of his hand, forming into a fist.

A moment later, still clutching at all his vanished hopes and dreams, his fingers were now curled round the iron door knocker of a tavern's wooden door. Now the camera craned upwards, following his gaze to the creaking sign of *The Hanging Man* slowly swaying backwards-and-forwards against the darkening sky.

The knight pushed open the door, breathing in deeply. In her imagination, Rose Thorn could almost smell the rich, yeasty scent of home-brewed ale, amidst the rise and fall of cheerful tavern voices. She watched as, stepping inside, Lanval's face began to tingle, and then revive with the warmth from the candle stubs on tables, on window-sills, and on the bar, as well as from the heat of the ruddy fire glowing in the hearth.

The other patrons turned to look at Lanval. Someone nodded a greeting, then returned to his drink. At the far end of the taproom, there was a strip of stage. A stocky young man with fair hair, who was wearing a Viking helmet twisted the wrong way round, stepped onto that stage and gestured towards the performer there.

The performer was wearing a shimmering gold dress and had hair of flame, with a proud look around the mouth that was reminiscent of Queen Morgana, though it was not her.

The youth began to speak.

'Ladies and gentlemen, knights and damsels, we're proud to welcome Florence the Siren, back here for one night only. Florence the Siren, who's taking time out from bewildering sailors and enchanting Ulysses on the high seas to delight our audience here tonight. So let's give a hearty Hanging Man welcome to Florence the Siren, ladies and gentlemen, purllleeease...'

After the clapping, cheers and catcalls had died down, the singer began:

*'Damsels fair on this dark night,
Guard close your heart from yon knight.'*

'Me?' thought Lanval, hovering by the stage, as the singer's soprano voice soared. She continued:

*'He'll sing and dance, drink and sup,
But break your heart, smash your cup.'*

The muted crash of a glass on the floor, seemingly in keeping with the words of the song, provoked laughter and a cheer. The young, fair-haired tavern owner shook his head in exasperation and hurried down from the side of the stage to clear away the broken shards. Meanwhile, the dark-haired barmaid, busy at the bottles and beer pumps, paused for a moment to listen to the end of the song, and her reflection in the sepia stained mirror lining the bar wall behind paused with her.

*'Damsels fair, on this dark night,
Better by far, you take flight.
Leave him to the song he sings,
Fly far away, find your wings.'*

When she had finished singing, more claps and cheers, a whistle or two, and then Florence the Siren stepped off stage and began to sign autographs for the assembled fans gathering round her. From his vantage point, Lanval tried to catch her eye, but she ignored him. Nevertheless, the barmaid smiled as Lanval approached her, and he nodded, as if to say, that's the first friendly face I've seen all day. He asked for a tankard of ale, which she fetched him, bless her heart, and by the time he was at his seat, a new singer had stepped onto the stage.

The new singer seemed not to merit the introduction, attention or applause of Florence the Siren. He was a dwarf with, thought Rose Thorn, a look of Merlin's Apprentice, though it was not he. There he was, on that narrow strip of stage, wreathed in smoke from the tables and patrons, his long jerkin augmented with a red scarf and Turkish slippers. Striking a mournful pose, he began:

> *'Gods of wine and gods of song,*
> *Tell me now, with smile or grin,*
> *Though I sing this right or wrong,*
> *When is my ship coming in?'*

Lanval took up his horn of ale and seemed to find it so much to his liking, that he poured it down his throat. Immediately calling for another, he sat back to listen to the dwarf's song. The notes from the accompanying harp were half-submerged in the hum of voices and chatter.

> *'Pheasant I want, and fine grouse,*
> *Red wine in a crystal glass,*
> *Hogs with apples in their mouth,*
> *And silver spits up their-...'*

The Hanging Man regulars started to laugh, and the camera showed Lanval grinning as he warmed to the song.

> *'Venison of generous size,*
> *Squires and page to bring it in,*
> *And I will eat up all the pies,*
> *And quaff draughts of finest gin.*

*If, gods of wine, gods of song,
You tell me, with smile or grin,
Though I sing this right or wrong,
When my ship is coming in.'*

And then, at Lanval's elbow, appeared the young, fair-haired man wearing the Viking helmet, and how warm and friendly he now appeared.

'More ale, sir?' asked the landlord, 'I have just fetched another barrel of it up from the cellar.'

'No, thank you,' said Lanval.

The landlord bowed politely and poured another horn. 'It's fine ale, sir.'

'Very nice,' said Lanval, draining it without looking at it.

'I'm glad to hear you say it,' said the landlord.

Now Lanval twisted the horn round and round in his hand, gazing into its depths. 'Have you ever,' he said, moodily to the landlord, 'have you ever been in love?'

The landlord smiled discreetly and poured another horn of ale.

By midnight, Lanval and the landlord were the only ones left in the taproom; the musicians, singers and other patrons had all departed. Only these two were left, sitting on opposite sides of the table, both looking red in the face. Now they were drinking mulled wine, with its mixture of wine, honey and spices. The clock struck midnight, and Lanval cried out, 'What am I to do?' He put his arms on the table and rested his head in them.

'Courage!' said the landlord. And then, 'Drink,' he said. 'Drink heartily. Seize your opportunities where you may.' A moment later, he added, 'There's a messenger at the door. I daresay his note is for you.'

And indeed it was, for on the outer side of the sheet of parchment was the flowing single word, *Lanval*.

'What does it say?' asked the landlord, who sat watching the man sat staring at the sheet of paper.

'Nothing,' said the knight, throwing the sheet of paper on the table.

The landlord picked it up and read it. 'It says your Lady Blancheflor is at the Castle of Chalis, seven miles from here, and she wants you. There are some kisses on it.'

'Well?'

'You dare not go,' said the landlord thoughtfully. 'Queen Morgana...'

'Ho, dare not I?' shouted Lanval, staggering to his feet. He lurched out into the darkness of the night, calling for a horse, Fauve, that once he had owned, a gift from his mother, years and years ago.

In the morning, Lanval woke suddenly in a strange room. It was quite dark, with tapestry curtains blocking out the light from the windows. From his grimace, Rose Thorn judged he had a headache behind his eyes, but no more than that, for his constitution was sound.

He clambered down from the dark oak bed and walked over to the window to hook back the tapestry curtains. A brief montage sequence recapped everything that had happened the previous night: the mysterious appearance of the tavern, the singers and the landlord, the many, many flagons of ale, the message from Blancheflor, and her warm, yielding body in the bed which he had just left. He lifted the tapestry and rested his forehead against the cool diamond-glass of the window.

'Blancheflor?' he said, after some moments.

At first, there was no answer. But after a moment, a small, sleepy voice sighed and mumbled, 'Lancelot?'

The voice was not Blancheflor's. He turned round and found himself looking at the girl, Elaine. She lay in the great bed, her arms holding the coverlet around her, her bewildered eyes fixed on his.

She looked small and scared, which Rose Thorn didn't like. 'I was closeted with my grandmother and her ladies here in the holdfast,' she said, at last. 'She kept giving me wine. And then a message came from Lancelot...'

Lanval's head tipped back, and his face took on a look of profound and outraged sorrow that granted him dignity despite the sunlight pouring across his naked body. Then he began to tremble. He steadied himself and walked over to the chest where his sword was lying.

'I shall kill her,' he said. 'Queen Morgana has stolen our honour from us both.'

'But if it is not our fault?' cried Elaine, 'if we were tricked?' She punched the pillow beside her. 'Is this pillow real? Is any of this real? Does what happens in the Collodian, really happen?'

'Yes,' said Lanval, soberly, 'it happened.'

Now the camera panned across his serious face and alighted upon the tapestry curtains' stitched foxgloves and snapdragons, mauve and crimson. Then the screen faded once more to black, and the closing credits rolled up, to the accompaniment of the plaintive sound of an oboe.

The lights went up in the starship's Viewing Theatre. Rose Thorn sighed and stretched her legs. 'No-one has called me Elaine for years,' she thought. 'So there's a slight chance the other crew members won't realise it was me. Because that was embarrassing. Even how they'd edited it, quite tastefully really, that was still embarrassing. Of all the memories they must have harvested, and they chose to broadcast that one? The one where Lanval and I... you know...'

Dimly, she recalled what her cousin Blancheflor had told her a few years ago, after this incident, after days of weary travel, when she and Lanval had found Lancelot again in a monastery, and they had finally reached the courtyard of the Winter Palace - and the Mothercrystal. There, Blancheflor had told them that the Collodian was also a kind of Purgatory. That Rose Thorn and Lanval, who had been without sin, must be rendered sinful, in order to be forgiven, so that, newly made pure and light, they could ascend upwards to the starry spheres.

Even at the time, Rose Thorn had been unconvinced. What if Queen Morgana were simply sacrificing everyone else's finer feelings to her own peculiar brand of voyeurism? Whatever the motivation was, Rose Thorn hadn't liked it then, and she liked it even less now.

Lanval and then Elaine had tried to say something appeasing to Blancheflor, but she just looked stony-faced. Then she turned away from them and pointed to the Arch of Regeneration, there in the courtyard, all painted over with symbols, signs of the zodiac, and hieroglyphics of prayers.

Elaine gave her cousin one last, beseeching look: there she was, proud and unhappy in her gown of red samite, with those rubies glittering like blood round her pale neck and a thousand eyes, cameras, shining down on her. But nothing. No gesture of reconciliation. And that was the last time Elaine had seen Blancheflor.

In that moment, when her cousin's feigned indifference most hurt her, Elaine decided she wasn't going to be Elaine anymore. What was the point of being some kind of ineffectual angel, beating luminous wings in vain, if people, her family, got hurt?

Then she, Lanval, and Lancelot stepped through the Arch of Regeneration, to find themselves in the lift, in Willis Towers, Ipswich. Lanval pressed the button that would take them to the eleventh floor, and they got out and made their way to *Office Suite E*. She gave her new name, which was spiky, like her hurt feelings, like who she was going to become, to the woman, Cordelia, behind the desk, then sat down in the waiting room.

Lanval was pleased to see Cordelia again, promoted perhaps, since she was no longer on the ground floor. He gave her a winning smile, which she ignored, and found out what time the officers' training programme began. Not for another couple of hours. 'Though,' said Cordelia, 'Officer Pluto has asked if you could sit in on a couple of interviews before that.'

Rose Thorn herself was interviewed by Officer Pluto, sailed through and accepted the position of flight navigation officer. A few days later, she started the induction programme, and a few days after that, she joined the ship's crew on board the *Joyous Gard*. Over the next few months, she spent quite a lot of time avoiding Lanval, and hoping that what had happened in the Collodian, stayed in the Collodian. Then, when she had set up the flight navigation programmes to her liking, and trained her replacement, she returned to Valerian, and her Sisterhood.

But now, five years later, that whole sorry story was there, harvested from Lanval's memories, and broadcast, larger than life, on the Viewing Theatre's vastscreen aboard the *Joyous Gard*, and, for all she knew, on all the televisions all across Avalon.

'I wish you'd warned me,' she complained to Aurélie in the officers' canteen, an hour or so later. The golden octopus melded to an anemone, on display with some exotic plants by the porthole, looked equally annoyed.

'Not my fault,' said Aurélie, taking another sip of her cappuccino. 'I'm running a starship. I don't have time for television.' She took another sip. It was good. 'I'm not going to sleep now I've drunk this, am I?'

'Who needs sleep?' said Rose Thorn. She suddenly grinned. 'I wouldn't say this to anyone else, but at least that TV show proves I'm the most exciting thing that's ever happened to Lanval. Out of all the centuries that he's lived in and all the people that he's known!'

Unable to share Rose Thorn's glee, Aurélie said slowly, 'About Lanval...'

'Yes?'

'Different people experience different effects with the harvesting process... since the queen's guards gave him back to us, a couple of weeks ago, he's mainly been in sick bay...'

'But what was he doing in Avalon, anyway?' asked Rose Thorn, twisting the handle round so her mug of tea faced her.

'He was there for Captain Dulac's wedding,.' Aurélie replied.

A pause the length of a heartbeat. 'Oh yes, I heard he got married,' Rose Thorn said at last.

Aurélie gave her a compassionate, sidelong glance. 'I'm sorry,' she said.

'What do you mean?'

'The way you and he used to look at each other sometimes... I thought...' Aurélie's voice trailed off into uncomfortable silence.

After a moment, Rose Thorn asked, 'Who's First Officer now instead of Lanval?'

'Officer Sophia James is Acting Lieutenant.'

'She'd be good at that, though, wouldn't she?'

'Yes - if anything, she's a big improvement.'

'Lanval is all right, though, isn't he?'

'No, not really,' said Aurélie, shaking her head. 'That's what I've been trying to tell you. You'll know, if you go and see him.' She took another contemplative sip of her cappuccino.

Lieutenant Lanval. There he was in sick bay, when Rose Thorn arrived to visit him the following morning. There was no natural daylight on this section of the starship, and the artificial lights above him were subdued.

As he sat there in his bed, his dark head resting against the headboard, he looked rough. Worse than that. Like he had the world's worst hangover. White, trembling, with a bandage round his forehead, and his eyes - those fine, dark eyes, now blank and unseeing, windows to a harvested mind. He had never thought he was the brightest button in the box, but Lanval had been convinced that serving on this starship would be the making of him. Now, however... he was just one more sorry reason for the Sisters of Valerian to locate those cylinders of missing memories.

And yet he stirred himself enough to stare up at her. 'I know your face,' he said, at last. 'Who are you?'

'I'm Rose Thorn,' she replied.

But the name meant nothing to him, and he shut his eyes and returned to sleep.

A book, that book with the purple cover, lay face down on his locker, its spine creased in half.

Honolulu Nights

Before she became a starship officer, Aurélie De Lys was at home in her Norwich attic, searching for that game of Jenga she had promised Guinan. All of a sudden, it happened again. That familiar feeling of heaviness and oppression, that sensation of pressure boring into her skull. Then a thousand scents assaulted her all at once - smells that were sharp, sweet, caressing, dangerous, disturbing. As vast as cities, as miniscule as atoms. As rough as cobblestones, as small and intricate as the filigree workings of a pocket-watch. Then the air turned on a dime, and became as hard as a metallic sheet, with surfaces, corners and edges.

It was as if her world were now comprised of polished spheres, fireflies in the cerebral sky, and crystal clusters, jagged and luminescent, darting across a spectrum of rainbow rays.

And she was forced to push her way through all of this, as if in a dream, or else not in a dream, since she was here in the attic, full of mum's furniture there was no room for in her retirement place, and that Aurélie didn't want either. And yet the whole experience only lasted for a moment.

She opened her eyes and cautiously felt her throbbing head. Another migraine. She been getting them a lot, just lately. Mum's legacy, perhaps, that made the world tilt on its axis, but before Aurélie could investigate it properly, the pain floated away, like so many statues on black water.

There was too much junk up here. All her box files from her recent amalgamation of Merlin and Morgana's spell books. Her notes from the History of Lady Elridge's Convalescing Home, that she had spent months trying to write. Oh - and look - pinned to a corkboard, a postcard from Violetta, that she had somehow posted across the centuries after Aurélie had taught her the Time-Writing spell.

'The summer nights in the latitude of St. Petersburg are a prolonged twilight.'

Yes, thanks for that, Violetta. It's been raining quite a lot here in Valerian. We're struggling to come out of lockdown, but the vestiges of it still cling, like cobwebs. I need a broom, give it all a good sweep.

Over there, beneath the sloping roof, and in its case, was the violin that had once belonged to her grandmother, Arabella, and before that, to Queen Morgana. Umber, amber, russet and gold. And over there, in a box beside it, was the mirror her grandmother had sent her from Avalon, which had arrived on the first day out of lockdown. On that day, she had been startled, then delighted to see a purposeful, forthright older lady peering up at her from the glass. But now, weeks had gone by, and she had not seen her Granny in the mirror again. This absence gave her an uneasy feeling in the pit of her stomach, made her heart sink with strange dismay.

Guinan had already told her that dark days were coming to Avalon: just, he had been curiously reticent about what that might mean. She shrugged. He would tell her in his own good time. Now she tried to re-work the thought into another Law for the Time-Traveller's Code, then shrugged again when she found she couldn't.

Anyway, over there, by the rickety filing cabinet, in a metallic freezer-bag with looped handles was Mum's old Sinclair ZX Spectrum. Not long before Aurélie had left home, the clean, white apartment she shared with her on the Ile-Grande, someone at the school where Mum taught had persuaded her to buy it. 'Mum must have thought it would be good for homework,' Aurélie decided, 'but I never got much beyond 10 print hello. 20 print goto 10. And then a whole screen of hellos!'

Then, in the summer months when Aurélie was waiting to take up her scholarship at the Valerian College of Arts, she mainly played games on it. She liked Slippery Sid, the snake eating up all the magic mushrooms, but her favourite was Leap Frog. She was pretty good at getting the frog to cross the road, despite the busy traffic. Using the arrow keys, she made him land on a series of fast-moving lily pads, until - one final leap - and then the frog was home. After that, the pixels settled into a beaming frog face that made her happy just looking at it.

After Mum had realised her daughter was unlikely to ever use the computer for homework, she didn't let Aurélie take it with her to college. Which was a shame. She missed that beaming frog face. She remembered it when her friend Harmony said, 'You have to kiss a lot of frogs before you reach the Prince.' They had both just recently embarked on a spate of dating, spurred on by that feeling of loneliness and alienation that only being single and twenty can create. Aurélie remembered thinking, never mind the Prince, I would just have been glad of a happy frog.

A happy, dancing frog? Because there, in a shoebox on top of the filing cabinet, were her old, red, dancing shoes. Her ruby slippers, she used to call them. She unwrapped them from their tissue paper cover and picked them up, so that her hands could make them dance. Wearing these, stamping stars across the dancefloor, she really used to think she was It. She used to match them with a red Brigit Bardot halter neck top and passion red lipstick, a level of attention to detail she fully intended to relinquish once she was married with three children.

Her hands inside the shoes stopped dancing.

Suddenly she remembered wearing them for a first date that hadn't gone too well. In fact, it had ended after forty minutes, and he'd gone to the loo four times during it. The only face she'd found herself sitting opposite on the train going home was her own mystified reflection in the glass.

Ah - look - the box of Jenga on top of the canvas cupboard from Ikea. If she stood on the wicker chair, she'd be able to reach it. And then, in moving the chair, she found a blue folder shoved under the wallpaper pasting trestle table, quite an important folder.

It was full of diplomas, certificates, references and testimonials. She would need it next week when she went for her interview at Willis Towers in Ipswich. The Conglomerate were recruiting across four hundred years for a History Officer for the starship, *Joyous Gard*, and Guinan seemed to think she was in with a chance. Of the job, too.

The following week, clutching this folder of diplomas, Aurélie entered Ipswich's foremost skyscraper, Willis Towers, all midnight smoky-black glass and concrete pillars, which she'd read online housed some 1300 staff in open plan offices over twelve floors.

As Aurélie walked inside, a cool blast of air-conditioning hit her. Marble tiles beneath her feet. Traffic noise suddenly muffled. Behind the front desk sat a receptionist. Above her, a row of clocks displayed the time in key world cities. London, Auckland, New York, Avalon, Paris. She picked her way towards him and announced her name, Aurélie De Lys. The receptionist checked his list, and assigned Aurélie a number, 13, then told her to take the lift up to the eleventh floor and find *Office Suite E*.

Aurélie stepped out on the eleventh floor, then stood outside the lift, looking up and down the corridor. A cleaner in overalls pushed a mop near to her new shoes, which were patent leather, glossy, and more stiletto than she would normally wear. She frowned at him, but he stared back, unapologetic and impassive, then swished down the corridor. Sighing, Aurélie headed after him, until she finally found a door with a neat sign taped over the nameplate. It read, in old-fashioned copperplate handwriting: *Office Suite E,* INTERVIEWS HERE.

She knocked, received no reply, then knocked again. Finally, a bespectacled man in his thirties with a name badge that read *Officer Pluto* jerked his head out of the door. 'The waiting room's down the hall,' he said.

She mumbled her apologies and went right to the end of the corridor, which opened out into a waiting room area filled with at least thirty people, sitting on orange, plastic chairs, stiff and awkward. She sat down. Glancing around surreptitiously, she surveyed the other candidates. Elves. Fairies. Someone young and familiar-looking, clean-shaven, and very short - another renegade dwarf? A beautiful, flaxen-haired girl who seemed to be meditating or praying. A tall, fair man with a vampiric look, glancing at a notepad and muttering foreign phrases. A golden monkey with jet-black eyes, chattering away in the corner.

The candidates cleared their throats, coughed or played with their hands. They flicked through magazines and tried to avoid making eye contact with each other. The sheer number of them was daunting. But Aurélie tried to reassure herself. Perhaps they weren't all applying for the same role. She didn't know how many vacancies there were on board the *Joyous Gard*. How many of them wanted to sail to the stars?

Presently, Officer Pluto poked his head round the door and called out her number, 'Thirteen.' She stood up and walked into the interview room, then sat down where he indicated, in front of a panel comprised of himself, and the two colleagues he introduced, Captain Lancelot Dulac to his left, and Lieutenant Lanval to his right.

'I will be conducting the interview,' said Officer Pluto, 'but the Captain and the Lieutenant will chip in if they have some questions. You should feel free to ask us any questions at the end, too.'

Three men thought Aurélie. Great. A nerd flanked by two American football players. Her heart sank again.

'Great,' she said. Was now the right time to ask them about the male to female ratio on board ship? About promotion prospects for women over the age of fifty-five? Probably not. She waited for his first question.

It soon came. 'How do you feel about warlords?' asked Officer Pluto, with a directness that was borderline insulting.

Then Aurélie remembered what Guinan had told her, that the Conglomerate were specifically recruiting in this age-range for the role of History Officer, judging her less likely to run away with a warlord, like her predecessor. Or was it a warlock? Still, positive discrimination was positive discrimination. She relaxed back into her chair and smiled brightly.

'I have no strong feelings either way,' she said, sincerely.

'Which is the correct answer, and we can proceed with the interview,' said Officer Pluto. 'Now, what do you understand of the Conglomerate's Mission?'

Unfortunately, not a great deal, since their website had gone down just when she had started researching for the interview. She tried to remember what Guinan had told her, that in the twenty-fourth century, population overcrowding was a huge issue - and 'The Conglomerate has been commissioned to seek out planets where life is sustainable,' she said.

Except she remembered now that there was some issue with some of Queen Morgana's future policies, about which Guinan had been a bit vague, actually. But from what she could gather, the Conglomerate were using some of the queen's resources to thwart her own policies.

'Isn't that a bit sneaky?' she had said. 'And aren't you a bit sneaky if you're part of it?'

Guinan had shrugged and given a sad smile.

'I support the good of the realm,' he said. 'That doesn't always mean the crown. Anyway, by the twenty-fourth century, Queen Morgana's a bit...

'A bit what?'

'You'll understand what I mean when you get to the twenty-fourth century,' he said.

'If I get the job,' she replied.

'Oh, I've no doubt about that,' he said.

Aurélie wished Officer Pluto felt the same, now.

'You can read that on our website,' he said sternly, 'or at least you could before they took it down. What else?'

'Partly this is a necessity since population overcrowding is a major issue by the twenty-fourth century,' she said, and then, working on her own hunch, she added, 'and partly the Conglomerate wish to establish their own policies there, which may not be strictly in line with those of the queen.'

'Very good,' said Officer Pluto, pressing his tapering fingers together in front of his face, and pausing to contemplate the resulting church steeple. 'And how do you feel about that?'

'I support the good of the realm,' Aurélie mumbled.

'Excellent,' said Officer Pluto, and Beefcake One grinned, while Beefcake Two pushed some papers around, importantly.

'Tell me,' said Officer Pluto, 'Ms er-,' he said, glancing down at the screen in front of him, so that Captain Dulac nudged him sharply and muttered her name. 'Ms De Lys,' Officer Pluto said, with a shade more respect, 'what do you know of the Collodian Program?'

A trick question, since the Collodian Program didn't exist until the twenty-fourth century, thought Aurélie. Besides, she was unauthorised personnel. She wasn't supposed to know anything about it at all.

'Absolutely nothing,' she said and then she thought back to what Violetta had once told her about her photography studies. 'Although the word Collodian means a kind of developmental film used in photography - and also a sort of bandage, to staunch a wound?'

'No embroidery lessons for her,' said Captain Dulac.

'She's needle-sharp,' agreed Lieutenant Lanval.

'You'll see from my CV, gentlemen, that I have some editorial experience,' Aurélie said, warming to her theme, 'and drawing on my etymological knowledge, I would surmise that the Collodian Program is an escapist and possibly controversial policy of the queen.'

'She's not wrong,' said Lieutenant Lanval.

Captain Dulac leaned over and whispered something in Officer Pluto's ear.

The officer tore himself away from the configuration of his delicate fingertips and glowered at the blonde woman from beneath his pale brows.

'How do you reconcile that with your own knowledge of Time Travel?' asked Officer Pluto then.

Cosmic string theory. Schrodinger's Law of Cats. Cat's Cradle. H G Wells... err... thought Aurélie. Then, finally, a lightbulb moment.

'When I was working as an administrator for Lady Eldridge's,' she said smoothly, 'I often thought how wonderful it would be if the elderly residents could re-visit the days of their lives when they were happiest. This inspired much of my research into the theory of Time Travel, in collaboration with Professor Guinan, who, you will see, is one of my referees. I would imagine that the Collodian Program has a similar desire to make people happy, but perhaps operates under a different, and highly flawed, premise.'

'You can say that again,' said Lieutenant Lanval.

'I'm not sure I can,' thought Aurélie.

'Yes,' said Officer Pluto, 'anything to keep the masses subdued.'

'And unfortunately,' said Captain Dulac, 'our research assistant, Dr Cordelia Maladroit, has informed us that Queen Morgana may have used some of your research to form the nucleus of her program.'

'Queen Morgana has no real respect for other people's intellectual or artistic property,' said Officer Pluto.

'Plagiarism is a terrible problem,' Aurélie agreed. 'But it seems to me that from what you say, I am the person who is uniquely placed to investigate Queen Morgana's program. Furthermore, my many years of experience of time-travelling, and my range of hobbies and interests, including, most recently, Samurai sword-fighting, and reprogramming Eighties technology, make me an excellent candidate for the role of History Officer on board the *Joyous Gard*.'

Officer Pluto licked the lid of his pen with the tip of his tongue. 'Which particular Eighties technology?' he inquired, in a breathless, slightly strangulated voice.

'The Sinclair ZX Spectrum,' she replied. 'Circa 1984.'

'Gentlemen,' Officer Pluto said, and then he paused, exhaling slowly, savouring the moment, 'I think we have found our new History Officer. Congratulations - and welcome aboard, Ms De Lys.'

'But aren't you going to interview the other candidates?' she asked.

'For other roles - yes,' said Officer Pluto. 'But you're perfect for this one. Isn't she just perfect?' he added, turning to the other two.

Captain Dulac and Lieutenant Lanval nodded politely in agreement, then each gentleman shook hands with her. Then she was directed to another office suite to complete some questionnaires ahead of the official induction in a few days' time.

The first thing Aurélie had to fill out was an Aptitude Questionnaire, but it was so similar to the job application she had already completed online, that she quickly grew bored. There in a dark booth, with a bright screen on the wall, she punched in her answers. *Height*: 5 foot 4. She deleted it. Actually, 5 foot 3. *Weight*: None of your business. *Dress size*: ditto. Then she thought it might be for a starship uniform, so she put 12/14 and hoped for the best.

Hobbies and Interests: She had already told them. *Star Trek*, all series, Scott Bakula, in both his Sam Beckett and Jonathan Archer incarnations, Samurai swords, writing, knitting, vampires errr… Then she remembered a dating website with similar questions, and the trouble it had caused her back in her twenties.

She was travelling home from that disastrous forty-minute date. Two men sitting on the other side of the train carriage, wearing short sleeved check shirts and jeans covered in brick dust seemed to be trying to catch her eye. Their interest had soothed her hurt feelings.

'You going out tonight?' asked the one with the grey stubble, whilst his skinny friend swigged some beer from a shiny blue can.

'I'm on my way home,' she replied, slightly bitterly.

The thin man turned his wrist to look at his watch, being careful not to spill his beer in the process.

'Can't have been much of a night,' he remarked, 'it's only twenty to nine.'

'Yes, my date ended early,' she said.

The two men looked at each other and the skinny one rubbed his jaw. 'How did you meet him?' he asked, smiling. One of his front teeth was missing and his tongue poked through it as he formed the words.

'Oh well, I've been signed up for this internet dating thing for a few months,' she said.

'Surely that's not necessary,' muttered the man with the grey stubble.

'You'd think not, wouldn't you,' she replied. 'I mean - I dress well... this is my best top.'

The man grinned. 'No, I meant it's not what we did in my day. We went to pubs, dances. That's how I met my wife.'

'We're not all as lucky as you,' said his friend. 'What happened?' he asked Aurélie.

'Well, when he was writing to me, he seemed really nice. Well, actually, no, not that nice, just ordinary really, but in his picture, he was incredibly good-looking. Like a male model. Or a knitting pattern man in mum's *Woman's Weekly.* And I thought, to hell with it, why not just be really shallow for once and go for looks.'

'But he didn't live up to his looks?' asked the thin man, with the trace of an Irish lilt that made his alliteration lyrical.

'No, he did. Apart from the lines round his eyes, and I rather liked them. Made him not too perfect. But maybe

I didn't live up to mine. He was the one that cut short the date. And we could have travelled back together on the same train, and he chose not to.'

The two men looked at each other again in blank incomprehension. 'But look at you, you're fine,' said the thin man.

'I know,' she replied. Then she smiled. 'Well, he was quite weird anyway. I think he was testing me to see how materialistic I was. And I somehow failed. He kept going on about giving up advertising to become a lumberjack. And I was like, yeah, be a lumberjack, be wild and free. Which probably wasn't the right answer. And another thing. He'd put on his profile that his favourite books were Kafka's *Metamorphoses* and Plato's *The Republic.* And I hadn't read any Kafka, but I'd read some Plato. So, I started talking about Plato's allegory of the cave.'

The skinny man's eyes glowed with blue fire. 'You mean that beautiful allegory, where beings are chained to a cave's walls, and mistake its shadows for reality, but their companion escapes to see the true light of day?' he said.

'That's it,' she said. 'That's it. Anyway, I was talking about it, in great detail, and I was being really enthusiastic, because, you know, it's one of my favourite things, and I was trying to, you know, make a connection, but then his eyes started to glaze over. So, I asked him what his favourite part of *The Republic* was. And he looked down at the table and told me that actually he's only read the first two pages. And that actually he has to go because he'd promised to meet a friend. Or a sick grandmother. Or something.'

She glanced down at her beautifully co-ordinated red outfit, at her slippers gleaming up at her consolingly. 'Maybe I'm just better read,' she murmured to herself, as the train pulled into Clapham Junction.

'We're going out tonight,' said the Plato-loving skinny Irish builder with the gappy teeth. 'Come dancing with us, instead.'

Hobbies and Interests: *Dancing. As fast as I can.*

'Have you finished, Ms De Lys?' asked Officer Pluto, poking his bulbous head round the side of the cubicle.

'Not quite,' Aurélie replied. 'I think there's still a bit more to write. Quite a lot, actually,' she added hurriedly, as his smile grew wider.

'Well, when you're done, there's a meet-and-greet with a few of the other officers in the bar downstairs. And me,' he beamed.

'That sounds wonderful,' she said, 'but I'm not much of a drinker these days. I want to keep a clear head for the induction.'

'But that's not until Thursday.'

'Still...'

'Soft drink?'

'No thanks.'

'Well, if you're sure?'

'I wouldn't have said it otherwise.'

Navigating post-lockdown socialising was going to be more slightly more difficult than she had anticipated, but there were really only so many conversations she could have about the Sinclair ZX Spectrum.

After Officer Pluto had gone, Aurélie stopped pretending to punch things into the screen. She started to rub her temple, the slight twinge that, if not caught in its tracks, heralded another migraine. Whilst she massaged her forehead, she returned to reminiscing.

Just for a moment, there they were, in her mind's eye, her ruby slippers, whirring and skimming across the dance floor with the Plato-loving Irish builder's boots. She let them sparkle and waltz there, stamping out stars in the dance hall with the thousand glittering lights.

Then she pressed the final button onscreen, collected her bag, and took the elevator down to the lobby. She would have to sneak out of a side door to avoid the officers.

'I got the job,' she announced to Guinan, who was waiting for her at a table in the café opposite Willis Towers. As she sat down with her cup of tea, she added, only half-jokingly, 'We should go out dancing to celebrate.'

'Congratulations, Aurélie,' Guinan said sincerely, 'I knew you could do it.' Then his face fell. 'The clubs round here frown on dwarves,' he continued, dolefully. 'And the few that don't haven't opened up properly from lockdown.'

'You dodged that one,' she said. 'Why do they frown on dwarves?'

'It's what happens when club bouncers look down,' said Guinan. 'But never mind that,' he continued, blowing the froth on his cappuccino. 'Tell me about the interview.'

'It was okay,' she said. 'Though Officer Pluto didn't seem to know who I was, properly, at least, not until Captain Dulac reminded him.'

'That's not great,' said Guinan, 'not considering how much effort you put into your CV - but I'll get Officer Pluto to buck his ideas up a bit when I write your reference.'

'If you can tear him away from the *ZX Spectrum Fetishists' Forum.* I know he's an acquaintance of yours, but he's a bit weird...'

'That's how you know he's an acquaintance of mine,' said Guinan, smiling.

Another thought that had been niggling at the back of her mind re-surfaced. 'Won't you get in trouble if you write my reference and then he finds out we're sort of involved?'

'If Pluto finds out we're sort of involved,' said Guinan, 'it might stop him from talking to you about ZX Spectrums.'

'Wasn't that your interview tip, though, to mention it?'

'Yes, but Pluto goes too far, sometimes,' said Guinan.

'Whereas you're a model of restraint?'

Guinan bowed his head over his cappuccino in agreement.

'Anyway, hopefully I won't have too much to do with him once I'm on board the starship,' Aurélie said. 'The induction programme starts later this week. Which means...' she leaned forwards, in what she hoped was a seductive way, 'there's plenty of time for you to take me out, on a proper date.'

'All right then,' said Guinan. 'No time like the present. Let's go and find a fancy bar and drink cocktails.'

'Right now?' she said. 'I'm not dressed for it.'

Guinan looked down again at his cappuccino and didn't reply. Then he glanced at his fingertips.

Meanwhile, Aurélie looked at a picture of a crane on the wall behind him, on a background of red and grey squares, wondering why he didn't speak.

Finally, she gave a loud, exaggerated sigh.

'Well,' she said, leaning forwards, less seductively, more annoyed really, and taking a gulp of her tea. But her skirt rustled strangely as she moved. She looked down at herself, then jumped up suddenly, in astonishment.

The mid-length grey pencil skirt and matching jacket she had worn for the interview was gone; in its place was a dress of dark blue silk, with spaghetti-thin shoulder straps. The skirt caught the light, and gleamed softly, like rain in April.

She glanced over at the sorcerer's apprentice, speechless.

'Do you like it?' he asked.

'Where...?'

'It's like a dress I saw a visiting princess wear once, at court in Camelot,' said Guinan, with satisfaction.

She looked down at the blue splendour of silk.

'I don't look like me at all,' she said.

'You're wrong, Aurélie,' Guinan said, softly. 'I think you look exactly like you.'

The evening itself passed by in a bit of a blur. They began in the Revolution Bar in the Old Cattle Market, but it quickly grew too hot and too crowded. Then onto the Rooftop Bar over in the town centre, which started out pretty well.

'May the best of your past be the worst of your future,' said Guinan, holding up his cocktail glass in salute, just before they drank their strawberry daiquiris.

'You can't add to the Time Travellers' Code with a drinking toast,' complained Aurélie.

'I just did,' replied Guinan, smugly.

They would have stayed there for the rest of the evening, but then the bar staff started to pin Elvis posters to the walls for the Elvis theme night. Aurélie caught a glimpse of *G I Blues* and some Las Vegas scenes.

'I thought you said it was classy here,' said Aurélie, crossly, because she had been enjoying herself.

'It is, usually.'

Since neither Guinan nor Aurélie were prepared to dress up as Priscilla or Elvis, they left, and wound up instead at the Aurora, by the waterside.

'This is better, anyway,' said Aurélie, glancing round. The white chrome bar was lit up with ultramarine blue lights, the tables and chairs were black or white, clean-lined, contemporary. Everywhere gleamed with sleek good taste, neither too plain, nor too fancy. Through large glass doors, they glimpsed boats and yachts on the river, some lit up with fairy lights, and there were friends sauntering between them.

'Better than lockdown, you mean,' said Guinan, 'though we might as well have stayed at the Elvis place if you're just going to drink Hawaiian cocktails all evening.'

'Mmm, pineapple,' said Aurélie.

'You're forgetting the rum.'

'The rum is the best bit,' said Aurélie.

'Try the next one with Martini.'

'Okay. It's funny, normally I can't drink too much, but here, I'm absolootely fine.'

'You can get the next round of drinks in, then.'

'I'm fine if I don't move,' said Aurélie. 'Otherwise, everything starts spinning.'

'Probably you haven't drunk enough, then,' said Guinan.

Some time later, when the Hawaiians had turned blue and Aurélie was twirling the paper umbrella round in her drink, Guinan said, 'Would you like to see the Aurora Borealis? When travelling gets easier, I thought about going to Iceland - or maybe, Alaska.'

'Oh yeah,' said Aurélie. 'We'd be Aurora hunters. That would be cool.'

Guinan took out his latest phone. 'I downloaded an App to track Kp alerts,' he said, modestly.

'Which are what, exactly?'

'The App tracks the Kp index. The higher the value, the more the lights can be seen.'

'Nothing to do with crisps, then,' she said.
'I think you're a little bit tipsy,' he replied.
'Yes, I am. Why aren't you?'
'Years of practice.'
'Still, the lights though,' said Aurélie, twirling the paper umbrella round and round, gazing at the luminous swirl of blue and green in the glass beneath her.

Morning arrived too early. It was breakfast-time and Aurélie wasn't hungry.

'What do you normally take for hangovers?' she asked, rooting through her kitchen cupboard, then, not finding much there of use, sitting down abruptly at the table.

'I don't get hangovers,' said Guinan. 'Like I said, years of practice.'

'Of drinking, too.'

'Haha. When's your induction?'

'Um... sometime this week. What day is it today?'

'Have some orange juice,' said Guinan, opening up her fridge and reaching inside for the carton. He located two glasses, poured the juice, then handed Aurélie's to her. 'And when you've done that, take a look at your calendar.'

After a mouthful or two, she said, 'I might just stay at the orange juice stage for quite some time.'

'Is that what I'm supposed to put in your reference? *Lightweight Ms De Lys, scuppered by a few well-placed rums and a shot of vodka...* I should probably send it off today.'

'What *are* you going to put in my reference?'

'I think it only fair that I should mention your disgraceful behaviour last night. But I will be pithy and precise. Then I will say something about how apart from me, no-one knows so much about Time Travel as you and your associate, Ms Valhallah.'

'She would have loved that bar,' said Aurélie. 'Did I ever tell you about that time with the cocktails and the gold lame bikinis?'

'Yes and the flamingos, that's not going in your reference, either.'

'But I count it as one of my finest achievements,' said Aurélie, standing up, walking over to the counter, and pouring out the last of the carton.

A day or two later, and Guinan was gone and Aurélie had nearly finished packing her bags for the induction day, and for the starship. Packing made her irritable; how to disseminate a life, to decide what was of value, and what should be left behind. She was glad to stop and give herself an early night, except that, after a few hours, she found she still wasn't asleep. So she texted Guinan.

'Are you awake?'

After a moment or two, he texted back. 'I am now... I was dreaming. Your text woke me up.'

'Oh, sorry. What were you dreaming?' Aurélie texted.

'Usual thing. Bright light all around me. A crown with six silver stars, and one bright gold one on my head.'

'You're winding me up,' she texted back.

'No, it's the same dream I've been having for years,' he replied. 'Sometimes I blame Merlin's whacky potions. Sometimes I don't.'

'All the same, you could ask Merlin about it,' she texted.

'I could, I could. When I get time. But now it's after midnight. You should go to sleep. Induction tomorrow.'

'But that's why I'm awake,' she texted back. 'Can't you come over?'

'I told you, I'm back in Avalon,' he replied. 'By the time I got to Norwich, you'd be gone.'

'You'd think I would have a better grasp of time zones by now, wouldn't you?' she texted.

'Yes, Aurélie, I would,' he texted. 'Good night 😊'

Aurélie fell asleep thinking about Guinan. Ever since she had known him, even back in those days at the circus, he had always had that bit of extra shrewdness, enough to make up for what the other dwarves, his companions and relatives, lacked. Despite this shrewdness, he never seemed to age, to the extent that at one point, he thought he had vampire ancestry.

He also wished his fellow dwarves to remain young with him. He had therefore persuaded Queen Morgana to allow the dwarves annual injections of DNA youth preserver (TM peptide cerato) which had already done such a good job of keeping her young.

Guinan still retained a fascination with vampires - as did Aurélie, herself. Perhaps that was why, when she was on the Induction Day at the Maiden Fayre Hotel, and skirting its courtyard on her lunchbreak, she found that she was actually drifting through the gardens of Violetta's home, Crowcroft Grange. The roses from the Lost Garden had spread far beyond its borders and now bloomed in wild profusion all across the outer lawns.

And there was Violetta, or perhaps a dream of Violetta, sitting in the shadows of a canopy of roses whilst the sunlight dappled across her face. She raised her head with its thick knot of gleaming dark hair from her book as Aurélie approached her.

'There you are,' Violetta said. 'At last.'

But before she could reply, Violetta was gone, and Aurélie was trailing through those rose petals, now brown and faded at her feet. Then she swept into a maze she couldn't remember having seen before. At the heart of the maze was a sundial, no, a moon dial, that told the time correctly for just one night of the year. There was a young girl leaning over the dial, her fair hair spilling across the numerals.

'Come back,' said the girl, looking up at her. For a moment, Aurélie thought she recognised her. Arabella? Or was it Frances? But when she looked again, the girl was gone.

And now Aurélie was no longer in the gardens of Crowcroft Grange but walking past the hotel's tennis courts. And her lunchbreak was nearly over; it was time to go back inside, text Guinan, fend off the advances of Pluto, then eat her sandwich and sit in a lecture room with all the lights turned out.

From the podium, the lecturer, Dr Donzel, a golden monkey with eyes like glittering coals, began to speak: 'One of the most significant developments in Earth history, and without doubt, the most dramatic in terms of the mobility of homo sapiens, was the introduction of the first hyperdrive engine by Henri De Vass in 2024 AD. Within a short space of time, this device had transformed your species' attempts to explore your extraterrestrial environment, so that the doorway to the stars was now open.' As Dr Donzel spoke those final words, she pressed a switch close to her lectern.

There, in the lecture room's recreation of inky night, to the assorted trainees' oohs and ahs, globes lit up, globes strung all the way across the ceiling: replicas of planets, Jupiter, Venus, Saturn, Earthsea, Mercury, Mars, constellations and untold stars.

A day or so after the induction, Aurélie and Guinan quarrelled, quite badly, their first argument, so there was no precedent to make it up. Then, a couple of days later, it was time for her to leave her home in Norwich and return to Willis Towers in Ipswich. From the rooftop of the building, she and the other crew members boarded the space cruiser that was to take them to the starship.

Half an hour later, and she caught her first glimpse of the *Joyous Gard* from the cruiser porthole. She automatically reached into her bag to find her phone and text Guinan. Then she remembered they weren't speaking, and let it drop.

For a moment, the glory of the starship faded just a little, for her.

And yet it was magnificent. Sleek, new, with starlight gleaming from its smooth flank. It had a wide-winged body, a long, slender midsection, and a spherical prow which gave evidence of the ship's descent from the usual design of the Conglomerate military. But the design had evolved to produce a unique ship, built for exploration and discovery, not intergalactic battles.

This was to be Aurélie's home for the unforeseeable future. She nodded to the fair-haired girl she had seen in the interview waiting-room, who was now wearing an identical uniform to Aurélie's: burgundy trousers and tunic. The Conglomerate's insignia was pinned to it: a triangle suggesting the potential union between Avalon, Valerian and the undiscovered planet. There was an R inside it, and a laurel, like her own, beneath it. An officer, then, thought Aurélie.

The girl nodded and smiled back, then, as the space cruiser drew closer to the starship, she stood up and touched a key to the locked hatchway. The key and the starship exchanged complex communication. Then, a few moments later, a hatch opened, and the cruiser glided into the starship's landing bay. Aurélie, the girl, who introduced herself as Rose Thorn, and a few of the others from the cruiser were escorted to the ship's bridge.

Here, Captain Dulac and Lieutenant Lanval were seated behind a control console, full of glimmering lights and sudden, warning alarms. When one alarm proved particularly persistent, Rose Thorn stepped forwards with a gracious smile, and took her place at her station as Flight Navigation Officer. With one touch of a button, the strident tone of the safety alarm ceased.

Meanwhile, a handsome young dwarf, whose ruddy auburn head reached just the height of Aurélie's elbow, stepped forwards. He had a frank, earnest expression, and Aurélie found herself liking him immediately.

'Officer De Lys?' he said. 'I'm Ensign Dagonet.'

'But we've met before,' said Aurélie, suddenly. 'Years ago.'

'No, I don't think so,' said Ensign Dagonet, politely.

'Yes, we have,' said Aurélie. 'The circus trailer in Astalot - and, before that, at the court of King Arthur?'

'That was you?' said Dagonet. He shook his head in disbelief. 'That beautiful, blonde girl?'

'Erm... to be so surprised is not quite flattering... besides, I'm still blonde.'

'No, I mean, it's just, well, I hear you've one of the most brilliant minds ever,' said Dagonet.

'Again, not quite the most flattering way to have phrased it,' said Aurélie.

'But gosh, darn it, I'm so lucky,' said Dagonet, 'I've been assigned to show you round the ship, and to assist you in your work.'

'That's very kind of you,' said Aurélie, 'or very kind of someone, at any rate.'

'Well, the Conglomerate want you to be happy here,' said Dagonet. 'And they've got a doozy of a research task for us,' he added.

'A doozy?' said Aurélie. She thought she had heard Guinan use the same expression, once. Must be a dwarf thing.

'Yes,' said Dagonet. 'They want you to research the purpose of vampires, and the benefits they might bring to the new planet, when we find it.'

'You sound pretty confident that we will,' said Aurélie. 'But why aren't vampires being granted automatic rights to live on the new planet?'

'Queen Morgana,' said Dagonet, pulling a wry face. 'You know... all her new policies about elf eugenics, and fairy racial purity.'

'Oh I heard about that,' said Aurélie. Guinan hadn't taken it very seriously; he had told her it was a temporary reaction to the death of Morgana's friend and lady-in-waiting, Étincelle, as well as her own Valerian marriage. 'But it's becoming serious,' Aurélie added, half to Guinan, who wasn't there, and half to Dagonet, who was, 'if she's now opposed to vampire emigration. Her own son Mordred and her grandson, Morleon, were vampires, after all.'

Dagonet glanced round the crowded bridge, quickly. But no-one seemed to have heard what she had said. 'That's classified information,' he said, hurriedly.

'Yes, but my friend Violetta was present when Mordred collapsed, with a stake through his heart.'

Dagonet's expression relaxed. 'Violetta? The Victorian vampire? I've only just started researching her, but I think she will be a really valuable case-study for the Conglomerate.'

'Strictly speaking, she's not actually Victorian,' said Aurélie. 'But I can give you plenty of first-hand, eyewitness accounts,' she added. 'Though that may not be enough for the Conglomerate. All right, you had better show me to my cabin, and then to my research department.'

'Research department? We don't...' said Dagonet, caught off-guard. 'Er... it's not quite ready for you, yet.' Then he grinned, with infectious enthusiasm. 'But it soon will be.'

And so, with the assistance of Ensign Dagonet, who proved to be an eager postgraduate with an MA, unfortunately, in Comparative Literature, Aurélie began to prepare the appropriate dossier.

The Vampire Rights Movements, dating back to the late nineteenth century, and even the post-lockdown demonstrations of her own century had made it clear that vampires don't need to be cured since they are already perfect, in and of themselves. Therefore, Aurélie knew she would have to write some sort of explanatory addendum about how she had once cured a vampire with the Holy Grail, emphasising, however, that this was at the expressed desire of said vampire, in accordance with her own free will.

Nevertheless, given her close friendship with this vampire, Aurélie was pleased to uncover the lecture notes of one Professor Dimitri Baladin from the Castle Archives in Kief. It was only a slight stumbling block that Ensign Dagonet didn't have sufficient academic credentials (*'Yet!'* he said, with touching enthusiasm, blind hope and a boyish grin) to access these himself. In the end, she gave him her password and keycode so that he too could download this key lecture from the Kief State Libraries Online Manuscript Collection.

Stirring stuff it was, indeed. If Ensign Dagonet had harboured any doubts *at all*, about pursuing a career as a research assistant, (low pay, short-term projects and contracts, and few opportunities for professional advancement), this manuscript laid them *entirely* to rest.

Vampirism In The Shadow Of Zamikova Hora?
- first in a series of occasional lectures.

Professor Dimitri Baladin,
25th January, 1888

Thank you all for inviting me to speak to you today on what is quite possibly my favourite subject: the former ninth century Regent of Kief, Violetta Valhallah, the erstwhile wife of Oleg the Vargarian and the daughter of Vladimir of the House of the Sabre. It is scarcely possible for me to express my unbounded admiration for her in such a short speech, but nevertheless, I shall try.

It was at the age of fifteen that this remarkable young woman first began to distinguish herself from her peers. Her father Vladimir wished her to marry a much older neighbouring landowner, presumably with the intention that the prospective groom's wealth should pass to Violetta and her family upon his death. However, the subject of our lecture today would have none of it and left her father's house in the dead of night, never to return.

Although records from this time-period are scarce, Violetta is next listed as working as a servant in the household of Zhdan. Upon his death, she nobly volunteered to sacrifice herself on the pyre of his burial-ship; we assume to spare her fellow-servants this same fate. However, accounts from this time claim that she and Daedalus, a young Greek goatherd now in the employ of Drozd, emerged, unscathed, from the flames.

It is this particular incident which first gave rise to the claims of vampirism which have subsequently haunted this young woman. My listeners will of course recall that nine hundred years ago, vampirism was rare, but not unknown. However, my own personal feeling is that such rumours were merely intended to strike fear into the hearts of her enemies, the Drevlians, of which more later.

Violetta next surfaces in historical records a scant few years later, as the wife of Oleg the Vargarian, a barbarian indeed, as some scholars have quipped. (*Pause for laughter.*) He was himself the Regent of Kief, ruling from the fine castle where I am now archivist. Following his death after ten years of marriage, in highly suspicious circumstances involving soothsayers, a dead horse and some asps, Violetta was proclaimed Regent of Kief. She then avenged his apparent murder by assassinating Drevlians in various ingenious ways, including death by poison, setting fire to bathhouses, and sending birds with flaming tail feathers to fly in wooden cities.

Upon the return of Igor, Oleg's ward, Violetta then renounced the Regency and set off, partly on foot, to the Port of St Petersburg, and to the ship awaiting her. This ship, *The Hummingbird*, was bound for Valerian's shores.

At this point, historical accounts differ. Some claim that Violetta died on her long sea-voyage and was then buried in a tomb-house in the graveyard of St. Swithin's church, in Lostwithiel. However, others have subsequently examined this tomb and since it now lies empty, rumours of vampirism have again swept through the historical community here in Kief. Only the other day, I was visited by a charming young woman who claims to be an ancestress of Regent Violetta, and who, in fact, bears the same name. Her likeness to her illustrious forebear is, quite frankly, uncanny. Whether she possesses the same determined spirit as Regent Violetta, or whether, as I sometimes imagine, she is in fact the self-same vampire of rumour and speculation remains to be seen. (*Pause here - 5 seconds?*)

But now, gentlemen, I have reached the end of my preliminary discourse on this most fascinating of subjects, and I thank you once again for your invitation, and for your close and careful attention this evening. (*Bow twice to applause, sign three autographs - but no more. Time is of the essence, etc.*)

Ensign Dagonet pushed the anti-blue-light glasses he wore for screenwork up from his tired eyes, rubbed them, then glanced round at what they now liked to call the research department, although so far, it consisted of one desk, one chair, one filing cabinet and one computer. There was also a single box-file which currently contained just two documents: some handwritten notes Aurélie had made from Sheridan Le Fanu's *Carmilla* before the computer had been set up, and a scribble in an unknown hand that had always bewildered her from the Lady Elridge Archives.

Dagonet opened the box-file now, to see if he could cross-reference anything there with the Kief Manuscript. From Sheridan Le Fanu, he read: 'The vampire is prone to be fascinated with an engrossing vehemence, resembling the passion of love, by particular persons. In pursuit of these, it will exercise inexhaustible patience and stratagem, for access to a particular object may be obstructed in a hundred ways. It will never desist until it has satiated its passion and drained the very life of its coveted victim. But it will, in these cases, husband and protract its murderous enjoyment with the refinement of an epicure and heighten it by the gradual approaches of an artful courtship. In these cases, it seems to yearn for something like sympathy and consent. In ordinary cases, it goes direct to its object, overpowers it with violence and strangles and exhausts it, often at a single feast.'

Dagonet sighed. How to reconcile this portrayal of the vampire with what he had read of Violetta Valhallhah? And in any case, it would be difficult to make any kind of argument about them bringing benefits to the new planet if this was how they behaved. He glanced at the other sheet of paper, which Aurélie appeared to have torn from a ring-binder.

To A., 25th April, 1891

'Ladies Fair, and Lady Dark,
Seek me while ye may,
Lady Crow and Ladies Lark,
Who knows what games we will play?'

But there, it was an incomprehensible scrap, after all. The Kief Manuscript was the thing to focus on. He thought he might make a start by compiling a list of all the positive adjectives he could find in the Professor's lecture, only to realise that his favourite pen was no longer behind his ear. He could have just typed or dictated the adjectives, but he was old-school, and he loved that pen. It was covered all over in beaten-gold dragon-scales, and the nib had adjusted itself nicely to his handwriting. He was going to have to retrace his steps from here back to his cabin and see if he could find it.

A few moments later, and there it was! Beneath the stool in the turbo-lift. It must have fallen down this morning when the lift gave that alarming judder. He really should have called Ship Maintenance about it, there and then, and indeed he might have done had he realised it had nearly cost him his pen. But the siren flicker of the vastscreen had lured him away from such practical, and rather dull, matters. Was there a moral to this sorry episode, he pondered, as he stepped out of the lift, only to have his thoughts disturbed by a voice which was distinctive, and, he judged, exquisitely modulated.

'Frightful!'

Ensign Dagonet turned, delightedly, to identify the owner of the voice. She had spoken in the vernacular of the nineteenth century. And there she stood, at the entrance to the recreation deck. She wore a dark purple riding habit, though the skirt was sufficiently voluminous that it covered all but the toes of her black boots. Beneath the jacket, there were glimpses of a white, lace blouse that complimented her white gloves. In one hand, there was a leather portmanteau stamped with the gold initials *VV,* in which he could just glimpse the dark cover of a journal. In the other hand, she carried the ivory handle of her parasol. Her hair was dark, and heavily coiled about her fine head, and there was an expression of alarm on her pale, oval face.

A Time Traveller, no doubt! Dagonet grinned with pleasure.

'It is a most disconcerting sensation,' complained the lady. 'But I believe I am in the right place, more or less. Young man, kindly conduct me to the domicile of your History Officer.'

'At least you didn't say *take me to your leader*,' said Dagonet. 'Some of the less experienced Time Travellers back in Valerian still do that. And less of the young man, please,' he added, drawing himself up to his full height of four foot seven, 'You can only be twenty-nine or so. I'm Ensign Dagonet, and I'm already twenty-three.'

'Oh, but I'm thirty,' said the lady, with a hint of tragedy to her manner. 'But before, I was - oh, can I tell you, can I tell you my great secret - yet, you have an endearing face, and who knows, we may yet become great friends, - very well, then, I shall tell you - no, no, don't try to stop me, for, dear soul, I was once...' she paused, impressively, 'an immortal - and a vampire.'

'Then you drank from the Holy Grail, and now you're human,' said Dagonet. 'Welcome aboard the *Joyous Gard,* Ms Valhallah.'

'But how did you know it was me?' asked Violetta, her mouth turning down.

'I believe you are a great friend of my boss, Officer De Lys. You are part of the dossier we have been working on, about vampires,' he replied.

'Oh really? You don't say?' said Violetta. 'Apart from our friendship, I wasn't aware that vampirism was one of her specialisms.'

'Oh yes,' said Dagonet. 'But she has so many. I feel I can learn such a lot from her. I'm going to help her with her addendum,' he added, proudly.

'You're her young protégé,' said Violetta, 'oh, how charming. But apart from the intrinsic fascination of the subject, why are you researching vampires together?'

'The Conglomerate is opposed to Queen Morgana's anti-vampire policies,' said Dagonet. 'Are you aware that ever since the death of her son, Mordred, Queen Morgana has been blaming vampirism for many of the ills in her family?'

'But I'm here on a related matter,' said Violetta, excitedly. 'Officer De Lys may have told you that Morleon, Mordred's son, disappeared into an alternate timeline. We have now had word that, in that timeline, he is turning asylum patients into vampires. The overall consequences could be disastrous.'

'How very odd,' said Dagonet, 'but then, they're an odd family,' he added. 'Did you know that Queen Morgana is now trying to deny vampires access to the new planet, when we find it?' His eyes narrowed, and for a moment, he looked older than twenty-three. 'Are you pro-or anti-vampire, Ms Valhallah?'

She paused, as if astonished, and, just for a moment, she lost her air of perfect self-composure. Then she discarded some of her affected manner, and said, more earnestly, 'I don't believe anyone should be made a vampire against their will. And I also don't believe that vampires should be excluded from the chance of a new life when the planet is discovered.' She paused again, a bewildered look in her fine eyes. 'Does that mean I'm a humanitarian?'

'I think it means you are a good person,' said Dagonet, kindly. Just then, Lieutenant Lanval, curse him, stepped through the door that led to the recreation deck, squash racket in hand, perspiring heavily. He shot them a curious glance, and nodded to the Ensign, but he was too out of breath to ask questions. All the same, it was enough to prompt Dagonet to say, 'Let me escort you to Officer De Lys right now.'

'Yes, do that,' said Violetta, eagerly. 'She really is most remarkable. I should have liked to have spent more time with her, but motherhood, alas, is not compatible with Time Travel.'

'Why not?' asked Dagonet, with the careless insouciance of youth. He ushered her into the turbo lift. 'Surely if you do it right, no-one ever knows you were gone?'

'It's a big *if*,' said Violetta, with growing candour. 'I'm not as good at Time Travel as Aurélie, or Guinan, for that matter, though don't tell him I said so. He's dreadfully conceited, already.'

'My cousin? said Dagonet, nodding seriously, 'you know him well, then.'

Violetta likewise nodded. 'He likes to call himself my mentor. Though I haven't seen him for many years. But perhaps it's just as well. For whenever I return from adventuring, I'm always so restless at home. It doesn't make for a peaceful existence. In fact, it's only because this is a matter of the gravest importance that I'm here, at all.'

The turbo lift began its slow descent towards the officer's quarters. 'But surely you're still an adventuress at heart,' said Ensign Dagonet. 'Why, you once slaughtered an entire race of Drevlians.'

'Young man,' said Violetta, pointedly, 'you know far more about me than I do about you. I fear it puts me at a disadvantage.'

Mildly abashed, Dagonet decided it would be ungentlemanly to pursue his line of questioning. As the turbo lift arrived at its destination and its doors slid open, he reached up for Violetta's elbow, and gently steered her out into the corridor, towards Officer De Lys's quarters.

He took great care, as he walked by her side, not to become entangled in the ivory spokes of the lady's parasol.

In the middle of the night, a dream. Violetta dreamt it was the Time of the Titrations. She was returning from the Lost Garden, stealing over to the couch where Lord Darvell lay, swooning from the loss of his blood. How silently she crept, careful to make no sound that might awaken him. She paused, fancying that he had stirred, then, since all was still, she crept ever closer.

In her dream, she leaned over him; her first hurried glance took in the pallor of his features. He was supposed to be pale; he had just sacrificed another quart of his blood, and yet, something was amiss. Her eyes roamed across his face. She started, then began to call his name, his first name, that she rarely used, for it brought him too close. When there was no answer, she grasped his arm, and cried out his name again, over and over, no longer afraid to waken him by any sound she could utter, by any movement she could make. She thought her lover dozed: in her vision, she found that he was dead.

Violetta sat up suddenly, bolt upright, on Aurélie's sofa bed in her cabin. 'Lights,' she called. All at once, the living area was flooded with intense luminosity.

'What'sa matter?' asked Aurélie, entering the room from her bedroom, rubbing her eyes. She walked over to perch on the side of her desk, near by the comm terminal and synthesizer unit.

'I'm going to die,' wailed Violetta. 'We're *all* going to die.'

'What do you mean?' asked Aurélie, moving now to sit down on the end of the bed. 'Are you sick?'

'No,' said Violetta, 'but,' she added, glancing down at the freckles on her pale arms, that were emerging from the sleeves of her nightdress, 'I'm getting older, and one day I shall die. And so shall they - all the people that I love.'

'You used not to be so histrionic,' said Aurélie. 'Why *are* you being like this?'

'Well,' said Violetta, 'for one thing, Aurélie, you're fifty-five. It's a bit of a shock to me.' She peered more closely at her friend's face and took a cautious sniff. 'Is that Oil of Olay you're wearing?' And then, 'What do wrinkles *feel* like?'

'Like an unmade flesh bed,' said Aurélie, drily.

'Arthur's friend, Miss Anning, thinks fossils are beautiful,' said Violetta, uncertainly. Her eyelids started to close but she forced herself awake. Aurélie was saying something. There was a chance it was important.

'I suppose they are,' Aurélie said, in a softer tone of voice. 'Intricate, whirling vortices. Like the Milky Way, solidified.'

'You have Miss Anning to thank for me being here,' said Violetta.

'I did wonder,' said Aurélie. 'You were too fatigued from Time Travel to tell me much, before.'

'Yes,' said Violetta. 'Well, you see, how it happened was, that Miss Anning wished to discover whether female palaeontology was more respected in timelines other than our own. She obtained the Time Travel spell from me to travel to different versions of *St. Cosmas & Damian*'s, intending to give lectures to the patients there.'

'I'm almost sure that's against Guinan's regulations,' said Aurélie. 'You know we're not supposed to disrupt other timelines.'

'But it's just as well she did,' said Violetta, 'for there was pandemonium in the timeline we had left behind.'

'Ah,' said Aurélie. 'That's not good, is it?'

'No,' said Violetta. 'It is not. In that alternate timeline, Miss Anning learned that Dr Charles Helton was no longer the acting supervisor at the hospital. He was apparently so alarmed by what was occurring that he fled to the Continent to recover.'

'I suppose it doesn't do a nerve doctor's reputation much good to admit he's suffering from an hysterical crisis,' said Aurélie.

'No,' said Violetta, 'especially when some of the other doctors are still there, and the orderlies and the Porter.'

'Oh dear,' said Aurélie, 'go on.'

'And Miss Anning found out that the sanatorium doors and windows were kept locked during the day, but were wide open at night,' continued Violetta. 'She even brought us a copy of the *Valerian Times*. Morleon had inserted a notice there stating that he wished to create a new vampire life for every vampire anarchist that had been lost. He claimed asylum patients were treated so badly that vampirism might seem to them a blessing rather than a curse.'

'I wonder why that didn't come up in our search engine?' said Aurélie. 'Maybe the alternate timeline software has a few glitches.'

'That's hardly the point,' said Violetta.

'On the contrary,' said Aurélie, 'it's exactly the point. I'm head researcher here, and my department can't be seen to be making those kinds of errors.'

'But you told me, your department was you and Ensign Dagonet, taking it in turns to sit in a broom cupboard,' said Violetta.

Aurélie grinned. 'Still,' she said, 'Morleon can't exonerate himself with such feeble reasoning, either.'

'No,' said Violetta. 'I'm sure he does though,' she added. 'The vampire conscience is as malleable as...' she paused and nodded in the direction of the desk, 'my gloves over there, and is, besides, entirely self-serving, my dear. The vampire can excuse any crime, justify any action, or, if he cannot, it is of no real consequence.'

'But you aren't like that,' said Aurélie.

'Not by the time you knew me, and bade me drink from the sacred chalice,' said Violetta, 'but I believe your young assistant has something to say on the subject of slaughtered Drevlians.'

'Actually, you're right,' said Aurélie, 'I tend to make a distinction in my mind between Regent Violetta of Kief, who committed all those atrocities - and *you,* yourself.'

'Lord Darvell does the same,' said Violetta. 'You both justify my actions out of your affection for me. Be careful. That is perilously close to the vampire's refusal to admit culpability.'

'Well. we don't need Morleon to admit he's wrong,' said Aurélie, 'we just need him to stop.'

'That's what Miss Anning said, too,' said Violetta. Then she added, slowly and impressively, 'What we *really* need is the Holy Grail. To make Morloen drink from it would be an entirely fitting punishment. But do Guinan and Pippin still have the Grail I gave them?'

'Guinan has the Grail, and Pippin, the Alternate Grail,' said Aurélie. 'Last I knew, they were using them to continue developing cures for covid, post lockdown, in the twenty-first century.'

'What do you mean, the *last* you knew? I thought you kept in touch with them?'

'I did,' said Aurélie, 'I do. But Guinan annoyed me dreadfully a fortnight ago, just before I joined the starship. So we're not speaking.'

'What did he do?' asked Violetta with interest, then catching sight of the look on Aurélie's face, she said, 'you don't have to tell me, if you don't want to.'

'He wrote my reference for this job, but he also wrote a joke reference,' said Aurélie, reluctantly, 'and they somehow got mixed up, *he says,* and he posted the wrong one - and it was all incredibly embarrassing. That was my professional career almost over before it had begun.'

'And you're worried it was deliberate sabotage?' asked Violetta.

Aurélie nodded.

'It seems strange he would try to help you and then ruin his own efforts,' said Violetta thoughtfully. 'I wouldn't have said he was malicious, though he certainly goes *much too far.* Still, you had better reconcile with him. We need the Grails.'

'What about my principles?'

'Principles are for when asylums are empty of vampires,' said Violetta. 'How do you communicate with him? Do you whistle?'

'The whistle is what he uses to summon Pippin,' said Aurélie. 'I usually just text. But he needs to say sorry, first.'

'Sometimes,' said Violetta, 'when Lord Darvell is at fault, and believe you me, it happens more often than you might think, I get round the awkward matter of an apology by demanding that he do something for me. He usually does, and then there is no loss of face on either side.'

'What sort of thing?' asked Aurélie, intrigued, despite herself.

'I'm not prepared to say,' said Violetta. 'And yet it is a satisfying solution.'

'I'm not sexting Guinan just to get hold of the Grail,' said Aurélie.

'No?' said Violetta. 'your choice of course, but I meant, just ask him for the Cup. He will relinquish it; he will feel happy; you will feel happy; and then together, we can resolve the Wrath of Morleon.'

'How happy was Lord Darvell when you asked *him* for the Grail?' asked Aurélie.

'Not very,' said Violetta, 'in either timeline - but then, the circumstances were quite different.'

Aurélie couldn't help it: she gave a sudden yawn. 'It's too late for all this,' she said. 'My head's spinning.'

'Would you like me to text Guinan for you, now?' asked Violetta, smiling at her friend.

'No,' said Aurélie. 'I wouldn't like that, at all. I'm going back to bed. I'll see what I want to do tomorrow,' she added, firmly. 'Good night, Violetta.'

'You'll have to show me how your phone works in the morning, then,' said Violetta, silkily. 'Good night, Aurélie.'

As it turned out, Aurélie didn't need to lose face by texting Guinan the next day. On the morrow, she, Violetta and Rose Thorn were sitting together in the officers' canteen, enjoying their breakfasts, grapefruit juice, croissants, cereal, when the subject turned, quite naturally, to the Holy Grail.

'Of course,' Aurélie said to Rose Thorn, 'you were the one to find it, originally.'

'And my Sisterhood continues to venerate its sacred properties,' said Rose Thorn, earnestly. 'When I was in the Collodian's Castle of Chalis just recently, I brought away a souvenir of the Grail, a beautiful woven tapestry. I thought it might look well in the Sisters' Ceremonial Hall.'

'You're with the Sisters of Valerian?' asked Aurélie, opening her eyes wide, impressed. She had heard of their subversive activities from Guinan.

Rose Thorn nodded. 'At some point, when all the flight navigation systems are set up properly and I have trained my replacement, I mean to return to the Compound,' she said.

'Before you do that,' Violetta said, firmly, 'I should very much like to see that tapestry.'

And so, later that afternoon, Rose Thorn brought the tapestry to Aurélie's cabin. Here, the Flight Navigation officer unrolled it and showed it to the two women. It depicted two dwarves, embroidered in bright silks, one older, one younger, walking out from a castle tower, each one clasping a goblet.

'But that's Guinan and Pippin,' said Aurélie, 'how did you not recognise them?'

'Well, they're embroidery,' said Rose Thorn.

'And look,' said Violetta, 'more importantly, there's the Grail, and the Alternate Grail.' She peered more closely at the tapestry. 'What do they think they're doing?' she said. 'Why are they hiding there?'

'What do you mean, *hiding*?' asked Aurélie. 'It's not real. They're *stitched*.'

'I used to think the things I stitched from the mirror and into my tapestry were real, the realest dreams that ever were,' said Rose Thorn. 'Then one day, Sir Lancelot...' she paused, and shook her head, 'woke me from my dreams.'

'Never mind that,' said Violetta, 'look at the tapestry. Look, Aurélie. Guinan's winking at you.'

And so he was.

'Like a frickin Ninety-Nineties dating emoticon,' complained Aurélie. 'Emoji. Whatever.'

'Oh, are you two dating, then?' asked Rose Thorn, her voice rising an octave with interest.

'Well we were,' said Aurélie. 'I don't know, though. He's dreadfully annoying at times.'

After she had uttered those unintentional magic words, quite by chance, all the stitched embroidery in bright coloured silks unravelled from the tapestry and scattered onto the wide sweep of the cabin floor. There they reassembled, from Turkish slippers and button boots curving upwards, into the size and shape of the two dwarves, Guinan and Pippin.

'What ho,' said Pippin, stretching out his toes in his button boots. His chalice was tied around his neck on a black cord, and he wore it proudly, like an Olympic medal.

'Hullo ladies, Violetta, Aurélie, Rose Thorn,' said Guinan, pleasantly enough, glancing at them, then all about the cabin. 'You summoned us?' he continued, quite as if he were a genie.

'Guinan,' said Aurélie, 'why are you hiding inside Rose Thorn's tapestry from the Castle of Chalis?'

'I'm an anti-establishment dwarf with a subversive ideology working in a school for magical miscreants that encourages ritualistic sacrifice,' he said. 'Obviously, I was checking out an appropriate escape route, should my brethren and I ever require it.'

'That makes perfect sense,' said Aurélie. She stopped. 'Oh, rats, I'm not meant to be speaking to you.'

'You are now,' said Guinan. 'Come on, admit it, Aurélie. Every moment without me has been an aching eternity.'

'I'm a Time Traveller,' snapped Aurélie. 'I don't do aching eternities.'

'I'm an Immortal,' said Guinan. 'I do.'

'Are they always like this?' Rose Thorn asked Violetta.

'Let's hope not,' Violetta replied.

'You sent in the wrong reference,' Aurélie said.

'You should be thanking me for that,' said Guinan. 'Hasn't Officer Pluto been much less frisky round you, since?'

'So, you admit it was deliberate, then,' said Aurélie.

'There are references, and there are envelopes, and there are dwarves with kind hearts and clever minds,' said Guinan.

'I wouldn't put you in either of those categories,' said Aurélie.

'Where would you put me?' asked Guinan.

'Excuse me?' said Violetta, politely, 'Even for Immortals and Time Travellers, there isn't enough life for all this. We need the Grail.'

'I thought I was going to be the one to ask for it?' wailed Aurélie, rounding on her friend. Really, nothing was working out this morning, the way she thought it would.

'You can *both* have the Holy Grail with our best blessings,' said Guinan. 'You will certainly have need of it on your travels,' he continued. 'I believe you are returning to the nineteenth century?'

'Yes,' said Violetta. 'How did you know that?'

'Why else would you be here?' asked Guinan pointedly, and then, cheek of the dwarf, he handed the Grail to her. 'After all, it's not only knights who are king slayers. The

103

ladies also must have their turn,' he said. 'But the Alternate Holy Grail stays where it is.'

Pippin nodded vigorously and tucked the Alternate Holy Grail beneath the collar of his shirt. 'Mine,' he said.

'Yours,' agreed Aurélie, in a calmer tone of voice.

Guinan gave her an approving smile.

'Now ladies,' he said, 'you know what happens next.'

'We don't need the chalk circle anymore since I made the compass,' said Aurélie. 'Panel,' she called, and a silver hatch near to the cabin entrance slid open. She walked over, and from it she retrieved a dome, something like a snowstorm, but with a Perspex, flip-top lid with a compass inside it. 'But we still need the objects for North, South, East and West,' she added, looking round wildly at her cabin quarters.

'I'll help you with North, Wisdom,' said Guinan. He walked over to her desk and began to scribble out some calculations on a piece of paper, which he handed to Aurélie.

'Thank you,' said Aurélie.

'What about South, Love?' asked Guinan.

'*Can* any one object symbolise Love?' asked Rose Thorn, wistfully. She glanced down at the skeins of tapestry silk now unravelled on the cabin floor, and wished she still possessed the silk case she had made for Lancelot's shield. Hours and hours it had taken her, to embroider all those heraldic devices, with their borders of branches, buds, flowers and birds with wings stitched in crocus-thread. She shifted her shoulder blades and slightly arched her spine. Her own wings lay the length of it, quietly folded.

'Well, there's still that piece of rose quartz,' said Aurélie, walking over and retrieving the rock from her desk.

'Oh, rose quartz,' said Guinan.

'What's wrong?'

'Nothing, nothing. I expect our Violetta can help us with East, Courage,' said Guinan.

'You can borrow this,' said Violetta, unclasping a locket from around her neck, 'as long as you give it back to me before we disappear.' She pressed the catch and handed it to Aurélie. Inside was a double portrait of two girls, the smaller one with a curl of blonde hair on her forehead. 'Arabella - and Frances,' she said. 'I didn't know what courage was until I had her.'

'Oh, I think you did,' said Guinan. 'Pippin,' he added. 'I know when you went to see Kilkenny last week, he gave you something. Would you mind lending it to the ladies, please?'

Pippin reached inside his pocket and took out the clockwork mouse. 'Mine?' he said, uncertainly.

'Sorry, Pippin, not today,' said Guinan.

'We're only borrowing it, Pippin,' said Violetta. 'Remember how I once borrowed the Grail, but then you got it back?'

'Don't tell him that,' said Aurélie. 'You gave it to a dragon.'

Pippin stuck out his lower lip and looked alarmed.

'No-one will give your clockwork mouse to a dragon, Pippin,' said Aurélie. She held out her hand.

'All right then,' he said. Slowly, reluctantly, he placed the grey, felt, object of adulation in her outstretched palm.

'Thank you, Pippin,' said Aurélie, then smiled at the fierce look of concentration on her friend's face. Evidently, Violetta was trying to recall the Time Travel spell.

'It starts like this...' Aurélie said, to help her, '*In siglia sela...*'

'That's right,' said Violetta. She mumbled a few more words, then smiled at the assembled company. 'Who needs the past to stay in the past, anyway?' she said.

'Sometimes we like it to jump about a bit,' Aurélie agreed. In unison, they continued the words of the magic spell:

'Monis Morgana
Sonor doni
Ex fugit sela.'

Then, Pippin reached out for his clockwork mouse and Violetta made a sudden grab for her locket.

Finally, to the astonishment of Rose Thorn, although not of Sir Pippin, Anointed Knight of the Realm, nor of his father, Ambassador Guinan Guineafowl, Professor of Time Travel *and* Queen Morgana's Visiting Envoy, there came a flash of bright light, a few green sparks, and then, moments later, Aurélie and Violetta vanished.

Sophia, Robot Girl

2025 AD. Three years into our Reign came the Explosion and then the Time of Ashes. They called it that. I did not. Could not. At that point, I was not alive to call it anything. Only when, a few months later, they began to rebuild me - finer, better, stronger - did I discover that Kensington Palace had been reduced to a heap of rubble, and that my husband, King Arthur III, was dead.

I could understand many things before I could say them. It took them many weeks to perfect the intricate circuits so that I could shape the words I thought. At first, they tried to argue that I was not thinking at all, that it was a simulation or byproduct of the neuropeptides they were injecting into my brain. But I knew I was thinking.

I knew, for example, who I liked, and who I merely tolerated. Whose hands were kind, and whose, impersonal. Who wanted to clip in eyes to restore my old, dark eye colour, and who laughed and said, 'Blue, brown, black, grey, or metal sockets, what the hell does it matter? She's a robot, for crying out loud.' But I knew, it did matter. Tentatively, I stroked my face. It would feel warm, not cold, when there was skin upon it.

When I had eyes, I could see these Men of Ash, though it was hard for me at first to tell one from the other. And yet I neither liked nor disliked what I saw. They all had grey hair, though one at least pretended he did not. Grey as cobwebs, but some spark of hope they must still have possessed to bring me back to life.

When I had a tongue to speak, they began to teach me. Their lessons were neither interesting, nor dull. From them, I learned, for example, that when meeting someone for the first time, or even the second, a weather conversation might be deemed appropriate. Daily study of meteorological charts will facilitate these conversations, which, with time and practice, might become quite complex.

Another time they wheeled in a vastscreen and showed me some footage of a dog who originated from the era and place of my birth, Victorian Valerian. A golden retriever, very elegant, who had become quite famous in Avalon. Uxbridge. A celebrity, in fact. I did not understand it at all. Why did they call him a clever dog? Already, I could do far more than he could. But seeing him there in black-and-white-and-sepia, barking, begging, jumping, jumping, begging, barking, reminded me of Arthur, and his tales of Dog Tray from Lyme Regis. I asked them then, 'Why did you bring me back? Why not the King?'

Collectively, they seemed to find it hard to reply. Perhaps they thought I was not ready for the answer. Or perhaps the reply was not rooted in what they knew, nanotechnology and neurocircuits. But the failure was in their words, not in my understanding.

At last, Ashley, the oldest of the three, judging by his beard and heavy eyelids, told me that King Arthur was steeped in so many legends, myths and magic of his own that there might come a time when he would resurrect anyway. Not as a robot, but as he once was, in all his glory.

'As a bear?' I said, for well I knew all the tales of his youth.

But this was too far a leap of supposition for these Men of Ash.

Austin, who had no beard, smiled and said he would see whether the fibre glass was ready so that my limbs could be attached to my torso. Ashley, kindlier still, wheeled me over to the window of their glass laboratory. As we trundled along, I glanced up at the complicated architraves soaring above me. A flash of memory then: a cathedral, a coronation, a crown.

When we reached the great, rectangular window, I could look at the white orchid nodding on the windowsill, and the view outside.

I stayed behind the window for a long time. When the colours went, they said it was night, and the night had a thousand eyes, and all of them were white.

Stars.

Wishthewishlwishtonight.

At that time I had no need for food or drink, although there was some talk of developing my technology so that I might have an appetite. This was so I would better understand the plight of the Valerian people, though, at this point, I did not know why they should be of any concern to me. Nevertheless, I liked to see the allotment outside the window, where the scientists were trying to grow tomatoes, potatoes, whatever they could, for the post-explosion soil lacked vital nutrients for plants. They called this place Greenwich, but there was not much green about it. However, one stunted tomato plant was still a hopeful thing compared to the charred remnants of buildings, the shards of breakage and detritus that lay beyond it.

And was not I, their hopeful thing?

They often made me feel like the only woman there. The reason I felt like that was because I was the only woman there. All around me were unfamiliar faces, men whose names began with A - and Sbud.

They gave me back my own name, Sophia, after the Greek goddess of wisdom, and it is true, my wisdom usually outstripped their own, even at the time when they had only completed half my neural circuits. Sometimes I used that name, and sometimes I called myself S for I disliked a superfluous number of syllables. 'Why was I created?' I asked them and just for a moment came a memory of the little girl in a pinafore that once I was, asking Nurse how babies were made. 'The stork brings babies,' she had told me - and I believed her.

These Men of Ash said something different. They said they had formed an alliance with the Sisters of Valerian in opposition to many of Queen Morgana's policies - Queen Morgana, whom, they reminded me, was my sister-in-law. The Great Explosion, for which she was believed responsible, as well as the development of celestine neurotechnology, and the new immigration policies she had begun to introduce after the death of my husband, had forced them to create some form of opposition.

I was that opposition.

I, Sophia.

I was to be their Robot-Queen. I had been created using the most skilled technology, the most advanced parts. I had been restored to rule over Valerian, to challenge Queen Morgana's dominion.

When I said I had no soul or mind to reign, but only to mourn, they said I had no real brain, no soul, no heart - everything I was had been created by them. I told them there was something wrong with their programming then, for I had all these things.

I marched away from them across the cracked tiled floor of this beautiful building made of glass. I would continue my contemplation of my orchid, and my study of the language of the Japanese.

'Do you think we made her too female?' asked Sbud. His voice sounded like it did when he claimed he had no grey hair. Though they had made it so, they often forgot how acute my hearing was, and maintained their habit of talking about me as if I were not there.

'I understood from contemporary records that Sophia James of both the nineteenth and the twenty-first century had quite a different personality,' said Austin.

'I expect elements of that personality will resurface eventually,' said Ashley, reassuringly. 'The celestine memory recuperation software we installed was so complex it hasn't fully downloaded yet.'

'What if we aren't making her at all?' asked Austin. 'What if she is making *herself*?'

'But it is our technology, our programming,' said Sbud, of the indifferent hands.

'And since when was the composition of haiku poetry part of our programming?' asked Austin.

'The neatness of that poetic form is not incompatible with the structure of her neural pathways,' said Ashley, thoughtfully. 'And perhaps a little personality in a ruler is no bad thing.'

'Careful, Pygmalion,' said Austin.

I understood the reference. By now my learning had far outstripped their teachings of 'The rain in Spain stays mainly on the plain,' or 'See the clever dog run and jump!' I had privately read or remembered most of the early Greek and Latin classics, although of course, it would be some months before I re-encountered the works of George Bernard Shaw. I dimly remembered meeting him once at a Fabian society dinner, but all I could chiefly recall now was the wisp of his beard and moustache, something like a charcoal sketch, at which I was becoming quite adept.

It was not possible to keep my proficiency at charcoal portraiture a secret for long. Charcoal ashes were my medium; the Men of Ash my subjects. And Ashley himself discovered his own portrait, pinned beneath my desk, when he was moving it closer to the bright window, so that I might get more sunlight. For, at that time, they would not let me venture outside. They had not yet perfected my anti-rain paintwork, and feared I might rust.

But the portrait! Just the right expression of sad wistfulness beneath bushy eyebrows, and the lines of his face, so noble, so expressive. Was it when he saw his portrait, that he truly believed I had a soul?

He took up the picture with trembling hands, admired it, then put it down, carefully, on the desk. He told me then that my late husband, King Arthur, had also possessed exquisite skills of draughtsmanship, although his preferred medium was pen and ink.

'Did he teach you to draw like this?' asked Ashley later, sipping his green tea from his Blue Willow cup. It smelt green and mysterious, of the mists of not-here places. And how I envied him his palate, and the roof of his mouth! But he had promised to develop my taste buds so that I, too, could become a connoisseur of such exquisite flavours.

Puzzled, I shook my head.

'I taught him,' I said. 'He could only doodle before he met me.'

Ashley twisted the empty porcelain cup round in his hands. I took it from him. It was smooth and fine beneath my fingertips. But if stars were made of porcelain, they might break. I wondered then whether my husband would have liked to learn Japanese with me, and whether he would have helped me find words of the right syllable for my haikus.

One time, when Ashley was posing for his silhouette portrait, whilst at the same time mending the nib of my calligraphy pen, I mentioned it to him. 'Is it not the duty and role of a husband, to share in all his wife's interests?'

Ashley blushed a little at my words, as pink as the peonies I had begun to embroider on his new slippers.

'Should you like to meet my mother?' he said then. 'She lives quite on the other side of town. We're lucky, the explosion didn't do much damage to our house.'

The word *mother* made me remember Nurse and her tales of the stork. Sometimes I liked to remember her. *Okaasan, sayonara.*

Ashley peered at me closely.

'Did that upset you?' he asked. 'It's hard to know, with girls, what does. That's why I didn't want you to have any emotions. I didn't want you ever to be upset.'

'Many things about me are hard to know,' I said. 'But I have begun writing my own manual,' I added. 'When I have finished, you may read it. Now hold still!'

But so far, it was a short manual. On the first page, I had written, *Sometimes it seems like I don't care when I do.* Then I had stopped. For that was the key to my whole personality, and I retained my dislike for superfluous words.

Next I tried to express the same sentiment in haiku.

'Glass laboratory
Where caring transcends the ash
The orchid unfurls.'

I was not sure about the final verb-choice. For was it not umbrellas that unfurl? I was growing impatient for the Men of Ash to complete the anti-rain paintwork and to allow me outside. When I suggested a kind of cloaking device that might prevent rust, Austin laughed and said I meant an umbrella. The next day, he brought one from his home to show me.

'One day, you'll be singing in the rain,' he promised, and he let me keep the umbrella. I put it in a vase and placed it on the window-sill.

Then he loaned me a disc of a film with the same name, and then, another one, just as brightly coloured, called *The Wizard of Oz.* Or at least, it was black-and-white, but then it was brightly coloured. It was kind of funny, but it was also kind of sad. One of the men in the film was a robot who wanted a heart. I am a robot with too much heart. How loudly it ticks! I found it hard, worrying so much about each member of my small kingdom.

It should have been exciting being the only robot woman alive, but often there were too many expectations. Three of them, and one of me. Sometimes there was talk of cloning me, and that may have been some kind of solution. But my learning was far outstripping what they could teach me, and I was almost at the point where I thought I could manage the process by myself. Then I would have no further need of them. Though there might come a day or a night or an evening when I would miss them, and then, where would I be, what would I do?

Alas, my orchid had no answer for me. Besides, the leaves of its petals were beginning to curl up and turn brown. I touched one with my fingertip. Too soft and unpointy a star. So instead, I went to sleep - sometimes I dreamed films.

Sometimes I preferred *Singing In The Rain*, and sometimes *The Wizard of Oz*. Sometimes I watched them on alternate days, and sometimes, one after the other. Austin said the discs came free with a newspaper; he had never watched them anyway, and I could keep them as long as I wished. I liked these kinds of thoughtful gestures, and I wanted to reciprocate. So I made it my business to discover the dates of the birthdays of all of these Men of Ash. Soon I was busy contriving suitable and appropriate gifts for them. Only I did not have a birthday myself, which was *fine*. They told me this was because I had evolved over many weeks and many parts, and indeed I was not yet fully complete. My knowledge of Etruscan pottery, for example, could scarcely be called comprehensive.

Although my mind to me was its own kingdom, and all that I required, nonetheless, I could not help but feel grateful when I was first taken to the observatory, which required us to walk down a long corridor from the laboratory. Sometimes we must leave our safe places and venture out among the stars. Besides, I had been asking them for weeks, ever since I had first seen the first star from my window.

Now I could see those great stars through the great telescope, which brought them closer, closer, closer, to shed their gold and silver light. And there they were again, glimpsed through the glass domed ceiling above. Ah, the beauty of those starry clusters among the blue and the dim and the dark. Half lights, guiding lights in the night, hopeful things indeed. And they gave me a sense then of being something above and beyond myself, or - as if they were a part of me, and I was a part of them. For though I knew I was made up of cogs, circuits and fibreglass, still, when I gazed at the stars, wheeling above me, I could not help but feel that a little stardust had got into the mix, too.

'There's something wrong with her eyes,' said Ashley then, peering at me anxiously.

'They're leaking,' said Austin.

'No, she's crying,' said Sbud. 'Why are you crying, Sophia?'

'It's a spontaneous overflow of emotion,' I said. 'It seems to come out of both my eyes.'

'Tears do that,' said Sbud. 'I'd cry too, if I had to put up with the three of us. Day in, day out, fellas, give the girl a break!'

Because of that day, Sbud decided I was a sensitive, indeed, a dignified young woman, and must therefore undergo a lecture series featuring the greatest minds of the twentieth and twenty-first centuries. So he spent most of one night building a mnemonic circuit board for the vastscreen from assorted laboratory detritus. The clanging and crashing was irritating, but Sbud was like that. I should have said to him then, it would be better to turn the palm of my hand into a movie miniscreen. What sights then, might I see? *'To hold infinity in the palm of your hand, and happiness in an hour...'*

When it was built, and he was choosing the first lectures, I happened to express a mild interest in the Object Relations theories of Melanie Klein. So Sbud uncovered three hours' of stock footage of mammary glands. He thought he was being helpful, and I allowed him to persist in that belief.

It was a small kingdom.

Also, I had learned another lesson about reigning successfully: Tolerance.

I still felt no desire to rule over all Valerian, but the Men of Ash said, keep taking these small steps. So I decided to attach some voice-circuitry to our toaster and see if I could persuade it to recognise me as queen.

After the laboratory had gone up in flames, and I, Sbud, Austin and Ashley stood there among its charred remains, out there in the rainy garden, I said to them, 'You all told me to take small steps. But even the toaster would not accept my dominion.' I unfurled my umbrella against the steady drip-drip of rainfall. 'I never wanted to rule, anyway,' I said.

I wrinkled my nose up at the scent of burnt toast and crisped cotton, for the first time ungrateful for the complex array of olfactory circuitry they had given me. My nostrils began to keen for rain, mist and the almost-scent of lakes of green tea, with willows dipping fronds into their depths.

'Well, what *do* you want to do?' asked Ashley in mild exasperation, as he clutched the scorched, tattered remnants of his lab coat closer to him.

I did not have an answer for him straight away. This was the first time I had ever been outside. The night was shiny and beautiful, and the air was rainy and cool. Over the glass dome of the observatory, the one part of the laboratory still intact, the moon was in conjunction with one bright star.

'For the first time this century,' said Austin. He pointed upwards. From that union emerged a comet, resplendent, blazing brighter than the laboratory fire. Like the golden tail feathers of the Phoenix, hatching, emerging, soaring.

'I want to be where that is,' I said, at last. 'I want to be *that*.' For why would I want to be Queen of the Ashes when I could be an Officer of the Stars?

Ashley said, 'But I had thought I might take you to my family home on the other side of the city. I know my mother would like to meet you.' He, being poor, had only his dreams but how graciously he laid them out before me.

'No,' said Austin.

'No,' said Sbud.

'No,' said I, and mine was the *No* that counted.

'We would do better to enrol her on a starship programme,' said Sbud, wearily. 'I hear the Conglomerate are recruiting across the four centuries. According to my observatory calculations, the *Joyous Gard* should be orbiting in our solar system in a matter of weeks.'

'And if we don't?' asked Austin.

'We'll know no peace,' said Sbud.

'Yes, stars please,' I said then, brightening, though the remnants of the laboratory smoked all around us. How good and kind and gracious were these Men of Ash, not to trample on my dreams! 'I'm sure they'll be glad to have me.'

Lady Elridge's Last Administrator

The same dream again. Six stars shining in the bright sky above him, and the seventh, gliding towards him, until it came to rest, unaccountably and spontaneously, on the crown he wore upon his head.

Guinan Guineafowl sat up with a start. Someone was knocking on the door. Darkness dissolved as he called for his cabin to illuminate itself. The cabin for Avalon's Visiting Ambassador, on board the *Joyous Gard*: his son's quarters were just along the corridor.

'Wait - just a minute,' he called.

Blearily, Guinan struggled out of his bunk and grabbed his dark green, brocade dressing-gown. He fumbled into it, somehow getting the heavy silk twisted and tangled until he had one arm in an inside-out sleeve.

He called out the door code, then yelled, 'Come in,' as he knotted his yellow cord belt.

A moment later, the door slid open. Aurélie stood on his doorstep.

'Well, hello,' said Guinan, 'you back already?'

Aurélie's green eyes widened. 'But I've been gone for an entire day at least,' she said. Then she stopped and shook her head. She had always found it difficult to fathom and then adjust to the temporal dislocations of Time Travel.

'Every moment without you is an aching eternity as far I'm concerned,' repeated Guinan, making it worse. He rubbed his eyes and yawned. Then he saw the chronometer.

'Great Valeria, do you know what time it is?' he said.

Aurélie shook her head. 'Obviously not,' she said. The irony of it made them both smile.

'It's the crack of dawn,' he replied, exaggerating only slightly.

'I really only just got back now,' said Aurélie.

'And you wanted to see me straight away?' said Guinan, preening.

'No,' said Aurélie, 'but my shower isn't working - and you know what happens when you take out vampires -.'

'A whole lot of gloop,' agreed Guinan. He stepped back from the cabin door and Aurélie entered. Since all the Officer Class cabins were laid out the same, she knew where she was going and headed towards the bathroom.

'Clean towels are in the cupboard under the sink,' he called after her, as with a swish of her blonde bob and a sway of her hips, she was gone.

He walked over to the synthesizer in the kitchen unit and tried to programme it to make him a cappuccino.

His drink arrived. He sat down in the lounge area, sipped it, then squawked in disgust. Mind you, the stuff was enough to shock anybody awake.

'Whoever designed the template for this got their idea of how it ought to taste from a Time Traveller's trip to Butlins, circa 1950, when they were having an Italian Night in between alternating rounds of spam and corned beef sandwiches,' he grumbled loudly to Aurélie, above the sound of the faucet.

'And never a lick of Angel Delight,' she called back. A moment later, she emerged from the bathroom wearing a robe, and a scrubbed-clean look that Guinan found youthful and appealing. She had towel-dried her hair and strands of it clung to her nape. She sat herself down in the black swivel chair opposite him, and, without meaning to, glanced quickly at the sheaf of papers on the black desk.

On a large sheet of foolscap, there was something that looked like the draft of a lecture. Guinan had written: *'Man's awesome scientific advances into the infinitude of space, as well as the infinitude of subatomic particles, seems more likely to lead to the total destruction of our world unless we can make great advances in understanding and dealing with interpersonal tensions... I hope for the day when we will invest at least the price of one or two constellation class starships in the search for a more adequate understanding of human relationships.'*

'What's that?' asked Aurélie.

'Oh, the University of Wisconsin asked me to speak in a personal vein in their Last Lecture series.'

Aurélie glanced at the notes again. 'You don't do personal.'

'Yep, that's sort of the whole concept. It's assumed that only under dire circumstances would a professor give away anything personal about himself.'

'Funny sort of comment on our educational system,' said Aurélie. 'And speaking of dire circumstances, I need something stronger to drink than coffee.'

'The drinks always flow freely at Chez Chief,' said Guinan, jumping up and heading over to the kitchen unit. Speaking sternly to the synthesizer, he ordered a rum and Coke. He walked back to Aurélie and handed it to her.

She took a sip, sweetly satisfying, then said, 'Thanks for that. And for the tandem, too.'

'The tandem?' said Guinan, opening his blue eyes very wide.

'Yes, that was your idea, wasn't it?'

'I don't know what you're talking about,' said Guinan. 'All the same,' he added, 'you and Violetta must have looked quite something on a bicycle together. What were you wearing?'

'Oh, a navy blue cycling outfit, quite long, with a slit up the - hey. It's not that kind of story.'

'What kind of story is it, then?'

'My own,' said Aurélie. 'And you had better let me tell it in my own way, or else I won't tell it at all.'

'Now that would be a real shame,' said Guinan, sitting down in the armchair opposite her, and continuing to eye her with appreciation as she began her tale.

'So, the tandem, then,' she said. 'I know you told me to take up cycling, but I wasn't expecting that. If your calculations had put us in a carriage instead, we wouldn't have had to wobble our way up a crowded thoroughfare.'

'I'm sure you handled it with aplomb,' said Guinan, as Aurélie took another sip of her drink.

'Sure - hansom cab drivers shouting where did we spring from, and one having to swerve his horse in order to avoid a collision.'

'And what did you tell him?'

'Heaven must be missing an angel,' Aurélie muttered. 'Two angels. And then I told Violetta she had better hurry up and do some pedalling - I was fed up with doing all the work...'

'Oh, am I supposed to pedal?' asked Violetta. Once she began to exert herself, Aurélie found their progress up the road became a little easier.

They cycled past some extraordinary houses, finished to look Gothic, quite crowded out with spires and gargoyles, scrolls, trefoils and traceries, everything that might once have stirred a medieval heart, but did what, exactly, for the factory worker, the industrialist or the city clerk? And then, the drivers of the hansom cabs would grant them no respite. One driver shouted out, 'Hi, hi,' not because he wanted room to pass, but in order to startle the lady cyclists.

As it was, Aurélie wobbled again, and it took the combined efforts of her and Violetta to steady the bicycle.

After that, they did their best to ignore the jeers and catcalls of the cab drivers, until one shouted something that sounded like, 'If yous ain't going to get control of yer veerhickle, me old chuckaboos, yous and me will be havin some right ole collie shangles.'

'What *do* you mean?' called back Aurélie.

'I meantersay, if you fall off that there veerhickle, you'll both be copping a mouse, make no mistake.'

'That sounds very rude,' Aurélie said to Violetta. 'Do you think it's meant to be?'

'I think it's a gross species of impertinence,' said Violetta, her colour high, her normally pale cheeks flaming. 'I fear that calling them hansom cab drivers is a real misnomer,' she added. 'Many are quite plain - and that fellow is positively hideous.'

'Cycling would be pleasanter,' Aurélie agreed, as they paused at the crossroads, 'if they would stop trying to kill us.'

'Yes,' said Violetta, 'for we have as good a right to our lives as even our arch-enemies.'

'Speaking of which,' said Aurélie, as another driver yelled at them to *keep moving or else get orf the road*, 'is the sanatorium really the best place for us to find out information about Morleon? He will be surrounded by his allies - all the vampires he has created.'

'What do you suggest, then?' asked Violetta, as she and Aurélie slowly began to pedal again.

'Maybe the PRB Headquarters that you told me about?' asked Aurélie. 'We could at least do a recce there before we go to the asylum.'

'You're right,' said Violetta. Then she added, vehemently, 'I never liked that sanatorium. Never. Not even when Dr Helton was in charge. I didn't think it right that Arthur should be sent there, not at all.'

'Well, he was very young,' said Aurélie. 'By the time I was administrator at Lady Elridge's, it was mainly for elderly residents.'

'Mainly?'

'And a few oddball eccentrics,' said Aurélie. Then she said, 'Violetta, on this tandem, in this time, we're the misfits. Shall we ditch the bike and proceed on foot?'

'But I was just getting the knack of it,' said Violetta. But she lurched forwards as Aurélie braked abruptly, then, a moment later, and more slowly, they pedalled up the dip in the kerb and onto the pavement.

Aurélie and Violetta climbed off the bicycle, then steadied it. They propped the tandem up against the brick wall of a haberdashers. 'By now, you surely know this part of London better than I do,' Aurélie said to Violetta. 'Come on, let's go to the PRB Headquarters.'

'Yes,' sighed Violetta, 'I suppose if we want to be truly elegant, we must walk.'

'Not at all,' said Aurélie. 'What's Guinan's Third Rule of Time Travel?'

'Don't use Time Travel when Public Transport will do,' said Violetta. 'All the same, it would be awfully handy if I could just send a message to Lord Darvell for the carriage.'

'He probably wouldn't send it in this timeline, though,' said Aurélie. 'We would sail up the avenue, but we haven't got a yacht... we would ride up the avenue, but the horse we had was shot...' she quoted.

'Oh well,' said Violetta. 'Didn't I tell you, I once walked all across Russia...'

'Practically barefoot,' said Aurélie. 'Yes, you told me. And,' she added, 'I read it in your journal.' Though for all Violetta's complaints of privations, Aurélie thought that Violetta and all of them at Crowcroft Grange were at the apex of the social pyramid; that Valerian of this era was a paradise for the well-to-do, a purgatory for the able, and a hell for the poor.

They marched on. Even without the assistance of Mrs Jenkins's map, by dint of careful inquiry, they managed to find their way to the nearest station. From there they bought tickets to Warren Street, noting the ticket seller's reminder to change at Paddington.

Presently, their train drew in at London Paddington, with its dark, glass hood. Among the calls of the porters and the clangs of the carriages, the train's hissing steam sounded like a sigh. They climbed out of their carriage and onto the crowded platform, to catch another train and then to emerge, some time later, at Warren Street Station. Thankfully, the guard announced the station name, for as Aurélie and Violetta saw, many of the station signs were still blacked out, to confuse the vampire anarchist bombers of this timeline.

They quit the station, and then Violetta led the way, down an alley and into a tangle of courts and side-streets. Here, ragged children jumped among the dust-heaps, or splashed in the streams of water that crossed the cobbles. Still, they did not have to walk far before they reached the mansions of Fitzrovia once more, more hybrid houses attempting to trail clouds of vanished glory into a world of machine-made facades.

'Your old stomping ground,' said Aurélie, gesturing towards the *Penrose Arms* across the way.

'No more, alas,' said Violetta, lightly touching the locket at the hollow of her throat that contained the double portrait of Frances and Arabella.

Another sudden twist brought them into Cleveland Street. A moment later, and they were stepping onto the porch and then standing on the doorstep of the artists' studio at *Number 2.* The Headquarters of the PRB.

Violetta rang the bell, and when there was no answer, she rang again. Finally the door was pulled open, creaking in protest. The two women found themselves looking into the glittering, treacherous eyes of a partially veiled, heart-shaped face, that seemed to curve into a decidedly pointed chin.

'Miss Dulcetta,' said Violetta in astonishment, 'what the deuce are you doing here?'

'I might say the same to you,' said Miss Dulcetta. 'Except that it's one of Lord Darvell's expressions.' She paused and her eyes gleamed darkly above the hem of her veil. 'As a result of your visit to him, in which you made it clear that I had taken the Grail, I lost my position at Crowcroft Grange.'

'*Stolen* it, not taken it,' said Violetta. 'And I thought he said that because you had cared for Arabella so diligently through the smallpox outbreak, he would not dismiss you.'

'But then,' said Miss Dulcetta, 'I borrowed a jacket from the nursemaid, Martha, that she was altering for herself. It had once belonged to Morgana, you see. When she complained to Lord Darvell about it, he said he would no longer keep a thief about the place.'

'Stealing from the nursemaid!' said Violetta. 'Her salary must be a pittance of yours. For shame, Miss Dulcetta!'

'It was fine, dark, embroidered cloth,' said Miss Dulcetta. 'More becoming to me, than her.'

'I think you only got what you deserved,' said Aurélie. 'But that doesn't explain what you are doing here.'

'After I left Crowcroft Grange,' said Miss Dulcetta, 'I remembered the stalls of the night-market, and I decided to see if I could sell a few items, knick-knacks, antiques, ornaments, that I happened to have in my possession.'

Aurélie assumed Violetta wanted to hear what Miss Dulcetta had to say, and so she restrained herself from asking whether these, too, were stolen from Crowcroft Grange.

'The stallholder told me that some of the bric-a-brac, or no, the *objets d'art*, he called them, might appeal to the painters and artists of the PRB. He directed me to the studios here - and here I met Neddy, that is to say, Mr. Burne-Jones, on the very day when he was looking for a model for his painting of Circe.'

'But what about the smallpox scars?' asked Violetta, seemingly unable to help herself.

'He says they add distinction to my features,' said Miss Dulcetta, removing her veil and tucking her hair behind her ears so that the scars were more on display. 'He seems, almost, to *like* them,' she added, drawing herself up to her full height. 'But now, may I ask, what are you doing here?'

'We have come to see the portrait,' said Violetta, quickly.

'Of Circe?' said Miss Dulcetta. 'But it isn't finished yet. Though Ned says it will be his masterpiece,' she added.

'No, no,' said Violetta. 'The portrait in the attic.' She began to extemporise. 'My friend Miss De Lys here has recently been appointed cultural historian at a... a fine museum... and she would like to write about the portrait for a paper she is compiling on the benefits of vampirism. Eternal youth, beauty, irresistible, magnetic charisma...,' Violetta continued, wistfully.

'Oh, vampires,' replied Miss Dulcetta. 'They're always hanging around, trying to host meetings here or organise protest rallies. I've no time for them, personally. I was glad when Morleon took a heap of them off to the, you know, that place - and so was Ned, too,' she added quickly. 'All that blood-letting for hungry vampires was distracting him from his painting. His veins are like ribbons!'

'So you keep a quiet house now?' asked Violetta, and when Miss Dulcetta nodded, Violetta placed her foot inside the doorway and said, 'then you can have no objection to us looking at the portrait.'

Miss Dulcetta stepped back in astonishment, and in that moment, Violetta and then Aurélie stepped swiftly into the house. Violetta led the way forwards, into the main building itself. They went past the studio, where they caught a glimpse of a short, young, refined-looking artist with sandy hair and whiskers who was setting up an easel in front of a raised platform.

For a moment, Aurélie remembered Miss Dulcetta as she had first read of her in Violetta's journal, that day at the Hawkins's photography studio. Might all this enmity have been avoided if Violetta had just taken a daguerreotype portrait of the governess? Would that have been so hard to do? Would it?

Aurélie followed Violetta past the studio, and up the staircase, towards the attic. There was a bar across the attic door, but, fortunately, the key was still in its lock. The work of a moment, then, they were inside the attic.

'Where is the portrait?' asked Aurélie.

'It should be under that cloth,' said Violetta, pointing to some purple velvet draped over a massive, life-size canvas, propped up against a window that was built into the arched, beamed roof. So saying, she threw the cloth back from the painting with a gesture that was decidedly theatrical.

The two women gazed at the splendid portrait of Dante Gabriel Rossetti in all the wonder of his exquisite youth and beauty. His hair was dark and curled yet shot through with sunlight; his painted dark eyes gleamed with the promise of a thousand summer days, and his full lips curved in an inviting smile.

Nevertheless, at the centre of the portrait, a knife remained embedded in Rossetti's heart. So life-like did the dripping-down crimson liquid appear, that Violetta touched it with her fingertips, to see if the paint was still wet. It was. Then her nostrils were assailed by the scent of metal.

'It is blood,' she said to Aurélie.

To Aurélie, the image, with its fountain of blood, reminded her of paintings and statues she had seen of the Sacred Heart of Jesus in her convent school days on Ile-Grande. The memory gave her an idea. She took the Holy Grail out of her satchel. A ray of sunlight suddenly shone through the high arch window. Its pearly light cascaded down onto the Grail, rendering it too beautiful even to describe.

'Let's see what we can do with this,' she said.

'Did you bring any holy water?' asked Violetta.

'Yes,' said Aurélie, 'I still have some in a vial that Father Simon blessed for me at the time of your transformation.' She reached back inside the satchel. 'Here it is,' she added. She unstopped the vial and began to tip the water into the Grail. A patch of rainbow sparkled as the water poured into the chalice.

Then she upended it and threw the holy water at the portrait so that it began to trickle down Rossetti's painted forehead. Where it trickled onto the dripping wound on his chest, the blood began to dry up, and the painted heart to heal. And then, the painted flesh so carefully rendered in brushstrokes began to split apart, and human flesh showed through.

The man inside the picture leaned back, flexed his shoulder muscles, then leaned forwards, and with one graceful, fluid movement, he stepped out of the confines of the antique gold frame. His dark, almond-shaped eyes widened in surprise at the sight of the two women.

'Miss Valhallah,' he said, with a slight, half-bow. 'And who is your companion, here?'

'I'm Aurélie De Lys,' said Aurélie. "It worked,' she continued with glee. 'So now we know we can genuinely use this with Morleon.'

'How do you feel, Mr Rossetti?' asked Violetta.

'Never better,' replied the young man. 'So glad to be free of the vestiges of vampirism and mouldering old paint. My heartfelt thanks to you both.' Rossetti stretched his arms out, then began to rock backwards and forwards on the balls of his feet. 'Forgive the gymnastics, dear ladies. My previous quarters were somewhat confined. Now, do you have anything to rid this house of riffraff?'

'Do you mean the vampires?' asked Aurélie.

'I mean the governess, or whatever she is,' said Rossetti, amiably. 'And why young Neddy thinks he can use my studio to carry on his strange liaisons, and all without a word of permission from me, beggars my belief.'

'They did think you were dead,' said Violetta.

'Why, Miss Valhallah, that's no excuse,' said Rossetti, firmly. 'Besides, I was right here, on this wall, the whole time,' he added, 'and yet you never came to visit me,' he concluded, wistfully.

'Well, you see, I'm married now,' replied Violetta.

'Unfortunate sort of business, I expect,' said Rossetti.

'But I'm completely happy in my present state,' she replied.

'In my experience,' said Rossetti, 'people who claim they are completely happy tend not to be. Else why would they feel the need to say it?'

'And your experience of married women is what, exactly?' asked Violetta.

'I believe my comment was general, rather than specific,' replied Rossetti, mildly.

'Then there was no need to say it,' said Violetta.

'I remain, as ever, grateful, for your advice,' said Rossetti, with a significant smile.

From her reading of Violetta's journal, Aurélie remembered that Violetta had once made editing suggestions for Rossetti's poem, *The Blessed Damozel*, in the interval of Madame Zozostra's spiritualist poetry recital at one of the Hawkins's Tuesday At-Homes. And indeed, his next words alluded to that time, for he said to Violetta, 'You can't go chasing after canaries anymore, I suppose?'

'Certainly not,' said Violetta, 'that would be very shocking,' but she was smiling now, too.

'But what about the canaries?' asked Rossetti. 'Surely to leave them thus forsaken and alone is too, too cruel.'

'Violetta,' said Aurélie, who had been listening to all of this with some exasperation, 'do you have an admirer in every single timeline?'

Violetta took the Grail from her and slowly rinsed it out in the basin that was overflowing with unwashed paintbrushes and tins of turpentine. When she had dried it carefully and buffered it, she turned back to her companion. 'Do you know,' she said at last, 'I really think I do.'

'That doesn't surprise me in the least,' said Rossetti, with another gracefully executed half-bow, then he escorted the ladies down the narrow stairway and into his studio.

The reaction to his appearance in the doorway of the studio would have been gratifying indeed to those who sought novel and alarming sensations. Miss Dulcetta, posing on the raised platform with her long hair falling thickly all around her, turned pale, and her jaw fell open. Noting her astonishment, the artist, Edward Burne-Jones, twisted his head away from the canvas on the easel and looked where she was looking. A moment later, his brush and palette had clattered to the floor.

'You!' he said at last, swallowing hard, then giving a convulsive shudder. 'You!'

'But they found your body in the attic,' said Miss Dulcetta: the timorousness of her companion granting her a modicum of courage.

'That was assuredly not *my* body,' said the young man. 'Come now, do you think that bloated buffoon bore any resemblance at all to me?'

To the question posed in such stark terms, Miss Dulcetta was forced to shake her head and, as her palpitations began to subside, she looked more carefully at Rossetti in all the bright, unblemished promise of his youth. Her own dawning admiration for him as he stood there, resplendent, was obvious to them all, so much so, in fact, that her palpitations began all over again.

'That's not bad, you know, Ned,' said Rossetti, taking a careless half-glimpse at the portrait on the easel. 'You've come on a lot.'

'Thank you,' said the artist, finding his voice at last, and glad even of this scant praise from his former tutor.

'Yes,' said Rossetti. 'It rather puts me in mind of something: - *Dusk-haired and golden-robed o'er the golden wine*/errr.../*She bends,* no, *she stoops, wherein distilled of death and shame,* /*Sink the black drops...*' He paused, waiting for the compliments he felt sure would follow.

'That's not bad, you know, Gabriel,' said Ned, grinning.

'Obviously, it needs a bit of work,' said Rossetti, a shade stiffly.

Violetta peered over at the canvas depicting Circe and decided it was not one of her favourites of the Pre-Raphaelite oeuvre. Later she would tell Aurélie how she had once discussed the Greek legends with Daedalus, and how Circe could not lure Glaucus away from the nymph, Scylla. Filled with envious rage, Circe went to a quiet grotto and poisoned the water where Scylla went to bathe. However, Ned's painting did not seem to capture any of that passion and drama. It merely depicted an ungainly woman in a copper-coloured robe, leaning over what may have been a panther, and pouring something, weedkiller perhaps, into a pot of sunflowers.

The only striking element of the painting was the woman's smallpox scars, painted with a certain amount of relish, granting distinction to her otherwise nondescript features.

Aurélie, trying to recall her art history classes from the Valerian College of Arts, began to wonder what would happen if the resin varnish mixed into its very colours. Would the picture so deteriorate that all the carefully transcribed reality of Miss Dulcetta in the flesh would vanish beyond reclaim? How might Violetta's former portrait painter, Fra Pandolf, have chosen to portray Circe? Perhaps Circe would be emptying a bowl of green poison into the waters, half-hovering, half-standing on the already transformed Scylla, writhing beneath the surface.

Aurélie glanced across at Miss Dulcetta, posed there awkwardly on the platform. She tried to imagine her with even longer hair, waist-length perhaps, billowing up and out, as if disturbed by a rush of deadly vapours.

Her gaze travelled from Miss Dulcetta to the artist, Ned Jones. The name Circe meant 'to secure with rings' or 'to hoop around.' She thought it unlikely, for these two.

A sudden, angry exhalation from Violetta made Aurélie glance across at her friend.

Her cheeks were flaming red, as if sudden fire was surging through her veins.

'What's wrong?' she asked Violetta.

'Give me the vial of holy water,' Violetta commanded her.

Aurélie knew better than to protest. Silently, she reached inside the satchel, retrieved the vial, then handed it to Violetta, who quickly poured some into the Grail.

Then Violetta stepped forwards and dashed the contents of the chalice full in Miss Dulcetta's face. 'There,' she said, and, 'take that, you vile woman,' as the liquid dripped down the former governess's forehead. 'You may not be a vampire, but there is your cure.'

Miss Dulcetta's hands flew to her wet face. A moment later, she cried out, 'My scars, my scars they are gone.'

'But how could that be?' asked Ned. 'Here, let me look,' he said, stepping away from the easel onto the platform. He held back her great swathes of hair and peered into her woebegone face. 'You are quite right,' he said at last. He let her hair drop as if he were the sea relinquishing despised and dishevelled seaweed. 'Then, my dear,' he added, 'I am afraid I have no further need of you.'

Miss Dulcetta gave a strangled gasp that ended in a sob.

Rossetti gave a bark of laughter, then put his arm round Ned's shoulder.

'What say we leave her to her packing, whilst we seek out a local hostelry? Do they still serve that ale you like at *The Blue Man*?'

Ned nodded enthusiastically.

'And then off to the painters' school in Red Lion Square! What toddies, what painting, what high, high jinks! Will you join us, Miss De Lys, and Miss - ah, no, but you're married now,' said Rossetti to Violetta. 'What is it you call yourself, these days?'

'Sometimes I'm Lady Darvell,' said Violetta, 'but my friends prefer Violetta.'

'I prefer Violetta too,' said Rossetti, smiling.

However, Aurélie was beginning to tire of these bohemians; indeed, she wondered how Violetta had tolerated their society for so long. 'It's very kind of you gentlemen,' she said, 'but we have important work to do and must not be long distracted from our purpose.'

'But surely you can make an exception for such a distraction,' murmured Rossetti, still looking at Violetta.

'Come on,' said Aurélie, and she pulled her half-unwilling friend towards the front door, then out of the studio, and down the porch steps.

'But I've never been to *The Blue Man*,' said Violetta, a shade sulkily.

'No,' said Aurélie, 'and I don't think you ever should.' Then she relented slightly. 'We can have a quick drink in *The Penrose Arms* first,' she said, 'and then head to the station.'

A few hours later, Aurélie and Violetta emerged at Shoreditch station, where they stumbled across the main thoroughfare and then crisscrossed a lattice of streets. After a few minutes' walk, Violetta located the sanatorium building she had visited once before, to inquire after Arthur. She shivered as they approached it, but Aurélie's widening eyes took in the sight of her old work-place with interest.

There was the main building, with its garden nearly a third of a mile long, and then, so many campaniles, cupolas, stone rustic quoins, cornices and ornamental trimmings that you had to wonder at the sense of those that put them there. Then too, there was the chapel, one last stable block that was still to be converted into a clinic, and the cemetery.

The path leading up to the sanatorium was new with yellow gravel. They proceeded up it, towards the big, staring, angular house. Then Aurélie looked up at the arched doorway, where the name was enamelled in red. Large, red letters, with a bright, red shine. *Saint Cosmas & Damian,* and underneath, *The Sanctuary.*

On either side of the door was a stone griffin. Aurélie wondered which griffin was Cosmas, and which, Damian. There was no moss or soft places on them, and their stone teeth looked sharp, ready to bite. Aurélie shivered and remembered what Bram Stoker had said before her, quoting the great Psalmist, 'that which should have been for their welfare, has become their trap.'

Violetta hung back, too. Perhaps, thought Aurélie, she was remembering how this was a place of many moods, and all of them, bewildering. All the emotions of all the different patients, all here at different times, spreading down from the slate roof at the top of the house, then past the attics, the three storeys, and sweeping right into the cellar.

Eventually, they gathered themselves, climbed the steps, pulled open the front door and peered cautiously inside. Not far from them was a grey, grizzled, heavy-set, bespectacled man in his fifties, sat behind a mahogany desk. In front of him was a sign that read PORTER, as well as a little brass bell, and to his left hand side, a pile of papers and an ornamental pen stand with quite a nice pen.

From where the Porter sat, he could see everyone who came in at the door and he stared hard at Aurélie and Violetta as they approached his desk.

'Beggin yer pardons, ladies, but please show us yer teeth,' he said.

Somewhat surprised, Aurélie and then Violetta drew back their upper lips and bared their teeth.

'No fangs,' said the Porter. The muscles of his face relaxed and he grew a little more cordial. 'Beggin yer pardons again, but what's two nice lady cyclists like yerselves doin' 'ere?'

Aurélie began to say something about the Conglomerate, but the Porter held up his hand. 'I don't care which charity you're from, kind words and baskets of posies ain't going to fix this.'

'We have no posies and we're not from a charity,' said Violetta. 'We are Voyagers of Space and Time, and we want to speak to Morleon.'

'Ah, then you're proper daft,' said the Porter, tapping the side of his head. He began to sort through the sheaf of papers on his desk. 'And is your friend here bringing you in, or is she crackers too?'

'You must believe us,' said Aurélie, earnestly. 'Where I'm from, time travel exists.'

'I've read H G Wells,' said the Porter, with dignity. 'I'm sure it does. But if yer want to see Morleon off yer own bat, you're proper off yer trolley, if yer ask me.'

'Your analogy leads me to believe you are a cricketing fan, Mr- er - Blake,' said Violetta, catching sight of the name badge pinned to his lapel.

'Sometimes I am, Miss, yes,' said the Porter.

'My husband is, also,' said Violetta. 'Many's the time I have watched him and his ward batting and bowling on the front lawn in the long summer evenings. And I know that cricketers believe in the quintessential Valerian values of honesty, decency and fair play. And that is what my colleague, Miss De Lys, and I, wish to restore to this asylum.'

'And how do you meanter do that?' asked the Porter.

'Show him, Aurélie,' said Violetta.

From her satchel, Aurélie removed the chalice, that was the most sacred chalice, that had once contained the most holy blood of all.

The Porter peered at it, took his spectacles off, polished them, then put them back on again. 'If that's what I think it is,' he said, 'it belongs rightly in a museum.'

'It belongs with us,' said Aurélie, 'and with it, we are going to cure Morleon.'

'Of being a vampire?' asked the Porter, carefully, for Vampire Rights Movements had made it clear that vampires were complete and perfect in themselves, though much vampire anti-discrimination legislation had yet to be approved.

'Of perniciousness,' said Violetta, firmly.

'Well, Miss, as to that, I really couldn't say,' said the Porter, 'but before you try anythink so bold, you may want to speak to Mr Dallas first.'

'Mr Dallas?' asked Violetta.

'Yes,' said the Porter. 'He's a vampire - but not a *pernicious* one,' he added, savouring the new word. 'In fact, he's what you might call a human sympathiser.'

'Oh yes,' said Aurélie. 'I've come across those in my research. In fact, there was a fin-de-siècle movement, intended to promote greater harmony between humans and vampires. These human sympathisers called themselves the Tudor Rose vampires.'

'That's right,' said Violetta, 'the scarlet petals of the Tudor Rose symbolised blood...'

'And the white petals symbolised human flesh,' said Aurélie, 'and each was contained within perfect, unbroken circles.'

'Like Snow White and Rose Red?' muttered the Porter.

'Not exactly,' said Aurélie, 'the Tudor Rose vampires were those who gave up drinking human blood.'

'Like with the Titrations,' said Violetta, eagerly.

'Yes,' said Aurélie.

'Yes,' said the Porter. 'Which is ter say - Mr Dallas is sortof drying out. Fell orf the wagon for a bit - some orderlies, a nurse, and not the best ones, neither... Soo - he might be a bit fragile, like. Have a little word with him, but mebbee don't speak too loud.'

'Where is he?' asked Aurélie.

'He might be resting in his room,' said the Porter. 'Number 13, straight down that corridor,' and he nodded to a part of the building that in Aurélie's time, was kept unoccupied. Then he glanced up at the clock overhead. 'Or he might be in the garden,' he added. 'He often is, this time of day.'

'Very well then,' said Aurélie, putting the Holy Grail back in her satchel and fastening the buckle. 'We shall go and find him.'

They paced down the dingy red corridor that the Porter had indicated. Its doors were shut all the way down, and their long skirts shushed against the uneven flagstones of its floor. Neither of them said anything. The drabness, the redness and the silence seemed to have swallowed up their voices. And there was no other sound except a humming from deep within the house, like the hum of a boiler.

'Here we are,' said Violetta at last, stopping outside a door with a small brass number *13*, and a little flap like a letterbox beneath it. Violetta lifted the flap, then let it drop, with a resounding rap.

Somebody moved inside, but no-one answered.

'Mr Dallas?' called Violetta. 'May we come in?'

'Yes,' replied a stentorian male voice. They pushed open the unlocked door and stepped into the room to be confronted by the sight of a bed, like a raft, in the middle of a pale, shiny floor.

On the shipwrecked bed, there lay a vampire, staring at the door. His eyes shifted as they entered, and he looked, first at Violetta, then at Aurélie. He smiled, like a weak sun.

'Violetta,' he said. 'So you're here, at last.'

'Daedalus,' said Violetta, slowly. 'Of course. I should have guessed it was you.'

'How are you?' he asked, crinkling up his eyes at her. The real smile had faded, but he was trying to hold onto it. The wide, shiny floor between them was like a deep sea.

Violetta approached the bed. 'I'm human now,' she said, uncertainly. 'So, it's just as well you're a - what was it, a Tudor Rose vampire?'

Aurélie nodded.

Violetta glanced over at the vase of red and white roses on the locker beside the bed.

'Who gave you the flowers?' she asked. They were dark, fresh ones, with little drops of water curling inside the petals.

'Someone puts them there,' said Daedalus, with an effort. He screwed up his face, as if he was trying to remember more. 'Nice, soft, little thing, from the country.' The thought of the roses seemed to make him tired. 'Every morning,' he sighed.

Aurélie and Violetta looked at him again.

His eyes were still like the sea when the storms have fled, but his hair was combed flat, in a new way, and it wasn't shiny anymore. He looked as though he'd been left out in the rain.

Violetta's eyes took on a dreamy, abstracted look. Aurélie wondered if she was remembering her time with Daedalus in the forests of Kief, how he had sheltered her from the rain with larch wood branches. Perhaps then, he had smelt of air and fields and trees, and sometimes of the blood from the hares he had trapped and slaughtered. Perhaps he caught her up in his arms, and wrapped her up in his smell, and the warm touch of his cheek.

Had he always pulled at bedclothes like that, and frowned over them, as if the neatness of the sheets was more important than Violetta? Aurélie looked at the shape of his legs beneath the sheet. They were very thin.

'How are you managing without human blood?' Violetta asked. 'And why are you?'

'I find feeding creates too many vampire children,' said Daedalus. 'I don't seem to have the knack of stopping when I ought. And then, they all side with Morleon, and when I learn of all the evil things they do...' His voice trailed off, then he steadied himself, and spoke more firmly, 'It's what I call the vampire's uroboros. If I create them, then I have at least some responsibility for them, and for all they do. But then, I also have some responsibility to keep humans safe from my creations.' Now there was sweat all over his face, like mist on a windowpane.

Aurélie glanced at her friend. From the tiny frown and the perturbed look in her eyes, it was obvious Violetta couldn't bear to see him like that.

'Can we go outside?' Violetta asked, at last.

'Of course we can,' said Daedalus. 'I'm not a prisoner. Not yet, anyway.' He pulled back the bedclothes and swung down his legs. He had all his clothes on in bed, even his socks. Aurélie and Violetta watched as his feet fumbled their way into his boots, as his hands shook as he tried to tie the laces.

The garden was a large, pale square of lawn at the back of the sanatorium, cut by paths and clumps of trees. There were long white chairs, set out in the shade, and pale vampires and patients lay in them with their eyes shut. A few were trying to walk about, but they didn't venture far, just round the same trees and chairs. The people and the vampires all had cloudy looks on their faces, as if nothing much made sense to them anymore. But they never collided with each other, just drifted around the lawn.

Did Daedalus know any of these people? wondered Aurélie. They did not seem like his sort, at all. But then, what was his sort? For now he stood in the middle of the grass, looking as if he did not know where to go.

Then it was all right. Violetta led them over to a maid who was setting out tea things on a little table. Daedalus seized some chairs and pulled them up round the table. They all sat down, and Violetta began to pour tea from the pot into porcelain cups. There were thin slices of pink-and-white cake on plates in front of them.

'Angel cake,' said Daedalus. 'Their sponge is very good.'

Suddenly, a very elegant lady got up from her chair beneath an oak tree, and swam towards them, her smiling face tilted towards the sun as if she were a sunflower, her eyes, half shut. One of her hands was held out, as if she were meeting them at a garden party, and her white dress seemed to float. There were light blue ribbons threaded through her hair, which was a fine heap of shiny fairness, as pale as hay. She smiled at them and shook Aurélie's and Violetta's hands.

'I am Mrs Goldstone,' she said. 'I expect Daedalus has told you *all* about me.' And she laid two white fingers on the vampire's sleeve.

'Not really,' said Aurélie, politely, 'we've only just arrived.'

A moment later, came a spot of rain. Up went Violetta's parasol, and she seemed determined then to draw

Daedalus under its wavery shade, whilst all the time she smiled, smiled, smiled at Mrs Goldstone, smiled until her cheeks must have ached. But after her initial greeting, Mrs Goldstone ignored Aurélie and Violetta, and kept her eyes fixed firmly on Daedalus.

'Of course, I shall be terribly sorry to leave,' she said, 'but Dr Helton was on the point of signing my release papers anyway. And Morleon - well, all he can offer me is vampirism.'

Daedalus gave a little bow from where he sat at the table. 'If you should feel any inclination in that direction, I should be more than happy to...'

'It's raining,' said Violetta, twisted her parasol so that it obliterated their view of Mrs Goldstone. 'We had better go back to our room, Daedalus.' She stood up from the table. 'Lovely to have met you,' she said, two bright pink spots of colour flaring in her cheeks, before she began to march back across the lawn. Aurélie and Daedalus trailed after her.

'She seems angry,' Daedalus observed.

'Yes,' said Aurélie, trying to recall something she had read in the Lady Elridge Archives. 'Daedalus, who is Mrs Goldstone?'

'Ginny Goldstone?' cried Daedalus. 'Why, only the most famous arsonist of this age. When her husband died, they were going to foreclose on the house. Rather than have the bailiffs take anything, she burnt the house to the ground.'

'That's a sad story,' said Aurélie, looking back at the fair-haired woman who had turned down a side-path towards the front of the house.

'Yes, it is,' said Daedalus, 'but, you see, she never wanted to leave.'

Aurélie and Daedalus passed a large flower-bed full of hyacinths bordered by daisies, with an ornamental weeping willow at its centre.

They walked on, past the hawthorn tree, and back onto the main path, and then finally, through the dark green door set into the wall, its top half hidden by shawls of ivy tendrils. They paused on the threshold. Now Aurélie could hear the scuff of mice and the squeak of bats in the attics above her, the creak and settle of the long rows of dormitories, the cry of rooks beyond the windowpanes. Then, back along the corridor, to Daedalus's room.

There was a light drizzle of rain outside, but it was cold and damp inside. Aurélie walked over to the hearth, to where Violetta, was already kneeling, coiling newspaper sheets into little balls to make a fire, catching here and there, the odd, alarming headline above the long, thick columns. ANNIVERSARY OF QUEEN VICTORIA'S DEATH; SUCCESSION STILL UNDECIDED; CRYSTAL PALACE BOMBING: ANARCHIST VAMPIRES QUESTIONED. Then Violetta made a pyre of the scrunched up balls of paper and balanced the kindling into a pyramid around it.

It was an instinct, thought Aurélie, knowing where to lay the flame of the Lucifer match so that it caught the draught and flared up against the spindles of white kindling. Soon the fire stirred, then began to roar. Now it was glowing big and orange behind the paper, singeing the sepia photo of a Russian aristocrat vampire. Count Fyodor Illich Pavia. He had fair hair and piercing eyes, an aquiline nose.

Although she wasn't bridge crew, Aurélie knew him quite well from the *Joyous Gard.* But before her friend could place him, the fire consumed his picture.

As Aurélie stood at the hearth, staring into the flames, something else occurred to her. 'In this time, isn't arson a crime punishable by a life sentence - or transportation to Australia?' she asked Daedalus.

'It is, usually,' he replied, 'except on the grounds of moral lunacy. Only - now - Mrs Goldstone is deemed fit enough to stand trial.'

Violetta turned round from where she was sitting on her heels. 'Enough of all that, Daedalus,' she said. 'Are you going to help us defeat Morleon, or not?'

'Well,' said Daedalus, and, 'yes,' said Daedalus, 'and oh - but - there are so many other things to attend to.' There were no chairs in the room and so he sat down on his bed and began to pluck at the counterpane.

'Such as?' said Violetta.

Daedalus nodded at a little chart pinned to the side of his locker, in which every hour had been allocated an activity.

9am Breakfast - Scrambled eggs, toast & milk
10 am Wash & Shave
11am Read the Valerian Times
12 noon Lunch - Bone broth & milk
1pm Dominoes
2pm Milk
3pm Walk in the garden
4pm Doctor's rounds & milk
5pm Game of solitaire
6pm Supper & milk (warm or cold)
7pm Lock windows, quiet reading

'What's all this?' asked Violetta, her voice perhaps sounding gentler than she felt.

But Aurélie wondered if Daedalus was happy in his own way, if this routine, with its clockwork regularity, sufficed for him.

'The doctor here - Dr Seward, says that by maintaining such a routine, I'll keep my vampiric impulses in check. However, it requires such intense concentration on my part that I have scarcely any energy left for anything else.'

'Such intense boredom,' muttered Violetta.

'Dr Seward?' asked Aurélie. 'Why didn't he leave the sanatorium when Dr Helton did?'

'Well, some doctors are still needed to tend to the patients,' said Daedalus.

'But I thought Morleon's plan was to turn all the patients into vampires,' said Aurélie.

'Yes,' said Daedalus. 'But - eventually. He hopes they will turn willingly. He said, for the sake of their souls, it's better that way.'

Suddenly, the door opened, someone entered the room, and his long shadow fell across the bed.

'Dr Seward,' said Daedalus.

Violetta and Aurélie looked up. Dr Seward was a tall, grey, sable pillar, leaning back against the blaze of the fire, one hand on his fob watch, the other, clutching a glass of milk, which glowed, slightly luminous, in the firelit darkness of Daedalus's room.

'Milk,' he boomed, with a half-smile on his keen, fox-like face. 'That's the ticket.' He took his watch out and held it up in front of Daedalus. Then he handed him the glass.

Daeldalus took a cautious sip.

'Milk - and the Weir Mitchell regime,' the doctor said, nodding. 'Excellent.' Then he was gone.

Daedalus put the nearly full glass down on the locker. He sat forwards on the bed. There were drops of sweat hanging like dewdrops in the fine web of hair above his forehead. He was about to reach for the glass again when, suddenly, Violetta stretched across the bed to the locker, and took it first.

Very deliberately, Violetta lifted it, held it high, then tipped it, until a slow, careful arc of milk poured from the rim of the glass onto the hard floor. She watched it make a blue-white pool that began to seep through the cracks in the floorboards.

Aurélie wished that she had done it.

Daedalus compressed his lips, then moistened them. 'Damn it, Violetta,' he said, and then, almost as if he couldn't help it, he smiled.

A log flared, fell, then cracked in the hearth. A moment later came the bell-beat of wings against the windowpanes.

'Make sure the windows are fully shut,' called Daedalus, so that Aurélie ran to the open casement and pulled it fast. 'Not all of Morleon's lieutenants share his views about informed consent. And here -,' he said, flinging open his locker and pulling out two minute scraps of paper. 'These should keep you both safe.'

Violetta glanced down and saw on each scrap of paper, a perfect drawing of a Tudor Rose, which appeared to be executed in vampire's blood, his.

'Finally, I recognise your penmanship,' she said as she and Aurélie each picked up their protective talisman.

'Yes,' he said, 'and now please will you go and check on Laura down the corridor?'

'Oh, so you've remembered her name now,' said Violetta, as she put the paper inside her reticule.

'My memory is my prerogative,' said Daedalus. 'But I don't have any more paper, and she's liable to forget what I say about keeping casements shut and wearing a crucifix. Such a shame, too, that the cook wasn't able to send up any more wild garlic from the kitchens this week.'

'Why not?' asked Aurélie.

'The cook is now a vampire,' said Daedalus.

'Oh,' said Aurélie. 'Well, why don't you go and tell Laura yourself?' she asked, turning over her scrap of paper between two fingers, before adding it to the front pocket of her satchel.

'Oh no,' said Daedalus, shocked. 'It's nearly time for my game of solitaire.' And now he reached inside his locker for a well worn pack of cards and began to lay them out in neat rows upon the counterpane.

As Violetta and Aurélie paced the length of the corridor, they hear a curious sound coming from one of the rooms, something like a gurgle, followed by a whimper.

'Do you think it's this one?' asked Aurélie, her hand pausing on the handle.

'We had better go in,' said Violetta, and so Aurélie pushed open the door.

They walked into a room, with archways that led to two other rooms, one on either side. One was the bathroom, with a great, white porcelain bath, whilst the other was a bedroom, though the bed had leather straps attached to it. It was there that they found two women, a younger, and an older, lying on the bed. The patient, and her attendant. The latter was covered in a white sheet, the edges of which had been blown back by the draught from the broken window. In this way, her drawn, white face was revealed, stark, with a look of terror frozen upon it. Dead.

By her side lay a girl with unruly, long, light hair. Her own face was white, and still more drawn. The red had departed from her lips and gums and the bones of her face stood out prominently. Her throat was bare, horribly white and mangled, with two little puncture wounds. And yet, from the rise and fall of her chest, they knew she was still breathing.

Violetta flew over to the decanter of brandy on the cabinet. Quickly, she poured brandy onto her fingertips and rubbed it into the prostrate girl's lips and gums. Then she said to Aurélie, 'This poor soul is nearly as cold as that dead one beside her. She'll need to be heated before we can do anything to help her with the Grail.'

Fortunately, there was a good fire blazing in the hearth, and with it, they were able to heat enough hot water to fill the bath in the other room. Then they carried the girl to it, just as she was, in her white chemise, and lowered her into the water. They began to chafe her limbs, and then, slowly, very slowly, they had the satisfaction of observing a faint flush of colour return to her cheeks and throat.

They removed her from the bath and sat her upon the couch in the central room. They sat next to her, and Violetta reached into her reticule and found a soft, silk handkerchief which she tied round the girl's wounded throat. Aurélie took the Grail from her satchel and poured a little of the holy water from the vial into it, then held it to the bloodless girl's parched lips.

Her struggle back to life was something disturbing to witness. However, her breathing gradually became more even, and from her renewed colour, they judged the pumping of her heart had improved.

The girl's eyelids fluttered open and when her eyes lit upon the two women, who, in truth, had nothing fearful about their appearance, they gladdened. But when she turned her head to look about her, she shuddered, then cried out, and put her poor, thin hands in front of her pale face.

Violetta poured the girl a brandy.

The girl took it from her, gratefully enough, but whilst she was drinking, her open mouth revealed the pale gums drawn back from her teeth, long and sharp.

'But she shouldn't be a vampire,' said Aurélie, bewildered. 'She just drank from the Grail.'

'She drank enough to restore her to a semblance of life,' said Violetta, 'but not enough to reverse her vampirism.'

'Then we must give her more to drink,' said Aurélie.

Violetta shook her dark head and now her voice sounded grim. 'We are not her judges, and she has committed no crime,' she said. 'It is a choice she must make for herself.'

Aurélie glanced around at the padded walls, the restraining straps upon the couch. 'Is it a choice she has the capacity to make?'

'A little vampirism does wonders for sharpening the wits,' said Violetta, a shade tartly, so that Aurélie wondered if she had been insensitive.

'You're Laura?' Violetta said to the girl, so that the newly-fledged vampire turned her pale face towards the dark, imperious woman.

'Yes, I'm Laura,' the girl said softly, with a slight country burr.

'And do you wish to remain a vampire,' asked Violetta, 'or do you want to be returned to human form?' Already her kindness, that she tried so hard and so unsuccessfully to suppress, was emerging.

'Being human?' said the girl. 'There ain't nothin human about the way I've been treated. A dog in my master's house is treated better. And they don't tell a dog that everything she thinks and feels is wrong, and when she be whelping, they don't put *her* out into the snow.'

'Is that what happened to you?' asked Aurélie.

The girl paused, then nodded. 'And then the baby died, poor little mite, cos what else could it do, it were that there cold. And then I were brought here, and there ain't no-one who would listen. Just I gotta be made useful again, what they call *well*, so I can go back to the master's house, or some other master somewhere else, no better, perhaps worse even, with even funnier ways, and more beatings besides, I shouldn't wonder.' Cautiously, she touched the handkerchief at her throat. 'So no, I don't want to be no girl again. I want to be-,' she paused, whilst she thought of the word. 'I want to be a *weapon*,' she said, at last.

'A weapon?' said Violetta, as if she were savouring the bittersweet word.

Laura nodded. 'And such great revenges will I have - and when I'm done with drinking all their blood, and I'm fat and happy, I'll dress me in,' and again she touched the handkerchief at her throat, as if the cloth were a source of wonder to her, 'the mistress's finest silk dress, and then will I sit me there by the fire, and invite everyone up from my village who wants to keep me company, and then anyone left alive in the house can serve me and mine.'

'As revenge fantasies go, that's not bad,' said Aurélie.

'I know something about revenge,' said Violetta. 'Are you quite sure your conscience won't trouble you after you have taken all those lives?' she asked Laura.

The fair-haired girl shook her head defiantly. 'It ain't no more than they deserve,' she said.

'Then that's her choice,' said Aurélie.

Violetta looked at her. 'When my first master died,' she said, after a moment, reflectively, 'it was the custom for chosen servants to burn with him on his funeral pyre.'

'And did you?' asked Laura.

'No,' said Violetta, 'I became a vampire.'

'Just as well,' said Laura.

'Laura,' said Aurélie, making her voice sound gentle. 'Won't you tell us something about what has been happening here? Who fed on you?'

'Fed on me!' said Laura. 'Drained me dry as hay, more like. If it hadn't been for you two… It was Morleon's lieutenants,' she added. 'They rank themselves like

150

they're soldiers - proper nonsense, that is. They thought they could drain us in here because we didn't want to be part of Morleon's master plan.'

'Which is, what, exactly?' asked Aurélie.

'A race of vampires that share his views, that will place him on the throne, where he can have dominion overall,' said Laura, with a dreary note to her voice, as if she were repeating something she had heard many times before.

'It's not far off your revenge fantasy of wanting to sit in a silk dress and play the great lady with your former household, though,' said Aurélie.

'My revenge is partikler to me,' said Laura, 'but Morleon's ain't.'

'Then he's in greater pain than you,' said Violetta. 'And perhaps has greater need of healing,' she added, remembering her one meeting with him, the tall, crooked vampire at the artist's studio, hunched over his own sorrow, with his creased black brows, thick, dark hair, hooked nose and sunken mouth. His eyes too, grey as the mists where he had got lost.

'All his jabbering on,' said Laura, 'it put me in mind of a jack-in-a-box I once had, a fairling. Then it broke somewhere inside the box, and he couldn't jump up no more. Perhaps Morleon's a bit like that too, broke somewhere you can't rightly see.'

'Do you think he would drink from the Grail, if we offered it to him?' asked Aurélie.

'You ain't gonna try that, are you?' asked Laura.

'What about the poor jack-in-the-box, all broken inside?' asked Aurélie.

'Bloody annoying it was,' said Laura, 'and then it broke. I didn't even want it, I wanted the gold-fish, but that's what happens when Jimmy Summat throws hoops for you at the fair.'

'I take it you won't be asking Jimmy to keep you company when you're the Vampire Duchess?' asked Aurélie.

'Oh, I don't mind,' said Laura. 'I him better than Bobby.'

At that moment, the Porter stepped into the room. He did not seem overly surprised to see Aurélie and Violetta there, since he nodded to them, then spoke to Laura.

'Beggin yer pardon, Miss,' he said, 'but Morleon has just heard two of his lieutenants came after yer. He sent me to check on you, and if you was all right, to take you to im so he can apologise.'

'Oh no,' said Laura, shrinking back against the cushions.

'Now Miss,' said the Porter, 'you know how I let you out in the morning for a breath o' fresh air and how I turn a blind eye to all o' them posies you pick. You know I'm not likely to let Morleon hurt you in any way.'

'And yet his lieutenants just drained her of blood,' said Aurélie.

'Well, she looks all right now,' said the Porter, dubiously. Then he seemed to change his mind. 'I don't know, though, ladies. I'm not sure this is the job for me anymore. My Missis sez it's changin me - and not for the better.'

'What would you rather do?' asked Aurélie.

'I don't know,' said the Porter, scratching his head, 'summat in the line of healing - or gardening. I almost never get a Sunday free to go up the allotment, these days.'

'There may be an opening for you on board the starship as a doctor,' said Aurélie. 'Of course, it would mean a lot of study, a lot of hard work to get you through the entrance exams...'

'And a tin foil hat so I could chat to the aliens on a Monday and Wednesday,' said the Porter with a grin, nodding as if he would like to believe her, but didn't, quite. 'That's the game Alfie and I play when it's just us at ome, and then we ave kippers for supper, - or boiled eggs and soldiers,' he added, with gloomy satisfaction.

'There are family quarters on board the *Joyous Gard*,' said Aurélie, 'room enough for all of you.'

'Sez the lady in the thruppenny cell,' said the Porter. 'Come along now, Miss,' he said to Laura, 'the sooner you've seen im, the sooner you don't ave to see im, if you see what I mean.'

Flakes fell from the burning logs in the hearth, curling in the evening.

Laura climbed down from the couch, grimacing when she realised exactly how wet her nightdress was, then, cupping the lower half in her hands, she squeezed as much water out as she could. The Porter opened the door, and she followed him out into the corridor.

Through the open door, they heard someone singing, or at least, the sound was pitched half-way between a song and a whisper:

'Ladies Fair and Lady Dark,
Seek me while you may,
Lady Crow and Ladies Lark,
Who knows what games we will play?'

'I found that verse in the Lady Elridge Archives,' said Aurélie, then. 'I didn't know how it got there.'

'No,' said Violetta, 'for you were in a different timeline. That means the singer - Morleon? - must know - or will come to know, the Time Writing spell.'

'But,' said Aurélie, 'only you, me and Guinan know that spell.'

'Which means,' said Violetta, 'that one of us will tell him. That's a great deal of effort he has gone to, Aurélie, to leave you that message. Writing across the centuries, across vast swathes of time. Why do you think that is?'

Aurélie did not like to hazard a guess, but as she stood up to pace the room, in her mind's eye, she glimpsed a pair of beseeching grey eyes, flecked with amber, and ringed with dark lashes.

Maybe another fifteen minutes passed before they heard Laura charging back down the corridor. Then the door burst open, and Laura came running into the room, as if she were half-startled out of her wits, so much so, that Aurélie wondered if more brandy was required.

'He's not right in the ead,' Laura said, 'he's not right at all!' She sank breathless onto the couch.

'What did he say to you?' asked Aurélie, sitting down again beside her.

'He said he admired me for bein unaffected by my own mortality,' said Laura. 'And when I said, what does that mean, he said I had a lot of life left in me, and then he called me dearie or Laura Bird or some such thing and said would I give him a kiss to show there was no hard feelings.

But then the Porter said that warn't right, and Morleon called him a fool, and said summat else besides, a spell or summat, and then the Porter couldn't move anymore, he was just sat there frozen-like in one of them flip up seats. But when Morleon came up close to me, I bit down on his lip, hard as I could, and then I ran back down here.'

'But why didn't Morleon follow you?' asked Aurélie.

'He was callin after me, that he had another bird to catch in his net, and that if we wanted the Porter back with us, unharmed, we had to send up Lady Crow, by herself.'

'Who does he mean by Lady Crow?' asked Aurélie.

'He means me,' said Violetta, 'He called me that once before.' She added, a trifle self-consciously, 'Well, my hair is black as crow's feather, and I do come from Crowcroft Grange.'

'Yes, he means you,' said Laura. 'B'ain't you afeared to see him by yourself?'

'No,' said Violetta. 'Just a little irked. Which way do I go?'

'Along the corridor, up the staircase, and into the attics,' said Laura. 'He's up there, in the old operating theatre.' She paused, swallowed hard, then spoke with a bravado that perhaps she did not entirely feel. 'But if you ain't back in half an hour, we'll come and get you. He's found out once already, he ain't the only one with fangs.'

In fact, they did not have to wait as long as that before Violetta returned to them and told them what had transpired. She had left them, to go out into the corridor, then up a narrow, wooden spiral staircase which twisted past one of the dormitory floors and into the attics. She had pushed open a door at the top of the staircase, which opened out onto the old operating theatre. Here, there were rows of seats, arranged in a semi-circle, around a central platform. The rows rose higher and higher into the darkness of the gods above her.

In front of her, Morleon was sitting on one of the seats closest to the operating table. The light from a lantern on the seat next to him illuminated the dark brow that topped his gaunt face, and the dark struggle of elf-locks clustered round his eyes and ears. In this light, Violetta discerned the shadows beneath his grey eyes, and his mouth, twisted into a strange, mocking grimace. The Porter sat next to him, motionless, with his wrists bound.

When he caught sight of Violetta, Morleon began to clap, very slowly. 'You came alone, as I requested,' he said. 'Bravo, Lady Crow,' he added, still clapping. 'I require courage in my adversaries. Come closer.'

Although she did not entirely want to, the rhythmic sound of his clapping drew her to him. Down the steps she went, as compulsively as a sleepwalker, until she reached the central platform.

'What do you want in exchange for the Porter's freedom?' she asked.

'Not a kiss,' he said. 'A man's life is worth more than that, even from lips as delectable as yours. No, I want -,' he thought for a moment, 'I want the Time Writing spell. If you give me that, then Jem Blake here can go free.'

Violetta mentally ran through all the Time Travel Laws that she could remember, then decided, perhaps it was already destined that Morleon should have the spell. Such would be her argument, she thought, if anyone ever challenged her actions.

'Let him come to me first,' she said.

Morleon sighed, but put his hand on the Porter's shoulder, and said, as if the matter, were of little consequence to him, after all, 'Jem Blake, no vampire holds dominion over you. You are free to depart.'

The Porter leaned forwards and rubbed his eyes, as if he was waking from a deep sleep.

'You here, Miss?' he said to Violetta. 'What happened to the young un?'

'She's safe,' said Violetta. 'We can go back to her now.'

'The Time Writing spell first, please,' said Morleon.

Violetta began to recite, '*In sigloi sera...*' Then, when she had finished, the Porter stood up from his seat as if to join her, and Violetta turned on her heel.

'Such haste to depart is scarcely flattering, dear Lady Crow,' said Morleon. 'Can I offer you nothing for yourself?'

Violetta turned back to him, shaking her head.

'Come now,' said Morleon, 'you trained as a photographer, did you not?'

Violetta nodded.

'And therefore you see all the beauty in the world that I do not. Suppose you allow me to look at the world through your eyes from time to time in exchange for - ah, now, what is it you most desire?'

'You can hardly expect me to tell you,' said Violetta, remembering the Tale of the Sandman that she had once read to Arabella. The Sandman steals the eyes of naughty children and feeds them to his own children, who live in a nest on the moon and open up their beaks, just like baby owls.

'No, but I can divine it,' said Morleon. 'I know that Jem Blake here, for example, wants to play spaceman, but his wife is expecting their third child. He is wondering if a starship is the best place to raise a family.'

'Just as well you gave him his freedom, then,' retorted Violetta.

'And you, Lady Crow,' he said, 'do you want your freedom?'

When she didn't reply, he said, 'Sometimes you do. And yet, I don't believe that is your heart's desire. No, what you want is - I believe, what you want is - to be immortal, once more.'

Still, Violetta did not reply, though now her heart beat loud and fast.

So Morleon continued, 'Make no mistake, I shall play no Tithonus-trick upon you. You shall live on forever, as young and lovely as you are now, but free from what you perceive as the taint of vampirism, in exchange for allowing me to look out of your eyes.'

'But my heart's desire is ever a shifting and kaleidoscopic thing,' said Violetta, finding her voice, at last.

'Then let the kaleidoscope align in my favour,' said Morleon.

Violetta shook her head. 'No,' she said. 'For what I want today, I will not want tomorrow. And my heart's desire is to have my own way, no matter how capricious it might be.'

'Then that is what I wish for you, also,' said Morleon, so graciously that Violetta was surprised. 'But before I allow you both to leave, you must agree to one thing for me.'

'What's that?' asked Violetta.

'That you tell Lady Lark, whom you call Aurélie, that if she wishes to see her daughter again, she must attend on me.'

Violetta's hand stole to the locket containing the double portrait of Frances and Arabella, which nestled against the lace at her throat. 'Aurélie doesn't have a daughter,' she whispered, in sudden fear.

'Oh, I think you will find, she did have, once,' said Morleon.

'How do you know?' asked Violetta.

'Oh, I think you will find I know everything there is to know about Aurélie Catherine De Lys,' said Morleon.

'Why?' asked Violetta.

'The vampire is prone to be fascinated, with an engrossing vehemence, resembling the passion of love, by particular persons,' said Morleon.

'I know my Sheridan Le Fanu as well as you,' said Violetta, 'but Aurélie will surely sleep better without you in her dreams.'

'But my dreams,' said Morleon, 'my dreams may be compared to Adam's. I wish to wake from them and find them truth.'

Violetta arched an eyebrow at the Keatsian reference but said nothing.

Morleon took advantage of her silence to dismiss her. 'Now run along, Lady Crow, there's a dear, and do as I say.'

'A crow of my feather is better than a vulture of yours,' was her parting retort. She and the Porter left the old operating theatre.

Aurélie and Laura both sighed in relief to see Violetta and Jem, returned to Laura's chamber in the sanatorium, seemingly unharmed. But when Violetta delivered Morleon's message to Aurélie, she sat bolt upright on the chaise, whilst Laura screwed up her pretty eyes and glowered, astonishingly grim for such a newly fledged vampire.

'I don't think you should go,' Laura said to Aurélie. 'A preacher man at our Sunday school said if the Devil came to town to tempt you, all in his fine, bright, clothes, you had to put summat between you and him. We was all girls there, and I thought he meant summat else, and it were already too late for that, but what if the preacher man didn't mean the Devil, what if he meant vampires?'

'But you're a vampire,' said Aurélie, starting to pluck at the skin of her thumbnail.

'Dun't mean I'm like Morleon, tho,' said Laura, 'nasty thing, he is.'

'What would you do?' asked Violetta.

'For once, it's not about me,' said Violetta, smoothing out the creases in her burgundy cycling outfit, 'but if you're as curious as Eve, you'll go.'

'Be careful, Miss,' said Jem, the Porter. 'He has such a way with spells, and of twisting words, it puts you all in a maze, like.' He held out his wrists to Violetta, who rummaged around and found a sharp pair of scissors in her reticule. She cut him free, and he fell to rubbing the veins of his wrists, gingerly.

'What'll you put between you and im?' asked Laura.

Aurélie thought for a moment, then said, 'You have your fangs, and Violetta her wits, but I, I, have the Holy Grail.' She patted the leather satchel where it lay, wrapped in a cloth of red samite.

'I doubt you will persuade Morleon to drink from it,' said Violetta. 'Not everyone wishes to relinquish *the cruel and terrible affliction of vampirism*, nor even regards it as such.'

'What else can I do?' asked Aurélie, shrugging. She adjusted the satchel's shoulder strap, nodded to the others, and then departed. Down the dark corridor she went, then up the creaking staircase, the way that Laura and Violetta had gone before. Once or twice, she fancied her doubt crept beside her, in a death-coloured cloak. She shook her head, trying to banish the words of Morleon's song, that she had read in the Lady Elridge Archives, and that had followed the others, mockingly, down the corridor.

'Ladies Fair, and Lady Dark,
Seek me while ye may,
Lady Crow and Ladies Lark,
Who knows what games we will play?'

She put her hand to her side, touched her satchel. The weight of the Grail inside it began to calm her heart's rapid beat. And there in the front pocket, she suddenly recalled, was Daedalus's Tudor Rose talisman, drawn in vampire blood, his, to keep her safe from those of his kind.

One step cracked like thunder, so then she edged back against the wall and proceeded to climb more stealthily, sideways. No need to announce her presence before she arrived.

Slowly, she pushed open the door to the attics. The scent of dust, mould and something unpleasantly metallic assailed her nostrils, hit the back of her throat, made her eyes water. She gagged.

The skylight, set in the slanted roof above her, showed silver-grey glimmers of light. It would not have been enough for former surgeons to wield their scalpels on unanaesthetised patients or possibly even cadavers, for the edification of their medical students, but it was enough for her to form an impression of the old operating theatre.

Rows of seats, arranged in a split, horseshoe shape, that led down into further darkness.

She reached into her satchel for her I-phone, took it out, then pressed the torch button. The light shone out, haphazardly, waking the birds nesting in the heavy oak rafters above. She heard the owl's screech, the high-pitched squeal of bats, then the rapid tumult and bell-beat of their wings. Now she directed the beam of light, away from the rafters, stained with bird droppings and dried blood, down into the stark shadows between the seats.

At last, it came to rest on the platform below, on the gaunt face and form of Morleon. He was standing beside the operating table, with his arms outstretched and his hands upraised. There was an air of showmanship, even gallantry, about the gesture, and yet, to Aurélie, he resembled nothing so much as a vast, crooked tree, twisted by an ill wind, but sustained by his own malevolence.

He winced, dropped his arms, then held his hand up to his eyes.

'Why, Lady Lark, you quite dazzle me,' he said. 'You will have heard that I have a special place for you in my heart?'

'Laura warns me your heart isn't to be trusted,' said Aurélie.

'You can discover that for yourself,' said Morleon. 'Or not. But I have made a grievous error. In my mind, you were already as I am, so that I judged your eyes to be attune to this darkness. Now I have realised my mistake, I ask you to switch off your torch, which is too bright for vampire eyes, and I will light my lantern.'

She did as he asked, and then, a moment later, in the darkness of the operating theatre, there came the sudden flare of a lit wick. It wavered through the dark, then steadied itself. Now Morloen's voice rang out.

'In any case,' he called, 'the spectacle of all I can offer you has its own, wondrous, pellucid luminescence.' Yet, to Aurélie's ears, the bombast of his rhetoric struck a false note, as if his pomposity shielded a deeper insecurity.

Nevertheless, Morleon held both arms aloft once more, and began pointing out different sections of the operating theatre: the gods, the upper tier of seats, where Aurélié now stood, the lower tiers, even the platform, even the operating table. Wherever he pointed, a Roman numeral appeared. When all twelve Roman numerals were glowing around them, like starry clusters in the sky, Morleon seized hold of the operating table and swung it round. Its solid timber groaned in protest, then obeyed his command.

Now the table lay at an angle on the platform, so that it cast a strong, slanted shadow.

'It's like the moon dial,' thought Aurélie, recalling the courtyard of the Maiden Fayre Hotel.

In that moment, a luminous being, radiant as the moon, began to materialise upon the operating table. Her hair was long and fair; her form was slight; her eyes were like opals, like Aurélie's own, but wilder.

Aurélie knew who this girl was, and how she had once loved her.

'I can give your daughter back to you,' said Morleon, softly.

In that moment, when the lost child's possibility of being was most strong, how tempted Aurélie was to say *yes*.

'What do you want in return?' she asked.

'Only that you abide with me for all remaining time,' the vampire replied. Then, when she glanced around again at the operating theatre, its rafters, beams, cobwebs, smelt the stench of their pine mingling with dried blood, he added, 'oh, I don't mean here. After I am crowned King of Valerian, we can go wherever you like. I - I have a place to the south of Avalon: a whitewashed villa on the shores of the Mediterranean. And there, we three little lambkins can live happy, innocent, and guarded lives.'

It was the strangest thing, but for a moment, she thought she could smell lemons, sweet and sharp, on a salt-scented breeze. She could taste them too, mingling with honey, as if the vampire had prepared his own drink to take away her pain.

'Guarded? From whom?' she asked.

'Why,' said Morleon, softly, 'from the wolves that do roam all the hills.'

As he spoke, Aurélie glimpsed a kind of dim, shadowy kingdom, a land of phantasmagoria, where pure, speculative reasoning was unknown, a domain of anarchic creatures, savage, sharp-fanged, yet, curiously abstract, subsumed by vague, visionary delights and pleasures. But after all, what else could Morleon offer, when he upheld that the only cure for this strange disease of modern life was vampirism?

'Why, why do you shake your head?' Morleon demanded now. His voice and hands quivered, so that the stars followed his movements, seemingly in obeisance. So then, in that one moment, how majestic, how magnificent, how like God Himself did he seem. His nostrils flared; his eyes blazed; yet still, Aurélie knew the Holy Grail possessed its own curative powers, and so she dared to speak.

'You are King Arthur's grandson,' she said, feigning a reverent tone. 'And it would be meet and fitting for you to drink from the most Holy Grail,' she continued, and now, with more genuine reverence, she began to remove the chalice from her satchel.

Morleon's grey eyes narrowed as she took the cloth of red samite from the golden chalice. How the cup gleamed in the silver-grey light: this phoenix that could grant him an undesired, unlooked for, unasked for, rebirth.

Aurélie strode forwards, down the steps. 'And if you could find it in your heart to drink from the Grail, then I would promise to support your claim to the throne, and, and… to stand at your side, your best earthly companion.' For after all, her best bargaining chip was not the chalice. It was herself. She began to walk down the central aisle towards him.

'Hold on a moment,' said Guinan, leaning forward so abruptly in his chair that he nearly spilt some of his drink. 'You told him, *what*?'

Aurélie repeated what she had said to Morleon.

'And you didn't think I might have something to say about that?' asked Guinan.

Aurélie gave a small, unhappy shrug. 'Morleon is King Arthur's grandson,' she said. 'He does have a legitimate claim to the throne. And I thought I could make things better, for the whole of Valerian.'

'The needs of the many outweigh the needs of the one? Is that it?' asked Guinan, wishing they had never started watching *Star Trek*.

Aurélie slowly nodded.

'But you didn't think about me, at all,' said Guinan.

'You weren't there,' said Aurélie. 'And just for a moment, everything I wanted, was.'

'That was part of Morleon's enchantment,' said Guinan. 'Neither of us can really hazard a guess as to how real it would have been.' He slumped forward in his chair. Then his eyes began to shift backwards and forwards, as if he were making rapid calculations of his own. He sat up straight. 'Aurélie, you know I can work magick too, don't you?'

'Show me when I've finished my story,' said Aurélie.

Guinan sat back in his chair, his eyes pleased and alert.

'Hurry up with your story, then, Aurélie.'

But Aurélie decided that she would take her own sweet time about it. So she tried to parody, as well as to critique, the Victorian Valerians who had so recently been the subject of her research. 'There's always the danger that one can enjoy the power of one's own rhetoric so much, that one forgets one does not in fact have much of worth to say.'

'Yes,' said Guinan, 'one's head can in fact disappear up one's arse.'

'And then,' said Aurélie, 'how would one send a postcard?'

'One would need a stamp and a-,' Guinan stopped. 'Aurélie, do hurry up, you look tired to death.'

'And I never have any stamps,' said Aurélie. 'But, to continue, Morleon didn't react so well to my wonderful proposal anyway...'

'Aurélie,' Morleon said, as she drew near, 'don't try me in this way. I am not a gentle-tempered man. I am not patient. I am neither cool, nor dispassionate. Out of compassion for me, and yourself, put your fingers to my pulse, see how it throbs, and - beware!'

He bared his wrist and offered it to her.

The tumultuous beat of his pulse slowed to her fingertips. 'You do not wish to drink from the Grail?' she asked.

He shook his head, vehemently.

Now the radiance of the child in front of them dimmed, so much so that Aurélié began to fear that she would forever be taken from her sight. Her heart ached. An old scar had become a pulsating wound.

And what of Morleon? Surely he suffered too. The blood was draining from his lips and cheeks; they grew livid, then yet, more pale. To agitate him so deeply felt cruel, but to yield when he would not drink from the Grail was out of the question. Not knowing what to do, she dropped his wrist. Then she cradled the Grail in both her hands, seeking reassurance from the touch and weight of metal.

When it did not come, the words, 'Help me,' burst involuntarily from her lips.

On impulse, she raised her head, and, through the skylight, she saw the moon, that is, the moon goddess Selene, a white hand breaking through sable, starry folds, then dispersing them. Now a white form was shining in the azure, inclining a glorious brow towards her, gazing upon Aurélie, the blonde woman whose own reflection was superimposed onto the glass.

She spoke to Aurélie's spirit, whispered to her heart.

'Daughter, flee temptation.'

'Mother, I will.'

Aurélie turned back towards Morleon.

He said, 'So all I can offer you is not enough?' and with another sweep of his hand, the constellation of numerals, and the child vanished. The flame in the lantern next to him went out.

In the darkness, Aurélie called out to Morleon, 'Are you still there?' - wanting him to be, wanting him not to be, but there came no reply. She stood there, alone in the dark, with the screech and ruffle of bats and owls above her, suddenly, painfully, aware of all that she had lost.

Presently, the silence was broken by a singing, hot noise, and after that, screams and shouts from below the attics. She heard a voice cry out then, and the voice might have been Morleon's. 'Run, run, the whole damn place is on fire...' She glimpsed fireflies above her head, which rapidly became a whirling blaze of heat all around her...

Afterwards, Daedalus told Aurélie what he thought had happened. *Ginny.* In the women's dormitory below the attics, empty now since so many had left, she had stood beside the curtains, where a lamp was burning. This was her home now: the long rows of empty beds, the steadfast lamp, the staircase beyond it. The clock was ticking downstairs in the hall. But she was tired now, very tired of thinking. She wanted to be in a room with sunlight pouring through the windows. But here, there were thin curtains behind thick curtains, that stopped out the sun.

So she must hold the lamp up to the curtains. She laughed when the brightness spread so fast, but she did not stay to watch it. She walked out into the corridor so fast, it was as if she was flying. But out there, in the corridor, she saw the ghost hovering above the dresser. A woman, with pale, streaming hair. She was surrounded by a frame, but she was a ghost.

Ginny called out then, 'Save me!' Then she saw that she had been saved, for there was a wall of fire protecting her from the ghost. Just it was too hot. So she went away.

There were some more candles on a table by the staircase. She took one of them and ran down a flight of steps. Lines of smoke drifted down after her. On the second floor, she threw away the candle. But she did not stay to watch. She had to get away from the heat and the shouting, for there was shouting now. She ran down to the ground floor.

There was no-one sitting at the Porter's desk. So she would sit in his chair and wait for him while flames brushed against the rugs. He was always so kind: he would know what to do. The clock was ticking louder now; soon it would be time to go out into the garden, walk among the tree ferns, silver and gold, or sit down in the shade, and have a cup of tea, a slice of angel cake.

See - there was Mr Dallas now, calling to her! He wanted them to go out into the garden, too. He told her to stay where she was; he would walk through fire to reach her. But the fire reached her first. She saw patches of tinder floating into the smoky air, which a moment before had been her dress. *How very pretty,* she thought, *how very pretty it all is,* then, nothing else, for though Mr Dallas carried her out into the garden, and laid her down gently on a stone bench, the cool air could not revive her.

Inside the sanatorium, the cinders still fell, in crepuscule showers, over charred and blackened bones. Up in the attic, Laura bundled Aurélie into the Porter's greatcoat and dragged her back down the burning staircase. On their way down, they could hear the patients whose relatives had not wanted them home, waking and coughing in their beds.

'Get out, get out,' Laura called. 'There's a fire.'

The ones who had not suffocated from the smoke in their sleep stumbled their way through the dark, then fought their way out through the flames. When the staircase to the ground floor collapsed, those now trapped in the lower dormitory had the idea to smash the windows and throw mattresses through them onto the ground. Then came panicked cries and shouts as people began to jump.

'It's the best way out,' Laura said to Aurélie. And so they rushed over to the nearest smashed window and leaned out. They looked over the edge, to the hard ground below. 'Aurélie! Aurélie!' A man was calling but though the sky was red, she could not see who it was. The wind caught in their hair, and it streamed out behind them. It might bear us up, thought Aurélie. Like Rose Thorn's wings.

'You scared?' asked Laura.

Aurélie shook her head, then Laura gripped her hand.

'Aurélie, Aurélie,' he was still calling her.

She cried out, 'Mother!' and then they jumped.

Aurélie felt a jolt of pain as her ankle folded beneath her when she landed, but other than that, she was unhurt. Laura was fine, stretching and bracing herself for the next challenge. Then the Porter and Violetta joined them, and hugged them hard, all huddled in blankets they had pulled from the bed in Laura's room. For a few moments, they stood and watched as the sanatorium blazed, turning the night sky, red, yellow and black.

'At least now there's a great ruddy fire between us and the Devil,' said Laura.

'But I thought I heard Morleon calling,' said Aurélie. 'Do you think he survived?'

Violetta gave her an odd look. 'Your memory, Aurélie! You'll recall vampires are immune to fire: *I* survived a burning ship,' she said.

Laura added, 'Besides, I think you'd know if he hadn't. Once he's left his footprints in yer mind, it's hard not to feel im.'

'And he has the Time Writing spell now, too,' said Violetta. 'I had to give it to him in exchange for Jem's safety.'

Aurélie said nothing for a moment, then spoke. 'You had better teach Jem the Time Travel spell, too,' she said, 'so he can go home and get his family ready to join us on the *Joyous Gard*.'

Dutifully, Violetta reached into her reticule for a little ivory-bound notebook with a gold pen tucked into its spine. She began to write out the spell for Jem in her finest copperplate handwriting, and with what she could remember of the instructions for saying it. Then she tore the page out of her notebook and handed it to him.

He took it, somewhat bemused, and read it carefully. Then he folded up the piece of paper and put it in his pocket. 'If yer don't mind, I'll stay and help out here ere a bit, first,' said Jem. 'I'm due to work a night shift anyway, so the Missis won't be fretting yet. And then, I s'pose there'll be some packing at ome to do. Can Alfie bring his cat to that there *Joyous Gard*, you called it?'

Aurélie nodded. 'We need a ship's cat,' she said.

'You might be gettin some ship's kittens in a few weeks, too,' said Jem.

'Oh,' said Violetta, in accents of great disappointment. 'I won't be able to see them.'

'Why not?' asked Jem.

'I won't be coming with you to the *Joyous Gard*,' she said, 'for, when this night is through, I will return to my home - and my family.' Her hand strayed once more to the locket around her neck. Then, as the stench of smoke and burning flesh reached her nostrils, she said, 'This fire was not of my making, but the end result is the same.'

'Those poor people trapped inside,' said Aurélie.

Laura stirred herself to return to the building to haul out survivors. Aurélie, Jem and Violetta tried to accompany her, only to find themselves beaten back by a wall of flame. Now the smoke was everywhere, thick and ugly. The faces of the emerging patients and vampires were clouded with it, and it poured out of the front door in waves. Then came another crash from inside the house, and someone shouted, 'The other staircase is gone.'

Aurélie, Jem and Violetta guided some of the survivors down to the river that wound its way through the forest to bathe their burns whilst cabs began to arrive to take those more seriously injured to a different hospital. The trio led those vampires and patients who were more scared than hurt to bed down in a stable block detached from the main building, which had remained largely untouched by the flames. Tirelessly, they worked through the night.

Towards dawn, Aurélie, half-dazed with smoke fumes, and covered in vampire blood, came to rest in the grounds for a moment's respite. The sanatorium was a blackened ruin. Nothing remained of the glass veranda, and the front of the house was the charred shell of itself, high, fragile, with the windows smashed out, and the roof and chimneys crashed in.

'It'll take a great deal of scrubbing to get that place clean again,' said Laura, appearing beside her.

'More than that, I think,' said Aurélie. 'The asylum will have to be closed down, its patients transported elsewhere, and then it will have to be rebuilt - and that could take months, years even.' She shivered as she imagined winter snow drifting through the void doorway; winter rain beating in through those hollow windows. But her reverie was shattered by someone throwing a teapot, cups and saucers out of the remnants of the veranda;

only one blush-pink, eggshell thin saucer survived, rolling out into the grass. Then a music-box was thrown out of a broken window frame and gave a musical cry as its tiny cylinders gave up their sound.

'I'll ave that,' said Laura, pouncing on it among the shadows of the lawn. She checked it was intact, the dancer still pirouetting inside, then said, with lowered eyebrows and a slightly ashamed expression, 'No but Violetta has kiddies, h'ant she? They might like it.'

'Where *is* Violetta?' asked Aurélie.

Laura peered into the smoky distance. 'Talkin to that fella, over there.'

'Who?' said Aurélie, looking in the same direction. 'It's not Morleon, is it?'

'No,' said Laura, 'it's Mr Dallas,' and she turned pink as a vampire can.

Violetta and Daedalus began to cross the lawn towards them, still deep in conversation, of which Aurélie caught the gist.

'They are all safe?' Violetta was asking. 'My vampire siblings?'

'A few of the less promising ones survived,' Daedalus replied. 'The orderlies, now known as the Emperor and the Hang Man, the former nurse, Madeline Kaos... It's a real shame. As for the others...' His voice trailed off, and he shrugged. Then he paused, and said more reflectively, and perhaps, more contritely, 'Better that than to be huddled together in ill-ventilated and undrained courts and cellars, or worse, in workhouses, or prisons.'

'Exactly how many vampire children did you have?' asked Violetta.

'I'm not sure,' he replied, shrugging again. 'Many. Feeding on those orderlies was probably a mistake, though. Vampire offspring with moustaches are disconcerting.'

Violetta hesitated before she spoke again, but finally the words came tumbling out. 'Sometimes,' she said, 'sometimes, I couldn't even see the sun, shining in the sky, Daedalus, I was staring so hard at you. But since I found you here, you're more like wine with too much water in it. Sort of - diluted.'

'It's hard to become who you're meant to be when - who you're meant to be with, isn't with you,' said Daedalus.

'As to that, we shall never know,' said Violetta, 'but I think it is possible to have more than one soulmate.'

'That gets you off the hook quite nicely,' retorted Daedalus. 'So I don't have your heart then?'

'You cut your teeth upon it,' said Violetta.

Not wanting to play gooseberry, Aurélie nevertheless chose that moment to step forwards and join them. Vampire flirting, she thought. Or at least, it passed as flirting, but it wasn't to everyone's taste.

'So you feel no compassion for my deep suffering, my wild woe?' asked Daedalus.

'I would feel more compassion if I were more thoroughly convinced of the authenticity of your wild woe,' replied Violetta. Then she added, 'And yet, Daedalus, you have lived nine hundred years whilst I have slept. You have known many lands and many people whilst I slumbered in my quiet coffin. If you have suffered, at least you have lived.'

'I have lived so much, I might envy you your quiet slumbers,' said Daedalus.

'Violetta,' said Aurélie then, 'enough! Stop exaggerating. You can hardly call Crowcroft Grange a quiet coffin.'

'Crowcroft Grange?' said Daedalus. 'You *are* going home, then?'

Violetta nodded. 'It's time.'

'But will I never see you again?' asked Daedalus.

'Never say never,' said Violetta.

'Write than in blood and I might believe you,' said Daedalus.

'I'm not sure I have your gift for penmanship,' said Violetta.

'Violetta!' said Aurélie, who had read many of Violetta's journals written in High Valerian, and who had admired, not only Violetta's tireless emotional energy, which had propelled her across acres, continents and centuries of passionate prose, but also, her beautiful, copperplate handwriting.

'I just meant, I can't draw Tudor Roses,' said Violetta, smiling.

'Lots of people are going to need those talismans,' said Aurélie. 'Jem, and his family, and, well, not Laura, but...' she sighed. 'I was supposed to be researching the benefits vampires would bring to the new planet. This hasn't exactly been their finest hour.'

'Oh, I don't know,' said Violetta, looking first at Daedalus, and then across at Laura, 'you might be able to write a few thousand words on Tudor Rose Vampires: Unexpected Acts of Heroism From Human Sympathisers.'

'You might need a catchier title,' said Daedalus. 'All the same, I should be happy to furnish you with a few of my select thoughts on the subject.' And before Aurélie could stop him, he launched into how he thought the fire had started, and all about his own (very courageous) attempted rescue of Ginny Goldstone.

'Well, thank you for your contribution,' said Aurélie, after she had politely allowed some time to elapse, 'but I was thinking more of - well, Laura ...'

The girl grinned, revealing the tips of her fangs, and then she grew pensive. She gave Violetta the music-box, and said, 'So you're orf now, are ya? It's always like that, you get to know someone, and just when you're likin em the most - ouf - orf they go!' She gave them each the biggest hug, her arms wrapping right round them, then added, 'Don't forget to look me up when I'm a Duchess!'

'But I will be in a different timeline,' said Violetta. 'Unless,' she said, glancing at Aurélie, then back at Laura, 'we can use the Time Writing spell across dimensions to stay in touch? And if I hang onto Guinan's calculations, then, yes, we might see each other again.'

'Duchess, eh?' interrupted Daedalus, a speculative gleam in his eyes. 'Perhaps I shouldn't hate where I'm supposed to be, after all.'

'I don't know,' muttered Violetta. 'Your timeline is going to seed.' She bowed her head, as if she didn't want to think about just how bad things were becoming.

But Aurélie was thinking something different, about the fickleness of vampires. What was it Violetta had said? *As malleable as a pair of gloves.* For just like that, Daedalus had transferred his dubious affections, from Violetta to Laura, for the sake of some possible pennies in his pocket and a new ribbon to tie on his frockcoat.

Then, somehow, Aurélie and Violetta found themselves hurrying under the trees, then out into the darkness, where sepia smoke with flecks of amber and grey rose up into the air... When they felt their feet leave the grass of the lawn and touch the soft mossy ground of the path through the woods, they stopped. Beneath the branches of a hawthorn tree, Violetta turned to Aurélie and said, 'Don't forget to...'

'And then Violetta said, Don't forget to...' Aurélie said to Guinan. She broke off, confused.

'What's wrong?' asked Guinan.

'How strange,' said Aurélie, 'I can't remember what Violetta said next.'

'But you're tired,' said Guinan, hurriedly. 'Or else the Time Travel spell worked before you could hear her.'

'Yes, but something must have happened next,' said Aurélie. 'I mean, after the asylum was set on fire, and Daedalus emerged from the flames, and then we talked to him, and we said goodbye to Laura, and then... then I must have said the Time Travel spell, because I was suddenly back in my cabin here, and the shower was broken.'

'Well,' said Guinan, 'you've certainly told me enough that I can make an official report. I shouldn't wonder if there's a promotion for you.'

'Thank you,' said Aurélie, pleased. 'As long as you post the right report, this time.' She paused a moment, then said, 'Although all I did was help a few survivors and save Laura.'

'Aurélie, Aurélie, Aurélie,' said Guinan. 'When you were writing your history of Lady Elridge's sanatorium, you didn't get very far with your research, did you?'

'Well, no,' said Aurélie. 'It got cut short because there were the spell books to edit and amalgamate, and...'

'In the Victorian era, *Lady Elridge's* was known as *Saint Cosmas & Damian*. But then came the fire, and the hospital was rebuilt - by Lady Elridge,' said Guinan.

'Yes, I know,' said Aurélie.

'But you haven't worked out exactly who Lady Elridge is yet, have you?' asked Guinan.

Aurélie shook her head.

'Lady Ottalie *Laura* Elridge?' said Guinan.

'Oh,' said Aurélie, 'so Laura did become a Duchess after all, and she rebuilt the sanatorium...'

'On modern and humane principles, yes,' said Guinan. 'By saving the murdered girl, you allowed her to become

Lady Elridge and carry out all the good that was in her heart.'

'But that was in the alternate timeline,' burst out Aurélie. 'The one where Queen Victoria was assassinated.'

Guinan paused and touched the tips of his fingers together in a gesture reminiscent of Officer Pluto. 'Laura was always destined to become Lady Elridge,' he said, 'in any timeline. In your timeline, don't forget, she wasn't murdered by Morleon's lieutenants. However, by your actions, you will allow the Conglomerate to discover the tremendous potential Laura possesses as a vampire. I am going to recommend that in this instance, Laura's alternate timeline is preferable to the birth and death of the hospital's mortal founder and benefactress. And Pluto, see, well, we can say what we like about him, and we do, but he's a clever chap… if he indulges in a spot of time editing…'

'Which is what, exactly?' asked Aurélie, stifling a yawn, but genuinely concerned that she was too tired to understand.

'In layman's terms,' said Guinan, not at all patronisingly, 'it's kind of a cut and paste job using Time itself. So, in that way, well, now Laura can become one of the Conglomerate's key vampire Ambassadors - in fact, when you get the chance, you should look her up and interview her for your report.'

'I could do that,' said Aurélie, nodding. 'Time editing,' she added, slowly. 'That could be very useful. Imagine being able to rewrite history. No World Wars, no Hitler, no 9/11, no Covid pandemic, no Great Explosion…'

'Aurélie!' said Guinan. 'Did you not listen to any of my Time Travelling Laws? Their principles still apply. Time editing is a new skill, and one that requires incredible delicacy and finesse. Whether Pluto will ever be able to develop a whole Time Editing Suite, as he claims, is very much a case for conjecture, and not one to be discussed in the officers' canteen, either,' he added. 'This is classified information. But at least Pluto has the correct cerebral aptitude and a proven track record. The Conglomerate certainly don't want any old Tom, Dick or Aurélie thinking they can just rewrite Valerian history willy-nilly.'

'Thanks for that,' said Aurélie. 'I am this ship's History Officer.'

'Not for long, perhaps,' said Guinan, smiling. 'I'll ask them to fast-track your promotion on account of extreme courage in the line of duty. *Past You Is So Proud of Now You, and Future You Can't Wait To Show You What Happens Next.* Fourth and Fifth Laws of the Time Traveller's Code.'

'Okay, okay,' said Aurélie. 'Thank you. Though it's a standing joke on board this ship that fast-track promotion takes five years.' Then she shook her head. 'I wish I could remember what happened properly after Daedalus said, *don't hate where you're supposed to be.*'

'You know, that would make a good Sixth Law of Time Travel,' said Guinan.

'Do you just make the Laws up as you go along?' asked Aurélie.

'Certainly not,' huffed Guinan. 'But sometimes, yes. I'm a cunning, careful planner filled to the brim with strategy, wisdom and wiles. Though that last one was Daedalus's, not mine,' he added, as if he were being generous. 'Well, the youngsters still have the capacity to surprise us - and then, I suppose he's come on a bit in the last few centuries.'

'Possibly,' said Aurélie. 'But what about my memory lapse?'

'Well, if you can't remember it, it's probably not that important,' Guinan said.

'Isn't that part of one of Queen Morgana's propaganda speeches for the Process of Memory Harvesting?' asked Aurélie. 'Though it's what my mother always used to say, too,' she added, rubbing her eyes. 'I'm hungry, Guinan. Would you make me an omelette for breakfast, please?'

'What happened to the promises of someday?' asked Guinan. He sighed. 'If I make it, will you stay awake long enough to eat it, hey?'

'I might,' said Aurélie.

'Then I might,' said Guinan, turning away and starting to rummage among the papers on his desk, so that she wouldn't see the grin on his face.

The Time Traveller's Code, latest edition.

An evolving work by Professor Guinan Guineafowl, Avalon Ambassador, Brunwych, and his associates. Suggestions welcome, usual address.

1 There's a Time to Every Purpose Under Heaven
2 But Now is Not That Time
3 Don't use Time Travel when Public Transport Will Do
4 Past You Is So Proud of Now You
5 Future You Can't Wait To Show You What Happens Next
6 Don't Hate where you're Supposed to Be. (Daedalus Dallas)
7 Is it nearly Time to go Home? (Pippin Guineafowl)
8 May the Best of your Past be the Worst of your Future.

Operation: Golden Claw

Five years later, the little emerald planet in the Delta quadrant gleamed at Lieutenant Rose Thorn invitingly on the starship's vastscreen. On her own console, Rose Thorn pulled up the standard astrobiology checklist and began to run through whether this planet was capable of sustaining human life. It did have a stable rotational axis. It did possess sufficient liquid water. Just, from the information available, she couldn't tell whether its magnetic field would sufficiently shield surface life from the lethal effects of charged particles in the solar winds and cosmic rays.

She pulled a wry face. The sensors weren't showing that there was enough high-frequency ultraviolet radiation to trigger ozone formation.

'*No* to this one,' she said, swivelling round in her chair to face Captain De Lys. 'Close - but no cigar.'

Aurélie mentally consigned the promising emerald planet to oblivion. 'At this rate, we're going to have to start investigating water worlds,' she said, trying to quash her rising sense of panic that they would never find the elusive planet. For her dreams had begun to trouble her, that she was spiralling upwards, higher and higher among the spinning planets, but never actually reaching them, never finding what she was searching for, leaving and losing everything among the detritus of the stars.

'Swampland might be our best option,' agreed Rose Thorn. She turned back to her own screen and caught sight of the time on its digital chronometer. 'Don't you have a qi gong class starting in a few minutes?'

'Do I?' sighed Aurélie. 'My energy doesn't flow in a punctual way. I'm nearly always late, and Sifu Wong nearly always says, 'You must respect *qi* before *qi* will respect you.'

'I'll walk you to the recreation deck,' said Rose Thorn. 'There's something I want to check out, too.'

She and Aurélie parted company at the door to the qi gong studio, then Rose Thorn slipped into the Viewing Theatre with almost the same feeling of reverence as if she were entering the Temple of the Sisters of Valerian. However, rather than repeat what she did last night, and wait for the lights to go down and the billed programme to start, she went and knocked on the door of the projection booth at the back of the theatre.

The door swung open to reveal a short man with a bulbous forehead, sharp, pointed, almost albino features, and pale blue eyes sitting at a rickety desk that filled the small room.

'There you are, Officer Pluto,' said Rose Thorn. 'Captain De Lys mentioned you were in charge of cinema projection.'

'Lieutenant Thorn,' said Officer Pluto, 'I heard you came aboard last night.' He gestured airily at the film reels piled high on the desk in front of him. 'Cinema projection, it's sort of a hobby of mine,' he said. 'I'm categorising some classics from the Seventies. Genre. Director. Star. I like films from that era, where the special effects are carried out traditionally, with back projection, travelling matte shots, blue screen and optical printers, all that sort of thing.'

'Oh?' said Rose Thorn, politely.

He seemed flattered by what he took to be her interest. 'Is it my imagination,' he continued, 'or do these old-fashioned effects have more weight and presence than those generated by CGI?'

'I quite like *Superman*,' said Rose Thorn, 'that's from 1978, so no CGI back then. And *Superman II*, with the triad of villains, that was probably the best of the trilogy.'

When he found she had nothing further to contribute to the topic, he said, 'At any rate, sorting through these is keeping me busy while I wait to start my new job.'

'Your new job?'

'Didn't the Captain tell you? Though I suppose it has been kept pretty *hush-hush.* Well, I'm going to be using the latest nanotechnology to iron out all the wrinkles in time,' he replied. 'Just the techbots haven't quite completed my Time Editing Suite to my specifications, yet.'

'That sounds pretty exciting,' said Rose Thorn. 'Will you be incorporating celestine or selenite astrotravelchips?'

'Now, now, Lieutenant Thorn,' said Officer Pluto, grinning hugely, 'you must know that's classified information.' He tapped the side of his nose. 'But apart from impart my deepest, darkest secrets to a woman, who, alas, I barely know, is there anything else I can do to help you on this bright and balmy morning?'

Was it her imagination or was there now an unwholesome twinkle in his pale blue eyes? Even as the Leader of nuns, Rose Thorn sometimes found she had this unwanted effect. Sometimes she wondered whether scrubbing herself down with carbolic soap and retreating to meditate in the Inner Compound for a century or two would get rid of all this unwanted attention - but she didn't want to. Life was for living.

'I've been on a mission to recover the Cylinders of Memory,' she said, at last.

'They're not here,' said Officer Pluto, quickly.

'No, I know that,' said Rose Thorn, more patiently than she felt. 'But because of that mission, and the time spent on retreat preparing for it, I seem to have missed out on quite a lot of current events. Would you be able to let me have, say, the last three months' worth of episodes of *Collodian Star*?'

'I don't think we have so many in stock,' said Officer Pluto, checking through the film cannisters. 'There's erm - oh, - the Lanval triple bill, including the one where you and Lieutenant Lanval...'

'Yes, I saw that last night,' said Rose Thorn.

'It wasn't bad, was it?' said Officer Pluto. 'I thought it was quite tasteful, some of the shots and angles - shows you can't believe what they say, about the camera adding five pounds...'

'Yeah, great *mise-en-scène* and all, but do you have any others?' asked Rose Thorn.

'There's the one with Sir Sagramore, and a short episode which is just Queen Morgana broadcasting from the Mothercrystal, outlining her new immigration policies and then there's a few reels about an ogre... and, oh, yes, there's Captain Dulac's wedding, Parts I *and* II...'

'Just *his* wedding? He married himself, did he?' said Rose Thorn. 'Match made in heaven. Yes, thank you, those would be useful to help me catch up.'

'They're a bit strange,' said Officer Pluto. 'I can only surmise that Queen Morgana allowed those particular memories to be harvested and broadcast as a demonstration of her power. Propaganda episodes, sort of...'

'I wonder that he let her...'

'I'm not sure he had much choice,' Officer Pluto replied. 'But, anyway,' he added, 'you'll know all about that from your colleague, Ms Jackson in the Collodian.'

'How do you know about her?' asked Rose Thorn.

'I watched you both during some preliminary equipment checks in the Time Editing Suite yesterday,' said Officer Pluto. When Rose Thorn made to protest, he added,. 'I'm *supposed* to know quite a lot about... quite a lot. It's part of my new job. To keep an eye on... our more *subversive* junior officers,' he said, giving her a nod that was almost respectful. 'And to prohibit, correct or, erm... adjust any further time displacements for the benefit of the Conglomerate.'

'Oh,' said Rose Thorn, feeling discomfited by *his* demonstration of power. 'Well, if you can please just play those wedding episodes for me, sir, errr, I'll leave you to it.'

'My pleasure,' said Officer Pluto, 'always happy to oblige *you,* Lieutenant Rose Thorn.'

Rose Thorn went and sat in one of the plush velour tip-up seats, waiting for the lights to go down. Up came the title screen, then flashes, zigzags, flickers, then the opening credits spelling out, *Collodian Star.* The production values seemed to be quite high for these particular episodes. The camera panned through a perfectly rendered model forest and came to rest on a replica of the Mothercrystal Broadcasting Studios, then swooped up and over the Winter Palace in Beaurepaire, the Castle of Chalis, and then the surrounding valleys of the Collodian.

Wheels and cogs turned to reveal the village of Beaumain, and then, sweeping through that village came a whirlwind with many heads, and they were all huge and hideous, all hurtling scorching fire, and each head's mouth had a demon's tongue, and the teeth and face of a leopard.

Finally, the camera leapt up, away from the whirlwind, and the screen shimmered as a ship set sail on turquoise rivers and seas that flowed out to Valerian, Ravenglass, the Westward Isles, and then on, to the wider world.

For the first scene, the camera pulled back to reveal Lancelot, Captain Dulac, asleep in his bed, with sunlight streaming in through high castle windows on every side.

Titles onscreen informed the viewers that he was in Avalon on a diplomatic mission, there to parley with his foster-aunt Morgana about some of her immigration policies.

Rose Thorn knew that Lancelot possessed dual Avalon/Valerian nationality, so he was exempt from some of the queen's harsher strictures, which had, for example, prevented Lieutenant Lanval from seeing his own wife, Blancheflor, for several years now. The junior officer wondered if Lancelot had meant to put in a good word for Lanval, if he got the chance.

But for now, onscreen, he was dreaming of that ship from the title credits, except that, in his dream, it was covered in black samite, and a girl was leaning forward at its prow, pensive at having been a-sail for so long. In his dream, the ship sped eagerly to where he was now sitting, on a bank beside the sea. As it reached the shore, the anchor was thrown overboard, the gangplank was set down, and the girl stepped down from the ship.

When Lancelot saw her approach, he moved to greet her, though he did not know her.

'Lancelot,' said the girl, 'I have travelled some distance to find you. How strange, you don't recognise me.'

Rose Thorn wondered for a moment if the girl might be herself, if Lancelot dreamed of her, as she still did, of him. But the girl onscreen was capricious indeed, for she averted her face when he tried to look upon her.

'By the faith I owe God,' said Lancelot, 'I don't know who you are.'

The girl took him by the hand. 'You have never seen me before, Lancelot?'

Now there came a sudden flashback. Lancelot was bride's escort, transporting the Lady Guinevere to Camelot, where she was to be married to his King, Arthur. And did not this girl now have a look of Guinevere?

Guinevere. Great, thought Rose Thorn. Let's pile up all the exes onscreen. Although, come on, this is Lancelot. The future monk. There can't have been *that* many.

Lancelot took hold of the girl and embraced her. Then she bade her elven retinue to pitch a rich and splendid pavilion for them. The elves laid out a sumptuous, embroidered quilt in the middle of the tent, and beside it, a table laden with the most delectable dishes imaginable. But, before they would allow him to partake of the feast, they stripped him of his arms. He and the girl sat down to eat, only, Rose Thorn noticed, there was no grace said, and no blessing.

After they had supped, they lay together, and the camera panned backwards to reveal the shape of the shadow of the Cross falling across Lancelot, although there was no crucifix in the Pavilion. In response to this falling shadow, Lancelot himself made the sign of the cross.

In the darkened theatre, Rose Thorn gasped, then held her breath, for it was this gesture which thwarted the enchantress, Queen Morgana, and not Queen Guinevere, at all!

Morgana leapt up instantly and swept away the dream pavilion and everything that it contained.

Onscreen, Lancelot woke up suddenly, anguished, sweating and penitent. He clasped his hands in prayer. He really had lain with Morgana, though all else was enchantment. As it was, he was an honourable knight, and when his foster-aunt appeared before him in the banqueting hall that evening, her flaming hair dimmed by a black veil spangled in starry, silver thread, her large eyes filled with mysterious sorrow, he knelt and asked her to marry him.

Cue closing credits. A flag with three lions rampant on an azure background unfurled against a darkening sky.

Part II should have been the wedding episode, but the reel of film was so badly damaged that after a few flickers onscreen, a few high-pitched screeches of violins and the tintinnabulation of bells, Officer Pluto brought the double bill to an abrupt end. Anyway, Rose Thorn had seen enough. She sat there for a few moments in stunned silence, ashen-faced, biting her lips, trying to still her beating heart.

The lieutenant made herself pace all round the Mezzanine Level until she felt calmer. A thought crossed her mind, if the Conglomerate ever attacked Morgana's Avalon openly, whose side would Captain Dulac be on?

Rose Thorn walked back down the corridors to the bridge to find Captain De Lys and First Officer Sophia James peering excitedly at the vastscreen in front of them. Rose Thorn caught a glimpse of a blue and amber planet onscreen, before some words began to flicker across it.

> TYPE OF SUN: *Gamma Sculptoris Class G8 Magnitude 1.1*
> POSITION: *Southern Hemisphere - Sculptor Beacon Code SSCL 87*
> DISTANCE FROM EARTH: *155 Light Years*
> TYPE OF PLANET: Class E9. *Escape velocity 8.9 M.P.S.*
> *80 per cent surface is water.*
> *10 per cent surface is under the northern polar ice-cap.*

'Captain,' said Officer James, 'I think we've found your water world.' She read out from the screen, 'The remaining land area is distributed round the globe in the form of thousands of small, swampy islands.'

Captain De Lys leaned forwards and scrolled up the text onscreen, to read out a warning: 'Only vessels equipped for liquid surface touchdown should attempt local landings.'

'That's just the Scout ships *Icarus*, *Ganymede* and *Perilous*, then,' said Officer James.

'No, just the *Ganymede*,' said Captain De Lys. 'The *Icarus* is currently being checked over, but Engineering are saying, it might have to be taken out of service.'

'What about the *Perilous*?'

'Engineering are putting the final touches to it. They've been remodelling it as a fast courier - its engines make it capable of warp speed.'

'So, I take the *Ganymede* then,' said Officer James, 'and an Away Team of Five?'

'Absolutely,' said Captain De Lys, 'after all, it's the chance you've been waiting for - to conduct your investigations at surface as well as orbital level.'

'I can bring back some new moss and algae specimens for the hydroponics department,' said Officer James, clapping her hands in delight.

'Yes,' said Captain De Lys. 'But I'm hoping for much more than that.' She dropped her voice to a confidential whisper. 'I'm hoping that this is the planet we've been searching for, for so long. The planet we can call home.'

Lieutenant Rose Thorn's heart plunged with misgiving at the Captain's words. But she didn't know why, and she didn't want to dampen their enthusiasm. So, instead, she said to Officer James, 'I did some of my initial flight training with the *Ganymede*. Mind if I tag along with you to the flight bay?'

'You would be most welcome,' said Officer James, with a graceful inclination of her head, which, just for a moment, reminded Rose Thorn of the undulations of weeping willows beside the river in Astalot.

Conglomerate Starship Officer, Eliot Pluto, stretched back, entirely at ease in his leather office chair, the proverbial cat with the cream. The techbots had finally replaced the damaged fluorescent light bulb overhead in the Time Editing Suite. Now the quality, the clarity of light was just what he required.

'How many techbots does it take to change a lightbulb? Answers on an icky sticky post-it note, ladies and gentlemen, pur-leassse.'

Beneath the beam of sulphur yellow light, he switched on the Time Editing Suite, savouring the sounds it made as it powered up. Like the swish-swish of taffeta skirts, of the women who had lost their way in the woods and hunted hopelessly through brambles and nettles for a way to escape, at first, dismayed, then disconsolate, then distraught.

Poor, lost, little rabbits. Poor, quivering crinolines. Victorian Valerians. They never *did* have much of a chance during King Arthur II's reign. Which reminded him - he was supposed to be working his way through the histories of the earlier, Precursor Valerians, to make sure that with so many different timelines opening up, there were no anomalies, no early errors in continuity to their histories.

He began to punch up the relevant files. Look, onscreen, there was Snow White, riding into the woods, accompanied by Hunter John. For her, at least, there was nothing to fear. No alterations to make. Everything was exactly as it was supposed to be. Or was it? Surely Snow White's hemline was a little crooked.

There. With one flick of a switch, she was herself again - perfect.

Now the seven dwarves stepped onscreen, the self-styled Travellers of Space and Time, marching through a grove of trees, through invented distances that kept receding before them.

Officer Pluto sighed. It was as if he were building a house of nets, hoping to bind the narratives in, hoping they would not escape through its interstices.

'What if he were not the right person for this new job? What if he caused... grievous harm?'

He clicked those early files away and opened another he had saved as *Astalot.*

Now Lieutenant Rose Thorn strode onto screen, her blue eyes shining like water. He understood, all too well, the nature of her appeal to him. She was so like Lavenza, from that other time, back when he was a boy, back when there was all the time in the world.

'There are some eyes that can devour you.'

Lavenza, his unnatural gaming avatar. Lavenza, his preternatural treasure. Lavenza, the very pinnacle of perfection, of everything he had created her to be. And there - there! - at the mercy of his hands.

When he was a boy, he'd dreamed of the day when technology would be far enough advanced that he could bring her to life. But as he grew older, he preferred her contained within the machine, genie in a bottle, whom he could summon at will.

If she were real, she might laugh at him.

And then, by the time he was well into his thirties, and first onboard the *Joyous Gard,* another gamer had drawn her to him with his magic lasso. She went to sing instead in his enchanted cage. Officer Pluto sighed again, strummed his fingers to the beat of his own melancholy tantivy: *'Too late to impress her now with those upgrades. She won't be coming back no more, no more.'*

Another unwanted, unbidden thought sprang to his mind: Lavenza, stripped to her last nakedness, her pearlized, pixellated flesh aglow onscreen. What obscene acts might she now be performing?

Better that he had never created her at all, than that it should come to this.

Unless-?

His hands were shaking now.

He closed down the *Astalot* file, then turned off the Time Editing Suite, then switched it on again, checked the drives for malware, then recalibrated some of the programmes.

There, onscreen, was his own timeline. There he was, a boy, Eliot, in striped pyjama bottoms, sitting at a computer desk in an attic bedroom, beneath a sloping roof.

The rain was dripping down onto a skylight that shed its light onto a ZX Spectrum keyboard. It was poised, in front of a huge, old-fashioned monitor, that was surrounded by a vast sprawl of other keyboards, with wires like snakes coming out of them, that twisted round to swallow their own tails. Then too, beside the desk were the lofty towers and turrets of old hard drives, treasure-houses of arcane knowledge.

From the Time Editing Suite, Office Pluto watched as the monitor of long ago gave out an ominous, cerulean glow. He noted the spotlight on his boyish, creased brow, his pale eyes' laser-like focus, the pinprick pupils beneath a slick of blond hair. And oh, the deft intricacy of his moving fingertips! He could have been a fine piano-player, with those hands, if only he'd bothered to practise.

Instead, young Eliot was putting the final touches to the creation on his monitor screen. *Lavenza*. He was combing the pixellated tangles of her pixie locks, whilst she gazed at him.

A boy could lose himself in the blue inward heavens of those eyes.

Back in the Time Editing Suite, Officer Pluto's bulbous brow furrowed.

Not this boy.

Not that day.

Officer Pluto hit *delete* for this section of his *own* timeline. Onscreen, cogs and wheels turned and hissed. Catherine wheels of centuries span fast, then slowed right down. With a flick of a switch, he reduced the pyrotechnics of infinite possibilities to cinders.

The gleam of that singular decade began to vanish.

He watched as, on the young boy's screen, Lavenza started to fade away, the tender ghost whom he had loved.

The last aspect of her to disappear was the hurt look in her eyes.

In the Time Editing Suite, Office Pluto punched down on the keys, clicking open another file, then another, then another. Now he was spinning them all around, correcting sections of people's lives, a difficult task, for they all enclosed one another, like a system of Chinese boxes. The intimate perspectives of these lives began to shift again, in infinite combinations, infinite permutations. It was his responsibility to create the best possible reality from the vast array of options before him - and yet, to maintain a sense of equilibrium, not to go *too far*.

He wasn't convinced he could do it. Morality, ethics, integrity, like so many spinning plates, and if he were to pause in his work, or allow his attention to be distracted for just one single nanosecond, they were liable to all come crashing down.

Besides, he knew he would never forget that look.

Deleting her was his first major transgression - in the brand new Time Editing Suite.

Lavenza.

Once they had emerged from the turbo lift, Lieutenant Rose Thorn and Officer James walked along the vast Mezzanine Level. When they passed the hydroponics suite, the usually reticent Officer James began to speak, at length. As Rose Thorn listened in astonishment, she realised, the robot girl's clockwork heart was overflowing.

'An orchid, once I had,' said Officer James, 'and on the windowsill of my laboratory, did I place it. And there it was, like a light beam from a sabre, a thing of beauty and solace. And since in this laboratory, there were three male scientists who were always trying to complete me, and were rivalrous besides, always felt I much need for the reassurance which only orchids can bring.

When first I came to this starship, I had a roommate who sometimes was cruel to me, and tried to convince me of things that were not true. And this was not a good untrue, like *Singing in the Rain,* that they tell me is really in a film studio, but a bad untrue, like when the wizard tried to convince them all was Emerald in the City when it was not. Even the Captain's first planet today was not an emerald, though she wanted it to be.

Sometimes, when my roommate was too full of lies for me to even look at her, I would take the turbo lift, as we have just done, to the hydroponics suite. The door of the arboretum would slide open, and I would step out into a place of many plants from many worlds. There was a little tree with sweet fruit, and if you cut the fruit open the right way, the pip-holes made stars inside. This was an apple tree. And there were cacti from a desert planet where sands and skies were striped the colour of a tiger. And there was a creeper which every other month blossomed

193

all over in great blue flowers, though when first I saw them, I mistook them for butterflies.

There were giant ferns, and sprawling conifers, and feathery vines, and the air was so damp and humid that glad I was that the Men of Ash had painted me all over with anti-rust paint. When I walked in the arboretum and thought of the great pains they had taken with my painting, then I felt sad, and wrote them postcards in my mind. *Wishyouwerehere...* And Arthur, I missed him too, though he never was there when most I wanted him. Arthur, who had never tried to learn the Japanese language with me: Japanese, flavoured beautifully, like the first sip of jasmine tea.

But - there is a boy here, or else, young man, I should say, for you cannot call men boys except you wish to vex or flatter them. And he told me that he remembered Arthur from a long time ago, and that Arthur taught him to write poems that did not rhyme. And so I thought this boy might become my friend, and I asked his opinions on haiku, and found he had many, and so was I glad.

Sometimes we walked together in the arboretum. Once, we found a space there where the gravity was quite different from anywhere else on the ship. And then my friend, Ensign Dagonet, launched himself into its empty space. He glided through the null-grav point, his movements as precise and perfect as a Kabuki dancer's.

As he somersaulted through the air, he plucked for me a single flower. He came to a halt an arm's length from me, still floating in zero gravity. Then he presented this flower to me.

Null-grav had made it grow in a strange way. It was a spherical, rather than a tapering bloom. I was grateful then for the olfactory circuitry that allowed me to comprehend its subtle fragrance.

Moreover, this was an orchid, transformed, exquisite. And this was the most singular, ineffable, perfect moment of my life.'

Officer James bowed her head again and spoke no more until they arrived at the ship's flight bay.

The *Ganymede* was pretty much as Rose Thorn remembered it from her training days, an angular craft designed for function rather than aesthetics, although it was obvious even to Officer James that she had a soft spot for it.

Officer James slid open the port-side hydraulic door so that Rose Thorn could climb up and take a look inside.

Just as the lieutenant recalled, the flight cabin opened out onto a main compartment with a workstation containing early warning, electronic countermeasures and other equipment. Then too, there were the port and starboard stub wings to provide additional lift during atmospheric flight, as well as winglets, to reduce drag and provide step access to the wings and hull. The junior officer felt a pang of envy when she saw the side-by-side seats for the pilot and ECO beneath the large bubble canopy.

'Great Valeria! I wish I was coming with you,' she said.

'Me too,' said Officer James, 'but the Captain needs at least one competent officer by her side.'

'Why, are you taking all the best ones with you?' asked Rose Thorn, climbing down from the scout ship.

'Yes and no,' said Officer James, scrolling through the ship's crew listings on her tricorder to select her dream team. 'Depends who's off-duty, who's on-duty, and who's available.' She pressed *send* on the display unit to summon her team to join her at the main launching bay. Her message of polite invitation was sent to:

1.   Dr Jem Blake, the ship's chief medical officer, whose knowledge of alien anatomy rendered him invaluable.
2.   Ensign Alfie Blake, his sixteen-year old son, specialising in technology at college, but, for extra credit, he was half-way through an Academy exam study of Terran and alien hybrid plant-forms.
3.   Count Fyodor Illich Pavia, bridge communications officer, a fair-haired, aristocratic, Time Travelling vampire who spoke seventeen languages and was also working on a prototype for a universal translator.
4.   Sister Scarlet Steel, a recent starship recruit, on sabbatical from the Sisters of Valerian and the Academy, who, Sifu Wong claimed, was the most skilful student of qi gong he had ever encountered.
5.   Ensign Dagonet, because no mission of hers, either now or in the future, was complete without him.

A few hours after these invitations had gone out, Officer James and her team were setting the *Ganymede* down on an atoll in the northern temperate zone of the new planet. Since the *Ganymede* was now the only functioning scout ship, it had been pre-programmed to return to the *Joyous Gard* after they had landed. The Away team watched, with a certain amount of trepidation, as it soared upwards in a powerful traction beam of light.

Then Officer James and her team began to check out the terrain on the banks of a lake that stretched out, limpid and sparkling. There was a point of land which jutted down into the lake, sloping down onto a sandy beach lapped by water. Like her crewmates, Officer James had spent weeks and weeks onboard ship. Now she noted the babbling of the streams, the plash of close-darting rainbow-coloured fish, the soar and song of the birds.

Ensign Alfie, a likable boy with ginger hair, freckles and stick-out ears, was just beginning to look for new plant specimens when he noticed several patches of bare rock near the water's edge. Quickly, he informed Officer James.

'It looks as though some of the vegetation has been scraped away deliberately,' he said.

Even as Officer James peered at the bruised, slimy carpet of tendrils, she could see that it was growing back over the bare patches of rock at what their tricorders affirmed was a detectable rate.

'That means-,' she began.

'Plant specimens were removed shortly before we arrived,' said Alfie, excitedly. 'Which means-,'

'Aliens!' said Ensign Dagonet, stepping up behind them to take a look at the rock.

Officer James called Fyodor, Jem and Sister Scarlet Steel away from the lake's edge. Then she said, 'If we set up base camp here with our long range detectors, we might discover advanced life-forms existing in the swamps and seas.'

Jem and Fyodor circled the clearing and selected the best site for the shelter. Soon the whole team were busy constructing the foundations of the camp. Now came the thwack of axes echoing in the open space, then tree trunks crashed to the ground. The underbrush was cleared; forked stakes were driven into the earth; cross-pieces were laid on them, and then poles, sloping back to ground.

Officer James had untold reserves of stamina, but even she was impressed by how quickly the team erected the skeleton of a house.

'It's like the Leader's Little Hut in Valerian,' said Sister Scarlet Steel, who had only joined the sisterhood a couple of years ago, after leaving school, and had only been there a year before entering the Academy and thence the Starship Programme.

'It still needs a roof and sides though,' said Officer James. She began to help Jem and Fyodor skin the trunks of the spruce trees. After they had skinned one apiece, there was enough covering for the roof. But though the planet's two yellow suns were shining now, all the same, she was glad of her anti-rust paint in case of rain.

Supper was regulation food pellets dispensed from cannisters, although Officer James had thoughtfully tried to synthesize for each crew member what he or she liked best. For Fyodor, some kind of spiced goulash, washed down with fiery schnapps, for Sister Scarlet Steel, great mouthfuls of Haloumi cheese sticks with a tangy Thai sauce. For Jem and Alfie, fish and chips, though Jem had beer-battered cod with ketchup, and Alfie, scampi, with a piquant tartare sauce. Officer James had no physical requirement for food, but she ate pellets of sushi to keep the others company. Ensign Dagonet ate sushi likewise and pulled out a flask of jasmine tea to share with his commanding officer.

Their campfire spluttered and flared in the clearing in front of them.

Whilst they ate, a drop or two of rain began to fall. The sky darkened; the wind rose up so that the trees around them shivered, then cracked, like whips. The team hurried into their shelter, taking the remnants of their supper with them, eating it as best they could. The green and purple rain fell harder; their fire began to fume.

Now tree branches were laden down with the burden of heavy-falling rain. They could not leave their shelter without getting drenched. The rain swirled into the shelter's open front and wet the bottom of their blankets.

In a huff, Fyodor pulled out his tricorder and began to tap out a report about unsatisfactory planetary conditions. Soon it was winging its way through hyperspace to the starship. Meanwhile, Jem felt a drop of water on his face, so he shifted his head to a dry place. Then, as dampness spread across his back, he discovered his blanket was drenched. Torn between wanting to complain, and not wanting to, he settled for scowling.

'Dad, dad, the roof's leaking,' Alfie said.

'Roof? Call it a sieve, more like,' Jem grumbled, shaking water out of his ears.

'Why all the fuss?' asked Sister Scarlet Steel, who was sitting in the only dry spot in the shelter, lighting up a cigarette with all the careless insouciance of her twenty years.

'Nessa,' scolded Jem, 'you do all those workouts and training, and then you wreck yer lungs with smoking.' He shook his head, showering her with drops of rain.

'Gis a smoke,' said Alfie, so she swung her plaits round and handed her one lit cigarette to him.

'In Russia,' began Fyodor, so that more than one of his listeners stifled a groan, 'I had palace, and many, many acres of land. Here, I share tent, ten foot square.'

'Yes, it's wonderful, isn't it,' said Ensign Dagonet, without a trace of irony.

'Sure,' said Fyodor. '*Vivere memento.*'

'That's the Brunwych school motto,' said Nessa, her momentary excitement overcoming her pose of cool nonchalance. 'But I don't remember seeing you there.'

Fyodor gave her a disdainful look, for he was obviously at least a decade older than her, and that was without considering any timeline anomalies. Nevertheless, she had at least provided him with a welcome opportunity to talk about himself. 'I was, what word you use, *home-schooled*,' he said. 'My mother came from a family ennobled by Catherine the Great and she wished to teach me herself. Then I had private tutor. I wanted to learn Art of Time Travel, and he taught me, a little, a very little.'

Nessa looked as though she wanted to say something, so Fyodor continued, 'Then I transferred to Brunwych Sixth Form after school became co-ed. My tutor said I had outstripped him in learning, and he could no longer teach me.' There wasn't a trace of modesty or affection to his voice; in fact, he sounded rather annoyed with his erstwhile mentor.

'Maybe he felt unappreciated and just confiscated himself?' muttered Nessa, but so quietly, that no-one except Alfie heard her.

Fyodor stared moodily into rainy space, imagining the golden curlicues and pendant crystal drops of his former rococo chandeliers, no doubt.

Meanwhile, Ensign Dagonet was no longer even listening. He was staring at Officer James, who, to the minor resentment of her colleagues, had unfurled her umbrella inside the shelter. But it was her face which had caught the Ensign's attention. She looked more alive than he had ever her seen before. Her brown eyes were wide open in rapture. Her lips parted, and, oblivious to them all, she began to sing, in a sweet, croaky voice, 'I'm singin' in the rain, /Just singin' in the rain/What a glorious feeling/I'm happy again...'

Whilst Officer James was leading her *reconnaissance* mission down on the surface of the planet, the bridge vastscreen flickered back into life.

Lieutenant Rose Thorn shifted over from the flight navigation workstation to Fyodor's communication panel. 'Hailing frequencies open,' she said, punching in an intricate sequence of keys and codes, grateful that all bridge crew were trained in standard workstation operations. 'An envoy from Avalon wishes to communicate with us.'

A moment later, a man's face painted in perfectly symmetrical black and white diamonds, with a pirate's hat perched on top of his dark hair, appeared onscreen.

'All hail to you, Captain De Lys,' he greeted the captain in her chair on the bridge. 'I am Admiral Tevlev of her Majesty's Royal Fleet. And it is on behalf of our most illustrious Majesty, Queen Morgana, that I greet you now. She wishes me to inform you that if you negotiate with her in person, her enemies, the Outer Reception, have declared they will temporarily halt their attacks on her domain.'

'What attack?' asked Aurélie. 'Nothing is showing up on our sensors.'

'Adjust your sensors then,' said the Admiral. 'The Collodian is under fire.'

Even as he spoke, the starship shook and shuddered so that she lurched forwards in her chair and the bridge crew were forced to cling to bars, desks, workstations, anything they could. The tube lights above them flickered, and the bulb above the magiscam blew. Warning alarms began to sound, *'Amber alert, Amber alert.'* The vastscreen juddered then steadied; finally, ship, bridge, and crew righted itself.

Aurélie adjusted the back of her chair, took a deep breath, then sat upright. 'And what is the Outer Reception?' she asked.

'Rebels, thieves, brigands, the lot of them,' said the Admiral. 'Traitors to Valerian and Avalon, who have renounced the authority of Her Majesty and her right to fabricate a better life though the warp and weft of the Collodian. Why, they mean to rip apart the Queen's Cloak of Dreams! But you will be safe waiting out the siege with us in the holdfast, my lady.'

'But how do we know it's the Outer Reception and not the queen herself who's carrying out this attack?' asked Rose Thorn of the Captain.

'On my honour as a pirate officer in her Majesty's fleet...' Admiral Tevlev began.

'Unfortunately, the word of someone unknown to me carries little weight,' said Aurélie. 'But if our previous ship's captain, Captain Dulac, will appear onscreen and guarantee my safety, and the safety of this ship and all its crew, then I will come and parley with the queen.'

'Very good,' said Admiral Tevlev. 'I'm sure Captain Dulac will be happy to do that. Afterwards, we will send over the co-ordinates so that you can land a scout ship away from the Collodian marshes.'

'All this had better be worth it,' said Aurélie, grimly. 'I have an Away Team exploring a water world. You're taking us eight light years off our course.'

'But surely there's no-where you'd rather be than... the Collodian,' said Admiral Tevlev, thinking himself very clever for parroting the weekly programme announcement for *Collodian Star*. A moment later, the vastscreen broke up entirely, so, whatever he said next, no-one knew.

The following morning, on the planet that Officer James had tentatively named Aquatica, the sky was still leaking, and so was the shelter. And yet, when she pulled back the blanket that was serving as a curtain, she wondered if the rain had temporarily ceased at some point in the night. This was because, beside the charred and blackened logs where the fire had blazed, there was now a huge footprint in the mud.

She took out her tricorder and began to measure the footprint. It was thirty centimetres wide and fifty centimetres long, splayed, hexagonal, and, she assumed, from a webbed foot.

As the suns began to dry up the rain and mists, the rest of the team slowly woke for breakfast. They were sitting and eating their food pellets, still beneath their shelter, when Ensign Dagonet called out, 'Look! Over there!' He pointed towards the exposed rocks jutting out of the lake. His crewmates saw then an amphibious form, perhaps seven or eight feet tall, emerging from the water to bask on the rock. It was roughly humanoid in form, but green and scaly, and yes, with webbed extremities.

'That can't be the only one,' said Sister Scarlet Steel.

She was right, for soon they caught sight of many more, swimming through the water in shoals.

'It seems they like to come to the surface as soon as the suns are out,' said Ensign Alfie.

'Must be that they're cold-blooded critters,' said Jem, 'er... I mean... life forms.'

'We don't have the resources here to investigate all this now,' said Officer James, clapping her hands, half in dismay, half in delight. 'We need to go back to the ship and order different investigative floating stations to be set up where we've made these sightings.' She began to imagine the full-scale research mission that the Captain would authorise, and that she, Sophia, would lead.

'Yes,' said Fyodor, 'and we don't know if species would share planet with us.' He began to wonder whether the amphibious beings would be willing to enter study chambers and submit to close examination, and, if they did, how on earth would he communicate with them.

Officer James sent off her report to the starship that a major new species had been discovered on a planet potentially capable of sustaining human life. She also supplied their coordinates so that the scout craft could return to them. Whilst they were waiting for the arrival of the *Ganymede*, they began to dismantle their shelter, which, only yesterday, had been a source of so much pride. Now, beaten down by the wind and rain, it seemed a shabby object, and the charred remnants of their fire heralded no bright promise for the future, but rather the extinction of life.

Nevertheless, as they soared back to the *Joyous Gard,* they were hopeful that their news about the planet might create a bit of a stir. Unfortunately, once the *Ganymede* had docked and they had been through the requisite medical checks and debriefings, they were dismayed to learn that Captain De Lys was no longer at the ship's helm. Lieutenant Rose Thorn thankfully relinquished the captain's chair to First Officer James, and quickly explained what had happened in their absence.

'So, the Captain took the *Perilous* down into the Collodian in the middle of an attack?' said Officer James. 'Who went with her?'

'There was a temporary ceasefire,' said Rose Thorn, 'during which we had assurances of her safety from Captain Dulac. So, she went alone.'

'How do you know that was Captain Dulac, and not a hologram, programmed to give those assurances?' asked Officer James.

'I don't,' said Rose Thorn, and with a sinking heart, she recalled the Mothercrystal where she had been held captive, and the hologram of her cousin Blancheflor, proud and beautiful, stationed there. 'But Captain De Lys insisted…'

'The Captain is inclined to be impulsive,' said Officer James, lowering her voice, so that only Rose Thorn and not the rest of the crew on the bridge could hear.

'Pot, kettle, black,' mumbled Rose Thorn.

'Meaning?'

'Didn't you once set fire to the laboratory *where you lived* by misdirecting a toaster?' asked Rose Thorn.

'A lifetime ago,' sighed Officer James. 'This is all very bad news though,' she added. 'Have we had any direct communication from the Captain since she left?'

'Before her communicator went out of range, she said she had landed safely on the planet's surface and that the Admiral was escorting her to the Castle of Chalis,' said Rose Thorn.

'The Castle of Chalis?' said Officer James. 'Not the Winter Palace? Is there anyone in the Collodian we can trust to liase with us about the Captain's safety?'

'There's Admiral Tevlev,' said Rose Thorn, doubtfully. Then, as she recalled his perfectly painted face dismantling on screen, she shook her head. 'No,' she said, 'better yet, there's Tallulah Mae Jackson, operating the Mothercrystal. Former Sister of Valerian. Codename: Golden Claw.' Privately, she hoped her hunch was right, that Tallulah would side with them to relay information about the Captain's whereabouts and safety. That Tallulah would side with them on what was taking shape in her mind as a very dangerous mission. But first, there was someone else, equally important, that she needed to contact.

Lieutenant Rose Thorn opened the hailing frequencies channel, and after she had located his coordinates, began a long, complicated conversation with Merlin, still in his eerie at Brunwych. After that, she dug out the coordinates for the Mothercrystal and tapped out a heartfelt message to Tallulah, following which, her friend called her, and the two women began to speak.

After she had disembarked from the *Perilous*, Captain De Lys was greeted by Admiral Tevlev, who had travelled to meet her by himself. They walked a little way across the valley that lay on the outskirts of the Collodian, then paused whilst Captain De Lys filled her gourd with the spring water that gushed from one of the rock outcrops. She tasted it. It was clear - and sweet.

'We need to follow the path beside the rail tracks,' he said, before they jerked backwards to avoid a crowd of spirits that had loomed up out of the gloom.

At one point, Aurélie espied the intertwined, skeletal branches of a grove of trees. Hanging from one of the branches was a pink neon sign that read, 'LOVE.' The O and the V were blackened and dead, but the L and E glimmered at pink half-power.

Presently, Admiral Tevlev led her into the courtyard of what Aurélie recognised from her research was the Winter Palace. The courtyard was immense and paved in coloured stones. Over there was the famous Arch of Regeneration, painted and beaded with strange symbols, and there, the imposing Mothercrystal, lit up by pillars of crystal, selenite and white limestone.

There were a thousand glass eyes shining down on the Mothercrystal, and Aurélie guessed that a broadcast was taking place. But she had little time to play tourist, since the Admiral led her out through the courtyard and on towards another castle.

As far as Aurélie could tell, this second castle was a strange amalgamation of different architectural styles, with Gothic spires, gargoyles and Tudor gables, that combined vanished glory with machine-made cogs, bolts and gleaming sensor displays. Above the drawbridge were carved three stone chalices, which made Aurélie pause, and wish she still had the Holy Grail with her. But she had sent it to the Sisters of Valerian years ago, not long after she had returned from Shoreditch. She believed it was now adorning an altar in their Temple, there for safekeeping, and veneration.

'Welcome to the Castle of Chalis,' said Admiral Tevlev, nodding at the stone chalices above.

The Castle of Chalis! That was where Rose Thorn had found the tapestry with Guinan and Pippin hiding in it, a few years ago. Aurélie had never discovered exactly what Guinan thought he was doing there, though she'd asked him many times. Despite his replies, she'd wondered if it was an undercover mission?

Guinan! It was months now since she'd last seen him. Queen Morgana had sent him to oversee a mining vessel on the far side of the galaxy, a job, he had angrily text-protested to Aurélie, was far beneath his abilities.

'What about your Professorship at Brunwych?' Aurélie had texted back.

'Short-term contract, came to an end,' he texted. 'They say I'm supposed to give the other fellas a chance.'

'Well, if Kilkenny can read now...' Aurélie texted back, doubtfully. 'And if you don't like the mining ship, you can always Time Travel your way out of it.'

'Time Travel isn't to be used for personal gain, Aurélie,' he text replied, sternly, in a way that reminded her of the old, venturesome days.

'Neither are the resources of the Alpha Centauri diamond mines,' texted Aurélie. 'But that doesn't stop Queen Morgana. I think you should give up working for her. Like I said, there's always a place for you here, on the *Joyous Gard,* if you want it.'

'We've been through this before...,' Guinan texted back. 'I need to stay in the queen's favour so I can best serve the realm.'

They left it there, since it was the same old argument that never got resolved. Still, he sent her a few pictures of the diamond mines, and a really sparkly one of the biggest diamond he had ever seen, except for the one that had crushed Clairmont all those centuries ago. Oh, and there was also a nice pic of the satellite mining craft orbiting Alpha Centauri by sunset.

Like this, they kept in touch.

What she wouldn't give now, the largest diamond that ever was, to see Guinan again, popping up out of nowhere, large as life but dwarf-sized. Instead, she was forced to follow on behind Admiral Tevlev as he led the way through the castle, pointing out places of interest as if he were a tour guide.

There, with three guards outside it, was the Queen's bedchamber, and there, just up ahead, the Queen's ballroom. As they went past, Aurélie glimpsed beaten silver mirrors behind wall sconces, which made the torchlight doubly bright. Its walls were panelled with richly carved wood, and above the main floor were some high arched windows and a gallery for musicians. Here, a servant led a girl with a lute around her neck down the gallery's spiral staircase.

But then Admiral Tevlev, all lanky six foot of him, ushered them on, into the square fortress that was Morgana's Holdfast, the castle within a castle, ten feet high, built of rough-hewn stone.

As they stood at the very door of the hall at the heart of the Holdfast, the Prince Consort hurried towards them, keen to greet his former History Officer. But before he could utter more than a few words, Admiral Tevlev turned to Sir Lancelot, now clad in full armour, and interrupted him.

'The Queen has summoned her ladies, and Captain De Lys, to wait out the siege here. You, sir, are required elsewhere.'

'Where?' asked Lancelot, gripping the jewelled hilt of his sword.

'The Wharves,' said Admiral Tevlev.

With a forlorn look at his former friend, Captain Dulac turned on his heels and departed.

The threshold of Compagnie Hall was guarded by two soldiers, and a minstrel, who sat at the foot of the door with a ceremonial trumpet across his knees. He rose when he saw Aurélie. Admiral Tevlev gave her a ceremonial half-bow of farewell, and then the minstrel ushered her inside.

Aurélie glanced all around the hall. Its interior was comprised of fine oak panelling, partly covered by heavy velvet draperies. These permitted no natural light to enter the gloomy hall and muffled the sound of war and prayer alike. Nevertheless, there were torches, which shimmered brightly against the darkness of those velvet drapes.

At the trestle table that ran the length of the hall, just about every noblewoman of Avalon was seated, every elf, fae, fairy, dame, damsel, mother, wife, daughter, sister. The menfolk must all be away fighting - who? Exactly? Admiral Tevlev had mentioned the Outer Reception. Aurélie wondered whether this was another name for the Renegade Conglomerate, and whether, by allying with Queen Morgana, she would be opposing everything that, ideologically, she held dear.

At that moment, the royal steward cried, 'All rise for Queen Morgana of Avalon.' The elves, fairies, faes all stood up, and smoothed down their skirts and wings.

The minstrel blew a resounding welcome on his trumpet as Queen Morgana entered Compagnie Hall. Her gown was forest green, stitched all over with gold, and her dagged sleeves showed a lining of gold satin. Masses of red hair tumbled to her bare shoulders in thick curls. Around her slender neck hung a rope of diamonds, twisted with rubies. The honey glint from the hall torchlight softened her, despite the hectic flare of colour flitting across her cheeks and the unearthly glitter in her eyes.

'Be seated all,' the Queen said, 'and Welcome.' Henri, her footman, held her chair back; Josef, the butler, more bird-like than ever, performed the same service for Aurélie at the queen's right hand side. And yet, thought Aurélie, was there fear in the eyes of Henri, now serving food and wine, and in the hacking cough of Josef? Even the queen's ladies and handmaidens did not dare to raise their voices beyond a stifled whisper.

Queen Morgana beckoned to her footman for another serving of wine, a purple vintage, bubbling as it was poured from the decanter to the very rim of her goblet.

'And one for Captain De Lys,' said the Queen, but the footman shook his head.

'That's the last of it,' he said, tersely, whipping the decanter away before the queen could check. After a moment's whispering to Josef, some more wine from another barrel was located, and another goblet, equally rich and bubbling was poured.

Aurélie took a few cautious sips, then gazed at the queen, who was drinking heavily. But the wine only seemed to make her more beautiful, for now her cheeks were flushed, and her eyes shone ever more brightly.

However, only Aurélie and the queen were drinking. None of the ladies of the court were even touching the broth that lay before them. To encourage them, Aurélie took a spoonful, and found it wholesome, hearty, and flavoured with tarragon. But their reluctance was more contagious than her enthusiasm, and after one mouthful, she put her spoon back down upon the table.

Somehow, more and more wine was being poured, and Aurélie found she was drinking it. Admiral Tevlev re-entered the hall to come and stand beside the Queen.

'The Summer Palace has gone up in flames, your Majesty,' he said.

'Not another conflagration,' sighed the Queen, whilst all the fairies flittered and fluttered.

'Well,' said Admiral Tevlev, 'apart from that one fireball destroying the palace, the Collodian and its valleys remain intact.'

'And my Lady Blancheflor?'

'She is within the Mothercrystal at Beaurepaire, recording her broadcast message. Tallulah has sent me word, the princess is doing a fine job of raising morale.'

'Which is precisely why she was chosen for the task,' said Queen Morgana. 'Anything else?'

'Your Majesty,' Admiral Tevlev added, 'the guards caught two of the grooms and a maidservant trying to leave the stables with three of your horses.'

'Traitors,' said the queen. 'The punishment is beheading. Take them to the dungeons with the other prisoners, until a date for their execution can be arranged.' Once the Admiral had departed, she turned to Aurélie and said, 'As a starship captain, I expect you know this already, but Fear is the coin that buys Loyalty.'

'I thought it was Love,' said Aurélie, 'and that Loyalty came free.'

The queen's face darkened. 'A captain and so naïve?' she slurred. 'But then, what do you know about love - or loyalty, for that matter? Why, I have seen and done such things - Henri, more wine!'

Henri stepped forwards to fill the queen's goblet, whilst other servants cleared the soup tureens and bowls, to replace them with plates of venison pie. Only the Fairy Bryony, who had a hearty appetite for one so dainty, took a few mouthfuls.

The last course was *tarte au citron,* served with great wheels of camembert, succulent and gooey. The scent of lemons drifted through the hall as the painted admiral returned once more to the side of the queen. 'The Conglomerate have landed men on the jousting field, and there are more coming across. The Gatehouse is under attack, but fortunately we had evacuated it some two hours ago.'

'So there was no-one there to defend it?' said the Queen, drily. 'Bravo.' Her eyes narrowed. 'And where *is* the Prince Consort now?'

'On your orders, he is still at the Wharves,' said the Admiral, 'unloading weapons from the cargo ships.'

'He is now needed elsewhere,' said the Queen. 'Tell the Captain of the Dragoons that Prince Lancelot is to be returned to his quarters so he can continue work on his defence plans.'

Horse. Stable-door. Bolted, thought Aurélie. Why am I here? What is all this? A setup?

'Very good, your Majesty.'

The queen turned and smiled brightly at the strangely silent assembled company. Then she reached out and touched Aurélie's hair, brushing it lightly away from her neck. 'And so, Captain De Lys,' she said, 'at last we get to the real reason why I have summoned you here.'

Aurélie flinched at the queen's touch, then recalled she was, in effect, a distant ancestor. 'I thought my presence was required to prevent these attacks from the Outer Reception,' she replied.

'It's much too late in the day for that,' said the Queen. 'You are here...' she paused, then said, all in a rush, 'you are here to become our latest *Collodian Star,* so that we can observe whether you suffer any ill effects from the process.'

'I'm almost sure I didn't sign up for that when I agreed to come here,' said Aurélie. 'You had better explain.'

212

The queen licked her lips, and now there was a cat-like glitter to her eyes. 'Following my orders, Ambassador Guinan Guineafowl placed an implant in your head, some years ago, just when Valerian was emerging from lockdown. Since that time, I have been tracking everything you do, and tonight, we wish to begin curating your memories for television broadcast.'

'I don't believe you,' Aurélie said.

'Don't you?' said the queen. 'Haven't you noticed any particular memory lapses?'

'No, what you said about Guinan, I mean,' said Aurélie. 'He wouldn't do that.'

'Wouldn't he?' said the queen. 'Who else has been that close to you, in all this time?'

'But I've known him for many years now,' Aurélie replied.

'Well, of course, he had to make it look convincing by building up a rapport,' said Morgana, 'and doubtless there were a few advantages for him along the way...'

'You're an evil woman,' Aurélie said, as sudden fear and anger rose within her, so strong it made her gag. After all, she had never been quite clear whose side Guinan was on. He said he served the realm, but more than once she had thought, he served himself.

'And *you*, my dear, *you* are our latest television star,' Queen Morgana replied. Her eyes, a smoky shade of tawny green, narrowed suspiciously. 'Come now, Captain De Lys, all this fuss, what memories are so precious to you that you fear losing them?'

Just for a moment, there they were, in her mind's eye, Aurélie's ruby slippers, whirring and skimming across the dance floor with the Plato-loving skinny Irish builder's boots. And above them, a glitterball, filling the dance hall with pink, red, and purple sparks, gleaming like a jewel, just beyond the wall of a cave. And then another memory, not of that time at all: a child with fair hair draped across a moon dial, a girl from long ago.

'Well?' asked Queen Morgana.

'None of your business,' Aurélie said, shortly.

'But we all have to make sacrifices,' said Queen Morgana. 'I myself have lost so many things, so many people that I loved, some might say I have elevated loss into an art-form.'

'You call your television show, Art?' Aurélie retorted. 'And in any case, how do your losses give you the right to harvest other people's memories? To deprive them of their choicest treasures?'

At the direct challenge, Queen Morgana looked suddenly bewildered. She sifted her hands through the air, as if they were nets to catch memories. 'But I have lost cities,' she said. 'Lovely ones, countries, continents. Old Valerian hardly exists anymore...' She held up a thimble she wore round her neck, to show the captain.

'The Great Explosion?' Aurélie said. 'But what caused it?'

'Increased combustion to generate...' Then her eyes narrowed again. 'I'm hardly likely to tell *you* that.' She continued, 'Avalon had to close its borders to refugees from Valerian. We simply don't have the space. So I began a starship programme to find anyone who wishes to go there, a new planet. But in the meantime, I need to give people Hope by broadcasting better times. Plug them in and let them dream. Maybe then they won't notice how bad things have become.'

'Oh believe me, we've noticed,' Aurélie said.

'*You* may have done, Ms De Lys, but you are not representative of the entire population. If you were, you would have signed up for the Collodian Program like so many others have before you. And yet, thanks to Guinan,

214

we have your implant, and after all, the art of losing isn't hard to master.'

'But I don't want to lose myself,' Aurélie said.

'I don't need your consent,' Queen Morgana replied. 'And besides, it's too late. Your memories have already been transferred to a celestine storage unit, and soon they will be broadcast. Though, since the regrettable consequences to Lieutenant Lanval, we too have learned a lesson, which is why you will be closely observed for any side-effects you may experience.'

'Observing brain damage does nothing to reverse it,' replied Aurélie.

A startled look slid into the queen's eyes, then she continued, as smoothly as if she hadn't heard, 'This implant is perhaps gentler than the celestine clips, less invasive, and so it may be that your memory loss is minimal.'

'But how do I know?' Aurélie asked.

'You don't,' said Queen Morgana, 'which is the beauty of the implant system. And now, Admiral Tevlev will escort you to your cell, er, medical observation chamber, for the night.'

Aurélie was led to a white-uniformed nurse in an antechamber. The nurse took her fingerprints, and there followed a few minutes in the BOSS chair (Body Orifice Security Scanner), a kind of metal detector. After that came a few precursory checks of her weight, heart-rate and blood pressure, and then Aurélie was told to enter a cell with bars and a bed.

The nurse left her there with a plate of ginger biscuits and a goblet of some herbal concoction she said was valerian, to help her sleep. Aurélie ate the biscuits but decided not to trust the contents of the goblet. Instead, she lay down on the bed and tried her communicator and I-phone again. Nothing.

So she drifted into sleep, and in her dreams, she had the strange feeling that she was twenty years old again, an art student. She was queuing up outside the Collodian Cinema on Manresa Road. Her date had gone to fetch her toffee popcorn. She had her whole life ahead of her. There was nothing wrong at all.

Then, still sleeping, she thought she heard someone say, loudly, *'Don't fuck it up.'* The voice sounded a bit like Rose Thorn's - or someone else's, someone sassy, like her. In fact, the voice sounded so loud, and so real, that it jolted Aurélie wide awake. It reminded her of that strange clairaudient moment years ago, when she'd thought Morleon was speaking inside her mind.

Was he talking to her now? After all these years? But to survive that fire at the sanatorium just to end up a prisoner in one of Queen Morgana's dungeons seemed a waste of good telepathy. So she tried to repeat over the Time Travel spell, to get herself the hell out of there, only to find she could not remember the second half.

What other memories had she lost? In the near-darkness, she shook her head in dismay. What should she do next?

'Have you tried praying?' asked Guinan quietly in the darkness, just inches from her ear.

Quickly, she lit the torch on her I-Phone (which needed an upgrade.) Her eyes adjusted to the beam of light, to take in his short, stocky frame, that began with grizzled grey hair and ended with the pointed curl of his Turkish slippers.

'Aren't you supposed to be orbiting Alpha Centauri?' she mumbled.

'Your friend Rose Thorn sent out a powerful distress signal,' he replied. 'And, obviously, I'm the answer to every distressed maiden's prayers.'

'The day you alight upon a maiden in this galaxy,' Aurélie retorted, 'you just let me know. Even Rose Thorn isn't Miss Butter-Wouldn't-Melt anymore. But how did you get here? There are guards outside... Queen Morgana...'

'Queen Morgana thinks I'm on her side,' said Guinan. 'I persuaded her that I might be able to influence you to join us.'

'But *are* you on her side?' asked Aurélie. 'She said... she said you put an implant inside my mind.'

'Well,' said Guinan, slowly, 'that's because I did. But that was partly to prevent the queen from doing anything worse to you, herself. She's no stranger to paranoia and suspicion. But this way, she's been able to see that your activities are sufficiently innocuous that you mean her no real harm.'

'Innocuous? Thanks. Traitor.'

'I always told you,' said Guinan, 'I serve the realm. And myself. And sometimes, just sometimes, mind you, Aurélie,' he scolded, 'long-suffering damsels.'

'I'm not one of those,' she replied, 'I'll be sixty this year.'

'All right,' said Guinan, 'You're not a damsel and I'm not long-suffering.'

'What do you mean?'

'Well, I meantersay, there I am, orbiting Alpha-Centauri, minding my own business, when your friend drags me away from my very important mining observations...'

'That you hate,' said Aurélie.

'Never mind that. You're in no position to argue with me. Because, as I was saying, your friend drags me away from my very important mining business, and I find you here, in the queen's darkest dungeon, wondering which of your memories have been wiped, *ergo* you are absolutely the most distressed damsel I ever did see.'

'Is that so? What about that green alien girl with the third...?'

'We're not in touch anymore. And we're not talking about her anyway, we're talking about you.'

'*I'm* talking about her,' said Aurélie.

'Only so you can win the argument,' said Guinan. 'But Aurélie, you must know, you get yourself into some terrible scrapes at times, you certainly do.'

'Maybe I should join the Sisters of Valerian, then,' said Aurélie wistfully.

'Or just rejoin the starship,' said Guinan. 'Shot of rum in the legit. Grail, knock it back quick, the implant will melt, and you'll be right as rain.'

'That's a fine idea,' said Aurélie. 'If only we had some rum. And if I hadn't sent the Holy Grail to the Temple of the Sisters of Valerian. Where's your alternate Grail?'

'Pippin borrowed it for *Show and Tell* with the kids at the school. But we can manage without it, just this once,' said Guinan. 'Because water into rum is quite an easy spell,' he added, 'and then, if I draw on the Process of Transubstantiation, all implants, alien and otherwise, should dissolve.'

'You're back in touch with Merlin again, aren't you?'

'We've been corresponding, yes,' said Guinan. 'In fact, I've been helping him out with a thing or two,' he continued, with a touch of the old pride that she liked to see. 'Now, water, please. Shake a leg.'

Aurélie searched around her cell, finally locating her gourd with the last of the spring water. Guinan waved his hands over it, muttering something that sounded a bit like, *forfuckssake,* but hopefully wasn't. Then he handed the entire concoction over to Aurélie.

'I don't normally care for spirits,' she said.

'Drink,' said Guinan.

So she did. The feeling of heaviness and oppression above her right eye began to ease, to melt away, in fact. Emboldened, she asked, 'Are you coming with me, back to the ship?'

'And bid farewell to my very important mining business?' he said.

She nodded.

'If I do that,' said Guinan, 'then I lose everything I've built up here, in Queen Morgana's realm.'

'Then lose it,' said Aurélie.

'It's true, I really don't like overseeing mining anymore...' mused Guinan.

'Is that a *yes* or a *no*?' asked Aurélie as she made the interesting discovery that she could now smile without her head hurting. So there in the darkness, with his reply just a few inches from her ear, she did.

Shortly before Guinan appeared in Aurélie's dungeon in the Castle of Chalis, Tallulah was busy fibbing to the three guards outside the queen's bedchamber. She was telling them she had brought the queen a message from her granddaughter, Blancheflor.

'Which is *what,* exactly?' asked the brightest of the guards. He was tall, with a gleam of low cunning in his dark grey eyes. Like the other guards, he wore a plush burgundy silk uniform, with gold embroidered buttons, piping, and epaulettes.

'Certainly not for *your* ears, Dillon,' said Tallulah, making her voice sound as shocked as possible. 'Say, when are you gentlemen coming by to our Harvesting

Chambers? I don't recall seeing any of your names on our lists. Dillon, Smudger, Polparrot...'

'The Queen's personal guards are exempt from the process,' said Dillon. 'In case there are any... you know...'

'Dangerous repercussions, side-effects?' said Tallulah, her dark eyes gleaming. 'But it's quite safe these days. Well, I say *safe* but there's always some collateral damage. Still, you don't need to worry about that. If it happens to you, you'll be way beyond feeling it. Besides, Her Majesty will be so happy to hear you've volunteered for the Collodian Programme.'

'What do you mean?' asked Dillon.

'I think you'll find if you don't let me in to pass on Princess Blancheflor's message, you'll be on the volunteer list for the Harvesting Chambers first thing tomorrow morning.'

'But that isn't what *volunteering* means,' spluttered Dillon scratching his head and turning to his fellows, who, alas, could not help him.

Though Smudger, a shorter guard, dumpy in his uniform, though proud of the beading on his cuffs, which he stroked with a certain, delicate relish, piped up, 'The Queen's asleep. They had to bring her in and lie her down on the bed.'

'Exhausted with the pressures of governance during a siege, no doubt,' said Tallulah.

'But she hates being woken up,' said Polparrot, the third guard, a look of genuine alarm flitting across his smooth face. 'She throws slippers and trays, and everything...'

'That's only at the Prince Consort,' said Tallulah. 'She won't do that to *me.*'

So, finally, the guards stepped aside to allow Tallulah to enter the darkened room where the drugged queen lay.

Tallulah's keen eyes grew accustomed to the gloom, and she was able to make out the shape of the four-poster bed, with a cabinet beside it, on a raised platform in the centre of the royal chamber.

She paced over to the window and looped back one of the heavy tapestry curtains. Now she could see to light a candle. That lit, she returned to the bed, and held it to the queen's sleeping face.

For a single moment, Tallulah felt a pang of that fatal emotion, *pity*. For, by candlelight, and in repose, the queen looked young, lovely and innocent, with the ruddy halo of her hair all about her, the pallor of sleep upon her cheeks, and her lips parted, as if in prayer.

She didn't look like a Collodian Star at all, thought Tallulah, not like one of those Technicolour high-definition 6D-er dames, hell no, she looked more like one of the old-time storybook princesses, like a precursor Valerian; hell, right now, she looked a bit like Blancheflor - or Rose Thorn, back when she was still Elaine.

'Trick of the light,' Tallulah told herself, firmly. She put the candle down on the cabinet beside the bed, and reached into the pouch that was clipped to her combat utility belt. Now she drew out the pair of celestine clips. These, she swiftly attached to one of the drugged queen's index fingers.

'Ravenglass next year,' the queen mumbled in her sleep.

'Whatever you say, Sleeping Beauty,' said Tallulah, touched, despite herself. Morgana's home with her first husband, King Urien, had been in Ravenglass. 'Whatever you say.'

But then, more to herself, she added, 'Don't fuck it up,' because the queen had slender fingers, and the second clip had already begun to slide off.

'For fuck's sake,' Tallulah cried. Her voice sounded loud in the quiet, candlelit chamber. She gritted her teeth, and then, once again, she gripped hold of the celestine clip between her fingertips. Hard as she could, she pushed down on its lever.

Whilst the denizens of Avalon lay sleeping, Lieutenant Rose Thorn was dreaming in her cabin on board the *Joyous Gard*. She dreamt that she was back at the altar of the Temple of the Sisters of Valerian. There she was, in the midst of dance. Her head was light, her body weightless, and, barefoot in her robes, she danced across the centuries.

Suddenly, in her dream, the queen's guards, closely followed by Queen Morgana herself, burst into the Temple. They began to remove the statues and incense, to hack at the precious stones that decorated the sacred altar - and even to chip away the name of the Goddess Valeria, worked in gold symbols in the mosaic floor.

'The Goddess Valeria is an ancient goddess, who protects our hearths and homes,' protested Rose Thorn in her dream.

'But she must give way to me,' Queen Morgana shrieked, the worst caricature of herself. 'I must have the worship of all my people. There can be no other god but me.'

Rose Thorn woke from her dream, bathed in sweat.

'Lights,' she called, and then she swung her bare feet out of bed, to fetch a glass of water from the kitchen area. She gulped the cool liquid down, as if it could quench, not so much her dream, but her sudden realisation that she really didn't want to return to the Temple of the Sisters of Valerian.

Ever.

In the Castle of Chalis, in the darkness of Queen Morgana's dungeon, Rose Thorn's friends were also finding it difficult to stay asleep. Or at least, Aurélie could have slept just fine, but Guinan wouldn't stop talking.

'The trouble with this bed, Aurélie,' Guinan complained, for the umpteenth time, 'is that it's very small.'

Aurélie thought to herself, well, no, it hadn't got any bigger since he'd last said it. 'And yet, Guinan,' she whispered, 'you're not very tall.'

'A scurrilous rumour put about by my enemies to discredit me,' he replied. 'Why aren't you asleep, Aurélie? Don't worry about a thing, I'll smuggle you out of here in the morning. It'll be easy when they're changing over the guards.'

'Yes, you could always disguise me as a boy - or a washerwoman,' she replied.

'Credit me with more ingenuity than that,' he said. 'Didn't I once dress you in dark blue silk? As I recall, you never looked lovelier.'

'That's right,' said Aurélie. 'Magick in the café, and then we went off to the Elvis bar.' She was just beginning to smile at the memory, when her smile was caught by something small and hard. 'Guinan,' she said, as she reached up to rub her cheek, 'why is there a pebble in your shirt pocket?'

'Lummy,' said Guinan, 'if I hadn't forgotten the celestine. Merlin sent it back to me. Living backwards as he does, he seemed to think I might need it.'

'The celestine?' said Aurélie. She frowned. 'Remind me again, what does it do?'

'Put your torch on again,' said Guinan, 'and I'll show you.'

He sat up on the narrow bed and reached inside his pocket. Aurélie shone a beam of light onto the palm of his hand. Now she could see a small, blue, unremarkable stone.

'Is that it?' she asked.

'Believe you me, the Celestine of Avalon is much more than just a lucky pebble,' he replied. 'Just as well Merlin made me memorise the spell to reactivate it.' Now he began to recite some ancient words of Avalon sea-magic that were mingled with a beseeching charm from a Valerian mage:

'Ula Ula Ulame,
Lallulume, Ula may,
Shirra, Shirra, Ula,
Ostende ostende, we pray.'

Then he said, 'Show us, celestine. Show us what we most need to know.'

The celestine twitched and quivered obligingly, then stretched out to the size and shape of an arch-shaped window. Through this vista, Guinan and Aurélie glimpsed something very strange.

Beneath a roof that rose upwards, to a point, there was a man seated at a sort of sloping wooden cabinet, with a look of Merlin about him. Or else, he was not like Merlin at all, though his beard was the colour of autumn and winter, and he wore a cloak covered in moons, stars, pentacles, pentagrams and phoenixes, all worked in pieces of quartz and moonstone.

In that chamber, there was a girl too, with hair the colour of ink, and skin as white as snow, resting on a chaise-longue. She asked the magician, or whatever he was, if he would play the glass harmonica for her again.

He nodded and began to pour water into glass goblets set in a frame on the cabinet.

'It's not so easy to balance the fluid levels,' he said. 'A little more in this one, tip this one into the next, until it's as close to the perfect balance as it is possible to achieve.' He touched his fingers to the water, to find out if it was as cold as it should be, presumably in order to conjure up the necessary quality of sound.

Now the magician passed his hands over the goblets until they were magnetised.

Then his foot began to pump at an iron spindle, a heavy percussion, whilst he rubbed his hands round the goblets' moist rims.

Soon the glass harmonica started to emit its pure notes.

Now the magician stood up and crossed over to where the girl lay. He passed his hands across her brows and temples, then massaged the outer corners of her eyes. Her eyes fluttered shut. She was coming back into harmony with the tides of the magnetic force that were guiding the poles of her being into sympathy with the forces that control the planets. For, in the sound of the glass harmonica, in the touch of his fingertips, there were stars, planets, comets, traversing the night-sky, comprising the harmonies intended to propel this girl and this magician on their voyage through the heavens.

'Well,' said Guinan, as the celestine arch began to collapse and fade. 'I don't know what to make of that. I lost touch with Snow White after she passed through the Arch of Regeneration. Still, it was nice to see her again.'

'That wasn't Merlin, was it?' asked Aurélie.

'I don't think so,' said Guinan.

'Well, I think we could do with seeing something more to the point,' said Aurélie. She took the stone from his hand. 'Show us, celestine. Show us how they are managing on board my ship, without me.'

Once again, the celestine doubled, then tripled, then quadrupled in size, then grew elongated and thin until it was the size of a serving hatch. And there was Sister Scarlet Steel, sitting down in the ship's *other* canteen at a Formica table, drinking a can of Red Bull.

A minute later and Officer James was bearing down on her with a huge smile on her face, and a cup of jasmine and lychee tea in her hand.

The officer came over, pulled out a chair and sat down opposite her.

'I believe,' said Sophia, without much preamble and still grinning from ear to ear, 'you're the girl my husband Arthur used to talk about. His foundling daughter. I recognised your name when Jem called you Nessa the other day, down on the planet's surface, and so I checked the ship's records.'

'So?' said Nessa.

'Don't you see, Nessa,' said Sophia, 'that makes me your stepmother.'

Nessa slammed down her can of Red Bull. 'You can't be my stepmother,' she said, her voice rising, a high, quivery, octave, 'because I don't want you to be. My mother was a queen, not a...' she glanced round the canteen until her eyes alighted upon something, 'tin of beans.'

'Beanz Meanz Heinz,' said Officer James, before she could stop herself. 'Oh, sorry,' she added. 'It's the Tourette's glitch in my programming. Whereas you, you're just rude.'

'Would you prefer it if I called you Ma Vader?' asked Nessa. 'Or no, how about, Robostepmum? Maybe we could rule the galaxy together.'

'Rude - and immature.'

'Immature? Me?' said Nessa, working herself up into a rage, 'I graduated first in my class at Brunwych High. People in tin cans shouldn't throw stones.'

'And I graduated first in Adolescent Psychology,' said Officer James, neglecting to mention that in the laboratory where she had studied, she had been the only student. 'I think you're just having a bad breast moment.'

The celestine shivered down to its original size. 'Okay,' said Aurélie, 'that was odd. Why did I need to see that?'

'Well,' said Guinan, 'clearly they're not managing very well without you. Maybe you could have a word with Nessa - or Officer James - when you get back.'

'It was so much easier when I was a History Officer,' grumbled Aurélie. 'I like archives. And pens. Your cousin Dagonet has a gold pen covered in dragon scales. I can relate to that. I don't want to have to deal with other peoples' turbulent emotions.'

'Do you know who you sound like, now?' asked Guinan.

'Who?' asked Aurélie.

'Me,' said Guinan.

'That's an excellent idea,' said Aurélie.

'Eh? What do you mean?' asked Guinan.

'Guinan, I would like to offer you a commission on board the starship, as the Pastoral Officer.'

'This is your revenge for my swapping... er... I mean, accidentally sending in the wrong reference that time, isn't it?'

'Come on, that was years ago.'

'Aurélies have long memories...'

'No, but just think, Guinan, I could send you all the cadets and Ensigns that come to see me. Often they're just homesick, or they miss the Academy, or their friends. I had a request the other day for someone's dog, Blue-toe, to be allowed on board ship. Apparently, Ensign

Blake's cat has created a precedent for pet requests and...'

'You're not really selling this to me.'

'But you'll think about it?'

'Can't I just buy you a pen?'

Meanwhile, in the royal bedchamber, Tallulah had finished harvesting Queen Morgana's memories. She removed the celestine memory clips and placed them carefully in the pouch that hung from her combat utility belt. Then, from a separate zip-up pocket, she pulled out a brown paper bag, untwisted it, and shook out a few white lumps.

'Rose Thorn said Merlin owed her,' muttered Tallulah. 'And that he'd suffered at Morgana's hands enough times himself. So hopefully this voodoo herbal shit RT got me to synthesize to his instructions will work.'

By *work,* she meant, send Morgana to sleep for a hundred years.

'And then, maybe,' she said to herself, 'without all of them bad memories crowding out her head, she'll wake up a bit - I dunno - a bit nicer?'

She removed a shallow, metallic dish about the size of an ashtray from her utility belt, as well as another stub of candle which she lit from the first. She put the white lumps in the dish and placed the lit candle stub beneath it so that the stuff began to swim in its own grease. As the lumps melted, the scent of roses curled into the room. To make the lumps, she had synthesized wild briar roses with sprawling petals, that were an intense shade of rose madder.

Now the stuff bubbled, and the fume of roses mixed with the fug of the room. In her sleep, Queen Morgana sighed once, and struggled. But eventually, as the white lumps continued to relinquish their odour, the lines on her face relaxed and she settled into her slumber.

Though she would have denied it if anyone had said, Tallulah had a touch of the artist about her. So when she saw a spiky thing lying at the foot of the bed, a spiky thing that looked like a spinning top, she had an idea. Because she knew what it was. It was a spindle. And so she placed it on the other pillow, next to Morgana's head, so that it would be the first thing the queen saw when she awoke. And, if the queen still remembered fairy-tales, (and there were some old stories circulating about her telling a Victorian Valerian kid a bundle of them,) then, by the symbol of the spindle, the queen would know what had happened to her.

Suddenly, Tallulah paused and looked doubtfully at the queen. What if she never woke? Her face was quite peaceful as she lay in her strange, terrible sleep. Her chest rose and fell evenly. Tallulah sighed, then folded the queen's hands across her breast. Round her neck, the queen still wore the thimble that represented for her the last of Valerian.

Finally, Tallulah put her ashtray, matches and candle back in the pouch and pockets of her utility belt then crept over to adjust the tapestry curtain against the onslaught of the rising sun. She glanced back at the queen. A pallor had fallen with the shadows, across Morgana's face. For a moment, she looked as if she was carved from mother-of-pearl.

Tallulah tiptoed from the room.

A moment later, she was sent sprawling when she tripped over the bodies of the guards sleeping in the doorway. She picked herself up and dusted herself off. Even when she reached the hallway, and discovered other sleeping bodies, she did not immediately understand what had happened. Only when she hurried through the musician's gallery and saw the flame-haired singer fallen prone across her lute did she begin to comprehend.

Though Merlin's enchantment seemed to have brought the siege to an abrupt cease, he had not otherwise overreached himself, as he was prone to do. Instead, all the courtiers and fairy-folk over whom Queen Morgana exerted her control, the puppet mistress of so many puppets, had likewise fallen asleep.

'That's better, I guess,' Tallulah muttered to herself, for she had been worried how Avalon's subjects would cope with a queen who slept for a hundred years. But now it seemed there would be no problem, since they could share their queen's slumbers. When the queen awoke, a century later, her court, and all the fairy-folk of Avalon, would wake with her.

For all her courage, Tallulah still howled when she ran through the barns and stables, the armoury, the dormitories of the military men, the kitchens, the granary, the orchards, to find that everyone and everything was asleep. Admiral Tevlev, the stable girls and boys, and all the fine horses in the stables. The Fairy Étoile at her loom. The Fairy Bryony, her fair hair falling into her bowl of curds and whey. The Fairy Chantelle, who had seemingly fallen asleep mid-song.

Everyone was asleep. Every living thing. Birds huddled under their wings in their nests. Spiders slept in their webs. Queen Morgana's hunting hounds lay indolently in the early morning sun, as unmoving as the carved wooden idols in the chapel.

The chapel! Now, more than ever, Tallulah felt the need to pray. She passed through the cloisters and entered its doorway. On a bench in one of the side chapels, there slept a priest, his mouth, slack-jawed, with drops of spittle wetting his surplice. Over there, in another side-chapel, kneeling and praying beside a votive stand lit with a thousand candles was the Prince Consort, Captain Handsome, Sir Lancelot Dulac himself, clad in a full suit of armour, and not asleep at all.

'Fuck,' said Tallulah, 'fuck, fuck, fuck,' and then, 'oh yes, of course,' because Queen Morgana had only been married to Sir Lancelot for a short time, so her mastery over him was not complete. Thus, she approached the Prince and touched him on the shoulder. He started from his prayer, opened his eyes, then smiled to see he was not the only human being left awake.

Tallulah began to tell him everything that had happened since the search party had found Rose Thorn breaking into the Winter Palace a couple of days ago. 'Since meeting Rose Thorn,' she said, 'I realised, all Queen Morgana had done with the Collodian Program was cut a window in our prison. There's stuff more real, and more beautiful, out there.'

She began to describe the embroidered shield-case which Elaine, as she was then, had once made for him, which, thanks to the celestine memory clips, had appeared on the Mothercrystal's vastscreen.

'I thank you right gladly for these tidings,' said Sir Lancelot, looking as if he wanted to hug her. But,

'Shit,' said Tallulah, before he could continue. 'The Mothercrystal! Princess Blancheflor must still be there.'

Guinan and Aurélie were still in the dungeon. Guinan had decided that he would remove Aurélie from there with the simple excuse that Queen Morgana wanted her for further questioning. He had intended to wait for the early morning changing of the guards, but then found there was no need. For when he poked his head out of the cell, the guards seated in the antechamber were fast asleep, their heads slumped on the table in front of them.

Cautiously, Aurélie and Guinan crept through the antechamber and out into the courtyard. How quiet everywhere seemed! Everyone was asleep, every living thing. The cattle in the byre; the chickens in their coop; the swans and ducks on the lake. Even the people that Queen Morgana had once changed into swine, Dame Ragnelle and Lady Suzanna, and all the rest of them, were fast asleep; even their piglets were laid out like flagons at their mothers' teats.

'What do you think happened here?' Aurélie asked.

'Some manner of enchantment,' said Guinan.

'Guess we don't have to worry about the siege anymore,' Aurélie added. For now there were no flaming fireballs falling from the sky, no cannons being wheeled out to the Wharves, no soldiers scurrying to obey their queen's commands. How still, how peaceful, it all was! The wasps were drowsing on the apples in the orchard. The bees were dreaming among the blooms. All the while, the bright sun shone steadily in a nearly cloudless sky.

'No,' said Guinan. Then he grinned. 'Maybe everyone got fed up of fighting and had a party instead.'

'Like the one you're going to have, with the other dwarves?' asked Aurélie. 'Out in the woods, with barrels of ale?'

'Aurélie!' Guinan sounded shocked. 'You know I don't just drink ale. But how did you find out about the party?'

'Are you kidding? You found you could get reception, so you spent half the night texting the lads, arranging it, and at one point you asked me how to spell *kumquat*.'

'Voldip wanted to know what he should bring,' said Guinan. 'It was a joke.'

'My watch said it was 3am,' said Aurélie. A thought occurred to her. 'Do you think they'll be awake for the party?'

'Oh yes,' said Guinan, 'they can handle a bit of late-night texting. They're used to it, from when I'm in different time zones. Sometimes we even Zoom.'

'Not what I meant,' said Aurélie. 'But never mind.'

They began to walk away from the castle, across the wide gardens and lawns, then beyond the walls, where the moat reached round them. The heavy drawbridge beneath the carved stone cups was down. Their footfalls thudded on its timbers as they crossed it, then grew silent as they walked out over thick swathes of grass. Here was a village of thatched cottages, their roofs glowing like spun gold, their walls lit up by the sun.

Beyond the village lay the outer walls, with low, massive ramparts, and a squat watchtower with a fanged portcullis. Beyond that was another bridge, and then a road which led out to the valleys and forests of the Collodian.

They walked on. Beyond the last bridge, at the limit of the castle lands, they paused in amazement. In front of them lay a waist-high hedge of briar roses, which rustled with savage life, pulsed with strange magic. Before their very eyes, it grew even taller.

The hedge stretched out in a wide circle, enclosing the outer walls, reaching back on either side of the shores of the lake. Now it was starting to hide the towers and turrets they had left behind. Tendrils reached upwards, like fingers, snarled in shawls, but clutching at the sky.

They pushed their way through, crying out as the thorns tore at their arms but thankful for their clothes' thick fabric. Once they were on the other side of the hedge, beyond the limits of the enchantment, they paused at the road that led into the forest. Guinan knew there was a clearing not far off, that he and the dwarves had discovered long ago. They used it to hide their treasures in, and sometimes, when they were weary of the always-puzzle of being and doing, to hide themselves in, too.

As they came out through the trees, Aurélie thought she glimpsed a shattered gleam of sun on a hill ahead, as though a man in armour had moved, and reflected the light. But a moment later, he had sparkled out of sight.

Another ten steps or so, and she and Guinan were standing in the dwarves' clearing, at the heart of the forest.

'Is this it?' asked Aurélie, glancing round.

'That it is,' said Guinan, with pride. 'Look, over there,' he said, pointing, 'that's the oak stump where we all carved our initials. And over there, by the nettle patch, that's where Kilkenny found the last bluebell.'

'Uh-huh. Okay. If I send Lieutenant Rose Thorn in one of the scout ships to pick you up from here, for this time tomorrow morning, is that long enough for you to say goodbye?'

'Some of the younger fellas might want to stop on a bit, but that works for me,' said Guinan. 'Thank you, Aurélie.'

'You don't need to thank me,' she replied. 'You'll be the one with a hangover…'

'I told you before, I don't get hangovers,' he said.

'I hope not,' she said. 'Because, in your new role as Pastoral Officer, you'll be in charge of liaising with the vampire contingent about whether they wish to join us on the new planet.'

'That sounds better than Ensign etiquette, or whatever it was,' said Guinan. 'The vampires are a bit hard to pin down, are they?'

'Yes,' said Aurélie. 'I thought you'd get on well with them.'

She brushed away some leaves and twigs that had snagged in his jersey, then started to walk away from him.

'Wait, where are you going?' he called after her.

'Over there,' she said, pointing to the oak stump. 'If you climb on it, I can kiss you goodbye.'

'You don't need to worry about that. Just bend down.'

So she came back.

After, she checked to see if her I-Phone was working again. Yes! She was back in the range of reception. Turning once to wave goodbye, she walked out of the forest clearing, navigating her way back to the *Perilous* scout ship. Half an hour later, she climbed into its cockpit and radioed the *Joyous Gard* to let them know of her imminent return.

Guinan watched from the forest clearing with a pang, as the scout shuttle soared into the sky, to disappear among a glow of stars.

Tallulah and Lancelot ran from the chapel and crossed over to the courtyard of the Winter Palace. Before they reached the luminous pillars of the Mothercrystal, Tallulah noticed something strange. The courtyard was giving out an odour she had always associated with the chapel, an odour of incense and - sanctity. Then too, there was a kind of golden mist swirling after them.

She looked up at the towers and caught her breath, for never in her life had they seemed so graceful. Over the garden walls, the willows dangled golden chains, lilacs bloomed in purple flames, and briar roses filled the air with their intense, heady fragrance. The sun slanted in from the east, making the orchards and gardens gleam.

For, ever since the wickedness had been harvested from the oh so-wicked queen, beauty was returning to Avalon.

There too, in the courtyard, was the Lady Blancheflor, with a thousand glass eyes shining all upon her. She sat at the heart of a dome of light, dressed in a deep red silken gown lined with new ermine. Around her throat, she wore a necklace of rubies, that had once belonged to Queen Morgana, and before that, to Morgana's sister, Morgause.

The rubies of protection thought Tallulah. They must be the reason that the Lady Blancheflor was still awake, though everyone else slept.

Blancheflor seemed in that moment, so pure a thing, so free from mortal taint that Lancelot was reminded of Elaine, as she used to be. He ran towards her, but the rays of light that encircled her were like swords, and he could not get within an arm's length of her.

'It is your sin that keeps you out,' said Blancheflor.

'I do not understand,' said Lancelot.

'Don't you know,' said Blancheflor, 'that this place, this Collodian, is also a kind of Purgatory, a place where you will learn to atone.'

'When will that happen?' asked Lancelot.

'When you have found the person to whom you must confess,' said Blancheflor.

'But all the priests inside the chapel are asleep,' said Lancelot.

'Those who were once under Morgana's control are asleep,' said Blancheflor, 'but if you journey to the outskirts of Avalon, you will find the right priest. Then, made pure and light by the act of confession, you can ascend once more to the starry spheres.'

'How do you know all this?' asked Lancelot.

Blancheflor frowned, and then, after a moment, gave a sudden, impish grin. 'Everyone is asleep,' she said. 'I thought it was a good opportunity to look in some forbidden files. You didn't know Queen Morgana kept a dossier on you?'

'I can well believe it,' said Lancelot. 'A man cannot sneeze but that his wife makes a note of it. *One for sorrow... Two for joy...*'

'I thought that was magpies - or crows?'

'And sneezes,' said Lancelot. 'But will you, Lady Blancheflor, accompany us? For we seek to return to the starship, *Joyous Gard,* where your husband awaits you.'

'I do not have a husband,' said Blancheflor, the smile fading from her face. 'The Queen annulled my marriage to Sir Lanval, some years ago.' Despite her words, Sir Lanval's face rose up before her mind's eyes. There he was, with the small scar on the side of his forehead, with a crow's foot of grey in hair that was otherwise chestnut and curling, and with hazel eyes that still shone.

'Dear Lord, I wish she had annulled mine,' muttered Sir Lancelot.

'I think you'd be granted an annulment on the grounds that your wife is going to sleep for a hundred years,' said Tallulah. 'You can ask the priest about it. And aren't you worried about Sir Lanval, Princess Blancheflor? That last time he came to Avalon, the memory harvesting process didn't go too well for him.' She bit her lip. 'I was off work that day. Bad shellfish. I don't think they should've attempted the process without me.'

'But how can I repair all that is broken between us if Sir Lanval lies comatose?' asked Blancheflor.

'This is your first marriage, ain't it honey?' said Tallulah.

Blancheflor nodded, her lovely eyes downcast.

'You'll learn,' said Tallulah. 'Some of my best conversations ever were with my sleeping husband. He didn't need to hear what I said, I just had to say it.'

At that moment, from the stables, the waving tail and elegant shape of a golden retriever came bounding towards them. It was Uxbridge. If his mistress wasn't asleep, then neither was he.

Within the Mothercrystal, Blancheflor adjusted a switch onscreen so that the forbidding swords of light disappeared, then she shot off her seat. She rushed over to her dog and began to pet him.

'Good boy,' she said as she patted him. 'Good Uxbridge. No nasty sleep for you, eh? Good boy.'

After the first flurry of licks, barks and strokes were over, Tallulah said thoughtfully, 'Yours and Lanval's dog? Like in that TV show, where Lassie hauls the kid out of the mineshaft?'

'Lassie was a border collie,' said Blancheflor, 'but yes...' She bent down again to pat the dog. Then, a moment later, she had dropped to her knees and was saying her prayers, her head pressed against the dog's flank. The spring sunlight slanted down onto her clasped hands and hair, rendering it a glory of sunshine. Her eyes grew heedless of her surroundings as she prayed.

When Blancheflor looked up again, her eyes were shining. 'I will cross the Collodian with you,' she declared, 'and I will go with you to the *Joyous Gard*!'

Tallulah made her way past the kneeling Blancheflor, entered the Mothercrystal and tapped something onto the screen in front of her. Then a series of messages passed back-and-forth.

Blancheflor clambered to her feet and stepped over to peer at what Tallulah was doing. Onscreen, there was a map of Avalon.

'She's a busy gal, your cousin,' said Tallulah, 'but I managed to get hold of Lieutenant Rose Thorn. She and I are arranging a pickup,' she added. 'The starship will send a scout ship to collect us tomorrow morning...' She glanced back at the screen, 'Oh - and she's just heard from Captain De Lys - so, it will be us, and Ambassador Guinan.' She grinned. 'It would be helpful if we could all meet in the same place at the same time.'

'Hear that, Uxbridge?' said Blancheflor. 'No running off after rabbits, eh, boy.'

As they crossed the courtyard, Tallulah turned back one last time to look at the Castle of Chalis. There, in the farthermost chamber of its Holdfast, the oh so-wicked queen would sleep on and on, a whole century of peaceful sleep. As her castle crumbled and decayed, birds might fly in and out of the places where its stones and fragments of stained glass had fallen, singing, and wondering when the queen might wake. And, like in the old-time fairy-tales, thickets of roses would grow all around her, and in their fragrance, the queen might dream herself at the heart of a flower.

Blancheflor, Uxbridge, Lancelot and Tallulah journeyed on through the Collodian, and everywhere they went, the streets were empty, not a man, woman or child to be seen. Blancheflor had read of a church, St. Boniface's, where the monks were particularly devout, and so less likely to be under Queen Morgana's control. Thus they made their way there.

Presently, they found this church on the outskirts of the valley. It was adorned with neither ornament nor tapestry, but only with wildflowers, that were forcing their way through the cracks in the stone flags. Periwinkles, daisies, ragwort, and even, a briar rose or two, though they did not grow in the same profusion here as around the castle they had just left. Then too, the church tower was open to the sky, so that, by looking up, they could see white clouds bearding the blue.

To them all, it seemed a better way to worship than to be grubbing among dusty pews and faded song-sheets.

Nevertheless, they entered the church to seek out a priest to whom Sir Lancelot might confess. Tallulah and Blancheflor sat down and began to pray. The bright sun shone through the stained glass windows, so that all its splendid dyes and vivid hues fell across them.

Sir Lancelot strode all around the church, looking for a priest, then stepped outside again.

Outside the church walls, shawled in ivy, was a little hermitage. Upon entering it, the knight found a priest in a dark robe, who was lighting silver tapers. Sir Lancelot approached him, and asked if he might make confession.

The priest, bald, with a tonsure of grey hair, introduced himself as Father Crispin, and agreed. He led the knight to a confessional, where Lancelot knelt down, and made the sign of the cross.

'Sir,' he began, 'I am Sir Lancelot Dulac, lately the Prince Consort. I confess to all my sins. That is - I repent of all of them, save one.'

'And which sin is that, dear sir?'

'Sir,' said Sir Lancelot, 'it seems to me the sweetest and most beautiful sin that ever I committed.'

'Dear sir,' said Father Crispin, 'sins are sweet to commit, but the reward is often bitter indeed, and no sin is ever beautiful or noble, though some are worse than others.'

'My tongue will tell,' replied Sir Lancelot, 'of the sin that my heart cannot repent. My lady was a queen, and I loved her more dearly than anyone else in the world.'

'You speak of your wife, Queen Morgana? Uxoriousness is not a sin,' replied the priest.

'No,' said Sir Lancelot, 'I speak of Queen Guinevere, though one of the finest kings alive, and my best friend, besides, had taken her for wife. Even now, my love for her seems so fine and noble that I cannot wholly forsake it - and it remains, even after all these years, so rooted in my heart that it can never leave me.'

Father Crispin looked grave at these words, as well he might, but because Sir Lancelot was so earnest in his manner, he allowed him to continue.

Sir Lancelot said, 'For so many years, I did believe that whatever was of worth in me stemmed from that love.'

The priest could bear it no more. 'What are you saying?' he cried. 'Nothing of any worth can come from such a love. The joy it gives is pure deception, and if you do not repent, you will pay for it dearly.'

'And yet,' said Sir Lancelot, 'there was so much beauty, worth, wisdom and courtesy in her, that no man on whom she bestowed her heart could abandon it.' But now there was some confusion in his manner, for he suddenly thought that he might more fairly have spoken these words of Elaine, than Guinevere.

'The more beauty and worth there is in her,' said Father Crispin, 'and in yourself, the more you were both to blame. For there is far less shame in a man of little worth, than in one who ought to be worth much.'

'I have no desire to renounce my love,' said Lancelot, 'though Guinevere is dead, and perhaps with the angels now.' Yet, in his heart of hearts, he knew that he had been consigned to the underworld for the self-same sin as Guinevere. He could only hope that her long years as a nun, and then as an Abbess, and her bitter repentance besides, had brought her some measure of redemption.

His words touched the kind old priest, who said, 'Since God is so gentle and good, he will perhaps have mercy on you. But know you this, because of your sin, you will never see the Holy Grail, even though it be passed freely all around you.'

'May the Lord guide me,' said Sir Lancelot, 'by his will and pleasure. But might it not be, if my repentance is sincere, I might one day be granted the gift of performing miracles, as I have longed to do ever since I were a boy?'

'May the Lord grant it be so,' said Father Crispin. 'Though these are strange times,' he added. 'I hear that many of my former congregation now sleep.'

'The people of Avalon sleep,' said Lancelot, 'as does Queen Morgana. I have heard it said this will be for a hundred years. And so I believe that my marriage to her, if such it was, must now be annulled.'

'As to that,' said the priest, 'it is not for me to say. But these are strange matters indeed. Come with me now to take Holy Communion, and when the wafer is upon your tongue, ask the Lord what you must do, and abide by the guidance you are given.'

Returning to the church, the priest took the communion wafer from the tabernacle. Lancelot knelt before him as the priest intoned: 'The body of Christ.'

'Amen,' said Lancelot, and in that moment, if it was not God that spoke to him, it was his heart, and his heart said, *Elaine.*

After his confession, and the receiving of Communion, the priest gave Sir Lancelot some food for himself and his companions: chervil, lettuce, cress and millet, bread made from barley and oats, and water from a clear spring.

Sir Lancelot quit the hermitage and found Tallulah and Blancheflor, still inside the church. After they had all eaten, they left this church, and though rebellion and repentance remained ever warring in Sir Lancelot's heart, still, he had also found a measure of peace.

On they travelled, ever hopeful that they would reach the pickup point by early morning light.

Now it was evening, and the dwarves were beginning to assemble in the forest clearing, and many were the 'Hail fellow, well mets,' hearty back-slapping and showings-off of drinking horns. Pippin had brought along the alternate Holy Grail, not to drink from, but to return to Guinan. He was still feeling glum that before he had even had the chance to carry out his *Show and Tell* class, all the little

First Year elves and fairies had fallen asleep, their heads tucked beneath their gauzy wings on their desks.

However, in the midst of all this revelry came an uninvited guest to the feast. A tall man, clad in a dark cloak, with a look of Sir Pinel about his grey eyes, though it was not he. But perhaps, thought Guinan, it was one of his descendants, for in one hand, he carried a basket full of poisonous plants, and in the other, a scythe.

The dwarf glimpsed some roots of mandrake peeping from the basket, and a few toadstools, their white spots stark against their crimson hoods.

Guinan remembered then what Sir Pinel had always said that herbs were like people, with the same capacity to perform good or evil existing within them - or else, like two warring kings camped in one man's will. But when the worse capacity is dominant, the plant rots, as though there is a worm inside.

'I think I know him,' Fieldung whispered to the Chief. He frowned and tugged at his earlobe. 'I think Queen Morgana introduced him to me at a school Prize-Giving ceremony. Back when I was still teaching the old *Resurrection of Cadavers* course.'

'Even if he's an old crony of yours, we don't want him *here*,' said Guinan.

The gaunt man was just beginning to scythe some mistletoe which had sprung up white and starry among the swathes of nettles, when Guinan approached him.

'Excuse me,' he said. 'This is a private party. Just me, and a few of the lads. Would you mind moving along?'

The man scowled, and seemed about to speak, but what he might have said was anyone's conjecture, for seconds later, a silver-tipped arrow, shot from the priest's unseen crossbow, came singing through the leaves. It pierced the heart of the poisoner, so that he sank to his knees.

'Perhaps I came to make amends,' he cried out, then smiled ruefully. 'Now Lady Lark will never know.' And he rolled over onto the ground, dead, with the arrow embedded in his heart.

'Fine start to a party, all this,' grumbled Guinan. 'Fieldung, Voldip, please could you drag the corpse out into the bushes.'

The undertaker dwarves nodded and moved to place their hands on the dead man's cloak, only to find there was nobody beneath it. So instead, Fieldung folded up the cloak, neatly enough, and placed it beneath a rock that stood sentinel to the forest clearing.

'Time to get some drinking in, lads,' said Guinan, firmly. 'Pippin, Cooey, do you think you can roll in that barrel that Kilkenny brought on the wagon?'

The younger dwarves jumped up, and with alacrity, rolled the barrel down from the wagon and into the centre of the clearing. Then they heaved it onto the oak stump and collected everyone's flagons and drinking horns. A few moments later, they had turned the barrel's tap, and everyone had a drink in hand.

'Do you remember when Dagonet fell into that barrel of cider?' asked Guinan, admiring the fine, foamy head on his ale. 'Now there was a lad with a powerful thirst. Though a little bird tells me, these days, he's gone all *literary.*' He sniffed and took a consoling gulp of ale.

'Like your good self, he always did have a way with the words,' said Kilkenny, tactfully. 'Do you remember when he wrote, I'm Dagonet, they say/Does it have to be this way? He was only a nipper then, too.'

'Knee-high to a grasshopper,' said Guinan, mollified. 'You did well bringing all this ale, Kilkenny. How did you manage it?'

'I have a tab at the tavern nearest the school,' said Kilkenny, 'and, well, everyone was asleep... so... I took what I wanted.'

'And I brought kumquats!' shouted out Voldip.

'That was a joke, though,' said Guinan.

'Yes, I know,' said Voldip. 'That's why I brought them. I ordered them off Amazon Prime, Next-Day Delivery, just before the site went down.'

'Ingenious, gentlemen, ingenious,' said Guinan. He held up his tankard. 'Let's raise a toast to...' He was about to say, *me,* but thinking better of it, he said instead, 'Absent friends.'

'Dagonet!' the dwarves cheered.

'Clairmont,' said Cooey, so that everyone went quiet.

'And, of course, the Chief himself,' said Fieldung, holding up his tankard and saluting Guinan. 'Till better times unite us,' he added. 'What do you think it will be like, on board the starship?'

'Well,' said Guinan, 'my girlfriend has put me in charge of persuading the vampire contingent...'

'Reeeeewind,' said Fieldung. 'Your *what*?'

'You heard me,' said Guinan.

'But is she an actual girlfriend or is it just like when Kilkenny learned how to write so he could send Madame Pomme love-letters?' asked Fieldung.

'Shurrup,' said Kilkenny. 'What I tell you when we're digging graves is private.'

'She's an actual girlfriend,' said Guinan. 'She's the Captain of the starship, actually.'

'The Fairy Estelle was going to be my girlfriend,' piped up Pippin, 'but she fell asleep.'

'That's a shame, son,' said Guinan, 'I think all the fairies are going to be sleeping for a long, long while. You'll have to see if you still like her when she wakes up.'

'At least my pony's still awake,' said Pippin, gesturing to the grey and white dappled horse tied to yonder tree.

'Nuff talking, more drinking,' said Voldip. 'Kumquat anyone?'

'Go on,' Guinan whispered to Pippin, 'have one. It'll make him ever so happy.'

Pippin took one and bit down into the small orange fruit. He wrinkled up his face. 'It's not bad,' he said, at last. 'Might try one with some lemonade.'

'Ale, lad, ale is what you need,' said Kilkenny.

'But I'm in charge of the pony,' said Pippin. 'I have to make sure none of you fall off.'

'I'll make you a shandy,' said Guinan. He nodded to the other dwarves, 'lad's not used to hard liquor.'

Guinan stood up then, and after he had made Pippin's drink, he walked round filling up everyone else's tankards and horns with ale. 'Bit of a change from broom sweeping, eh lads? But I'm going to miss you all, I really am. You're all... you're all... so... what I'm trying to say is, well, I love the bones of each and every one of you.'

He stumbled then, with drink, or emotion, and the celestine fell out of his pocket. Since it had been activated the previous night, it was primed to answer questions, and the last one was Kilkenny's, 'What do you think it will be like on board the starship?' Obligingly, the celestine twitched, quivered, shimmered, then grew to the size and shape of a large window.

'Coo, look at that,' said Cooey, peering through it.

'Well I never,' said Kilkenny.

For what they could see through the celestine window was the viewing screen onboard the *Joyous Gard,* showing stars, constellations, the powerful beauty of space at warp speed. And standing there, transfixed, were Aurélie and Guinan, bathed in the steady glow of the stars in all the colours of the universe.

'There's lovely,' said Fieldung.

'It is, isn't it?' said Guinan.

'No, I meant the captain,' said Fieldung. 'She's like that girl we saw in the circus trailer in Astalot, all those years ago.'

'It *is* Aurélie,' said Guinan, pleased. He walked over to the celestine, bent down, picked it up, and put it back in his pocket.

'She hasn't changed much,' said Fieldung. 'I would know her, anywhere.'

'Hey,' said Guinan, 'why are you so interested in *my* girlfriend, all of a sudden?'

'S'cuse me, I haffta take a leak,' said Fieldung, standing up, then staggering, with dignity, to the thickest hedges, at the edge of the clearing. When he had finished, he walked over to the pony. 'Hey Pip, your pony has two heads,' he called out. He reached out to pat one of them, but somehow, in doing so, he collided with the tree where the pony was tethered. A low branch caught the bridge of his nose, hard, and out popped an eyeball, which flew through the air into the very centre of the clearing.

The other dwarves gazed at it in horror, whilst a dazed Fieldung wiped his bloody nose on his sleeve, then felt around the socket where his eye had been.

Guinan walked towards the centre of the clearing and peered down. 'It's an android eye,' he said, at last. 'Come over here, Fieldung.'

So a bruised and bloody Fieldung stumbled towards the Chief, only to have Guinan punch him hard in the chest.

'Ouch,' said Fieldung. 'What was that for?'

'I wanted to see if you were made of flesh and bone, or wheels and cogs,' said Guinan. 'It's all right, lads, he's more-or-less dwarf.'

'What about that eye, though?' asked Cooey, pointing at the android eye, still whirring, buzzing and ticking next to the tree stump and barrel.

Guinan thought for a moment. 'This all reminds me of something Aurélie once told me - about a vampire that wanted to look out of other people's eyes. Fieldung, that fella that came to the school that time, that just died by the silver arrow, did he try and talk to you by yourself?'

'Well,' said Fieldung, trying to think through a haze of ale, 'well, I meantersay, I'm really not sure. Mebbe. For a few minutes. He was asking me about my cadaver lectures.'

Guinan pondered some more. 'And did he try to make a bargain with you, or give you anything?'

'Oh yes,' said Fieldung, brightening, 'he asked me what was my heart's desire, and when I told him, he pulled a clockwork mouse out of his pocket and gave it to me. But I thought it was a joke. Then he gave me a sort of playful slap on the side of the head, and, do you know, my eyesight was never the same after that. I was even thinking about going to see Merlin for some of those owl-glasses.'

Guinan cleared his throat. 'Gentlemen,' he said then, 'I think that the man who just died in our midst was the same man who replaced Fieldung's eye with an android iris.' He paused for further effect. 'The vampire, Morleon.'

'Oh,' said Fieldung, dubiously, 'but why would he do that?'

'To spy on our dwarf revels?' said Guinan. 'Perhaps even to learn more about Aurélie.'

'But he said he came here to make amends,' said Pippin, in a small voice.

'He said, *perhaps* he came to,' said Guinan. 'That word makes a world of difference.'

'What happens now, to the android eye?' asked Cooey.

Fieldung went to the centre of the clearing, undid his

breeches, pulled out his member, and peed on it. As the android eye sizzled beneath the jet of piss, it ceased whirring and buzzing. The eyelid closed, and it was still. 'That's dealt with that,' he said, pulling up his breeches. 'But I'm going to need a pirate eyepatch, for a time.'

'Dr Blake on board the starship might be able to do something for your eye,' said Guinan. 'I'll ask him when I see him. But now lads, let's play a drinking game. We sit round in a circle, and we each have to say something. The others have to guess if it's *Truth or Lie*. If a dwarf guesses right, he has to down a horn of ale. If he guesses wrong, he get a slap.'

'I might sit this one out,' said Fieldung. 'I've already been punched once, I've lost an eye and I've got a bloody nose.'

'Count me out too,' said Pippin, and he and Fieldung climbed up onto the pony, and stroked his mane and chatted to him. But the other dwarves were more than willing to play, and soon the party game was in full swing.

In the sober light of dawn, Tallulah, accompanied by Sir Lancelot, Princess Blancheflor and Uxbridge, marched into the forest clearing that was close to the pick-up point for the scout ship. Glancing all around, she surveyed the carnage that the dwarves had wrought, the blood, the battered drinking horns, the broken barrel, the gouged-out eye.

'Who hit who with which horn?' she asked, clicking her tongue. But the dwarves didn't answer, since they were mostly asleep, or hungover. 'That must have been one hell of a party,' she added, shaking her head.

'They're not giving me much confidence that they will cope *sans* supervision,' said Blancheflor. 'What will happen to them, without Ambassador Guinan?'

'Ambassador Guinan's over there,' said Tallulah, pointing to the grey, grizzled dwarf, who had somehow wrapped himself in the poisoner's cloak.

'And the drinking game was his idea,' muttered Voldip from the other side of the clearing, rubbing his sore head and black eye.

Guinan opened one eye. 'Tattletale,' he mumbled.

'They could come with us to the starship,' said Lancelot, 'and thence to the new planet.' A smile twitched at the corners of his mouth as he surveyed the wreckage of the drinking party. Yet for all that, his heart was heavy. These dwarves reminded him of court, of Camelot and Cardoeil, when Guinan was Merlin's apprentice, and little Dagonet, now an Ensign, went skipping in corners, to tunes of his own devising.

'I'm not sure there's room in the shuttle for all of them,' said Tallulah. 'And at the moment, we don't even know if there's going to *be* a new planet.' She paused for a moment, thought about it, then said, 'They could all stay at my house till we locate the new planet. It's big enough, and there's a pool out back.'

'That's very kind of you,' said Blancheflor.

'Well, with nearly everyone else asleep, I think they need somewhere safe to stay,' said Tallulah. 'And my house is certainly that. I could see the way things were going with the queen and all those fireballs, so I had an air-raid shelter built. *And* it's well-stocked with food.'

'Don't be misled by their size,' said Lancelot. 'I know from Captain De Lys that dwarves can eat *a lot.*' But were not these dwarves the emblem of his own lost innocence, and of all the bloody battles since that time? Once he had been a boy, even as Pippin, now sleeping on the back of the pony. Except, unlike the dwarf-knight, he'd had a kettle-drum for a helmet, peering into a well to admire his own reflection, with a dream of glory beating in his heart.

Once, as he had told Father Crispin, he had even dreamt of performing miracles, more priest than knight perhaps, riding from village to village, intending to heal the sick, to give succour where he might.

'Good,' said Tallulah, 'there's plenty there to eat.' And so she walked over to Kilkenny, whom she judged to be the most competent since he had placed a compress of dock leaves on his swollen jaw. Or, at least, he was the best of a bad bunch. She gave him her house and car keys, and some directions as to how to get there, which he made a note of for Pippin and the pony. 'And,' she added, 'there's a kind old priest, Father Crispin, living in a hermitage outside St. Boniface's church. It's only a few miles from here. He would probably help you, if you got really stuck.' And again she provided directions.

'Cool,' said Kilkenny, his bleary eyes brightening, 'a new drinking buddy.'

Lancelot shook his head. Did the dwarf lack proper reverence? The thought led him back to the subject of Miracles, which he had wanted to perform for so long, but which could only be carried out by the pure in heart, as Father Crispin had implied. And that purity had been sacrificed on the altar of his great love for the queen, for twenty years or more.

Unthinkingly, he walked over to Fieldung, whose head was slumped forwards against Pippin's back as they dozed on the pony. Sir Lancelot had no real plan in his mind except to give comfort where he might.

'I'm sorry about your eye,' he said humbly in the sunlight. He reached over and gave the dwarf an awkward pat on the shoulder. Then he twisted his fingers in supplication, glanced at the pony's strong reins, and with the words of the priest still echoing in his ears, prayed as hard as he could. *'If you will heal this dwarf, for this knight's sake, dear Lord, I pray thee, please do.'*

When Fieldung finally opened his sleepy eyes, where once there had been a gouged out hollow, now was there was the full iris of a blue lake.

And so at last Sir Lancelot had his Miracle, and his heaviness of heart began to lift. He moved away from the pony and knelt down in the clearing to give thanks, weeping in a secret way that the others might not see. Then the rest of the dwarves began to wake up. When Fieldung jumped down from the back of the pony to show them his restored eye, how did they jump, then cheer, then exchange hearty thumps and backslaps, whilst Tallulah whooped and even Blancheflor cracked a smile. They did not know that the miracle was, that Sir Lancelot had been allowed to perform his Miracle.

Just then, Pippin, still slumped on the back of the pony, woke up. He lifted his head. 'It's very noisy here,' he said, crossly. Then he pointed at Uxbridge. 'Doggy,' he said, and fell back to sleep.

Into this haze of sunrise, came a dark shimmer, accompanied by a rapid, bell-beating sound, as if a bird of prey were circling above them. A moment later, and the scout ship *Ganymede* had landed on the outskirts of the forest clearing.

Lieutenant Rose Thorn opened the port-side hydraulic door and let down the steps. Her passengers climbed aboard: first, Ambassador Guinan Guineafowl, the new Pastoral Officer, grizzled and careworn, then Princess Blancheflor of Avalon, as lovely as ever, and accompanied by her elegant hound, Uxbridge, then the dark-splendid Sir Lancelot Dulac, former Prince Consort of Avalon, and finally, Ms Tallulah Mae Jackson, who had sacrificed her job, home and car to be there.

Ambassador Guinan, blinking, bewildered, and clutching the Grail, nodded to Lieutenant Rose Thorn. Sir

Lancelot, who could not see the Grail, though he had made a dwarf see, smiled at her with all his heart, as if she, herself, were the sacred chalice. Actually, he was trying to decide if he liked her short, spiky haircut, but then he realised it made her eyes look more like lustrous violets than ever.

However, her cousin, Blancheflor, gave her a nod of proud, chilly disdain, whilst Tallulah whooped again, and high-fived her.

'Bet you've never flown so many bigwigs before,' she said.

'Where's Rapunzel, and - Cinderella?' asked Rose Thorn. Then she added, 'No, but I always wanted to sail to a heavenly city in a boat shaped like a silver star.'

'That's from the Creed of the Sisters of Valerian,' said Tallulah, giving her a respectful look and then heading towards her seat.

'It's also from Grail-lore,' said Guinan, earwigging. 'It makes me think that you, not I, would be a fitting guardian for the Grail.'

Rose Thorn's heart leapt up at the sight of the sacred chalice, that she had once journeyed throughout the Kingdoms of Valerian and Avalon to find. 'It could go back to the Temple of Valerian,' she said, 'except - I was thinking that *I* wouldn't, that I would remain on the new planet, when we find it.'

'You were?' said Sir Lancelot, moving to the front of the scout ship so that he could sit beside her in the cockpit.

As Rose Thorn nodded, he held her gaze, those lustrous eyes, slightly longer than was strictly necessary.

'That's a big decision to make, though, honey,' said Tallulah. 'You're their Leader.'

'Yes,' said Rose Thorn. 'About that. I was thinking to have a chat with you at some point...'

'Enough of the chitter-chatter,' said Guinan. 'I have new and important responsibilities awaiting me onboard ship,' he continued, puffing out his chest. 'So, the Grail's yours again, dearie.' And before she could say *yay* or *nay*, he had handed the chalice over to her, and was pushing his way to a quiet, dark seat at the back of the scout ship.

'I see no Grail,' said Sir Lancelot, sitting down and rubbing his eyes.

Rose Thorn sighed. 'Can you all take your seats please?' she called into the *grande mêlée*. '*When* you have fastened your seatbelts, we can take off.'

'You have confessed your sin,' said Blancheflor to Lancelot from the seat behind them, 'but the original condition has not been lifted. Perhaps you have not truly repented in your heart.'

'And yet I healed a dwarf,' said Sir Lancelot.

'Oh?' said Rose Thorn, turning to face him. 'You did? But which particular sin are we referring to here?'

'I'm not meaning to be sexist,' called Tallulah from the seat in front of Guinan, 'but, honey, he's a guy. There'll be millions of them.'

'You're very tolerant, Tallulah,' Blancheflor replied.

'It's only you Precursors who look for perfection,' said Tallulah. 'Not that there's anything wrong with that,' she added, hastily. 'Just, I didn't grow up in a perfect world.'

'That's what the new planet is supposed to be,' said Rose Thorn. 'Now, if everyone will just shut up for a minute, I can take off and get us all back to the starship.'

'The *Joyous Gard,*' said Lancelot, a pleasant Avalon inflexion to his pronunciation. 'My first command - named for my castle.'

'Captain De Lys's first command too,' muttered Guinan from the backseat, his hackles rising. But he tucked the poisoner's cloak behind his head to use as a pillow and went back to sleep.

First command thought Rose Thorn, moments later, after the *Ganymede* had taken off. Then she glanced over at Sir Lancelot beside her: *First love.* But a bright comet blazed out of nowhere, just ahead of the scout shuttle, so that she was forced to swerve, or else perish in the collision. As she regained control of the juddering craft, the Grail tumbled from her lap to the floor at her feet.

'How am I going to get the Grail back to Valerian?' she thought then.

An hour or so later, after she had guided the *Ganymede* into the landing bay of the starship and helped escort its illustrious passengers to their respective cabins, she was free to talk to Tallulah and then to Sister Scarlet Steel.

She messaged Tallulah to come and meet her on the Mezzanine Level, and her friend showed up pretty soon.

'So, whaddya gotta say?' Tallulah asked as they began to walk to the recreation deck. 'And don't think I don't know where this is going.'

'Er, game of Jabberwocky?' asked Rose Thorn.

'Got me there, I wasn't expecting that. Yes, all right then,' said Tallulah. 'But I warn you, I used to be pretty good.'

'I can believe that about you,' said Rose Thorn, wondering if she should throw the game. She did have a particularly big favour to ask.

They collected their net, shaped like dragon wings, and paddles, carved like dragon claws, from the games cupboard in the rec room and set up their table. Then Tallulah flipped a coin to see who would go first. 'Heads,' called out Rose Thorn, and, yes, the coin landed heads-up, Queen Morgana's side profile, wrought on a heavy gold sovereign. So Rose Thorn tossed the fireball then smashed it with the paddle so that it hit her side of the table, then bounced over the net and hit Tallulah's side.

Tallulah's eyes never left the fireball. 'Point to you,' she said. Then, 'Let's play to 11.' Maybe it was years of operating the celestine clips, but she had powerful wrist action, and deftness and precision with the paddle. The fireball was moving fast: she kept it low. Her back hand was strong; her forehand was strong; sometimes she sent the fireball spinning across to Rose Thorn.

'That was a killer serve,' said Rose Thorn. 'You were right: you're pretty good.'

'Yeah, but why aren't you, honey?' asked Tallulah. 'And is it on account of my Jabberwocky skills that you want me to be Leader of the Sisters of Valerian? High Priestess Ping-Pong herself? Can I say that? I think I can say that.'

'How did you guess that was what I wanted?' asked Rose Thorn, dishing out another easy serve, and wondering when, and if, she should take control of the game.

'Back on the scout-ship, you weren't exactly subtle. Still, at least it gave me some time to think about it,' said Tallulah, smashing back the fireball. 'You don't need to throw the game on my account, either.'

'Then I won't,' said Rose Thorn, gearing up for a proper match.

'But you remember what I said, about the sisterhood and the Grail?'

'Sometimes what people *say*,' said Rose Thorn, smashing the fireball herself, 'and what they *feel* aren't the same. I'm offering you power,' she added, smashing the fireball as it came back at her again, 'and responsibility far beyond what you possessed working for Queen Morgana.'

'But why?' asked Tallulah, hitting the fireball back.

'Because,' said Rose Thorn, 'you're strong, you're smart...' and now she put a gentle spin on the fireball, 'your heart is as big as your house.'

'Hey, you've upped your game,' said Tallulah. She hit the fireball back, but her mind was elsewhere. 'I can't deny I'm not tempted,' she added. 'But I'm known as Queen Morgana's treacherous henchwoman. How will you explain that to the Sisters of Valerian?'

'You mean, you're Sister Golden Claw, who left the Compound after years of devoted service to infiltrate Queen Morgana's closely-guarded Collodian Program and bring about her downfall from the inside?' said Rose Thorn. She gave the appearance of a slam, then dunked the fireball, 'Somehow, I think they'd be cool with that.'

'Are you always this good at getting your own way?' asked Tallulah, for now the score was in Rose Thorn's favour.

'Always,' said Rose Thorn, as she sent the fireball crashing back, 'except once, when it really mattered.'

'Ah shit, you've won,' said Tallulah, laying down her paddle. 'And - you've won. When do I travel to Valerian?'

'I need formally to resign as Leader, first,' said Rose Thorn, 'and... I want to introduce you to the Compound crew *and* the Custodians of the Temple, and this far out in space, it may take some weeks before I can set up a panel meeting. Oh - and I need to speak to Sister Scarlet Steel, as well.'

'Who she?' asked Tallulah.

'Hopefully, the Cup Bearer,' said Rose Thorn.

'Shit, you mean, like in Grail-lore, 'the chalice shall pass from Holy Fool to Wise Dwarf, and from those dwarfish hands, the Guide shall take it and bring it at last to the Cup Bearer, and thence to its true and final resting place?' asked Tallulah.

'Yes, but that's just from the abridged version,' said Rose Thorn. 'The Grail *and* The Alternate Grail have passed through more than just dwarfish hands. You're forgetting Queen Morgana, Lord Darvell, Violetta, Miss Dulcetta, Mordred and Captain De Lys, as well as all those who were cured from covid. Really Tallulah, you'll have to brush up on all of this if you're going to be the Leader.'

'Don't push it,' said Tallulah. 'But I'll read over it all in time for the panel meeting. Say- do they have any clothes shops on board this starship? I'm gonna need to dress smart.'

'The panel will only see your head and shoulders onscreen,' said Rose Thorn, 'but yeah, there's some Terran boutiques on one of the upper decks.'

'I am going shopping,' said Tallulah, 'I am going to be spending the big advance on the big salary that the Conglomerate are going to be paying me; I am going to get my hair done, and if I can find a beauty salon, my nails too, and if, at the end of all that, I can't pass for my own daughter, I'm going to do it all over again.'

'Yeah, we like our Leaders vain, shallow and materialistic,' said Rose Thorn.

'Shut up,' said Tallulah.

'You shut up,' said Rose Thorn. 'You'll look great, you'll do great, you are great.' She picked the paddles up from the table, and swinging them backwards and forwards, she sauntered over to the games cupboard.

After she had left Tallulah to mull over her defeat *and* her victory, Rose Thorn checked over the ship's rotas, and worked out that Sister Scarlet Steel would be off-duty. She poked her head round the door of the hydroponics suite and the Viewing Theatre, then finally wound up in the ship's *other* canteen. The one where the officers didn't go. Here, there were no rare plants from Nova Nevada, no display cabinets of Murano glass ornaments or crystals from the mining planets, not even an aquarium with an octopus melded to an anemone.

Worse than that, there didn't seem to be any of those thick, dark slabs of gooey chocolate cake, only a few wan crackers and crumbs on the scratched silver counter, over by the vending machine.

Nevertheless, Nessa had chosen to be there, with a plastic cup of coffee and a red sweater on the Formica table in front of her. She was hunched over a small screen, reading intently.

Rose Thorn bought her own coffee from the vending machine, then made a beeline for her. 'Mind if I sit down?' she asked.

'I'm off-duty,' scowled Nessa. 'I'm *reading.*' She nodded at the trashy rom-com vampire novel on her Kindle.

'Without wishing to pull rank,' said Lieutenant Rose Thorn, 'I'm your commanding officer on board this starship, and I'm *also* the Leader of the Sisters of Valerian - who, I might add, have been informing me about some irregularities to do with your rather lengthy sabbatical from the Compound. Two years, isn't it? So, if I want to sit down here and talk to you, you say, Yes Ma'am.'

'Sheesh,' said Nessa. 'Sit down, *Ma'am.'* And then, as Rose Thorn pulled up a chair, she added, 'What is it with you officers here? Officer James yesterday, now you... seems like all you want to do is tell me what to do.'

'Yes,' said Rose Thorn, with a patience she did not feel, 'it's called chain of command. What did they teach you at the Academy?'

'I was only there for a year,' said Nessa, flatly.

'And before that, you were with us in the Sisterhood,' said Rose Thorn. 'Have you given any thought to going back?'

'Why? asked Nessa.

'I want to be part of the quest for the new planet,' said Rose Thorn. 'So I'm stepping down as Leader.'

'And you want me to be the new Leader, is that it?' asked Nessa.

'Hardly,' said Rose Thorn, before she could stop herself. 'Er - I mean, I have someone else in mind for the position. But she is going to need a certain amount of assistance. I thought you could use this voyage to get to know her, and then go back with her to the Compound.'

'What's in it for me?' asked Nessa.

'Extensive pilot training, to get you back to Valerian - and the chance to really hone all your other skills. Because you would be next in line for leadership. *And* you could restore the Grail to the Temple.'

'The Grail?' asked Nessa, with a sudden, yearning note to her voice.

Lieutenant Rose Thorn removed the Grail from the towel in which she had wrapped it before placing it in her sports bag. As she held the chalice up to show Nessa, it glowed so brilliantly that the aluminium lights above them lost their brightness, like the stars or moon when the sun rises. For this vessel was made of purest gold, and it was inlaid with jewels of many kinds, the richest and most precious stones in the earth or the sea.

'Niiice,' said Nessa, and now there was a note of reverence to her voice.

'Really?' asked Rose Thorn.

'No,' said Nessa, back pedalling, 'I meant, nice... of you to use a religious artefact to manipulate me into doing what *you* want.'

'You're very... smart,' said Rose Thorn. 'You and Tallulah both. Won't you at least think about it? I was going to say, you could hang onto the Grail while you decide, but you might think I was manipulating you.'

'Well,' said Nessa, 'at the very least, trying to get your own way.'

'We're girls,' said Rose Thorn, 'it's what we do.'

Nessa grinned then, as if she couldn't help it, and Rose Thorn thought, that's the first time I've seen the kid smile.

But then Nessa said, with so much self-possession, it was unnerving, 'Rose Thorn, Rose Thorn. Nice name.'

'Er, thank you?'

'Actually, Rose Thorn, I looked you up and I found out, you're the daughter of my grandmother's best friend. And,' said Nessa reflectively, 'I love my Granny.'

('I loved mine, once, too,' thought Rose Thorn, sadly.)

'So,' said Nessa, 'I'll think about it.' And she took the Grail from the lieutenant, and then carefully, so carefully that Rose Thorn grew more hopeful of what her eventual answer would be, she wrapped it up in her red sweater.

Later that day, Sister Scarlet Steel was to be the subject of another heated conversation. Back in her rightful place in the captain's chair on the bridge of the *Joyous Gard*, Aurélie pored over Officer James's report, that a wealth of advanced life-forms existed in the opaque seas of Aquatica, a planet that, moreover, seemed capable of sustaining human life.

'Of course, I'll put in a request to the Conglomerate to fund a full-scale research mission,' she said to Officer James. 'On one condition.'

'What's that, Captain?'

'That when you set up the floating stations, you're partnered with Sister Scarlet Steel.'

Officer James's robot face fell. 'I was hoping for Ensign Dagonet...'

'Ensign Dagonet is devoted to you,' said Captain De Lys, 'as he was to me, when he was my research assistant. I have no doubts about him, none whatsoever. But though Sister Scarlet Steel is brilliant, she's... a bit of a loose cannon, too restless, too *maverick*. Maybe you can... I don't know, steady her up a bit.'

'Don't you mean, she's an insufferable brat?' asked Officer James. 'In my free-time, I'm a horticulturist, not a babysitter.'

'I have every confidence in you,' said Captain De Lys. 'And you might just find you learn something from each other.'

'Last time someone tried to persuade me to do something I didn't want to do,' said Officer James, 'the laboratory blew up.'

'I thought it was just the toaster?' said Captain De Lys.

'No, the whole laboratory burned down,' said Officer James, not without a certain amount of pride.

'Thankfully then,' said Captain De Lys, glancing back at the report on her screen, 'Planet Aquatica is eighty per cent water.'

That afternoon, the formidable trio, Captain De Lys, Lieutenant Rose Thorn and Tallulah-Mae Jackson somehow persuaded Officer Pluto to withdraw the double bill he had been intending to show, a recently restored *'Starflight or Dragonflight?'* and, in black-and-white, a rare classic, *'An Officer and an Alien'* (not to be confused with its prequel, *'An Alien and A Gentleman,'* made by the same director, Otto J. Octopus, five years later.) Thus the Viewing Theatre was free for the three women to watch Queen Morgana's harvested memories on the ship's largest vastscreen, in complete comfort.

Tallulah had tried to harvest only the queen's bad memories, the death of her first husband, King Urien of Ravenglass, the death of her first son Ywain from the plague, the death of her daughter, Rose Red, her growing enmity with her second son, Mordred, and then her own death in Valerian during the Victorian era which had rendered her a ghost in that land.

'She was never the same after that,' said Rose Thorn.

Then came the Vexatious Complications of trying to restore her stubborn brother Arthur to the throne several times over, as if he were a mere Pretender, when in fact he was Rightful King of All Valerian. And of course, throughout her long reign, there were all the various poison and assassination attempts. However, despite Tallulah's precision, inevitably a few other memories had slipped through the celestine net, memories from when the queen was at her most vital and vibrant. Watching those onscreen saddened the three women, and made them wish they had known her, in other, better times.

One of these memories was from a ball held by Queen Morgana's second husband, King Leopold. From her seat in the viewing theatre, Rose Thorn was thrilled to see her mother, Rose Red, onscreen, looking very young and very lovely, dressed all in crimson, with crimson cochineal upon her lips, and her dark hair swept upwards into a tiara ornamented with jewels like rosehip berries. The ball was in honour of Rose Red's dear friend, Princess Snow White, who had just become betrothed to Hunter John.

Tallulah also liked to see these old, storybook Precursor Valerians dancing. Glimpses of other peoples' harvested memories had made her realise that there was a once-upon-a-time Valerian, but she had never seen it so clearly before, so brazen and beautiful onscreen.

Onscreen, a lead violinist appeared, perspiring heavily on his rostrum. He struck up a lively Tarantella, in which he was soon joined by the other members of the orchestra. Now Queen Morgana began to move in time to the music, and then to twist like flame. As she span, sparks emanated from her layers of charcoal-grey silk and feathers, and from the pointed toes of her glass slippers. Tallulah began to feel uneasy then, right down to the pit of her stomach. Her palms started to sweat, and the rapid beat of her heart took its rhythm from the music.

Onscreen, Queen Morgana was still dancing. Like the tongue of a darting match, her dress flickered in the ballroom. Then it seemed her red hair was also ignited, and then, whirling faster-and-faster, her long arms uncoiled, and her dress fanned into passionate flames. Now she moved with complete and perfect confidence, and the slash of scarlet that was her lips became an exultant smile.

There she was, all at once, completely aflame - a sheer wall of lambent fire that hurt the eyes of its beholders. But, as the flames dispersed, the ballroom guests were astonished to discover that the wicked queen had completely disappeared into the dark, quiet night.

As the screen faded to black and the lights in the Viewing Theatre came up, Aurélie sighed. 'That was one incredible dance,' she said.

Tallulah got up from her seat and walked over to the projection room, where she unhooked the celestine clips from the projectoquartz. How cold, fine and delicate they were beneath her fingertips. Then she turned and came back to Rose Thorn and Aurélie.

'Well?' she said. 'What the hell do I do with the queen's memories? If I destroy these celestine clips, I'm doin' worse to her than she did to Lanval, and all those poor others.'

'I'm not sure she'd be glad to have all those memories back,' said Rose Thorn. 'There was a lot of darkness there.'

'Can you have the light without the dark?' asked Aurélie.

'Maybe I should just toss these clips out of the airlock,' said Tallulah, because feeling compassion made her cross. It didn't lead to an easy life. Hell, she had somehow agreed to become the Leader of the Sisters of Valerian, when all she really wanted was to float around slowly, maybe paddle about a bit, in her nice big swimming pool out in the yard.

For a moment, she imagined the celestine clips turning perfect somersaults among the stars.

'Let the stars decide their fate,' she said.

Her suggestion was greeted with silence from the other women.

'Or maybe,' Tallulah sighed, 'I can store them in a Cylinder of Memory. I know the process, though I wasn't part of the original team that shipped the cylinders out for storage. Everything was on a strictly need to know basis, so goddamn hush, hush in that place.'

'But if you do that,' said Rose Thorn, 'what happens to her stored memories when the queen wakes up in a hundred years?'

'She gets to choose for herself, I guess,' said Tallulah, 'if she wants the bad stuff back again, mixing in with the good.'

'Would you want to be a fly on that particular wall in a hundred years' time?' asked Aurélie.

Rose Thorn and Tallulah both shook their heads.

Aurélie paused to reflect. 'Still,' she said at last, 'it feels like the right decision. Her memory is her prerogative.'

Cylinders Of Memory

Sister Scarlet Steel had returned to the discipline of qi going for the answers she sought. Inside the qi gong studio on board the starship, behind a screen that was covered in blue lotus flowers, she bowed her head, and listened to the sound of her old teacher, Sifu Wong's hypnotic voice, intoning, 'Now we are going to do the spontaneous five animal movements. Qi Gong, Ching Chi. Now, stand in relaxed posture. Now, breathe deeply through your nose, fresh air...'

Barefoot on the coconut matting in front of him, she inhaled deeply.

Sifu Wong continued, 'Breathe out through your mouth, dirty air. Now, look forward. Bring your eyesight back to yourself and close your eyes... Now tell yourself in heart, I'm very happy, I'm very comfortable, very calm and relaxed. My body is floating on a cloud...'

As Nessa went through the warm-up routine, she took in the qi energy, feeling it energising her system.

'I am going to circle you with my qi to try to help your qi,' said Sifu Wong. 'Let go of yourself and then your body will start to move spontaneously with the qi in the music.'

To the sound of a bamboo flute, Nessa's body began to pass gracefully through the Five Animal Movements routine. Her arms stretched out wide to either side, as if she were a bird, soaring out into the sky, with sunlight on her wings.

Next her arms came down and her shoulders hunched. She began to shuffle forwards, heavy-footed, strong and swaying like a bear. But as the flute music swirled round her, her movements grew lighter, and she bounded forwards, a deer. Then she dropped to the ground, feeling herself consumed by the energy of the tiger. On all fours, she bared her teeth, ready to spring forwards, to pounce.

But there came a lilt and a lift in the music, and she rose back onto her heels, and began to gesticulate, like a monkey. Only as the music rose an octave, her arms didn't feel quite right. The qi was pushing them forwards, but another force was pulling them backwards in a series of graceless, senseless gestures. Unnerving. But Nessa fought for control and persisted with the routine as best she could.

Finally, the music of the bamboo flute came to an end, and Sifu Wong guided her through the last part of the meditation.

'Open your eyes,' he said at last, and they bowed to each other. 'Very good,' he said. 'Excellent - but last movement, not like your usual monkey movement.'

'I don't know what that was,' said Nessa, 'my arms kept twisting back. It felt -,' she paused, and shook her head, 'it was the strangest feeling. Like someone was trying to control me.'

'But that is nature of qi energy,' said Sifu Wong.

'No, but this was something different,' said Nessa. 'Qi energy has a wonderful feeling of power to it, but this felt more like someone was trying to *rewind* me.'

Sifu Wong looked grave. 'Officer Pluto has charge of Time Editing Suite now?'

'Yes,' said Nessa, 'for the last few weeks, in fact.'

'That man, he Devil-Tiger,' said Sifu Wong. 'The more power he have, the more he seize.'

'You think the strange movements are something to do with his new job, then?' asked Nessa.

'Yes - other students say same thing happening to them. And last night,' Sifu Wong paused impressively, 'Officer James and I drank full pot of jasmine and lychee tea.'

'So?' said Nessa.

'Officer James is robot. I, old man with leaky bladder. We *never* drink so much tea. Someone rewound us to make us drink more, and, end of evening, pot was empty!'

'As far as plans for world domination go, that's not terrible,' said Nessa.

'No, but is indicative,' said Sifu Wong, 'a little power here, a little control there, I tell you, that man Devil-Tiger.

He not just correct timelines. Soon, he make everything how *he* want it to be.'

'He needs to be stopped, then,' said Nessa.

'Yes, but we need him to correct timelines first, all in terrible muddle.'

'What if he had an assistant, who could learn from him, and then take over when we - we...'

'Put him in airlock,' said Sifu Wong.

'You really think he's that much of a threat?' asked Nessa.

'He came to my class once. Bad energy crackle from him. He cannot hide it. Qi gong bring it out. So then, I watch him like hawk these last years, and I see... so much wickedness. But on this ship, no-one challenge him. They need his skills. Who, who here as clever as Officer Pluto?'

'There's Alfie Blake,' Nessa said, at last. 'He has a couple more computer assignments to do for college, but frankly, he's reached the point where he knows more than the tutor.'

'Him!' said Sifu Wong. 'Very good plan. Flatter Pluto's vanity. Give him excellent young assistant. And then - Airlock!'

Nessa looked at her teacher thoughtfully for a moment, before she nodded her head in acquiescence. Then she went to collect her shoes from the other side of the blue lotus screen.

Later that day, the doors of the turbo lift made a fluttering sound as they opened and Ensign Blake stepped out onto the lower decks, looking as if he were scared the lift computer might tell him off again.

'Thanks for coming,' said Sister Scarlet Steel, crossing the mezzanine floor towards him, 'what's with the frown?'

'On the way down, I tried to instal some software to improve the running of the lift,' said Alfie. 'Computer said *No.*' He shook his head, ruefully.

'Really?' She was about to ask him why he would bother, then stopped. She knew the answer. Alfie was *helpful.* 'Never mind that now, Alfie,' said Nessa, trying to make her voice sound more authoritative, like Officer James or Lieutenant Rose Thorn, talking to *her,* 'have you given any thought as to what you'd like to do when you finish college?'

Alfie's eyes widened in surprise. This was not the conversation he had been expecting. When he'd spent time with Sister Scarlet Steel on Aquatica, they'd shared a cigarette, and she'd taught him how to blow smoke rings.

'I dunno,' he said, at last. 'A desk job on board this ship would suit me, I suppose. Why all the interest?' And then another idea took root in his mind, that girls liked boys with drive and ambition, and his eyes gleamed.

'Oh, you know,' said Sister Scarlet Steel. 'Have you ever thought of dropping off a CV with Officer Pluto? Sifu Wong was telling me the timelines are in a real mess. I'm sure he'd be glad of an assistant.'

'It's a good idea,' said Alfie. 'We were learning about the Travellers of Space and Time in college the other day,' he added. 'My tutor said they were why we needed a Time Editing Suite. I'm redesigning some of its primary configurations as part of my final year project,' he continued. 'The Time Editing Suite is *awesome*!'

Sister Scarlet Steel walked him over to a complicated-looking console set into the wall of the corridor and started to type. A few minutes later, she said, 'Okay, that's your cover letter drafted. Can you attach your CV?'

'Sure,' said Alfie. He had been watching how fast she typed. 'Say, your nails are cool.'

'They are, aren't they?' said Nessa, fanning out her fingers and admiring her black and silver nails, decorated with dragon and jewel motifs. 'A new salon just opened up in the ship's Terran quarter. I went with Tallulah Mae Jackson,' she added, trying to impress him.

'Oh,' said Alfie, who didn't know who Tallulah was. He located and attached his CV from the Ensign Files, then hit *send*. 'I hear they have a new retro arcade up there, too. Care to hang out, sometime?'

'Are you into retro?' she asked.

'Are you?' said Alfie.

What was the polite response, here? Nessa chose her next words carefully. 'Not so much,' she replied, 'but Officer Pluto is.'

She took in his crestfallen face. She was four years older than him, and, she flattered herself, the very pinnacle of sophistication. Perhaps that was why she didn't have too many friends. And whereas she could be picky and awkward, Alfie was... Nice. Wholesome. Easy-going.

'Hanging out,' she said, at last. 'That could be cool.'

A couple of weeks later, they had run the gamut of the arcade's games machines: *Street Fighter* and *Street Fighter 2*, *Mortal Kombat* and the *Tetris* inspired *Klax*. Now Alfie was trying to get her interested not only in fighting games, but in beat em ups, too. He also really liked the *Teenage Mutant Ninja Turtles* game, was trying to introduce *Cowabunga* as a legitimate swear word and had got her to agree to takeaway pizza every other day.

'But the turtles don't actually eat pizza in the game, though,' Nessa protested.

'Obviously they don't,' said Alfie, 'but I really like that bit in the movie when they order pizza and they each get a slice, and the cheese is really stretchy and they all look... happy... hey, don't laugh. It's a cool moment.'

'So eating pizza is kind of your tribute to the Teenage Mutant Ninja Turtles, then?'

'You could put it like that,' said Alfie. 'Look, my little brothers think it's great, okay?'

'I can be cool with that,' said Nessa. 'And the Ninja stuff is awesome. Sifu Wong is going to teach me more fight moves,' she added.

'Why?'

'Not every villain is an inch high and pixellated.'

There were to be no more episodes of *Collodian Star*. The Conglomerate's blue-eyed girl, Lieutenant Rose Thorn, her friend, Tallulah, and even the wizard Merlin had put paid to that. Sorting though film reels in the projection room, Officer Pluto sighed. For all that he venerated the wizard, he had heard that Merlin was as much in thrall to Rose Thorn as all the rest of them. Thanks to them, Queen Morgana was to sleep for a hundred years. And since just about everyone who mattered was ideologically opposed to her television show, no more of it was to be made. Even though, Officer Pluto told himself, some of the episodes had genuine, artistic merit.

He certainly found them compelling. But he was meant to be one of the Conglomerate's rising stars himself: he wasn't supposed to be seduced by the very television show his colleagues had fought so hard to ban. Still, the temptation... the temptation to start making his own episodes now he had all the resources of the Time Editing Suite at his disposal was becoming unbearable. Sometimes he rewound his colleagues, made them carry out random, bizarre acts, just to take the edge off. If Officer James started to clip the heads off dahlias she had previously cherished, would that be so terrible?

Now he pounced on a particular cannister with alacrity. Ah, what had he got here? Oh. Nothing much. Just a lot of old footage from Lieutenant Lanval's harvested memories: well, he had lived for centuries. And a few random reels of a giant playing a bugle. Could he do something with them? What if he spliced the film reels with some of the Time Editing Suite's files? Strictly forbidden of course, but it was only a relatively minor transgression, of the kind at which he excelled. Since many of the morning crew were likely to be at their workstations or breakfast, he could hurry over there now and begin work undetected.

A moment later, and he was gone from the projection room, gone from the Viewing Theatre, leaving its double doors still swinging. Down the corridor, into the turbo lift, and then, with trembling, sweaty fingers, he punched in the code to open the Time Editing Suite. Its doors slid open, and he hauled the bag of film cannisters over its threshold.

He sat down in front of the screens and powered up the machine. Ah, that delicious sound, the swish of taffeta petticoats.

Now Officer Pluto plugged his old ZX Spectrum keyboard into the matrix of the Time Editing Suite. Then he flexed his fingers until his knuckles cracked, the great composer at work. A single, quiet breath before he placed those fingers on the keys. He could feel the letters raised within the rubber merge with the whorls and vortices of his fingertips. *Lavenza.*

Impatiently, he clicked open a file, then another, then another, splicing the film reels with what he found there, rearranging the lives of his colleagues, twisting them, tilting them into new patterns. As he became absorbed in his task, the tension started to dissolve from his arms and shoulders. But it took several hours of rearranging, refabricating, recalibrating, before there emerged something he deemed worthwhile.

Over on the Time Editing Suite's main vastscreen, Lieutenant Lanval once more appeared, walking with, yes, it was, it really was, Merlin, though it had been hard to tell at first, since they were both surrounded by thick, murky fog.

Officer Pluto had never met the wizard, but he had always wanted to. He imagined Merlin as someone akin to himself, touched by the warped hand of genius, the blessing or curse of a cruel destiny. In an online auction, Officer Pluto had even bid for an early edition of *Golden Spells For A Golden Age,* an amalgamated version of Merlin's and Morgana's spell-books: he had gone as high as three months' salary before he was outbid.

Now he watched as the duo onscreen approached a bank that ran around a well, from which the upper half of a giant's body towered. If Nature didn't repent of her creation of whales and elephants, surely she must have repented of her handiwork with this creature, thought Pluto. He could discern the giant's face, his shoulders, his chest and a good portion of his belly, and, fastidious as ever, he did not like what he saw. For, magnified many times over onscreen, the pores of the giant's skin were like the horns of a frog, or a toad, or even a hound-fish. The giant's arms hung down at his sides, and downward from the place where men clasp their cloaks, there was a generous thirty hand-spans of long, flowing hair.

The giant bent down from his great height towards the little men.

'Have you come at last to slay me, King Arthur and Sir Bedivere?' he spluttered.

Merlin called up to him then, 'Hold your tongue, you blathering idiot. Arthur slayed you at Mont Saint Michel these many years hence.'

'Was that where I had my nice little cave?' asked the giant. 'Ever so cosy it was, like a socket in a skull.'

'Oh, I know who you are now,' Lanval declaimed. 'I remember the song Dagonet used to sing at court,' he continued, warbling, *'The King broke armour of crocodile-skin/And ended this life of terrible sin/Sir Kay and Sir Bedivere compliant/In beheading this Horrible Giant.'*

'Me too, me too,' said the Giant. 'I like to sing.'

'Stick to your bugle,' said Merlin, 'and when you feel a great and tremendous urge to sing, search around your neck and you'll find the strap it's tied to. Take the impulse out on that.'

'Poor, muddle-headed soul,' he added, turning to Lanval. 'Let's leave him alone and not waste our breath. There's only nonsense here.'

As they departed, the stooping giant drew himself up as tall as a ship's mast. With the call of his bugle, it was as if he were trying to pipe them back - as if he were his own bosun's whistle.

Not bad, thought Pluto. Not bad at all, for a first attempt, considering the unpromising source material. Emboldened by his own success, he decided to embark on his Grand Design. There would, of course, be an aesthetic rightness to it. And if that meant, for example, that he became the Captain of the *Joyous Gard,* or that Lieutenant Rose Thorn, or even Sister Scarlet Steel, evinced a sudden, irresistible attraction for him, then so be it. For he would be Star, Director, Auteur.

The glimmerings of an idea for the stand-out episode of his own series, *Planet Pluto,* began to take shape. Of course, that unfortunate haircut of Lieutenant Rose Thorn's would have to go. She would be as she had been before, blonde, lissom, lovely. And what if he could contrive it so that she had never left the *Joyous Gard* at all?

Life, Mediated by His Art. His Purpose. His Destiny.

Slowly, savouring the moment, he clicked open the *Astalot* File, ready to merge the first images. A minor pang of conscience began to trouble him, but he shook his head, shook it away. *So, I'm complicated. Their ways are not mine. It takes all sorts. A little leeway. A little compassion, purrlease. Not everyone has their own castle, and a starship named after it.*

From somewhere inside the whirring machine, the tender ghost whom he had deleted, although not from the memory cloud, watched over him, with a great ache in her heart. Surely, she thought, surely her heart would break, at last.

Lavenza.

Nessa had to put her plans for Officer Pluto on hold, since she and Alfie were chosen to take part in Planet Aquatica's continuing research mission. Trying not to look too excited, they climbed aboard the *Ganymede* with

Officer James and the rest of her team. The scout craft was to take them to the outskirts of their former camp on the planet's surface.

Three floating surface stations had arrived ahead of them and were now situated on the lakes and seas where the most frequent creature sightings had occurred. Officer James assigned the three senior members of the team, that is, herself, Dr Blake and Count Fyodor to head the stations, to be assisted by Sister Scarlet Steel, Ensign Alfie Blake and Ensign Dagonet, respectively. And in fact, almost before the teams had settled into their floating stations, the creatures began arriving to investigate these curious structures.

One enterprising amphibian started trying to scale the steep, metallic sides of Dr Blake's station. 'So there'll be no trouble gettin' the critters to come inside for a look-see,' announced the chief medical officer to them all over the communications system that Count Fyodor had rigged up.

Dr Blake was right. In the days that followed, it became apparent that the amphibians had an intense capacity for accelerated learning. Using a decompression flask which harnessed the power of blue agate crystals, Count Fyodor and Ensign Dagonet adapted the communications system so that it translated concepts into images. They were pleased to discover that, using this system, the amphibians were able to provide valuable information. Soon reports were heading back to the starship that the Aquaticans possessed their own comprehensive language, and advanced social structures, and that, in every respect, they qualified for the status of sentient beings.

Captain De Lys then sent authorisation for Officer James to hold a meeting with the Aquatican leader, in which she should use the communications system to inform him what it would be like if his people joined the Conglomerate. The Aquatican sat there in the hub of Count Fyodor's floating station, patient enough, whilst

275

she turned dials, pulled levers and pressed buttons, then switched the whole thing off in frustration.

'Take a look at it for me, Fyodor, would you?' she said, for though Ensign Dagonet was far more helpful, Fydor was more knowledgeable.

The Count switched the communications system back on so that it whirred and juddered into life. 'You need to wait until the amber light has gone off before you twist that dial,' he admonished her.

'Oh, right,' said Officer James, 'sorry.' Cautiously, she turned the dial, then punched symbols onto the screen that were intended to represent the protection that the Conglomerate could offer. However, the image that came up was her umbrella.

She sighed.

Next, she tried punching in symbols that meant sharing this planet, and the screen showed a disc world, sliced up like pizza, with different hands reaching for a slice.

However, the Aquatican proved to be better at conveying his meaning using the new system. After he had punched the screen, it revealed ruined cities beneath the sea, and a shadowy race that lived there. Then a mysterious being appeared onscreen. He had the head and torso of a man, but the lower half of his body had been washed away, as if someone had spilled water onto a watercolour portrait.

'Who is that?' Officer James asked Count Fyodor.

Count Fyodor stared at the screen, unwilling to admit his new invention wasn't flawless. 'We don't have word for it in any Earth language,' he said at last. 'Maybe *Mer-Magician? Sea-wizard?*'

The Aquatican pressed some more onscreen buttons to reveal an image that looked like glass cylinders, each being filled with differing amounts of water.

Count Fyodor recognised the cylinders, since Animal Magnetism or Mesmerism had formed part of the advanced syllabus of vampire studies at the Academy.

'Mesmer's glass harmonica!' he said. He frowned. 'What he mean?'

'The music of the spheres? The celestial harmony of the planet?' suggested Officer James, who had studied the same syllabus. 'Which would be disrupted by alien entities. In other words, *us*.'

The Aquatican could not understand exactly what they were saying, but there was something about the hushed, reverential tone of their voices which made him feel that he had successfully imparted his message. So he nodded, for he had been wonderfully quick at realising that this was the Terran gesture of assent. Then they all three stared at the images flowing onto the screen, of a mysterious, enigmatic people, at one with their dream-like world, reflecting the same mysterious qualities as the seascape they inhabited.

That night, in the hub of their floating module, Count Fyodor and Ensign Dagonet sat up late, looking through the further eerily beautiful images the Aquaticans had provided of this Kingdom Beneath the Sea. This was an ancient kingdom awash with waves, set amongst immense rocks covered in hooded clusters of barnacles and green sprawls of seaweed or purple sea-wet heather, with slippery fronds. Birdfish flew and swam, cyan seahorses and seven-pronged starfish ebbed and flowed, and porpoises drifted through vapours, shadows and miasmas.

'What I wouldn't give to go and explore there,' said Ensign Dagonet, twisting the stem of his glass between his fingers so that the sea-world onscreen sparkled through its crystal. A steady flow of equipment had been arriving in the Gamma Sculptoris system, including heavy-duty submarines and Officer James had ruled that soon they could begin their study of the sea's mysterious lower levels.

'Well, if *you* ask Officer James, sure she say yes,' said Count Fyodor, nursing his schnapps and his sour temperament, 'though I hear she and Steel girl have first submarine mission.'

'I don't begrudge them that first trip,' said Ensign Dagonet. 'Think how exciting it will be for them.'

'Then you better man than I,' said Count Fyodor ruefully, and he raised his glass to chink it with that of the young Ensign.

In fact, there were opportunities for all of them to take the submarine below the surface of the water, except that, during these first few excursions, they couldn't locate this kingdom beneath the sea. And then, a couple of weeks in, Ensign Alfie was recalled to the starship to take up his new post with Officer Pluto in the Time Editing Suite. He took the webbed wombat-tribble he had found on Aquatica with him. In their absence, Dr Blake often called on Ensign Dagonet to assist him.

By the time of their second trip in the *Poseidon* submarine, Count Fyodor and Ensign Dagonet realised their sensor equipment was detecting the movement of a huge entity, some way off, in the distant gloom. But they could not reach the creature, since it could move much faster than they, in this, the Conglomerate's most powerful submarine.

However, on another chase, Officer James and Sister Scarlet Steel stumbled across an extraordinary reminder of the civilisation of sea magicians. The submarine's sensors began to flash, registering the presence of a large construction in the nearby darkness.

'Do you think it's the sea-creature?' asked Nessa.

Officer James nodded, uncertainly. 'Though the temperature reading isn't right for a mammal,' she said. 'But let's alter the submarine's course to pursue it.'

As they surged forwards through the water, a beam of light blazed into existence, so startling them that they hurled the submarine away from its source. Seconds later, the light flickered out, and the submarine made another cautious approach.

Once again, the beam of light blazed out.

This time, however, Sister Scarlet Steel took charge of the controls, and slowed the submarine so that they ventured forwards, to the point where the light had originated. There, rising from the ocean's depths, was a massive stone pyramid. On its luminous white, central lateral face was carved an apple tree. Only, the apples were eyes, engraved among the leaves. Once again, light shone out, and they realised it came from these eyes.

'Do you think this pyramid ever stood above sea-level?' Nessa asked Officer James.

'Maybe,' said Officer James. 'It was certainly built to last. What do you think it's for?'

Nessa thought long and hard. She remembered a lesson her Headmistress, Arabella, had taught them at school, about the Pyramids of Egypt, the great pharaohs and their treasure-houses. Of course, centuries later, Arabella would lose her job for refusing to declare her support for the Collodian Program. Just before Nessa had left Avalon, she had seen her former headmistress on television, at a protest march, carrying a banner, which read, 'Memory is the guardian and treasury of all things.' All these thoughts coalesced now in Nessa's mind., so that she said,

'The apple tree reminds me of the sacred grove that once used to exist in Avalon. And the eyes remind me of the Pharaohs of Egypt. Do you think...,' she swallowed, 'do you think this Pyramid might be where the Cylinders of Memory are hidden?'

'Maybe,' said Officer James. 'I'd almost given up thinking about them. I thought if Lieutenant Rose Thorn couldn't find them, no-one could.'

'Well, we weren't exactly looking,' said Nessa. 'But how do we get inside?' For there was no visible entrance.

In answer, Officer James began to punch figures onto the onscreen navigator, which using GPS digital technology, put the pyramid's height at 60 meters, with a base of 8000 square meters.

Suddenly, out of the darkness, a vast, monstrous shape, the sea-creature they had been searching for, swept towards them. Beneath a pair of pale eyes, each as large as knight's shields, it possessed huge, scaly mandibles which grasped the submarine and shook it from side-to-side. It was only when they fired torpedoes into the scarlet roof of his mouth that he dropped them, suddenly, like a dog drops a bone. And yet the conflict had made the sea-dragon lash out its baleful tail, which had opened a secret trapdoor at the base of the pyramid.

They stationed the submarine and climbed out of it in their diving suits. Together, they swam over to the trapdoor and hauled it open. Once inside, the time-carven floor beneath their feet thrummed and thrummed. They began to make their way along the pyramid's bewildering tunnels.

Inside the pyramid, nothing ran straight. All the tunnels curved and split, interlaced and looped, tracing round elaborate concentric circles. And so they walked on and on and on, hoping that they were going in the right direction, through caverns, corridors and doorways that were all alike, and on through watery darkness.

Now they suddenly entered a tunnel, and here, their torches picked out strange wall drawings of winged beings with dark eyes, mournful and beguiling. Sister Scarlet Steel shivered when she saw them, for they reminded her of the undead souls she had glimpsed when escaping across the borders of the Collodian.

Down they went, along slanting passages and through cavern chambers overgrown with springy moss and sea anemones, lit up by only the faintest glimmer of approaching light. But at the last turn of a corridor they halted, then very slowly they took a final step into a faint, surprising bloom of light...

Before them shone a world of muted blues and greens. And now the dancing beams from their torches lit up what was already illuminated by pillars of emerald and jasper, and encrustations of topaz and sapphire, immense and glittering. It was a cavern-palace of such dazzling beauty that their hearts ached to think they might otherwise have missed it, had not the lash of the dragon's tail revealed its lustre.

In a state of wonder, Officer James and Sister Scarlet Steel passed through this cavern with its jewelled statues of ancient gods and goddesses, funerary figurines and elephants of ivory and jade. Then they drifted out into darkness again, guided only by the occasional glance of light from their torches. On and on like this they swam, slowly, steadily, until finally they reached a series of rocks, that burned with a phosphorous glow.

Here, there was another boulder in front of another trapdoor. They were weary now, and it took considerable effort from both of them to push the boulder to one side.

Then, as they hauled open the trap-door, an amber radiance fell all around them, as a sea-wave falls in sunlight. They tumbled into this light, their shadows racing across them into the carven traceries and glittering crevices of this vast chamber at the heart of the pyramid.

In this chamber, there stood a man with the look of a magician about him, a sea-mage, with long, tangled hair and a beard the colour of rust and sea-mist. He was broad-shouldered, and narrow waisted, and his skin, though wrinkled like a sea-apple, was supple, too. His eyes were piercing and luminous, yet even though he started at their arrival, still, he did not take his gaze away from the girl who was seated there in front of him.

She was sitting at a sort of wooden frame with an iron spindle, which contained glass cylinders. Her face was an ivory rose, shadowed by hair as dark as raven wings. Her expression was thoughtful, contemplative even, as she poured water from a flask into one of these cylinders.

This girl was the Guardian of the Cylinders of Memory, though she did not know what that meant.

All at once, Nessa shouted out, 'Granny!' and the spell was broken.

The girl seated at the wooden frame which held the Cylinders of Memory turned towards her. For a moment, she was confused, for she was emerging from a trance. Then the expression on her face cleared and her eyes shone.

'Nessa,' she said, 'there you are! But you're very thin, child. What have you been doing with yourself? And where's the dear little beastie that sits on your shoulder?'

'Oh Granny,' said Nessa, 'Farlight's gone.' Her voice rose up in a sort of sob. 'I don't have him anymore.'

'Did Queen Morgana take him from you?' asked Snow White.

'I don't know,' said Nessa. 'Maybe. I wondered if it was because I refused to take part in the Collodian Program. Because Farlight always slept at the end of my bed, and then, one morning when I woke up...' she paused and gulped, 'he was gone.'

Snow White stood up from the wooden frame, stepped towards her granddaughter and gave her a consoling hug.

'And yet, it would be very unusual for one witch to try and steal the familiar of another,' said the sea-mage. His eyes shifted over to the visitors, taking them all in, fixing on nothing.

'That's Merrick,' Snow White said. 'Trust him. He knows things.'

'He doesn't seem to know that Queen Morgana will now sleep for a hundred years,' said Officer James.

'Really?' said Merrick. Now a look of glee lit up his face that had seemed grim as midwinter. 'That's wonderful news. Why, it means, my dear,' he said, turning to Snow White, 'I can release you from your role as Guardian of the Cylinders of Memory.' He waved his hands in sweeping gestures across her face. 'I now revoke all enchantments placed upon you. You are free to leave.' And when Snow White made no attempt to move away, he added, 'You can go with your granddaughter now, if you wish.'

'But won't you tell me what it is I have been doing here?' asked Snow White.

'Queen Morgana appointed you the Guardian of the Cylinders of Memory,' said Merrick. 'She knew that only someone pure of heart could be trusted to care for them, and she bound you to the task with magic.'

'But how will we return all those memories to the poor souls who have had them stolen?' asked Snow White.

'Lanval, too,' said Nessa, remembering something other than her own grief.

'Oh, gracious, my poor grandson,' said Snow White.

'Lieutenant Rose Thorn wanted to organise a programme whereby the Sisters of Valerian would redistribute them...' said Officer James.

'I'd like to help with that,' said Nessa. 'I never got the chance to know Lanval much, but he's my half-brother, and... it seems like it would be a good thing to do.'

'Yes, but it would take years to help everyone,' Snow White objected.

'And there is a simpler, better way, besides,' said Merrick. He fetched a jug, filled it with water, and began to pour it into the glass cylinders. 'It's not so easy to balance the fluid levels,' he said. 'A little more in this one, tip this one into the next, until it is as close to the perfect balance as it is possible to achieve.' Then he touched his fingers to the water, to find out if it was as cold as it should be, presumably in order to conjure up the necessary quality of sound.

Now the magician passed his hands over the cylinders until they were magnetised.

Then he took Snow White's place at the wooden frame, and his foot began to pump out a heavy percussion on the iron spindle whilst he rubbed his hands round the cylinders' moist rims. Soon, the glass harmonica began to emit its pure notes.

The sound of Merrick's music started to seep through the interstices in the walls and trapdoors, rising upwards in a spiral towards the apex of the pyramid, and then out and upwards, to twist its way through the water, to the surface of the planet. Then it moved like smoke all across

Aquatica, turning through its islands and floating stations, sometimes cascading down to the water, then spiralling up again, towards the heavens and the stars.

Now the sound began to soar out across the galaxy and reach those poor souls in Avalon and Valerian whose memories had been harvested. The music made its way to Tallulah's swimming pool in her backyard on the outskirts of the Collodian, where Pippin was trying out his new water-wings. It restored those memories to him that had been taken at such a young age, he had never even known they were gone.

On it soared, to Aurélie, sitting in the captain's chair on board the *Joyous Gard.* Now she remembered the Time Travel spell, and the purposes of celestine, and everything else she needed to know. Then the sound reverberated through the corridors of the starship and into the medical chamber, where Lieutenant Lanval lay sleeping. Thus, without knowing it, he was infected by the sound, and in his dreams, his memories began to return.

'It may take a little time,' Merrick said, as on he played, 'for those whose ears are not attuned to the music of the heavenly spheres to hear it. But in this sound, there are stars, comets, planets, traversing the night-sky, comprising the celestial harmonies that will bring them back to themselves once more.'

'Why now?' asked Officer James. 'Why didn't you do this before?'

'Queen Morgana had to be stopped first,' said Merrick, 'or else none of this would have been possible - and besides, no-one was ready to listen to my music before.'

'It's very beautiful,' said Nessa, without a trace of her customary arrogance.

Merrick turned swiftly towards her. 'Yes,' he said, as he brought it to a close, 'it is.' Then he looked at her more carefully, as if he were examining the contents of her heart, and what he found there made him speak more kindly. 'I think it's almost worse to steal a familiar than it is to steal memories,' he said. 'It's like taking a part of your soul.'

'Yes,' said Nessa. 'And without Farlight, I feel so lost.'

'Nessa,' said Officer James, 'I had no idea. You should have said something.'

'There wasn't much point,' said Nessa. 'What can you do about it?'

'Orchids are sometimes consoling,' murmured Officer James.

'They're nice an all,' said Nessa, 'but Farlight was *everything* to me. Without him, the last few weeks at Brunwych were a bit of a blur. Then I thought, well, perhaps the Valerian Sisterhood would give me some kind of structure. But I couldn't keep my mind on Valerian Grail Scripture. So then I signed up for the Academy, where they said I was *brilliant but erratic,* and could I go somewhere else please, and then, finally, the starship, mainly because Sifu Wong, my old qi gong teacher, was now the fitness officer onboard - he'd always been good to me.'

'I suppose qi gong is another kind of helpful discipline?' asked Merrick.

'Yes,' said Nessa, 'but more than that, Sifu Wong knew me from before, knew how I used to be. Sometimes he gave me a dragon meditation to do, and that helped a bit. That used to give me something like the kind of feeling I had with Farlight.'

'I still can't fathom why Queen Morgana would steal your familiar,' said Merrick, then.

'If she did,' said Nessa. 'She was my fairy godmother, after all.'

'Perhaps she was worried by how powerful you might become, with Farlight at your side,' said Snow White. 'To her way of thinking, you had already rebelled against her.'

'I'm no lover of Queen Morgana,' said Merrick, 'but perhaps we had better not accuse her until we know the truth. The Celestine of Avalon would assist us in discovering it - or else, this would...' And he removed a small rose quartz pendulum set on a silver chain from a little drawer in the carven wall.

'Let me give you this,' he said to Nessa. 'You ask it a direct question, and it moves backwards and forwards for *yes*; side to side for *no*.'

'Ooh I know about these,' said Nessa, 'we did them in First Year Introduction to Magick.'

She took the pendulum from the wizard, and straight away she asked, 'Did Queen Morgana steal my luck-dragon?'

The pendulum moved backwards and forwards. *Yes.*

'Sometimes,' said Merrick thoughtfully, 'even great queens can be reckless and wilful. She should not have done it, but perhaps she regrets it now.'

'*Does* she regret it?' Nessa asked the pendulum.

The pendulum span round in slow circles. *Maybe.*

'Ah,' said Merrick. 'Well, rose quartz is a wonderful, soothing crystal to lay upon your heart,' he added. 'And you may find that in a hundred years or so, you don't mind, quite so much.' Then he began to frown and cudgel his brains. 'I have an idea,' he said, at last. 'There is a sea dragon who circles this pyramid.'

'Yes, we were chasing him in our submarine,' said Officer James.

'Don't do that!' said the wizard. 'There are so few dragons left now. But each dragon feels the call of his brother in his blood. He should be able to tell you where to find Farlight.'

'Why would the sea-dragon help me?' asked Nessa. She glanced over at Officer James. 'We *were* chasing him.'

'Do you have anything you could give him in exchange?' asked the wizard. 'Dragons like precious metals, jewels, gold doubloons.'

Nessa reached into the pouch at the front of her diving suit. 'I have this,' she said, taking out the Holy Grail. 'I think it's made of gold, and look, it's covered in jewels.

But Lieutenant Rose Thorn entrusted it to me. I don't think I should give it away.'

'The Grail!' said Merrick, and he made the Sign of the Cross. 'No, child, you should not give away what was entrusted to you. But this dragon has long held a fascination with the Grail, and it may be that if you grant him the sight of it, he will help you.' He smiled again, and in the reflected glow of the Holy Grail, his face became less like winter, and more like autumn, when the leaves are bright, russet and ruddy, when fires curl and crackle in the hearth, when chestnuts gleam and roast. 'Although the Grail is also a symbol of hope, of everything you can become. If you become that person, then you no longer need the symbol,' said Merrick.

'The Sisters of Valerian cherish the Grail,' said Nessa. 'It is the lodestone and polestar of their Creed. And I am supposed to place it in their Temple.'

'Be that as it may,' said Merrick, 'perhaps one day, there will be no need for Creeds or Temples. We will all worship as we best see fit, within our hearts. Because I think that all the old prophecies are starting to come true. I think we are just now entering upon a time when we are all going to be granted our heart's desires.'

'I thought happy endings were just for fairy-tales,' said Nessa.

'Some might argue that the trials and tribulations of Avalon and Valerian *are* fairy-tales,' said Merrick, 'that your grandmother Snow White is a fairy-tale heroine, that the cloud-capped towers, the gorgeous palaces, the solemn temples are all the stuff of which dreams are made.'

'And me?' asked Nessa, in a small voice. 'And Farlight?'

'Well,' said Merrick, kindly again, 'perhaps if you love someone or something enough, they stop being a fairy-tale or a dream, and become real. And so - let's go and search out the sea-dragon.'

Meanwhile, on board the starship, over in sick-bay, Lieutenant Lanval had heard the call of Merick's music from his bed. As its sound swooped and soared all around him, he began to dream about who he used to be. Although he did not know it, Blancheflor was sitting beside him, clutching his hand, and her presence too permeated this twilight state between dreaming and waking.

Blancheflor was wondering when and if he might wake, and whether a little forgetfulness were a better thing, since like smoke hiding a flame, it would conceal his shame from him.

Sir Lanval was dreaming that he was back in the Collodian, with Sir Lancelot, and Elaine, as she was then, for it was in the time before they had enlisted for the starship. He had, all unwittingly, spent the night with Elaine, and now she did not wish to talk to him overmuch, and it was a strange, sad, sorrowing time for both of them. But in his dream, they wandered on some little way through a celestial forest, which tempered its thick shade with mossy greenness.

Presently, Lanval walked from them to fill their gourds with fresh water from the fast running river. When he had finished, he looked up, and there was a beautiful lady, clad in a robe of spring-green on the other bank. He thought that she was singing, and he called to her to cross over the bridge and come to him, that he might better hear her song.

She turned her face towards him, and he thought that love's beam shone from her eyes. He knew then that she was his own wife, Blancheflor. But the sound he had mistaken for a song among the ebb and eddying of the river was actually a sob.

In his dream, Blancheflor began to walk away from him, against the current, heading far up the verdant river. He tried to follow after her, when there came a flash of light. This lightning began to unfold itself like a bolt from a cloth of gold, illuminating the green boughs of the trees all around them. Now Lanval could discern seven trees of gold, blazing out against the sky.

His wife called out to him, 'Why do you look on these living lights, and not on what follows?'

And Sir Lanval beheld then two boys, clad in radiant green and white, embroidered all over in fleur-de-lys, which was the emblem of his wife's house.

From the other side of the bridge that she had not crossed, Blancheflor cried, 'This is a vision of what might be. Don't you know that your happiness is here?' But she would not take one step to join him, and try as he might, he could not cross the river to join her on the other side. Each time he dipped his foot into the water, the water spat him out.

Finally, Blancheflor seemed to take pity on him, for she said, 'A little while, and ye shall not see me. Again a little while, and ye shall.'

Lanval felt then such a sense of joyous gladness that it propelled him forwards to the bridge, where she was waiting on the other side. And though she could not cross over to join him, yet now could he place his feet upon its slats.. He trod the bridge, with steady, measured pace, and when he reached Blancheflor's side of the river, he took her in his arms.

'It was a cold heart I kept towards you,' said Blancheflor, 'and in that time, I could not forgive you.'

'And am I forgiven now?' asked Lanval. 'Merlin told me my sin would be forgiven.'

'It was not for him to say it,' said Blancheflor, with a sudden flash of anger. 'And yet I find that my life without you is sadder than when we were wed. You know that my grandmother annulled our marriage?'

'She should not have done that without our consent,' said Lanval.

'Alas, she had mine,' said Blancheflor. 'So, you see, there is something too for you to forgive.'

'I think perhaps I should wake up now,' said Lanval, 'so that we can try to put back together the pieces of our lives.'

Thus, like Adam, Lanval awoke from his dream and found it truth, for there was Blancheflor beside him. Now she reached across the bed to enfold him in her arms, and, if each of them wept in that moment, they can be forgiven, since the intermingling of their tears was healing.

Beneath the seas of Aquatica, Nessa followed Merrick the sea-mage back through the labyrinthine corridors of the pyramid, to its very threshold. There they stood, and there Merrick waved the point of his staff in three concentric circles, then shouted:

'Khrilgharran, I call out your name and summon you now, here to me.'

His voice fell short against the sound of waves beating against the pyramid, but dragons have sharp ears. What Nessa had mistaken for part of a ruined tower in the water slowly began to shift its shape, so that she saw the shoulder of the Dragon Khrilgharran as he uncurled his bulk and lifted himself up.

The dragon's scaled head, crowned with spikes, rose higher than the broken tower's height, and his taloned forefeet rested in the detritus of the ruined city below. His scales were a burnished blue-black, catching the sea-light like broken slate. Lean as a greyhound he was, and immense as a whale. Nessa stared in awe. Merrick had told her little about the dragon, and what he had told her, had not prepared her for this sight. Almost she stared into the dragon's eyes, but Merrick pulled her aside, for one cannot return a dragon's gaze.

Merrick held up his staff, that now looked like a twig, a splinter.

'You will not win my hoard with that,' said the great dry voice of the dragon.

'You should know me well enough to know I do not want your hoard,' said Merrick.

Phosphorous smoke hissed from the dragon's nostrils: that was his laughter.

'Would you, would *both* of you, like to come with me now to my sea-cave and see my hoard? It is worth looking at.'

'No, Khrilgharran,' said Merrick, and the sound of his own name repeated seemed to subdue the dragon.

'Where is your greed?' he muttered. 'Your race loved bright stones when I was young.' Then he turned his attention to Nessa. 'But *you* are very young,' said the dragon, 'Is there no bright circlet or bracelet you have set your heart upon?'

Nessa shook her head, finding it hard not to look into the dragon's watchful eyes.

'I did not know females came so young into their power,' said the dragon.

'But I have lost my power,' Nessa said, at last. 'For I have lost my familiar, Farlight, a luck-dragon, who meant all the world to me.'

'You should not have been so careless, then,' said the dragon cruelly, and his upper lip twisted into a smile, and yellow smoke curled from his nostrils and then above his long head and out into the water.

'I wasn't,' said Nessa then, full of her own fire, 'he was taken from me.'

'And it is to ask for my help that you have summoned me?'

Nessa nodded.

The point of the dragon's tail arched up over his mailed back, like a sword held aloft in front of the ruined tower. Dryly he spoke: 'What have you to offer me in return for my help?'

Merrick placed a hand on Nessa's shoulder. She said then, 'I... I have nothing to give you.'

A grating sound came from the dragon's throat, like an avalanche far away, stones falling among mountains. Fire spurted along his pronged tongue. He raised himself yet higher, so that he loomed over the ruins of the city.

'Surely this wizard must have told you, you do not approach a dragon, empty-handed.'

'I have the Grail,' she replied, her voice shaking, but her words emerging clear and true.

At the sound of the name of the sacred chalice, the ancient sea-dragon became still, utterly still.

A minute went by, then another, and then, finally, Merrick smiled.

'You have the mastery of him now,' he whispered to Nessa. Then he called out to the mighty dragon, 'She will show you the Grail, that you may see it with your own baleful eyes, and then live to be the most honoured, the first among your kind, if you will grant her the favour we ask. Khrilgharran, where is Nessa's luck-dragon that she calls Farlight?'

When thus the wizard spoke the dragon's name for the third time, it was as if he were tightening the leash that held fast the huge being. There were the steel talons, each as long as a knife, and there, the chainmail scales, and the embers of fire that lurked in the dragon's throat, yet still this leash tightened.

'Might I see the Grail?' asked the dragon now.

'After you have helped her, yes,' said the wizard, clutching his staff to him, standing as still as the dragon stood.

Flames broke suddenly loud and bright from the dragon's jaws, and when they had died down, he said to Nessa, 'Was there ever anywhere that Farlight used to hide?'

'Sometimes under the bed in my dormitory at school,' said Nessa.

'Then, by the call of his blood to mine, I tell you, that is where you need to look now.'

'But how can I?' asked Nessa.

'The sea-mage and I will help you,' said the great, dry voice of the dragon, and he called out the name, *Farlight,* and in that great calling, more and more flames unfurled, and then Merrick held aloft his arms, and with his staff, drew three great circles in the air. When he brought his arms down again, Nessa found she was eleven-years old, and peering under her bed at school.

Farlight was there, in the darkest, most difficult to reach corner, curled up on an old pink sweater of hers. But she was able to crawl under the bed and haul out the sweater, and since his sharp talons were snaggled in it, Farlight came too.

And then the little mauve luck-dragon was in her arms again, and she hugged him so tightly, it was as if she would never, ever let him go.

Then, somehow, she did not know how, she and Farlight were standing at the entrance to the Great Pyramid beneath the sea, and Merrick, the great sea-mage, was smiling beside her, and she heard the dragon say, 'See, little wizard, sometimes things are much simpler than you make them.'

'But now is the time,' answered the wizard, 'the time of which the Living Scrolls of the Sea have prophesised. Everyone who has suffered and strived will now be granted their hearts' desire. For Nessa, her Farlight. For her good crewmates - well, they each will know what it is they most desire. It will all happen, just it was always supposed to.'

'And me?' said the mighty sea-dragon. 'What about my heart's desire? Was I not promised another glimpse of the most sacred, Holy Grail?'

Nessa moved Farlight to her shoulder. His pale gold wings brushed against her hair, and he chittered against her ear. Then she reached into her pouch for the Holy Grail and brought it forth, the rich and precious Grail, encrusted with jewels, the sacred receptacle of the blood of Christ.

Khrilgharran's great eyes were reverent as he stared at the Grail. 'I am an ancient dragon,' he said at last. 'I am what you now call a Precursor Valerian, brought here to advance the magical explorations of the sea-wizards. But when I behold this sacred chalice, it seems to me I glimpse again the Valerian of Old.'

'Apart from the Compound and Temple of the Sisters of Valerian,' said Nessa, 'Valerian is wasteland now and so it will remain.' For she had heard the rumours that Valerian had shrunk to the size of a thimble and was worn around the sleeping queen's neck.

'They said something like that once in Arthur's time,' said the dragon, 'at the Court of Cardoeil, from which I was exiled. And yet, when the Grail was restored to its rightful place, birds began to sing, and blossoms to bud, and flowers and fruit grew in rich and ripe profusion.' He sighed at the memory, and his sigh emerged as further sparks of flame.

'Do you really think that can happen again?' asked Nessa, and Farlight lifted his head at the unfamiliar, excited lilt to her voice, then nuzzled back into her neck.

'Only if you take the Grail back to Valerian,' exhaled the dragon.

'Then, so will I,' said Nessa, her eyes shining.

The submarine brought Nessa, Officer James and Snow White to the surface of the seas of Aquatica. Thanks to the information which Merrick and the Aquatican had provided, this planet was judged unsuitable for the Valerians, and although a few researchers elected to remain behind to forge closer links with the planet's inhabitants, the mission was deemed complete. Everyone else returned to the *Joyous Gard.*

After a few happy weeks with her granddaughter on board the starship, Snow White chose to return to Avalon, to keep company with Rose Red, who was a Daughter of the Air in that sleeping land. Lanval had given her the very last stump of his Travelling Candle, since she had a superstitious dread of her atoms hurtling across space in any other way.

Once her beloved Granny had departed, Sister Scarlet Steel felt more inclined to discuss the side mission with her teacher, the thought of which had already given her a few sleepless nights. Only her utter conviction in the goodness and integrity of Sifu Wong persuaded her that this was indeed the right course of action.

'Can't we just abandon him on some rotten old planet with an oxygen cylinder?' she asked him after some further training exercises in the qi gong studio.

'That man like bindweed,' insisted her teacher, putting down his bamboo flute. 'However you cut him down, he spring back.'

'But all they did to Queen Morgana was let her have a nap for a hundred years, and she's *worse,*' said Nessa.

Her teacher looked at her drawn, anxious face and relented. 'Your gold heart get you into trouble one day,' he said. 'Okie-dokie, oxygen cylinder, pre-programmed parachute, and - out he go.'

It was easy enough to persuade Officer Pluto to accompany her to the Viewing Theatre on the pretext that something had gone wrong with the film projector. The cinema was showing what was purported to be the last ever episode of *Collodian Star,* but now the protagonists onscreen, an ogre with a bugle round his neck, and a small boy leaping onto him from a table, were flickering wildly.

Officer Pluto entered the projection room to examine the film reels. Following behind him, Sister Scarlet Steel cut the lights.

In her mind, she ran through the different animal movements of her qi gong training. The bear, the crane, the deer, the monkey, the tiger. She altered her mind to bird vision. Now she could see in the dark. Officer Pluto could not.

He emerged from the projection room, flailing everywhere. She ducked down quickly. She decided the bear was strong enough to tackle this officer. Like that, she could deal a powerful blow. She curved her hands, then struck at him with the heel of her palm. Her paw.

He staggered to one side and then her paws became a tiger's, and her claws raked across his throat, pressed against his windpipe. Now he was gasping for breath, but somehow he jerked his head free and then as the screen flickered into life, there was enough light for him to charge her.

She edged backwards, then sideways, her every movement flowing seamlessly into the next. Yet there was something ritualistic too about the movements she made, those powerful, soft strides, which were also like the dance before the altar dedicated to Valeria.

Now she breathed deeply into the qi and then she emerged from her corner, a roaring tiger. Again she swiped at him with her paws, again and again, so that he could neither shake her off not muster his composure sufficiently to counter-attack.

Onscreen, the small boy sat on the ogre's shoulders, and put his hands over his eyes. The ogre seemed cross and sat down on the sofa with the boy still on his back.

To Officer Pluto, Nessa was a veritable cyclone, and even as the blood began to splatter from his nose and split lip, still, she did not cease. For the tiger only grew more fierce, more determined at the sight and scent of blood. And so she roared again, and in that savage sound was the hunt and hurt of decades.

She took his head between her paws and twisted it round.

There came a crack, and she wondered if his neck was broken. But no. Though he collapsed onto the floor of the Viewing Theatre, still, he was breathing. He lay on his back, his nose and mouth bleeding.

Now he was docile enough for her to turn on the overhead lights and summon Sifu Wong via her communicator.

The teacher joined her quickly with the pre-programmed parachute, constellation class, and the lightweight oxygen cylinder in a backpack with food and liquid pellets from the synthesizer. Sifu Wong had no desire for there to be more suffering than was strictly necessary, to draw it out, to render it a lingering revenge.

At the sight of his old adversary, Sifu Wong bowed slightly. 'Officer Pluto,' he told the barely conscious man, 'thanks to this girl, today you say no to death.' He nodded to Nessa. 'Compassion also is honourable.' Then the two of them fitted the backpack and parachute to the crumpled body and began to haul it down the corridors of the starship, towards the airlock on the recreation deck.

An open door: a blast of air and Officer Pluto was gone; his parachute opened out so that he shot up into the sky; his aching bones and bruised flesh relinquished to the reviving air and suffering stars.

Lieutenant Rose Thorn insisted that Tallulah Mae Jackson, Sister Scarlet Steel and Farlight should take the *Ganymede* back to Valerian. It was the scout ship she had trained in, she knew every inch of it, and so she trusted it above all others. After she and Officer James had walked to the flight bay to make their farewells, she clapped Nessa on the shoulder.

'You've come on alot,' she said to the girl. 'I almost like you now.'

'The feeling's mutual,' said Nessa as Farlight squirmed in her arms.

'I'm sorry I wasn't the stepmother you wanted me to be,' Officer James said to Nessa, attempting to give her a hug.

'That's okay,' said Nessa, wriggling free from her clasp, and setting the luck-dragon on his usual perch. 'If it's any comfort, I didn't want Arthur to be my teenage stepfather either, when I was at school. You can't be much older than I am.'

'Whereas *I*,' said Tallulah, 'am old enough to be everybody here's mother. FFS.'

'You look good for your age, though,' said Nessa. 'When we went to the beauty parlour, the nail technician thought you looked young enough to be your own daughter.'

'Wherever the hell *she* might be,' said Tallulah. 'Running round Old Valerian's ruined churches, last I heard.'

'All of us who have encountered the Grail will retain a certain youthfulness,' said Rose Thorn then. 'I'm so grateful to you two for taking over the running of the Temple of Valerian. You'll do a much better job than me.'

'Yeah, lightweight,' said Tallulah. 'Enjoy your time gallivanting round the new planet with the one with the face - Prince Lancelot.'

'*Captain* Lancelot,' said Rose Thorn. 'He's given up his old title.'

'I'm more interested in his looks,' said Tallulah.

'It's just as well you're going back to Old Valerian then,' said Rose Thorn. 'To be a nun.'

'There's no requirement to take a vow of chastity in the upper echelons of the Sisters of Valerian,' said Tallulah. 'I read that in the manual.'

'There *isn't*?' said Nessa. 'I mean, there isn't. And we get holiday leave, right?' That was the one thing she had told Alfie that had managed to reassure him that he would see her again.

'Six weeks' holiday, and a pension plan,' said Rose Thorn. 'We're not medieval.' She walked over to the *Ganymede*, there, across the bay, darkly shimmering. She slid open the port-side hydraulic door and located the lever that let down the flight of steps.

'Your chariot awaits,' she called across to Tallulah and Nessa. They crossed over and after several further hugs, they climbed inside, with Nessa taking the pilot's seat.

'Radio me if you hit any turbulence,' the lieutenant said to her, poking her head inside the cockpit. 'You soared through the preliminary training programme, but it was only six weeks.'

'I'm a fast learner,' said Sister Scarlet Steel as Farlight breathed hot air against her cheek.

'Yeah, when you bother to read the training manual,' said Rose Thorn.

She came out of the cockpit, the steps went up, the door went down, and then the lieutenant activated the control panel to open the starship's doors. The *Ganymede,* with its precious cargo, and the alternate Holy Grail, shot out into the sky.

Some weeks later, after the Compound's matin prayers and rituals were over, Nessa took the alternate Holy Grail down from the shelf in her chamber and buffered it with a soft cloth. Then she turned it this way and that, letting it sparkle in the light. Farlight stirred sleepily at the end of her narrow bed, but he was not required for today's events.

Then Nessa began to walk through her domain, the Temple of the Sisters of Valerian. First, she went to a little half-loft, over one of the robing rooms in the hinder part of the Great Hall. There, she carefully selected a long, black, ceremonial robe, encrusted with topaz and dark amethyst. A mirror with a mosaic frame hanging beside the chest where the ancient robes were stored gave her back herself: her dark hair, parted over a pale, oval forehead, her eyes, dark also, full of purpose and reverence for the sacred task that awaited her.

When she was robed, she proceeded past the treasure-house with the alternate Holy Grail. Here, some of the Treasures of Old Valerian still remained: the burnished armour, the broken plumes of helmets, buckles and brooches, copper, silver and solid gold. One day, Rose Thorn's shield casing, embroidered all over in crocuses and singing birds would find its way here, and even Sir Lancelot's shield itself, with its three golden lions rampant on an azure background.

High up in the temple rafters above her, owls perched, blinking their yellow eyes. Early morning sunlight shone down in between the tiles in the roof, and then a little rain came down, fine and cool as the ancient silk against her skin. She walked on, noiseless on bare feet, black-clothed. At the very last turn of the passageway, she halted, then very slowly, she took the last step, and looked, and saw.

There, at the heart of the Temple, at the end of a vast hall between double rows of marble columns, were seven steps, austere and gleaming with crystal, which had driven out the ancient darkness with their glory. Above these steps was the altar to the Goddess Valeria.

To the sound of beating drums, Nessa began to walk the length of the hall. Torches held by dark-robed girls threw out their red light onto the Cup Bearer as she approached the altar.

Alone, she climbed the first four steps whiles the drum beats quickened, and the priestesses began to chant: *'From centre to the circle, and back, /From circle to the centre, water moves, /In the sacred chalice.'* On the fifth step, the Holy Grail sent back by Captain De Lys had been set down. Nessa picked it up, so that now she was cradling both chalices, Then she did something which no priestess there, not even Rose Thorn, not even Tallulah, had ever done before. She climbed the final three steps to the altar.

Now she turned to face the assembled women gathered in the Temple. She turned and held aloft the sacred chalices, one in each hand, so that they gleamed with a thousand scintillations, sending a thousand lights dancing among the shadows and the torch-flames.

And there were priestesses who claimed the sight dazzled them, and those who claimed it blinded them, but when their vision cleared, they saw Nessa place those two chalices in the altar alcove.

Finally, she descended the steps and came and walked among them, and now they knew her, not as Nessa, not as Sister Scarlet Steel, not even as the Cup Bearer, but as the reincarnation of the Goddess Valeria, come at last in answer to their prayers.

In Guelder

Inside her cabin on board the *Joyous Gard*, Lieutenant Rose Thorn was dreaming again. Her dream took her back to the time of her Grail quest, when, on the outskirts of Avalon, at the end of a grove of apple-trees, and at the very borders of Valerian, she had seen a huge and leafy oak tree. On that oak, there were more than a thousand candles of miraculous size, twenty or thirty on each branch, all ablaze. Except that when she approached them, the candles proved to be fire fairies.

In that fair light, the luminous beings coursed in gracious and rapid circles.

Upon waking, she was perplexed. If only the Goddess Valeria would come and whisper the meaning of the dream in her ear. But the Goddess was often silent now, as if Lieutenant Rose Thorn, by acting according to her own intuition, had finally become her own best guide.

That day, the lieutenant had arranged to witness the ceremony in which Nessa placed the two Grails within the Temple of Valeria. From her velour seat in the darkened theatre, Lieutenant Rose Thorn watched as, to the sound of her sisters, beating drums, the girl paced the length of the Great Hall. Torches threw out red light onto the Cup Bearer as she approached the altar.

Just then, the onscreen picture froze, and the Captain announced over the communications system, 'Lieutenant Rose Thorn and Officer James to the bridge, please.'

'Lights,' sighed the lieutenant, and as they came up, she stood up, shuffled sideways, then made her way back down the Viewing Theatre's central aisle.

'There it is,' the Captain said gleefully, a few minutes later, pointing to the bridge's vastscreen. 'The planet we've been searching for. There it is, at last.'

From the vastscreen, the planet was shining down on them, blue and green, with its seas beneath them like sapphires, and its land, all the gorgeous emeralds of a Paradise new-created, with the dew of Eden not yet dry.

On her own console, Lieutenant Rose Thorn began to run though the standard astrobiology checklist to see whether this planet was capable of sustaining human life. Stable rotational axis? Affirmative. Sufficient liquid water? Affirmative. Suitable magnetic field? Affirmative. Sufficient high-frequency ultraviolet radiation to trigger ozone formation? Affirmative. Then she looked through the readings for Type of Sun, Position, and Type of Planet.

'This all checks out, Captain,' she said, at last. 'This planet seems ideal.'

'I know, I know,' said Aurélie. 'It's fully capable of sustaining human life. There's enough oxygen, enough water, and it's the right distance from the sun for us to be warmed, not toasted.'

'How soon can we send a preliminary scout party down there?' asked Officer James.

'I'm going to message Dr Blake now, ask him to assemble a team of engineers and medical personnel to go down to the planet's surface,' Aurélie replied. 'Blake's seven.'

However, the captain's preliminary messages soon evolved into an urgent, excited conversation over the communicator. 'Okay, okay, Jem,' she said at last, then turned to her officers. 'Which one of you two wants to pilot the scout ship?'

'I'll sit this one out - it's Lieutenant Rose Thorn's turn,' said Officer James, graciously. 'Aquatica was mine.'

'You've a good heart,' said Aurélie.

'Yes, filigree gold for the mechanism, and it has a loud tick,' said Officer James.

So the Captain told Dr Blake that Lieutenant Rose Thorn would be flying him and his Away Team in *Pegasus*. A moment later, she shut down the communicator, and looked up again, grinning. 'This is it, Rose Thorn, Sophia. This is it! After all the false starts and red herrings. Our new home!' As the ship slowly circled round its sphere of splendour, the bridge crew gazed in wonder at the green and blue planet onscreen.

Though the crew did not know it, on the surface of that new planet, a great king was waiting to be found. He had been gone for such a long time that he had stopped believing in himself, becoming a stone likeness of who he used to be. And these doubts about his own existence had caused great holes to form in his cloak and armour. But now, as the starship continued to circle the planet, he knew he was ready to be found.

He was longing indeed to be set free from the stone, so still and cold, to feel once more the blood singing in his veins. He knew the star seekers' renewed faith in him would grant him such strength that when he next appeared in front of them, he would cease to be a liminal being, tattered and torn he would be, once more, their King.

'And so, on Planet Guelder...,' began Dr Blake, a few days after his return from the planet's surface. He was speaking to a group of Ensigns and cadets assembled on the lower deck's mezzanine terrace.

'S'cuse me,' said Ensign Dagonet, 'but why are you calling it Planet Guelder?' He, like many of them present, had not been part of the initial scout party's exploration of the planet.

'Because,' said Dr Blake, 'when we went down there, we found a shrub that looked like a guelder, like honeysuckle, with white flowers, and scarlet fruit. Besides, it's less political than calling it New Avalon or New Valerian. Any more questions?'

'No,' said Ensign Dagonet amiably, 'carry on.'

'Well,' Dr Blake continued, 'on their return, the scouts all passed their medical fitness tests, so we know the air on the planet is capable of sustaining life. Of course, some of Planet Guelder...' he paused for a moment and glared at Ensign Dagonet, but there were no further interruptions, 'remains swampland, and some of this will have to be drained. Then we can plant new woodland areas, so that those from Avalon can worship in their sacred groves of apple trees. We also propose to plant hazel, hawthorn, spindle, downy birch, field maple, and fruit trees, including the crab apple, wild plum and cherry.'

'Why those trees in particular?' asked a furry mauve being who resembled a warlock.

'Because we've got those seeds and saplings in the hold,' Dr Blake replied. 'Any more of you lot need to know anything else? No? Good. Because, surprise, surprise, you cadets and Ensigns are the ones who'll be doing all the digging. We will assemble in the departure bay at 1400 hours.' His communicator bleeped, and he sighed. 'And now, gentlemen, if you'll excuse me. Tests to run, results to process. Ensign Dagonet, you can walk with me to the medical lab, please.'

Dr Blake's impatient strides made no allowances for Dagonet's shorter legs, so the Ensign was forced to break into a half-jog to keep up with him.

'I read your completed report about whether vampires should be allowed to join us on the new planet,' began the Doctor. 'From what I read, you and the Captain seemed to have turned in a wholehearted verdict of *yes*. But don't you think her personal friendships with vampires may have biased her a little?'

'The Captain is nothing if not impartial,' huffed Ensign Dagonet, trying to catch his breath.

'I know, I know,' snapped Dr Blake, 'and when she shits it smells like golden roses.'

There was a silence, then the doctor sighed. 'I may have overstepped the mark there,' he said. 'Just I've got to be very careful. I'm responsible for the medical well-being of the ship's entire crew. I have to make absolutely certain that if we introduce vampires to the new planet, we are not jeopardizing ourselves in any way.'

'To speak of Jeopardy is a little harsh, don't you think, Doctor?' said the Ensign. 'We might become ferocious ourselves if we were starving.'

'Yes,' said Dr Blake. 'About that. When I was talking to you all just now, I received a message to say that Lady Elridge has arrived onboard. After Fyodor was found to have a rare, incompatible vampire blood-type, she kindly consented to take part in some trials for us.'

'Oh?' gasped Dagonet.

'Yes,' said the doctor. 'So that we can work out how to synthesize a kind of blood substitute that will provide vampires with the correct level of nutrients.'

'Is that even possible?' asked Ensign Dagonet. He stopped half-jogging and clutched his side, forcing Dr Blake to stop, too. 'Stitch,' he said, apologetically. 'Big mind, little legs.'

'Sorry sonny,' said the doctor. 'I was too wrapped up in what I was saying. Which was, yes it is: with a few minor adjustments here and there, we certainly have the technology. And with Lady Elridge's assistance... have you met her?'

Dagonet shook his head, then he and the doctor began to make their way down the corridor again, to the medical lab.

'She's not the most disagreeable vampire I've ever encountered,' the doctor replied. He grinned. 'I knew her when she warn't much more than a kid. Always one for the posies!'

'She's Head of the League of Tudor Rose vampires now,' replied Ensign Dagonet, thoughtfully.

'Dr Blake spent hours this morning trying to synthesize an appropriate food substitute for us,' said the vampire to the dwarf. 'The Conglomerate must certainly be anxious that we should accompany your crew to the new planet,' she added, glancing down at her manicured nails. Too long? Too intimidating for her present company?

She peered round the starship interview room, the sliding doors built into an archway, the vibrant orange prints of Nova Nevada on the otherwise plain walls, the circular walnut table where she and the dwarf now sat opposite each other.

He nodded.

Whilst she waited for him to finish unpacking his briefcase, her gaze fell on the porthole opposite, with its view of the passing stars. Then she turned back to him. On the table in front of them, there was now a dark, rectangular box, a panel of buttons and wires, and what looked suspiciously like a microphone.

'Does the Conglomerate get to hear *everything* I have to say?' she asked then.

'Well,' said the dwarf, sounding flustered as he checked that the carnelian batteries were sufficiently charged, 'at least if it's all unedited, you can't complain about being misrepresented.' Good. They were. 'Oh, beggin your pardon,' he added, 'just I worked with a fella once, on a project about the implications of using crystals to power handheld technological devices. I knew about the crystals, see, on account of my mining background, whereas this fella, Pluto, was stronger on the tech side...' Warming to his theme, he failed to notice that Lady Elridge was suddenly sitting absolutely still. 'But hangingman me, when it came to presenting our findings to the panel, he'd only gone and edited out most of the shots of yours truly, and my mining crew. Just kept a hand here, a helmet or a pickaxe there. So, all in all, you see, I'm a bit suspicious of editing now.'

'I'm sorry to hear of your experience, Ambassador Guineafowl,' said the vampire. 'Or is it Officer?'

'Guinan, please,' said the dwarf. 'And to think we then let him loose on the Time Editing Suite! It's my big heart, and trusting nature that's to blame, for sure.'

'I would have thought you were pretty shrewd,' replied Lady Elridge, after a pause.

'Well,' said Guinan, 'I like to see the good in everyone, even when they've done me wrong. I hoped it was just a little bit of professional rivalry, and no-one could deny, Officer Pluto was a clever chap. We needed what he could do for us. But you see, Lady Elridge, what I think is...'

'Do call me Laura,' said the vampire.

'Very well then,' said Guinan. 'Well, Laura,' he continued, warming to his theme, 'what I meantersay is, it's a bit like life. Life should be unedited. Lived in the raw, if you see what I mean.'

'I'm not sure I do, Guinan,' said Laura, glancing down again, and flicking a speck of imaginary dust from her long, black dress. Then she straightened up and adjusted her dark glasses. The fluorescent lights onboard ship were too bright for her sensitive eyes. 'Especially as I understand my presence here in this timeline is in fact the result of some of Officer Pluto's prior editing.'

'Ah,' said Guinan, looking abashed and taking out a pocket handkerchief to mop his brow. 'You're not wrong,' he added. 'I'm a Professor of Time Travel and all this stuff still has the capacity to fry my mind. Aurélie's, too.'

Laura nodded, then, noting his discomfiture, had the grace not to pursue the topic. 'Have you started recording, yet?' she asked instead.

'The thingummyjig is going round the wotsit spool,' said Guinan, peering at his equipment. 'So yes, yes I have. You'll have to forgive me, Laura,' he added then, recovering his aplomb, becoming suddenly as expansive as the game show host on the *Collodian Star* spinoff, *Neural Reapers,* 'but all this tech stuff isn't really me. I wasn't born in this era. I'm more of a Renaissance man.'

'No more was I,' said Laura. 'I was born in Victorian Valerian, and I was a servant in many different households. And if I hadn't become a patient at the sanatorium, then had my entire life history rewritten, I wouldn't be sitting here now.'

'Yes,' said Guinan, playing his trump card a little earlier than he had intended, 'your early history, dear Laura, is not too dissimilar to that of Violetta Valhallah, Lady Darvell, whom I believe you know.'

'Yes,' muttered Laura. 'Daedalus says she's my stepdaughter.'

Guinan raised a quizzical eyebrow but continued with what he had to say. 'And, through the medium of Time Writing, Violetta has contacted me, requesting that she and her family be allowed to join us on Planet Guelder.'

'Yes, but Violetta and her family are *human*,' objected Laura. 'Whereas the Earl of Elridge and I remain vampires. As long as we can continue to locate sufficient sources of blood for feeding, we have no need to emigrate.'

'Elridge? Elridge? How did you and Daedalus come up with that name?' asked Guinan then, curiosity overcoming politeness.

'Well, my initial is L and - never mind,' said Laura. 'The Earl and I see no need to leave our current mansion, our charitable projects or our efforts on behalf of the League of Tudor Rose Vampires.'

'If I thought like that,' muttered Guinan, 'I'd still be in the Wild Welsh Woods. Laura,' he added firmly, 'we have so many Valerians wanting to join us on the new planet, there's now a waiting-list. And if everyone does leave, your blood supply dwindles to a few unwanted, possibly rabid, mice and rats.'

'That's a fair point,' Laura conceded.

'Besides,' wheedled Guinan, 'your modern psychiatric knowledge, and particularly your training with trauma survivors, would be invaluable. So many people who have had their memories harvested could really do with your help and support. Already we're planning to set up special clinics to assist them on the new planet.'

'But it would mean starting all over again,' said Laura, frowning behind her dark glasses. 'Even after all the work of the League of Tudor Rose Vampires, and, you know, we joined the Conglomerate back in 1981, still, it's very hard to get people to trust a vampire psychiatrist. On a new planet, without all their familiar support systems in place, it might be even harder.'

'True, true,' said Guinan, pressing the tips of his fingers together so that they resembled a church steeple. 'I certainly wouldn't want to diminish your concerns, Laura. Have you ever considered the Holy Grail option of becoming human?'

'I'm not Violetta,' snapped Laura, so vehemently that Guinan wondered if there was a rift between them. However, Laura's next words made the source of this apparent enmity a little clearer, 'And Daedalus is no Darvell.'

'Well no,' said Guinan, peaceably. 'But I'm sure there are many ways in which you can *all* contribute to the greater good of the new planet. Just think what a wonderful opportunity it would be to promote the Tudor Rose vampire values of tolerance and equality. For where you and Daedalus lead, others will surely follow.'

'His other vampire offspring, you mean?' asked Laura, dubiously. 'Because we've had more than a few problems with them.'

Guinan nodded.

Laura was silent for a moment, growing fascinated by the spools, spinning round and round.

'I wish I could say you present a compelling argument, Ambassador Guinan,' she said, at last.

'I try,' said Guinan. 'I believe that's why Aurélie chose me for this assignment - I'm the Pastoral Officer, now.'

'Dear Aurélie,' said Laura, a note of genuine warmth creeping into her hitherto carefully modulated voice. 'I've often thought about her - just, I get so busy.' She removed her glasses and began to rub her eyes.

Guinan noticed that there were dark circles beneath them, which made her appear oddly vulnerable. 'You ladies do far too much,' he scolded then. 'I'm always telling Aurélie she should delegate more. But no. She'll go her own way - as I expect you will, too.'

'And yet,' said Laura gently, 'whatever way I decide to go, I hope to cross paths with you and Aurélie again in the future.'

'That sounds like a *yes* to me,' said Guinan.

'That sounds a bit presumptuous to me,' said Laura. 'But you've certainly given me a great deal to think about - and to discuss with the Earl.'

'Well, if you do insist on bringing him...' said Guinan, with only the slightest hint of gallantry to his voice, for after all, he was a boyfriend now, with all the values, duties and responsibilities that the role entailed.

'Certainly,' said Laura, 'and if we do make it to the new planet, I think it would be very nice if the four of us all had dinner together, sometime. Perhaps Jem will have found an appropriate blood substitute for us, by then.'

'I think it would be very nice too,' said Guinan, 'and on that note, I hereby conclude this interview with Lady Ottalie Laura Elridge on board the *Joyous Gard* at 17 hundred hours.' He leaned over to click the *off* switch on the recorder.

'How was that?' he asked Laura, then.

'If I didn't know that was impossible,' said Laura, 'I'd swear you had some vampire blood. You're very persuasive.'

'Ain't I just,' said Guinan. 'And that's why the Captain of *this* ship *is*...' and he pointed to his chest proudly, '*my* girlfriend.'

'I sort of guessed that during the interview,' said Laura.

'Yes, but I still get a kick out of telling people,' said Guinan. 'And now, since it's just gone five o'clock, there's a chance that she'll be off-duty and I can take you to her. She'd love to see you again,' he added, and he began to pack the recording equipment back into his briefcase, then fastened its leather strap, that was stamped *GG*.

On Tuesday, Dr Blake and his Away Team were again down on the surface of Planet Guelder. Dr Blake was supervising, and the cadets and Ensigns were digging. Eight hours in, and Ensign Dagonet leaned on his spade, and, with the back of his sleeve, wiped the sweat from his brow. He glanced at his wristwatch. Ten past five.

'Permission to knock off now and explore here-and-thereabouts?' he asked Dr Blake.

'But we've got supper in the picnic hamper,' said Dr Blake, nodding towards an imposing wicker hamper beneath a sprawling chestnut tree. 'The Kitchen Team have packed us some nice chicken sandwiches and bottles of ginger beer. Why go exploring?'

'I promised Officer James...' said Dagonet, and then, mumble, mumble, mumble.

'You promised her *what,* sonny?' asked Dr Blake.

'I promised her I would look for a blue rose,' said Ensign Dagonet, all in a rush.

'In Great Valeria's name!' said Dr Blake, 'what made her ask for such a thing?'

'Well, she's been reading Japanese fairy-tales, you see,' said Dagonet, as if that explained everything.

'Er, no,' said Dr Blake.

'Well,' said Ensign Dagnonet, huffing, puffing and starting to turn red. 'She's been reading a fairy-tale where the Princess of Japan agrees to marry whoever brings her a blue rose. And so her suitors, they bring her a blue porcelain rose, a sapphire jewel rose and a rose poisoned blue, with flies still buzzing around it. But only the gardener brings her a real rose - except that it's white. But she marries him anyway cos she's the princess and she's smart, and if she says it's a blue rose, no-one is going to contradict her.'

'So, why does Officer James want you to find her a blue rose?' asked Dr Blake.

'Well,' said Ensign Dagonet again, 'she said she never had a birthday in the laboratory where she was created. So she has chosen a birthday for herself, which is in a few weeks' time. And she said no-one had ever bought her a birthday present, before. So, she would like me to put a lot of effort into this quest, as she calls it.'

'Synthesizer?' asked Dr Blake. 'Replicator? We have the technology onboard the ship.'

'Dr Blake!' said Dagonet, 'that would be cheating! No, I must find her the blue rose, in time-honoured and traditional fashion, and then present it to her, with a certain amount of decorum, flourish and pizzaz on her birthday.'

'I see,' said Dr Blake, and he did, at last. 'Very well, then. You have my permission to take a look-see for a posy for a lady.'

Four hours later, and Dr Blake was growing worried. It was nearly nine o' clock and the enthusiastic Ensign had not yet returned. 'I should never have let him go alone,' Dr Blake scolded himself. And he went back to their makeshift tent and found his torch and his stout walking-boots and stick, and he set off in search of Dagonet. But as he was walking up the path, there was Dagonet walking down it, and when they collided, the good doctor clapped him on the back. Then, as they walked back to their base-camp, he demanded to hear all about the quest.

'Well,' said Dagonet, 'I travelled north. I travelled south. I travelled east. I travelled west. I braved the high seas and the low tides. I waded through fire-swamps and swung through trees. I fought with dragons and tussled with unicorns. But wherever I went, and whoever I asked, not a single scout could tell me where to find a blue rose. I was on the point of abandoning my quest and coming back to get a tattoo, when, all of a sudden, I found myself standing in a field of wildflowers. So I dug up the largest one I could see, and here I am.' Feeling rather proud of himself, he took the flower out of his rucksack. It was the size of a dinner-plate, and more like a daisy than a rose, with soil-encrusted roots dangling down.

'Okay,' said Dr Blake carefully, 'but that's not a rose, and it's not blue.'

'Ah-ha,' said Ensign Dagonet, looking and sounding very pleased. 'But I shall tell her that on this planet, this is what roses look like.'

'Do you think she'll believe you?' asked Dr Blake.

'Oh yes,' said Dagonet.

'Very well,' said Dr Blake, 'but still - the colour...'

'Ah-ha,' said Ensign Dagonet again. 'Only Officer James's closest friends will know this, but actually, she's a big fan of *The Wizard of Oz.*'

'So?' said Dr Blake.

'Well, in the book, *not* the film,' said Ensign Dagonet, 'they are all given green-tinted glasses so that they see the Emerald City as... well, emerald. And so, I shall synthesize for Officer James a pair of blue-tinted glasses for her to look at this flower, and I'll tell her that this is all in homage to L. Frank Baum's Oz.'

'Do you think your plan will work?' asked Dr Blake.

'I think she'll be so pleased, she'll marry me,' said Ensign Dagonet.

'Well, if you're sure, sonny,' said Dr Blake. 'You know her better than I do.'

On Officer James's birthday, there was salted caramel cake in the officers' canteen, and candles to stick in the icing. Ensign Dagonet had resisted the temptation to arrange them himself, because he knew that Officer James would take great pleasure in the careful placing of the *sticks of flaming light.* After this part of the ritual had been completed, and she had blown out all the candles, and wished for, ah, but that would be telling, you're not supposed to tell, else it doesn't come true, Dagonet slid a small, slim, rectangular box across the table.

Officer James licked the icing from her fingers, then untied the ribbon, peeled back the wrapping paper, and opened the glasses case. From it, she removed the blue-tinted glasses from their velvet swaddling and balanced them on the bridge of her nose.

'These are wonderful,' she cried. 'If I had known they existed, I would have wished for them.'

'But that's not all,' said Ensign Dagonet, gleefully, and he brought the big white daisy in its plant pot out from underneath their table. She gazed at the flower and clapped her hands in delight. It was blue! The bluest flower that ever there was. Then she took the glasses off. The flower was white! As white as white could be! Then she put the glasses back on. By some miracle of tinted glass, blue, once more!

'How, how can this be?' she asked. 'By what magic have you granted this, the first of my heart's desires?'

'It is a daisy,' said Ensign Dagonet, wanting to be honest about it, 'but on Planet Guelder, daisies are roses. The queens of the flowers.'

And so Officer James spent many happy minutes taking the glasses off, looking at the daisy without them, then putting the glasses back on again, to see how the flower had changed colour.

Half an hour later, she spoke again: 'This is the single most sublime moment of my life.' Then she leaned across the table and kissed him.

Dot. Dot. Dash. Dot. Dot. Squiggle. A code. A corruption of Morse code, mixed with some arcane hieroglyphics of stick figures that may, or may not, have been a man picking a flower. These were all being tapped out to Ensign Alfie Blake. Ever since the Perturbing Vanishing of

Officer Pluto, as Merlin called it, Alfie now had joint charge of the Time Editing Suite with the great Magician himself, who was working remotely from his eyrie in Avalon. With a certain amount of trepidation, the young Ensign leaned back in his swivel leather office-chair and began to decipher the incoming message.

*'Wild and free, wild and free,
Restore my dear liege lord, to me, to me.'*

Alfie sighed. The message was the latest in a series from Merlin, each written in a different code. As soon as he had deciphered each one, he found it was not in fact a message, but a spell. And once he had decoded the spell, it was too late. Things started to happen, whether Alfie willed it, or no. Now he thought the new planet, Guelder, would have a king, regardless of whether his subjects actually wanted one or not.

Yet, just for a moment, he allowed himself to get caught up in the glory of his own vision: King Arthur, restored to the throne for the fourth time. He had developed a fascination with the monarch on account of his fascination with Nessa, and from her, and from his own reading, he knew of Arthur's different reigns in different eras of Valerian.

Now Alfie scrolled through the Time Editing Suite's list of contacts and paused at *N. Nessa.* She had attended Brunwych High, where Merlin now was, and she had some training in magick, so she might be able to help him. Except that she had returned to the Sisters of Valerian, and now her hours were not her own. Besides, how powerful would she have to be to withstand the mighty Merlin?

Alfie sighed again. When he had first heard that Merlin was to assist him in running the Time Editing Suite, he had hoped that the magician would command space and time in a magnificent, magical way. Perhaps he could even solve the mystery of the mournful sobs that Alfie sometimes heard, as if there were a ghost, trapped in the machine. Instead, all he got was this artful jiggery-pokery, that meant he would now have to contact the wizard himself. He pressed the communication symbol, a whirling squiggle that looked like a conch, and waited for the necromancer to pick up.

Merlin shimmered, bad-temperedly, onto the vastscreen. He had a shocking cold: his eyes were watering, his nose was red. To make matters worse, none of his own herbal concoctions had helped, to the extent that he was glad everyone else was asleep, since he was hardly a good advertisement for his own remedies. He had already tried a sweet yarrow infusion, rosehip tea, fennel tea, and an extract made from purple coneflowers, all to no avail.

'Yes, boy?' he snapped. 'Out with it. I'm very busy, you know. Very busy, indeed.'

'If you please sir,' began Alfie, 'we are supposed to be *collaborating* on the timelines.'

'Yes, yes, we are,' said Merlin. 'What of it?'

'Well sir, it's just you keep sending me all these disguised spells, and when I decode them, they all have dramatic and far-reaching consequences that I couldn't possibly have predicted.'

'Yes,' said Merlin. 'They're supposed to be like that. They're very good spells.' Now he raised his hands to the heavenly moons and stars of his hat, as if the spells might be there for him to gather, then dropped them abruptly, to catch a sneeze.

'But sir, I do think you might give me a bit of a warning first,' said Alfie. 'Otherwise, it's sort of like you're...' he paused, swallowed hard, then continued, bravely, 'tricking me.'

The thought of tricking Alfie tickled Merlin immensely. He began to rock with laughter, so much so, that he knocked his own owl-rimmed spectacles off. Settling them back on the bridge of his nose steadied him up, slightly. 'Well, yes,' he said, at last, 'I suppose that is what I'm doing.' When he emerged from a sudden, immense series of sneezes, he sounded more reflective, 'Well done, young Alfie. I would have had to turn Arthur into an eagle or something, to get him to think things through, and then stand his ground, like that.'

Alfie couldn't help it; he began to imagine himself as Merlin's eagle, soaring close to the sun above lonesome lands, whilst the sea crawled beneath him, until down, down he swooped, the entire length of the mountain, falling like a thunderbolt. But he managed to direct his thoughts back to the matter at hand. 'So you won't send me any more spells hidden in codes, then?' asked the young Ensign.

'Oh no, I'm not going to promise that,' said Merlin. 'My word is my bond, you know. I don't make promises lightly.' He gave another almighty sneeze, but this time his handkerchief rather than his beard was its receptacle. 'Tell me, young Alfie,' he continued, to the dumbfounded Ensign, 'Did mustard plaster foot-baths and wrapping one's head in vinegar and brown paper, as Arthur recommends, ever cure colds in your original era? I can't seem to shift this one, at all.'

'I don't think so,' said Alfie, trying to sound sympathetic. 'But are you sure it's a cold? When our cat gave birth to a long-haired kitten, mother kept sneezing. It turned out that whenever the kitten washed itself, mother was allergic to a chemical in its spit.'

'Really?' said Merlin. 'Because, of course, I have been looking after Rose Red's cat whilst she and Snow White are conducting a tour of Avalon. Bit of a holiday for the girls. There are so few of us left awake that she can ask to cat-mind, you see.'

'Well, I can ask my dad to talk to you,' said Alfie, 'and he can dispense you some antihistamines.'

'Really?' said Merlin. 'You'd do that for me?' And the part of him that was more man than mage or merlin felt a little ashamed.

Alfie nodded.

'Then, my boy,' said Merlin, skilfully side-stepping what Alfie had actually asked him to do, 'by the power invested in me as a fellow Grand Operator of the Time Editing Suite, I now grant you a half-holiday.' And when Alfie made to protest, Merlin shook his beard. 'No, no,' he said. 'No need to thank me. I shall fix it all up, right as rain.'

'But why do I need a half-holiday?' asked Alfie. 'There are so many interesting things I can do here.'

For a moment, Merlin was slightly at a loss, for, under his tutelage, Arthur had always known how to spend his holidays. As a bear, in a cave. As an owlet, in a barn. As an eagle, circling the sky. Then he glanced out of the arch-shaped window of his eyrie, and feeling somewhat inspired by what he saw, he said, 'The sky between the stars is now of the fullest and deepest velvet. The hunting-dog star is on the chase, and Orion is soaring through the pure serene, trailing fire. It's all out there for you, my boy,' he continued, warming to his theme. 'Space. Eternity. Inspiration. The scintillating lights, the glitterance of comets, the divine dazzle of it all. And if you find the right telescope or observing screen, stars hovering above you, like moths. As if you could just reach out and touch them...'

Later that day, Lieutenant Rose Thorn emerged from the *other* canteen with her own eyes streaming, so much so, they obscured her vision and she collided with Captain Dulac. When they had disentangled themselves, and she had picked up her cup of spilt coffee, he peered at her closely.

'What's wrong?' asked Captain Dulac. 'Have you been crying?'

'No, no,' said Rose Thorn. 'Alfie was Facetiming Nessa in the canteen just now, that's all, and I sat down to say hello. Just he had brought that wombat-tribble with him, that he found on Aquatica. He wanted to show it to her luck-dragon. And it had a sort of skunk aroma, that made my eyes water.'

'Then *I* am no longer worthy of your tears?' asked Lancelot.

'Anyone that makes you cry is not worth crying over,' said Rose Thorn. 'Besides, you're hardly on your death-bed, for me,' she added. 'You look very well, in fact. Particularly hale and hearty. Avalon obviously agreed with you.'

'But am I supposed to be?' asked Lancelot.

'The way you look makes it difficult to believe you ever suffered a single day, over anyone,' replied Rose Thorn.

'But why does suffering demonstrate sincerity?'

Before Rose Thorn could reply, she let out another almighty sneeze. Sir Lancelot reached into his pocket for a cambric handkerchief, a gentlemanly action that was more of a reflex. In doing so, he dislodged a sheet of paper covered in his own scribbles, that fell out on the mezzanine floor. Rose Thorn took the handkerchief, then pounced on the paper.

'Don't read them,' said Lancelot. 'They are but some halting verses composed in the modern vernacular.'

'Let me see,' Rose Thorn said.

Lancelot sighed. 'My own heart betrayed by my own hand. Very well. As long as you're aware, they're not my best effort.'

Rose Thorn read:

'O my fallen angel
You've cut off all your hair.
I don't know what to make of you -
You just don't seem to care.

O my fallen angel
You never seem to sing,
I don't know what to make of you -
Why the one singed wing?

O my fallen angel
I've not seen you around.
I don't what to make of you -
Where is your starry crown?'

'Are these about me?' asked Rose Thorn, at last. 'When did I ever wear a crown?'

'Ever since you were queen of my heart,' said Lancelot. Too much?

Rose Thorn grimaced.

Too much. 'What's wrong?'

Rose Thorn sighed. '*Queen* Guinevere? *Queen* Morgana? I'm not them.'

'Thank the - Goddess Valeria for that,' said Lancelot.

Rose Thorn glanced down at the scrawl on the paper again. 'Maybe change that last line of the final stanza to - '*Is your scout ship on the ground?'*

'I don't think that would improve the verses overmuch,' said Lancelot.

'No, but it would make more sense,' said Rose Thorn, folding up the paper. 'Can I keep them?'

'Yes,' said Lancelot, 'by all means.'

'Which reminds me,' said Rose Thorn, 'Dagonet and Sophia are running a Haiku Circle tomorrow night, if you felt like going? Last chance to do something like that before we set up camp on Guelder.'

'I prefer villanelles. I find haikus a little controversial,' said Lancelot, 'but yes, if it would please you.'

The following evening, Count Fyodor and Dr Blake didn't get the chance to attend the Haiku Circle because they were in the medical lab. Dr Blake had earlier discovered some bloodroot plants in the hold, and he had learned from Alfie via Merlin that these were often used as a replacement for blood in magical spells and rituals. Dr Blake was therefore attempting to mix the plant in a 1:10 ratio with wine to create an appropriate nutritious drink for vampires. After the tests were complete, Count Fyodor was to sample the first batch.

'I believe you're something of a connoisseur of wine,' the Doctor said eventually, pouring him a glass of the bloodroot concoction from a conical flask.

The Count held the ruby liquid up to the light. 'See, swirl, sniff, sip, savour,' he said. He swished his glass round, flared his aristocratic nostrils, sniffed, took a small sip, and let it glide across his palate. 'Not bad,' he said at last. 'It may need a little time to mature but - it's eminently quaffable.'

'And it would provide you with all the requisite iron of human blood, as well as a range of other vitamins and minerals besides,' said the doctor. He glanced at the notes on his clipboard. 'It's toxic to humans though - it can cause vertigo, cell death and necrosis.'

'Ha!' said Count Fyodor. 'Aren't vampires toxic to humans also!'

'Well, *you're* all right,' said the Doctor, 'in small doses.' He grinned. 'Speaking of which, would you care for another glass?'

'Certainly. But you're not drinking,' said the Count. 'Oh, not the bloodroot,' he added hastily, 'but perhaps, a medicinal glass of wine?'

'I've never needed an excuse,' said the Doctor. 'Don't mind if I do,' he added, and he poured them each their drinks, pleased that the discovery of bloodroot would now make the emigration of the vampires to Guelder so much more straightforward. 'Cheers,' he added.

Apart from the doctor and the count, nearly everyone else had decided to attend the Haiku Circle. There they all were, all sat round a long row of tables that had been pushed together in the Officers' Canteen: Alfie with his wombat-tribble, Lieutenant Rose Thorn wearing mascara and eye-liner, and Captain Dulac sitting next to her, smiling, whilst opposite them, sat Lieutenant Lanval, grinning, and Princess Blancheflor, darting dagger-glances at her cousin. Next to them sat Aurélie, wearing a long, dark, blue silk dress, with spaghetti-thin shoulder straps, and Guinan, who was scowling at his spiral notepad whilst his Turkish slippers kicked her kitten heels beneath the table.

'Thank you all for coming,' said Dagonet from the head of the table. 'It's good to see so many of you, as well as so many newcomers, here tonight. Those who attend regularly will know we normally like to start by hearing everyone's compositions from the previous week, before we move onto something new. But since this is the last night onboard ship for many of us, Sophia and I,' and he glanced at Officer James, sitting at his right hand, and tried to ignore the few raised eyebrows, 'would like you to write a haiku on the theme of - this starship.'

'It has been our home for so long,' chimed in Sophia, musically, sadly. 'What does it mean to you? How do you feel about leaving it?'

'I didn't know I'd actually have to *write* something,' Guinan muttered to Aurélie.

'What did you think you were going to do?'

'Clap, nod, smile. Buy you a drink, if you were lucky.'

'Spoilsport. Captain Dulac has brought along a fine quill pen.'

'Never judge a wordsmith by the size of his pen,' said Guinan.

'What's wrong?' asked Aurélie, putting down her own neat biro and turning to face him. 'You've been like this all day. Don't you want to be here? Don't you like the ale? You can go back to our cabin, if you like.'

'It's not that,' said Guinan. 'I mean, it's not *here* that's the problem.'

'Well, what is it then?'

'It's Guelder,' said Guinan. 'What if I don't like it?'

'Now?' said Aurélie, exhaling slowly, 'you want to talk about this, *now*?'

'You did ask me,' said Guinan.

'I wasn't expecting a fireball in response.'

'I thought I was supposed to be honest about my feelings,' said Guinan.

'Yes, but not *now*. This is the wrong time and place. Am I supposed to announce to everyone, hey, listen up, Guinan's written a beautiful haiku about how he *doesn't* want to come to the new planet with all of us?'

'I don't think I'm in the mood for writing anything, anyway,' said Guinan. He put down his own pen, saying, 'I'll see you back at the cabin.' He leaned over and gave her a kiss on the cheek.

'I think maybe you had better sleep in the Ambassador's quarters until we can sort this out,' said Aurélie. 'The door code is still the same as before.'

'Really?' said Guinan, looking suddenly crestfallen. 'Of course, there is a possibility that I've grotesquely mishandled the situation,' he added, but still, he nodded to everyone, then departed, leaving Aurélie staring down at her blank sheet of paper.

'What's up with the Chief?' called out Dagonet.

Sophia nudged him hard in the ribs. 'They've had a fight,' she hissed.

Dagonet continued, oblivious, 'Didn't he like the ale?'

'No, not really, he said it's given him a funny tummy,' lied Aurélie.

'Strong ale and strong emotions don't mix,' agreed Dagonet. 'It's an odd night for all of us.'

'Can you all please be quiet?' said Alfie, unconsciously copying Nessa's intonation. 'I'm *writing.*'

For another ten minutes or so, everyone was quiet, so that the only sound that could be heard was the scratch of pens on pads or the tapping of fingers on consoles or keyboards. After Alfie's comment, no-one felt like dictating their haiku. But when the time came to read out their contributions, the crew-members were shy. Yet Princess Blancheflor surprised them all by volunteering to read out her haiku first:

'Hologram handbag
Discarded in the garden:
New explorations.'

Everyone clapped politely. The general consensus seemed to be that some deep emotion had prompted this, even if no-one could entirely work out what it was, or why they should care.

Captain De Lys then volunteered, because she felt she should, because it was *her* starship:

'We search through the stars.
We soar through clusters of light.
Our home, day and night.'

Now the applause was more enthusiastic. Aurélie added, 'It's really hard, saying what you want to say, in so few syllables.'

'That is the nature of the art-form,' said Officer James. 'I myself have been writing haiku for many years, and it is a discipline to which my neural pathways are well-adapted. Since I don't wish to discourage you all, who are just putting a foot on the first rung of the ladder, I will not read mine tonight.'

An uncomfortable silence followed, which only ceased when Lieutenant Rose Thorn volunteered to read her haiku:

'I dreamed of this ship,
I dreamed of a Goddess Bird,
Now I dream better.'

'That one, I like,' said Sophia. 'Simple, but effective. The repetition of the word 'dream' works well.'

'Thank you,' said Rose Thorn. 'Er - perhaps Lancelot has a sonnet he would like to share with us?' She gave him an arch smile.

'We've been through this before, Rose Thorn,' said Sophia. 'Writing in another poetic form is against the rules of the Haiku Circle. But he can contribute to our Poet's Page, if he would like.'

'No, I wouldn't,' said Lancelot, with some of the old authority of his captaincy. 'But it's been a fine evening, and good to see everyone,' he said, as he began to gather his papers together. 'Dagonet,' he added, 'you do need to sort out that barrel of ale.

'Yes, er, Captain,' said Dagonet, feeling relieved, nonetheless, that the evening had passed off so well. With so many ladies present, he had wondered.

On Guelder the next day, the selected crew members felt as if they were walking out of winter. There was the evening breeze of May; there was the breath of spring all about them: floral, floating, herbal, green. Then too was the scent of unfolding flowers, of currants, wild cherries, plums and hawthorn. Whilst most of the ship's crew remained on board the starship, Captain De Lys had divided her most trusted officers into separate teams. They were all instructed to *rendez-vous* at eight o' clock at the scout ships' landing site, to report on their findings.

For the time being, Sir Lancelot had resolved not to question this captain's right to command, and so he had elected to join the scout party headed up by Lieutenant Rose Thorn and Lieutenant Lanval, accompanied by Blancheflor and Uxbridge. Officer James and Ensign Dagonet chose a different path.

Having apparently reached some kind of understanding after yesterday's row, Captain De Lys and Ambassador Guinan set off together. However, the Captain was held up by her communicator, relaying multiple messages from the ship's crew, so Guinan ended up charging off on his own.

As they began their exploration of the new planet, Rose Thorn broke into a delighted smile. 'Oh look,' she cried, 'there the linnet and there, the throstle.' The others looked to where she was pointing, to birds in the curves of the drooping chestnut tree, that spread its shade over the amber river. 'Whenever I see beauty in the world, my heart gladdens, and I must give thanks,' she said.

The team walked on.

But presently, Rose Thorn was forced to halt because her white tunic, that was buckled with a golden clasp, had become entangled with some reeds that clustered among the moss at the river's edge. The others marched on without her, and it was only Captain Dulac who noted her absence, and turned back. He approached her, then stooped to help her free her tunic. In doing so, their fingertips touched, and then, as they straightened up, it seemed only natural that he should take her in his arms and bestow all that remained of his heart in a single kiss.

A moment later and Lanval was calling, 'Lancelot? Where are you?'

Each sighing, they drew apart and went to rejoin Lanval, Blancheflor and the dog. But often over the next few hours, Rose Thorn felt her hand stray to her lips, to relive the memory of that kiss.

'What's that up ahead?' asked Ensign Dagonet as he and Officer James, in full space suits, waded through mossy swampland.

'It seems to be,' said Officer James, peering into the distance. 'How strange - it seems to be a sort of statue of - well, except that it's full of gaps, I would say it resembles...' She paused then, overwhelmed.

'It's a sort of ghost statue,' said the young Ensign.

'I think it is,' Officer James said, at last, 'a statue of Arthur.'

'I think you're right,' said the Ensign, scrutinizing it as best he could. 'And - it's trying to step down from the plinth.'

'Something like this has happened before,' said Officer James, trying to remember. 'Arthur told me about when some statues in a park came to life. But they were statues of Merlin and Morgana.'

'Do you think this has something to do with them?' asked the young Ensign.

'Well, they were always so keen to restore him to the throne - but Morgana is asleep now, and who knows the ways of the Merlin?'

'I do,' said Dagonet. 'I knew him well, once. He's a wily old one, that wizard. This has to be his doing.'

'Then my husband is returning to life,' faltered Officer James. With trembling fingers, she began to tap out an urgent message on her communicator to Lieutenant Rose Thorn.

'Think about this for a minute,' said Ensign Dagonet, 'you haven't seen him for several hundred years and you are now a robot. So, if the other officers can go round annulling their marriages on even more spurious grounds, you can too.'

She stopped texting. 'You have an invested interest in this though, my dear,' she said, after a moment.

'I would prefer it if you weren't married to the returning phantom monarch, yes,' said Dagonet. 'Anyway, I remember, when I was researching vampire history, I discovered that Lord Darvell used to be married to Morgana, but once she returned to Avalon and became a ghost in Valerian, he wasn't. So...'

'But aren't we being selfish, just thinking about ourselves?' said Sophia. 'What about poor Arthur? After all he suffered, with Guinevere... to deny him the love of a good robot seems cruel.'

'Whatever I say now will sound wrong, callous even,' said Dagonet, 'so actually, when all's said and done, the choice is yours. Go and speak to him and then...'

'And then?'

'Come back to me. Please.'

Rose Thorn tapped into her communicator. 'Captain? Have you been able to proceed?'

'Yes,' came back Aurélie's reply, 'I found a clearing, by a stream. The water's good. I'm going to send these coordinates back to the starship, get some cadets down here to start building.'

'Excellent. Oh - and Officer James seems to think King Arthur might be on this planet.'

'King Arthur? Surely not?'

'That's what her message said,' replied Rose Thorn.

'I used to know him. I'll message Officer James, see if she's all right.'

'Great. Her messages were a bit jumbled up, not like her. And what's happening about the vampires - and Violetta?' asked Rose Thorn.

'The Darvells weren't travelling with Lady Elridge and the Tudor Rose Vampires. We had to requisition two separate scout-ships for them - there's been a bit of a beef, apparently. Hopefully, they'll be able to sort it out here,' replied Captain De Lys.

'Hopefully...' Rose Thorn tapped, and she remembered then a prophecy she had read in the Grail-lore, that had formed a more obscure part of the doctrine of the Sisters of Valerian: *'Here is the rose, in which the divine incarnates, and here are the lilies, which herald a new way of life.'* That was too long for a text message, so instead, she tapped, 'How's Guinan?'

'He took off in search of a campsite for the dwarves. They'll be arriving from Avalon in a week or so. And he says he *is* going to stay here, after all. He likes it.'

'How did you manage that?!!!'

'He says he was just winding me up before. He says he always intended to stay. You know what he's like.'

'He wouldn't be Guinan without a few last minute U-turns and the odd existential crisis,' texted back Rose

Thorn. 'Oh, sorry, didn't mean to be rude. But, see, I *do* know what he's like.'

'He says he can't help it, it's his vampire heritage. I say bollocks to that.'

'And so say we all. Over and out, captain.'

Rose Thorn clipped her communicator back onto her golden belt. Once, she thought, her heart had been open to the spirits of the air, and she had the gift of transforming herself into a nightingale, eloquent in song. Now she was eloquent in other ways, and all the better for it.

As Officer James neared the statue, its stone appeared misshapen to her. Beneath the cascading lines of the shoulders, there were carven descents into nothingness. And yet there remained a crown upon the statue's head, and his head was set square upon his broad shoulders. And even where there were gaps of cloak and torso which should have encased the busy workings of his organs, still, there was the curve of his breastbone, and the curve of his loins.

The Robot girl paused for a moment in her thoughts. From her human memories, she recalled the act of love, but not the feelings that accompanied it. From everything she had read, she imagined it to be like a star bursting from the borders of itself into a fuller radiance.

It was only when she was standing square in front of the statue that she realised her mistake. For the name at the base of the plinth read not ARTHUR but UTHER PENDRAGON.

She bowed her head. She did not know what to say.

And yet the statue's eyes were gleaming, as if he was suffused from within by a lamp.

Eyes, that were familiar to her, and yet strange. Eyes that watched her closely. Their gaze, reading the contents of her soul, and, she hoped, approving of what they found there.

'You're here at last,' said the King. 'The first of my subjects.'

'Are you to rule this planet?' asked Sophia. 'We had hoped to hold an election...'

'Your looks and words are strange to me,' said the King. 'But let it be known throughout the land that we are to return to the golden era of Valerian's history.'

'But this is a new planet,' said Sophia. 'Surely we should look to the future, not the past.'

'Rex quondam, Rexque futurus,' announced the King.

'But isn't that supposed to be Arthur?' asked Sophia, with the persistent pedantry that some found irritating, and others, endearing, 'the Once and Future King?'

'Well,' said Uther, blustering only slightly from his plinth, 'not to take anything away from the boy, but he's already been resurrected twice. Merlin says the definition of insanity is to keep doing the same thing over and over and expecting different results. So - Merlin thought - well, actually, *we* thought, Valerian under my reign had a certain glory to it, a certain grandeur, and we said... well, let's make the realm magnificent again. With *me*, as its ruler.'

Sophia was too polite and too perplexed to persist with the subject, so moved onto what was, for her, a more pressing concern.

'But where is Arthur, then?' she asked, glancing all around.

Uther's eyes took on a puzzled expression. 'I find him a little difficult to keep up with myself,' he admitted. 'But I believe Ensign Blake, under Merlin's close supervision, has been carrying out sterling work in the Time Editing Suite. And so, as I understand it, Arthur will be arriving on this planet in a scout-ship with his foster-family, the Darvells.'

'So my husband will be here soon?' Officer James inquired.

'*Your* husband?' said Uther. 'Oh no, my dear. Dr Muir is married to his boyhood sweetheart, Miss Mary Anning.'

'But he married *me*,' said Officer James. 'My father came to the church. My mother, no, not my mother - my nurse, too.'

'Ah. You think so?'

Officer James nodded.

'It may be that Ensign Blake hasn't finished deleting all of that timeline yet,' said Uther, 'or it may be, that since you are wired a little differently, you retain vestiges of memories of things that haven't happened.'

'*Beamz Mean Heinz,*' said Officer James.

'But I can assure you, my dear,' said Uther, 'that after much prevarication and deliberation, you know what he's like, Mary Anning was his choice.'

'And Arthur is not mine,' said Officer James, with relief. 'For my heart is a pocket-watch and my midnights are not for him.'

All the same, it was a pocket watch of gold, for she helped Uther Pendragon down from the plinth. And at her kind touch, the phantom aspects of his form fleshed out, and he stood before her, no longer the stone wraith of himself, but every inch a monarch. Yet his legs were stiff from standing still for so long in stone, so he shook them, to pump back the blood and feeling.

Officer James remained with him a little while, watching as he took his first steps on this fair soil, King of this new realm.

Then, when she was sure he would not stumble, she tapped out a reply to her captain's anxious inquiries and returned to Ensign Dagonet.

'You came back,' he said.
'I never went away,' she replied.

Sophia began to tell Dagonet what Uther Pendragon had told her, about Arthur and his bride, Mary. Dagonet, who had once loved his liege-lord right well, began to imagine himself sailing with Arthur until the boat arrived on the looming shores of the new planet. It was a daydream, but sometimes daydreams have about them the truth and stir of day. Next the dwarf imagined himself waiting with a crowd on the dockside to greet the king's barge. Now Arthur stepped out onto the quay, a modern gentleman, of stately port and bearing. All the people clapped and cheered, shouting out, 'Prince Arthur is here at last: Prince Arthur cannot die.'

A hundred bells began to peal, and at the sound of those bells, a woman stepped from the barge. She put her hand on Arthur's arm and looked up into his face. Her eyes were fierce and loving, dark and luminous as thunder clouds, at war with the sun.

Together, Ensign Dagonet and Officer James decided that when Dr Muir and his bride had arrived on Guelder's shores, granting them proof that the last of the old timelines had faded, they too would be wed, in a little chapel that had not yet been built.

'Besides,' Dagonet said to his cousin Guinan, later that day, at the camp-site the Chief was attempting to set up for the incoming dwarves, 'how can I have a stag party before the other lads get here?'

'They can bring some of the good cider and ale from Avalon, too,' said Guinan, in between hammer blows. He was attempting to hammer a stake into the ground. 'It's all right for a tent here, isn't it?'

'Yes, there's a stream there, and a field of cows over there. They'll love it,' replied Dagonet.

'Just till we can build something better, mind,' said Guinan. 'Some log cabins here might be nice... Aurélie always wanted a log cabin...'

'Did she? Have you two any thoughts of nuptials yourselves, Chief?'

'Many thoughts,' said Guinan, 'and such they will remain, for Aurélie says I've shown more commitment to my Turkish slippers than I have to her.' The hammer crashed down on his thumb. 'Ouch.'

'That's a shame,' said Dagonet.

'All the same,' mused Guinan, laying the hammer down, and standing back to admire the one stake he had set in the ground, 'when I was on the mining planet, the crew dug out the most beautiful opal I ever did see, and I had it set in a ring, just in case, you know, because I thought I might find someone just as beautiful who wanted to wear it - and, of course, Aurélie and I were still in touch, and so - why are you smiling?'

'Just, Chief, you might need to work on your proposal, a bit.'

'Yes, Aurélie said that too,' said Guinan. He peered down dolefully at the curled points of his toes. 'And I don't know what she's got against these slippers. I've had them for centuries.'

'Just I prefer moccasins,' Aurélie said, choosing that moment to step into the clearing. 'Well done - this is better than the place I found. It's a great spot for a log cabin - or several.'

Guinan may have worn the same slippers for centuries, but what was happening right now, in the present moment, had its own radiance. For now, on Gulder's soil, there was a breeze, blowing gently, lightly rippling the

335

feathers of the wings that lay across Rose Thorn's back. Slowly, for the first time in a long time, they began to unfurl.

Rose Thorn glanced over at Lanval, jocund and blithe. He was wearing a hat of rich cloth upon his head, and a tunic coloured with a fine, deep dye, that was girdled with a belt of which the buckle and all the links were likewise made of bronze. He had clipped a leash to Uxbridge's collar. Blancheflor walked beside them, clad in a robe of spring and flame, with pearl earrings, shaped like lilies, dangling from her ears.

Rose Thorn thought Blancheflor still hadn't entirely forgiven her, but the lieutenant was starting to admire her cousin's obstinacy. Perhaps she wouldn't be so quick to forgive either, if what had happened, had happened to her. So Rose Thorn nodded at her cousin and smiled, and Blancheflor scowled, but then, maybe because the air was so fresh, fine and bracing, and Rose Thorn, so genuine and warm, the princess half-smiled in return.

'One thing I don't understand,' said Lanval to his wife, for so he still thought of her, since they had decided to ignore the annulment on the grounds that *a)* he hadn't agreed to it, and *b)* the queen was still asleep and so couldn't be expected to issue a decree to reverse it.

'Just the one?' she replied, 'what is it?'

'Apart from her haircut, you and your cousin are alike in every single way - and I can testify to that. So why don't you have wings?'

'I'm not an angel,' snapped Blancheflor. 'I'm fairy-born and fairy-bred, but my father renounced Avalon for Valerian, and my mother's genes were recessive, so I didn't even inherit her fairy wings. And *yes*, I do mind.'

Lanval remembered then what Merlin had once told him, about angel wings unfurling on new soil, so that in that moment, he would finally understand what he had never known before.

'You may not be an angel,' Lanval said to Blancheflor then, so that she braced herself in anticipation of one of his compliments, 'but your new loveliness gives me ample proof that I am in Heaven.' His gaze took in the sun-illumined gold of her hair, and the deep blue lustre of her eyes.

When Blancheflor didn't respond, Lanval frowned.

To help him out, Rose Thorn said, 'It *is* beautiful here.' Then, more to herself, she added, 'Just I don't think it's Heaven.'

'Where do you think it is, then?' asked Captain Dulac.

'You and I are Precursor Valerians,' Rose Thorn replied. 'They may call this place Guelder, or even Paradise, but don't you think its energy feels more like Valerian - the Valerian of before, before lockdown, before the energy bill crisis, before the wars, and famines and plagues...?'

'How could that be? asked Captain Dulac. He was thinking that, despite the unfortunate haircut, her forehead was still whiter than snow, her mouth, still red and curving, and her cheeks, like the blended tints of a rose on a May morning.

'I remember Aurélie telling me about the bridge between Avalon and Valerian, that her edited spell books created back in the twenty-first century,' said Rose Thorn.

'Yes? What about them?' asked Captain Dulac.

'Well, when I was studying navigation history, I read that when the bridge collapsed, some of its steel was incorporated into the manufacture of starships. What if it was used for the *Joyous Gard*? Perhaps that was why I had the vision of the Bird of the Goddess. And then, maybe, just maybe the starship brought us here, back to the dawn of our own time,' said Rose Thorn.

'Yes,' said Captain Dulac, 'when I did my training, they said something like that about the steel. And - what about the nestling I found?'

'Oh, you mean Nessa, Sister Scarlet Steel?'

'Yes, Nessa. Well, didn't you notice that at the very moment when you were in the Viewing Theatre, watching the live broadcast from the Temple of Valerian, this planet was discovered, and the captain summoned you to the bridge?'

'Yes of course I did,' replied Rose Thorn, 'what of it?'

'Perhaps,' said Lancelot, 'when Nessa took the alternate Grail to the Temple, it healed the Kingdom of Valerian so that we star seekers could discover it anew, and it could become our home.'

'Does that mean the Temple of Valerian is *here,* on this planet, too? And that we'll see them all again, Nessa, Tallulah, all of them?'

'There's only one way to find out,' said Lancelot.

'Which is?'

'We keep exploring.'

'And the end of all our exploring will be to arrive where we started, and know the place for the first time,' said Rose Thorn. 'Which means...,' she continued.

'We have finally found the place where...'

'Where?' said Rose Thorn.

'We can all be happy,' said Lancelot.

'I'm already happy,' said Rose Thorn.

Now the dog who had been ambling beside them suddenly stopped and barked and barked and barked.

'What's up with him?' Lanval asked his wife. 'What's up, hey boy? What's up, Uxbridge?'

'A kitten just ran past,' said Blancheflor. 'Must be a stowaway. An Ensign's cat keeps having kittens, apparently.'

'Do you ladies like kittens?' asked Lanval, then.

'No,' said Blancheflor.

'Not particularly,' said Rose Thorn.

'Anyway, we've got a dog,' said Blancheflor 'that's enough. We wouldn't want to upset Uxbridge.'

'*I* quite like kittens,' said Lancelot. 'When Galahad was a little lad, we had a striped kitten that used to bite our fingers so much, we had to wear chainmail gauntlets to pick him up.'

'Your son should be arriving soon,' said Rose Thorn then, 'he crossed over from Cardoeil to travel here with the dwarves.'

'I do not think you have seen him since the quest for the Grail,' said Lancelot to Rose Thorn, 'which reminds me, what your cousin was saying before, about angels... does that mean *our* children would or wouldn't have wings?'

'I can think of only one way of finding out,' said Rose Thorn.

'Such thoughts ill befit your maidenly...,'

'Lancelot, I'm twenty-five. If I'm still a maiden, you're still a monk.'

'You *were* a nun, though,' said Lancelot.

'No, I was the Leader of the Sisters of Valerian, which isn't quite the same thing. Once you reach the higher echelons of the sisterhood, chastity isn't required on the grounds that it's an unrealistic expectation.'

'That's quite enlightened, for nuns,' said Lancelot. 'So, angels don't have to be chaste, either?'

'Not particularly,' said Rose Thorn. 'I mean, it depends on the context, and your theological stance, really.'

'Just as well,' said Lancelot. 'Er - I mean, the wings are most becoming. It would be a shame to forfeit them.'

And so, after everyone's bickering, grumbling, and smiling, and more particularly after that last conversation with Lancelot, to her great surprise, Rose Thorn's bare feet began to skim the surface of this planet, Guelder, or Valerian, call it what you will. She skimmed and skipped, and each time she skipped, she rose a little higher in the air, and then, for the first time in a long time, she rose right, right up, her wings unfurled completely and - she flew.

They that gazed up at her, her fellow crewmates, friends and family from the *Joyous Gard,* thought, for one, bright, shining moment, her wings might touch the familiar stars.

But before anyone could marry anyone, the chapel needed to be built. And when it was built, some months later, people wanted to use it for memorial services for their loved ones, for Guinevere, who had died, and for those others so far away, Snow White and Rose Red in Avalon, and even the sleeping Queen Morgana.

At Queen Morgana's memorial service, when Rose Thorn saw all the votive candles blazing on the altar-stand, it reminded her again of that tree she had once seen in Avalon, that turned out to be lit by the flames of a thousand fire fairies. She wondered if that tree had been set there as a premonition of this moment, and as a source of consolation besides, for guides and spirits of the air can work such marvels, if we care to let them.

So many candles were lit for the sleeping queen, and so many prayers were said for her, that she might perhaps have been surprised to learn how many people, Rose Thorn, Arthur, Arabella, Lord Darvell, Violetta, had once deeply loved her.

Standing there beside a rough-hewn pew in Guelder's first, simple chapel, Lord Darvell remembered his first summer with Morgana, when all he could hear, all he could see, all he could feel was her. Ah, she had bewitched him indeed, body and soul. If he had known their time together was to be so short, he would have made more of it, if such a thing were possible. Losing himself in the red tumble of her hair, drowning in the green depths of her eyes, she was smoke and flame to him, hearth and home.

After a year or so of marriage, there came that horrendous night. As the maids were changing her blood-soaked shift, Lord Darvell stared blankly into the fire in the next room. In his hand he held an envelope, on which Morgana had written, '*To be opened in the event of my death.*' When she had first given him the envelope, he had wanted to laugh and reassure her, but he had not. They were both aware, enough women died in childbirth, even with the best medical attention. And Morgana, so rarely superstitious, was nevertheless superstitious about intermarriage between those from Avalon and Valerian.

'I'm an ogre, then, am I?' he had grumbled.

'Sometimes, yes,' she had replied, dropping a light kiss on his head.

His heart lightened briefly at the memory. He wanted to smile, but he could not. He glanced across the room at his friend, Dr Charles Helton, a dark rook staring out of the window. For once, the good doctor was silent, rubbing at the pane with his finger as though he could wipe away the looming fog, through which he dimly discerned the horses and carriages passing by in the street below.

Now Lord Darvell ripped open the envelope.

Inside was merely a single sheet of foolscap paper in which his wife had requested that her clothes be given to the servants as they wished, and for her jewellery to be placed inside her casket, with her. For her funeral itself, she requested that he summon the undertakers, Messers Kilkenny and Fieldung, old family friends now living in Avalon.

When Lord Darvell met these undertakers, of course he had reservations as to the wisdom of her choice. Not because they were dwarves, oh no. But because their snufflings and lip tremblings, their copious handwringing and application of none-too-clean pocket handkerchiefs to their red-rimmed eyes, seemed, at the very least, somewhat distasteful. Still, Morgana had always known her own mind, and if this is what she wanted, then he would honour her wishes.

There followed some discussion with the undertakers as to whether Morgana's casket should be transported to Waterloo Station on a barge on the River Thames, but they had declared that Morgana had no wish to repeat the actions of her ancestress, Elaine of Astalot.

'She who once found the sacred chalice,' said Lord Darvell, glancing up at the gleaming cup in pride of place among his trophies in the cabinet. It would ever be a comfort to him now, he thought, never to be let out of his sight, a memento of Morgana.

'The very same,' said Fieldung, who, despite himself, felt a sudden pang of sympathy for the great, foolish six-footer.

'So what are Morgana's wishes?' asked Lord Darvell then.

'She has left instructions for a state funeral,' said Fieldung.

'And then,' said Kilkenny, 'she wished for her open casket to be placed on a train, the London Necropolis Railway, running from Waterloo to a cemetery in Avalon.'

'Oh?' said Lord Darvell. 'A state funeral? So she's a queen now, is she?' Referring to her in the present tense also comforted him.

Kilkenny's eyes flew open, startled, as if he did not know how to answer the question. Fieldung twisted the brim of his top hat round and round in his hands. From their reactions, Lord Darvell began to surmise that his late wife had perhaps been a more important person in Avalon than he had ever realised.

And yet the dwarves remained curiously reticent about her final resting-place. All Fieldung would say, softly, is, 'Where she is going, it will always be spring, and the plants and trees will be of the fairest and finest.

'With saplings sprung from the sacred groves of Avalon itself,' added Kilkenny, with such aplomb that it made Lord Darvell suspect he was inventing it on the spot.

On the morning of the funeral, Lady Morgana Darvell was laid out in her open casket in the front parlour of Crowcroft Grange, as she had requested. Lord Darvell could not recall ever having seen her so peaceful before, except once, when he had watched her as she slept. Her crimson lips were curved in a tender half-smile; the flame of her hair lay a placid gold against her cheeks.

As the servants piled in to pay their last respects, they too thought they had never known their tiger mistress so tame.

'God bless you, Ma'am,' said Martha, the housemaid, arranging the jonquil lace at her mistress's throat, so that it lightened the cut and colour of her severe black gown. 'And God keep you from harm,' she added, pushing back the lace so that Morgana's carcanet of rubies could be seen by all the mourners. Morgana's rubies, which she had always hoped would protect her.

As he watched mistress and maid, Lord Darvell began to wish that he had taken some of Morgana's fears more seriously. But who wants to bring shadow to a bright summer's day?

The funeral service was held at St George's Church in Hanover Square, where they had been married. As arranged, a hearse drawn by six magnificent black horses with scarlet plumes between their twitching ears carried her casket to the Cemetery Station in Waterloo. Onlookers lined the streets to watch the carriage go by, as Morgana must have hoped they would, but they were moved not to tears, but rather to a deep, heartfelt sympathy which they themselves could not understand.

The carriage entered through a pair of ornate iron gates; thence was her casket removed and taken through a grand entrance hall and raised up to the second floor by a steam-powered elevator. Then it was taken out onto the platform and slotted onto the train. The dwarf undertakers, now impeccably dressed in full mourning garb, dissuaded Lord Darvell and Arthur from boarding the train on the grounds that they had already said their last farewells in church. 'Better to remember her in the sound of church-bells and song,' said Fieldung, so that, for the first time, Lord Darvell felt that he liked the cunning little dwarf.

The train passed through the Necropolis Junction into the dense city, and then out into the verdant countryside. Faster than witches, faster than fairies, the queen's beautiful corpse passed villages, cottages, farms, fields, open tracts of country. Painted stations whistled by; a railway child, clambering, scrambling, paused in his gathering of blackberries to watch the train go speeding by; so too the damsels gathering daisies in green fields, the solitary tramp, standing, gazing, even horses, cattle, sheep turned their heads at the departing fairy queen's train. A glimpse of majesty, and then, was she gone - gone forever?

On she sped, past carts, past mills, past distant woods and heathery uplands. Beyond rivulet, river and sedgy pool, all silvered in the sunlight, beyond wildflowers, wafting their scent from hedgerow banks, from fields, from blossoming hedge, into the dun heath, and among the stalwart rocks upon the moors.

Now the train made its rugged ascent, slowly, with difficulty, and then at last, *Vale Valerian,* for it was unlinked, and glided down gently into the undulating plains of Avalon.

At the end of the line, as Prince Nikolai had once before, so many years ago, the queen sat up in her casket. The undertaker dwarves placed a little stepladder beside it and helped her to climb down. Another few steps and she was off the train. And thus at last another horse-drawn carriage transported her to the Summer Palace.

Upon her arrival there, how her fairy maids did fuss and flitter about her hair and gown! And if, in her heart, Morgana felt a pang for the grief that Lord Darvell must be suffering, still, she was Avalon's Queen. Her duty, like her oak throne on the raised dais, lay before her. That is what it means to rule.

Some weeks after the funeral, in one of those oh-so Victorian gestures of mourning that were half ostentation and half genuine grief, Lord Darvell commissioned a portrait of Proserpine, Queen of the Underworld. However, apart from a certain fierceness about the forehead, the finished portrait looked nothing like Morgana. Nevertheless, there was something about the frankness of the model's dark eyes that Lord Darvell liked. He hung the portrait, by D.G. Rossetti, in his study, and he found her face brought him solace, although he did not know why.

That was the face beside him now in the chapel, here, in Guelder. He reached for her hand, then raised it to his lips and dropped a light kiss upon her knuckles. She turned to smile at him, and the smile chased away the serious expression in her eyes. Dark eyes, in the perfect oval of her pale face, dark hair with scarce a trace of grey, accentuating her pensive features. *Violetta.*

Nettled

When my brother and I were little, we were allowed to play outside, but our world was circumscribed by one lamppost halfway up our road, and another lamppost at the bottom of it. As we grew older, our boundaries became subsequent lampposts. So when Sharon-Next-Door told us we must never go to the King of Co's land by ourselves, we hoped the rules might one day change.

Sharon wasn't a grown-up, anyway, she was only eighteen months older than me. Only, when I was five, and my brother was four, she was by far the worldliest and most exciting person we had ever met. Thanks to Sharon and what was, at the time, the only video recorder in Vicarage Close, I watched *Blue Lagoon* at far too young an age, and still managed not to understand where babies came from. 'That girl,' my mother and godmother would sniffily agree, 'is *precocious.*' When our mother said, 'Don't talk like Sharon,' she meant don't be clever; don't answer back.

The infamous Sharon was the daughter of Michael the police-man, and Janice, his wife. They had a golden Labrador called Krystle, named after Krystle Carrington in *Dynasty.* Their living room looked like a palace to me, since it had deep burgundy curtains of an uneasy velvet we weren't supposed to touch, and a chandelier that chinked and sparkled above us.

However, the King of Co's domain was a patch of wasteland that could only be reached through a hole in the fence behind the grounds of some private flats, *For Residents Only*. That was printed on a big yellow sign on one of the flat's exterior walls, but my brother and I didn't know what *residents* meant. Besides, Sharon and her father had taken to walking the dog, and sometimes us, round these grounds, and it was on one of these expeditions that we spied the hole in the fence.

The next day, minus the police escort, we children climbed through that hole in the fence. Our skin had toughened with sunburn and nettle-stings, but still, this jagged hole, with spiky green wires round it, could tear our clothes, tear us, if we let it. On the other side, the wasteland seemed immense and overgrown, a tangle of sweeping grass and overripe weeds, sweet-smelling, effulgent, foul. Then too, there were sheets of rusting, corrugated iron, and stretching out for miles and miles, rows of crooked electricity pylons with zigzag cables. I had never seen so many of them before. If I held my breath, I could hear them hum.

I'm not convinced that we thought this was a beautiful and enchanted place; only that, in the absence of anything better, we wanted it to be. Otherwise, our world of gap-tooth pavement, tarmac street and marmalade lamp-post light would have been very small. Occasionally, the neighbours, including the local Franciscan friars came round to visit, but we knew them all: this was a suburban childhood, sherbet sweet.

In contrast, the wasteland was the vast unknown. And my bare legs seemed long in those days; my summer sandals were snug on my feet; if I walked far enough through the long grass, I might reach Erith Station, meet my dad coming back from work with the *Mr Men* books he had promised us.

Sharon owned an impressive collection of *Flower Fairy* books. When it was the Royal Wedding fancy-dress street-party, she had gone as the English Rose fairy, which meant wearing a dark pink dress, with matching flowers in her long, black hair. My costume was not much more inventive: I had a silver foil crown and a blue dress with a scratchy elasticated bodice, but I did have a purple cloak. My brother had the best costume: a cowboy outfit, but his guns and holsters were so heavy they kept pulling down his trousers. He finished the street-party *sans culottes.*

Since Sharon had been the English Rose, 'the Queen who everybody knows,' as she liked to recite, she had taken to writing plays. My brother had to rehearse, over-and-over, until he could roar, with gusto, his single line: 'Stop! She's the fairest.' Sharon had also decided that she was married to the King of Co, and that together they reigned over the wasteland. For reasons I don't entirely recall, the King of Co was occasionally trapped inside some of my brother's larger marbles: the swirling patterns of the cool glass rolled beneath our fingertips were his distorted face.

Sharon's decree came about because she said she had to order the king's guards away for us to be permitted into the wasteland. We must have feared and respected her enough that we waited some months, until she was on holiday for a week, to crawl through the hole in the fence by ourselves.

But where was the King of Co? Was he still trapped inside my brother's best marbles? And as for the guards, why were there only nettles, a stalwart sentry of sharp stingers, with their tang and scent of metal? And why, without Sharon, was nothing as exhilarating as it was before? One sky, blue, bearded by a few white clouds. One patch of grass, yellow, its scent of withering hay pricking our eyes. One crow perched on a pylon, caw-cawing. A few early knobbly blackberries sprouting on far-flung brambles, too acidic to swallow, entirely unsuitable partners for our sweet-sour Granny Smiths.

A cabbage white or two fluttered by, but no red admirals.

We were just crawling out of the wasteland - in fact, I was already safely on the other side, picking gravel out of the ridges in my sandal soles - when an old man began waving a stick at my approaching brother.

'Don't you know, it's very dangerous there?' he rasped. 'No place for children to play,' he continued, in a voice that sounded like the end of summer. And when we returned the next day, the hole in the fence had been boarded up.

We weren't sure we believed in the King of Co anymore, but all the same, we hoped he would be all right.

At the end of the week, Sharon came back from her holiday. She could do joined-up handwriting now. Her mother told her to give my brother his marbles back.

By the same Author:

In Valerian - Part I of the Valerian Trilogy

The Dragons of Blue Lias - Part II of the Valerian Trilogy

Keeping French Time

Printed and bound by CPI Group (UK) Ltd, Croydon, CR0 4YY
10/06/2024
01011742-0008